He dodged, Lindsay's dagger only sliced air, and he retreated. She was able to follow him and get away from the
wall to give herself room. Jenkins tried to circle again.
Suddenly she wished for her old mace, for it had a longer
reach than the knife and she had more fighting experience
with it. And with a cold smile she relished the image of
Jenkins' head smashed like a watermelon. In conscious imitation of Alex, she straightened from her guarded crouch,
went loose-jointed and deceptively insouciant, then pressed
him and swiped her dagger at him.

Jenkins dodged again, and on his riposte she dodged
backward, then stepped in to shove him around with his
own momentum and stab. She caught him in the back, a
good, solid stab . . .

Knight's Blood

JULIANNE LEE

ACE BOOKS, NEW YORK

THE BERKLEY PUBLISHING GROUP
Published by the Penguin Group
Penguin Group (USA) Inc.
375 Hudson Street, New York, New York 10014, USA
Penguin Group (Canada), 90 Eglinton Avenue East, Suite 700, Toronto, Ontario M4P 2Y3, Canada
(a division of Pearson Penguin Canada Inc.)
Penguin Books Ltd., 80 Strand, London WC2R 0RL, England
Penguin Group Ireland, 25 St. Stephen's Green, Dublin 2, Ireland (a division of Penguin Books Ltd.)
Penguin Group (Australia), 250 Camberwell Road, Camberwell, Victoria 3124, Australia
(a division of Pearson Australia Group Pty. Ltd.)
Penguin Books India Pvt. Ltd., 11 Community Centre, Panchsheel Park, New Delhi—110 017, India
Penguin Books (NZ), 67 Apollo Drive, Mairangi Bay, Auckland 1311, New Zealand
(a division of Pearson New Zealand Ltd.)
Penguin Books (South Africa) (Pty.) Ltd., 24 Sturdee Avenue, Rosebank, Johannesburg 2196,
South Africa

Penguin Books Ltd., Registered Offices: 80 Strand, London WC2R 0RL, England

This is a work of fiction. Names, characters, places, and incidents either are the product of the author's imagination or are used fictitiously, and any resemblance to actual persons, living or dead, business establishments, events, or locales is entirely coincidental. The publisher does not have any control over and does not assume any responsibility for author or third-party websites or their content.

KNIGHT'S BLOOD

An Ace Book / published by arrangement with the author

PRINTING HISTORY
Ace mass-market edition / March 2007

Copyright © 2007 by Julianne Lee.
Cover art by Judy York.
Cover design by Annette Fiore.

ISBN: 978-0-441-01485-9

ACE
Ace Books are published by The Berkley Publishing Group,
a division of Penguin Group (USA) Inc.,
375 Hudson Street, New York, New York 10014.
ACE and the "A" design are trademarks belonging to Penguin Group (USA) Inc.

PRINTED IN THE UNITED STATES OF AMERICA

10 9 8 7 6 5 4 3 2 1

In memory of
Don Richardson,
Michael Thoma,
and
John Peck
of the American Academy of Dramatic Arts

ACKNOWLEDGMENTS

Folks say "Write what you know." But if I only did that, I would never write anything. I am ever in debt to those who know more than I do. Among those who have helped me in writing this series are: LCDR Alan R. Bedford, Sr., USNR (Ret.); Teri McLaren; Judy Goldsmith; James A. Hartley; Trisha Mundy; Diana Diaz; Joyce Coomer; Maggie Craig; Susanne Dhomhnallach; Liz Williams; and the lovely crowd at the 2005 Milford Workshop in Snowdon, Wales.

As always, many thanks to my editor, Ginjer Buchanan, and my agent, Ginger Clark.

For information about future books in this series, visit julianneardianlee.com.

CHAPTER 1

"Strike, Saber One Zero Five. Seven zero miles north-east with four, released from BARCAP, state seven point zero."

"Saber One Zero Five, roger." The strike controller then cleared Alex's formation of F-18s inbound to his ship and directed him to switch to marshal frequency. He switched, checked in, and the voice of the ship's controller came over his radio.

"Saber One Zero Five, marshal. You're cleared to marshal on the two seven zero radial, angels fifteen." There was a slight pause, then, "Expected approach time four five. Altimeter is three one point zero two."

Alex led his formation in compliance with the directions, then the controller said in a conversational tone, "No excitement this trip?"

Alex snorted behind his face mask, a harsh sound of mild disgust he'd picked up in Scotland, then keyed his mike. "Nope, the bad guys are fully cowed today." Today's barrier combat air patrol along the Iraq-Iran border had been uneventful, and that was lucky for him. After two years on the ground, in a place and time where the fastest transportation on the planet was a galloping horse, the supersonic speed of the F-18 had taken getting used to again. Not the least like riding a bicycle. The plane Lieutenant MacNeil flew was the Navy's top-of-the-line speeder, and acting fast was the only way to keep it from smacking into things. He'd been rustier than all hell on his return from the past, and it had taken him a while to feel truly comfortable again with a stick in his hand.

His preoccupation with Lindsay didn't help matters. There had been a time when he'd taken his reflexes for granted, but no more. Coming up to speed without letting the Navy know he'd gone two years without a hop had been a tense, dangerous thing, but he'd pulled it off. His trap scores weren't up to his previous standard, but at least he was still flying. Not dead yet.

The controller then said, "We'll see you on deck. Got some news that might perk up your day."

Alex frowned, wondering what news. Then it hit him, and a charge surged through him. "What news?" He knew what it had to be. It was time.

"Belay that, Lieutenant." The other voice was a lieutenant commander also working in marshal control. A guy named Bannister. "Make your trap and never mind."

"What? Is Lindsay all right? The cat's out of the bag. It's Lindsay, am I correct?"

"Your wife is fine. They're both fine," said Bannister.

"Both . . ." A wide smile pressed against Alex's mask, and a loud laugh burst from him. "What is it?" When there was no reply, he added, "Seyeth ye freeleh; I moot ken." He bit his lip for having lapsed into Middle English again, and though nobody laughed on the frequency, he figured they were all sniggering behind their mikes now. The guys thought it was British slang he'd picked up from Lindsay, but the truth was sometimes he used archaic vocabulary without realizing it.

He pressed the controller again for news, and translated his lapse. "I wish to know now, sir."

"A boy. She had a boy, MacNeil. He's healthy, she's healthy, so don't worry about them; get yourself onto the ship in one piece."

Danu had been right. She'd told him months ago it would be a boy. A son. He was the father of a baby boy. He let out a whoop and a long, hearty laugh that contained not a little relief. A son. Now he couldn't wait to get back to the ship.

Contrary to the fears of the controllers, Alex's recovery was perfect. Screwing up and killing himself now was just not thinkable. Once on deck, he climbed from his cockpit and took his helmet off to tuck it under his elbow. Some pilots on their way to the catapults stopped to applaud and slap him on the back. The guys from his patrol and his own Guy In Back joined them, voices all loud and cheerful, but their eyes betrayed their real thoughts and Alex couldn't stand to see them. The congratulations rang false—were false—for none of them believed Alex was the father of Lindsay's baby. And there was nothing to be done about that. As far as they knew, he'd only met his wife three months ago. There was no way he could tell them about the two years he'd spent with her, a year of it married and a year of it as knights fighting for Scottish independence under Robert the Bruce.

How nuts would that sound? To be sitting around a table in the wardroom, telling his buddies he'd once been whacked on the back of the neck by the flat of a broadsword blade, and by that action had become a member of medieval Scottish nobility. Later on, he'd been made knight banneret in the midst of the most famous battle in Scottish history, and after that battle had been handed over an entire island in the Inner Hebrides. At the very least it would sound like bragging, but more likely the Navy would take a dim view and send him to a shrink if he uttered such a story. That would certainly be it for his career.

No, better they should think he was a cuckold than a nutcase. Instead of protesting, he pretended he couldn't hear the hint of scorn or pity in their voices. He had faith

he must be the baby's father, and that was enough for him.
Lindsay had been his wife longer than he'd known some of
these pilots, and had proven herself to him more times and
more fully than any of them had. So he thanked them all,
ignored the odd looks, and walked away to the ship's island
and the escalators to the wardroom.

Behind him he heard one of them say in an exaggerated
accent that may or may not have been meant to mimic
Alex's own slightly Southern speech, "That there boy is off
to get hisself some phone."

Alex grinned. That much was true. After his debriefing,
Alex headed straight for a pay phone in the wardroom and
called London. The hospital where Lindsay had planned to
have the baby. It seemed to take forever for the call to go
through, but Alex had patience, for he knew what it was
like not to have a phone at all. Had the baby been born
while he was deployed by King Robert, more than likely
he wouldn't have known it until the boy was several months
old. He could wait a minute or so to hear Lindsay's voice
through a wire.

The patched-through call was not a good connection,
and an annoying delay caused them to interrupt each other
with false starts, but Lindsay's gentle voice calmed Alex's
soul. Still wearing his zoombag and sidearm, looking like a
well-used rag and feeling the motion of the ride from which
he'd just returned, he leaned his forehead against the bulk-
head and pressed himself to the phone as if he could hug his
wife through it. He wished he were in London.

"Is he—"

"Where are—"

Alex tried again, and this time was able to get out an entire sentence. "Is he healthy?"

There was a pause, and he let it ride for the delay to
pass. Then came, with a slight echo that emphasized the
distance between them, "He's perfect." Even with the crappy
connection Alex could hear the joy in her voice. "I didn't
get a very good look at him, and was fairly drugged up at
the time, but he's absolutely beautiful." She still sounded a

little drugged up, speaking slowly, almost haltingly. But her joy made him grin wider.

His heart swelled, and he glanced around to see if anyone in the wardroom could tell his throat was closing up. He tried to stifle the smile stuck to his face, but it was impossible. A table of lieutenants across the room were snickering into their coffee. Jake, Alex's Naval Flight Officer, was there with them, but he wasn't laughing.

Lately Jake had become distant, though they'd been good friends before Alex's two-year hiatus into the past. Gave him weird looks just short of the hairy eyeball whenever he lapsed into Middle English. Alex had tried to pass off his misspeaking as humor, but Jake never seemed to buy that. Neither did he seem to accept Alex's claim that new scars that looked like old scars were actually old scars Jake had not noticed before. There were too many of them. Alex could see he wasn't fooling his Guy In Back.

Alex turned back to the wall and murmured, "I can't wait to see him."

"Where are—" She went silent again, having been interrupted, and he waited. Then she repeated, "Where are you?"

"You know I can't tell you that. But I'm going to take some leave. I'm coming to see you and the baby."

There was a sigh that sounded like relief. Lindsay had never been one to cling to him, or anyone, but the final months of her pregnancy had been tense. He had a sense she resented the way he'd been able to regain his old life, where she hadn't. She'd had to take maternity leave from her job as a reporter for the *London Times*, and wasn't sure she'd be able to go back to it later on. Travel would be difficult with the baby, not to mention the chances of a conflict of interest between her job and his were high. Alex knew she feared her career was over. Or at least it would be stunted and at odds with his own. Even so, all she said now was, "It will be good to see you."

"I miss—"

"I'm afraid—"

"—you, too."

And then she said something that was swallowed up with static, but he guessed she said, "It's terribly hairy."

"What's hairy? He's got hair? He's not bald, then?"

There was a silence, then, "What was that?"

"What did you say?"

The silence fell again, then she said, more clearly, "Yes, he's got hair. It's dark, like mine."

Alex nodded though she couldn't see him. "Good. I like that. What color are his eyes?" He hoped for green, for that was the color of his own eyes.

"Blue." He felt a twinge of disappointment, but then Lindsay added, "All babies have blue eyes. We can't know what color they will be for a while yet."

"Oh." Good.

The static returned, and worsened so that Alex knew they were about to be cut off. "Listen, hon, I'm going to lose you. Give him a kiss for me, and I'll see you both in a couple of days."

"Right. Love you."

"Love you back." He slipped the receiver from his ear to the phone hook and stood motionless against the wall, thinking about the enormity of what had just happened. In the twenty-first century he routinely flew thousands of feet above the earth, at speeds faster than sound. During the fourteenth century he'd been in battle, wielding at various times both sword and dagger. He'd been knighted by Robert the Bruce, for a year had been laird of an entire island off the coast of Scotland, and had once enjoyed the prospect of eventual elevation to the Scottish peerage. But today his world had been rocked by a child.

Alex pulled himself together and turned around, threw a grin at the cluster of fellow officers, then hurried away to request his leave.

Like everything else in the military, Alex's trip to London was a hurry-up-and-wait. It was three days later that he arrived at Lindsay's flat, which had become his also when they'd married again three months ago. A plain place and there was no lift, and like everything else in London it cost more than Alex thought it should, but the building at least was clean. The landings on the stairwell were papered in green plaid that made him goggle and blink every time he saw it, the halls being so narrow and the walls so close. Tacky, he thought, but once he was inside the flat he wouldn't have to look at it.

He climbed the three flights to their floor, shifted his bag to his left hand, and turned the doorknob, but the door was locked. She wasn't home.

Huh. Lindsay should be there by now. Perhaps she was out. Groceries or something. Dang, he wanted to see the baby right away. With a sigh, he reached into his jeans pocket for his keys.

The door to the next flat opened, and its tenant emerged. James, Alex remembered from his last time here. Fortyish, he wore a slightly rumpled black trench coat and collarless white shirt that gave him a Eurotrashy sort of look. He held a cigarette between two fingers, which he put in his mouth to lock his door, then dragged on it. He turned and noticed Alex, and said, "Oh . . . hello, MacNeil."

Alex knew James to be an utterly pleasant fellow, contrary to appearance. But today there was an odd note in his voice that caught Alex's attention, and instead of going on his way, James stepped toward him. Alex's hand paused before his key reached the door. "Hi."

"I'm terribly sorry for your loss."

All Alex had in response to that was a blank look. He had to swallow a "Huh?"

"The baby."

Thundering terror nearly knocked Alex sideways. Struggling not to show how stricken he was, he gripped his keychain hard so the key blades bit his palm. "Excuse me?" Anger rose that lately he seemed to be the last to know anything.

Now it was James' turn to look stricken. "Oh, I'm deeply sorry. I thought you knew."

"Knew what? What happened?" And how did James know and himself not?

James was turning red and looking around as if he wished he could run away down the stairs, but he faced up to his responsibility for what he'd said, and replied. "Your wife spoke to me as she was leaving."

"Leaving?"

"Yes. Just this morning. She told me the baby has been abducted. I'm terribly sorry."

Somehow that was a relief, and Alex let out in a sigh the air he'd been holding in. Not dead. The baby could still be alive and well, and so was Lindsay.

But then the words sank in, and he realized the child was missing. And so was Lindsay. "Where did she go? Did she say when she'd be back?" Soon, he hoped. Then they could figure out what to do.

James' discomfort seemed to grow. Now he sidled toward the stairs as if readying to dash down them. "She didn't say. She had a bag with her." He blinked as if just remembering something, then reached into a pocket. He fished around and came up with a single key. "She asked me to hold the key to your flat."

Now nothing made sense. Bag? Key? Where on God's earth could she have gone? Alex blinked at James, at a loss for what to say.

"Here." James held out the key. Alex took it and stared at it stupidly.

"Why? What's going on?"

James pressed his lips together and for a moment looked as if he were going to clam up. But instead he said, "I don't know what this means. You understand she was quite upset at the time. But she blurted something about ears. And she said she was going to get someone. It was almost as if she knew where the baby had been taken and was going there to retrieve him. Don't know how, but she seemed determined."

Alex knew Lindsay was always very determined. If she knew where her child had been taken, it was a lead-pipe cinch she would go there and get him. That gave Alex hope. He said, "Ears?"

James drew on his cigarette and shrugged, struggling now to regain his well-cultivated insouciant air. "I've no idea what it means."

"What, exactly, did she say?"

"I don't remember. Not exactly. As I said, she was quite upset and, well, not terribly coherent. I reckon she'd been crying for hours. Seemed in pretty bad shape, I'm afraid."

Lindsay crying. That didn't happen often.

Alex wished for more information, but James seemed tapped out. He stared at the key in his hand. "Thanks. Have the police been notified?"

"I don't know. I've told you everything she said. She ran out of here awfully fast."

Alex nodded. "All right. Thank you."

James headed for the stairs, then paused and said, "I hope you find your son."

"Wait!" James waited. Alex continued. "Did she say anything about a name? We haven't named him yet." For months Lindsay had changed her mind on a daily basis, and Alex couldn't remember most of the ones she'd picked and discarded.

"I'm sorry. I couldn't say. There wasn't a lot that made sense in what she told me."

"I see. Well, thanks."

James nodded and hurried down the stairs, leaving Alex breathless. It was with fumbling fingers he slipped the key on his chain into the door lock and turned it. He entered the flat, let his bag slip to the floor, and looked around.

The place was a wreck. Not large to begin with, and the furniture crowded it a bit, but also clothes lay scattered about and breakfast dishes on the dinette table gave the place the close, dank smell of a Dumpster. This was very much not like Lindsay.

In the bedroom he found the bed rumpled and the closet spilling over with clothes torn from hangers and dropped to the floor. A new, white, spindled crib stood against the wall by the window. It was covered with dust. Not dust settled over time, but a thick coat of it splattered all over as if a vacuum cleaner bag had exploded. Alex felt it, and it was gritty like fine sand. His heart lurched and his stomach turned. This was too weird, in a way that gave him the sort of creeps he hadn't experienced since . . . well, since the fourteenth century.

In search of answers—or even a clue—he picked up the phone and called Lindsay's mother. But on hearing the old lady's cheerful voice full of congratulations, he knew she hadn't been told any more than he had. He wasn't about to say anything, not with the paltry information he had, and so he let her go on in a chirpy, excited voice and plummy syllables until he could get her off the phone.

When he hung up, he stood in the living room, alone and struggling to know what to do. Or even how to feel. Lindsay hadn't told James where she was going. Hadn't told her mother anything at all. Hadn't even waited until he would be off the ship and on the ground before tearing off to God knew where in search of the baby, and that astonished him more than anything. Why would she do that? He looked around the room, wishing something informative would leap out at him, but it didn't. Desperate for something constructive to do, he went to the table and cleared the dishes to the kitchen. They went into the sink with some hot water and soap, and he went to the window to crack it open and perhaps let some fresh air into the flat. It was a relative thing, but the noise and fumes from the street below were an improvement over stale food.

There on the kitchen counter was a photo, one of those routinely taken of newborns. Alex snatched it up and held it to the light from the window for a good look. His son. It had to be. It was a pink-faced baby with a fuzz of dark hair, eyes squinted shut and tiny fist closed near one ear.

The ear was pointed at the top.

Alex stared at it. Pointed. He blinked, then held the photo closer to the light, but the ear still curved forward at the top and came to a distinct point. Like Mr. Spock. Like . . .

Cold sweat broke out, and an unwanted image came to

his mind. *Nemed*. That blasted elf. Alex's chest tightened, and he backed against the counter. His world twisted into shapes he'd never known it could. It had been Nemed, the elfin king, who had taken himself and Lindsay to the fourteenth century. Nemed and Lindsay: he'd dreamed it once—a nightmare—but hadn't imagined it could have been true. Obviously he'd been both right and wrong. Nemed and Lindsay. It sickened him. His throat began to close, and breathing was an effort. *Nemed and Lindsay.* Now he knew where she'd gone and why she hadn't so much as left a note.

He tossed the photo onto the counter and headed for the bedroom. A wooden crate sat at the bottom of the closet, and he shoved aside the clothing and shoes on top of it to haul it out. The clothes stored inside, the hauberk, sark, trews, and tunic he'd been wearing on his return from the past, were missing. He knew where Lindsay had gone, and why.

"Oh, man." She really had gone to Nemed. Alex sagged where he knelt. "Oh, Lindsay." Despair closed his throat and it was hard to breathe. He didn't want to believe it was true, but hard-won faith crumbled. His mind struggled for an explanation for this, but every avenue of thought led him back to the photograph, the ears, and the same conclusion: that Lindsay and Nemed were lovers, and they'd both taken the baby back to Scotland's past.

As the truth hardened in him, the heat of anger kindled and his skin began to flame with rage. There was no way he would let this just happen. He couldn't let that slimeball do this to him. Nor Lindsay. She was his wife, and he'd trusted her. They would both answer for this, but first he had to find them.

His medieval clothing was gone, so he rose to look through his civilian clothes for something approximating what he would need. A pair of brown sweatpants and a long-tailed linen shirt looked good. Then a leather belt, with an oversized buckle that was nevertheless too small to be fashionable where he was headed, would have to do.

She'd taken his gauntlets as well, and he cursed. He liked the spiked knuckles on those gloves. He'd have to find a new pair once he got there. His green plaid was still there on the sofa, lying in a crumpled heap where it had functioned as a throw during the short time he'd had with Lindsay here. He grabbed his bag, dumped out the change of clothing he'd brought with him from the ship, and stuffed in the plaid and the quasi-medieval items.

Hungry and tired as he was after his flight in from the Persian Gulf, he couldn't think of stopping to eat or sleep. He took his bag, locked up the apartment, and headed for Heathrow to catch the first available flight to northern Scotland. Eilean Aonarach, the island he'd once ruled as laird. Danu was there. The faerie was immortal; she would surely be there still. She would know how to find Nemed. And therefore also Lindsay, and probably his son.

His wife's baby, in any case.

CHAPTER 2

The ferryboat bobbed on the Sea of the Hebrides, calmly on a calm though steel gray summer's day. By modern standards the vessel was tiny, though it wasn't much smaller than the sailing ship that had brought Alex the first time he'd seen this place. The island it served was also small, but small by any standard, not just modern ones. Only a few miles long and one or two across. There were no bridges to this remote chunk of granite among many such dots scattered northwest of the Scottish mainland. Alex watched the cliffs approach, and examined the silhouette of it. Of course, it had changed over the past seven centuries. There were fewer trees and many more structures, and even the profile of mountains seemed different. Softer. He was certain he didn't care for that, as if his island were melting away.

At first the castle wasn't apparent. As he searched for the outline of crenellated battlements, he found none and was disappointed. His castle was gone. Or ruined, rather. Closer now, he found a wall cresting one of the hills near where the quay should be. But, again, there was nothing left of the quay but a gray-black rubble crumbling into the surf.

The ferry headed for a modern dock off to the west, and Alex moved to the rear of the boat to keep sight of the place where his castle had once stood. Remnants of walls clung to rock like old food to a pot. He thought he caught a glimpse of the dark hollow where the master's chambers had been. His bedroom. His and Lindsay's. A weird nostalgia washed over him, as if it really had been seven centuries since he'd last seen the place, though it had only been a few months by his own reckoning. When he was the laird here, his castle had been a lively, thriving garrison teeming with men at arms, servants, dogs, chickens, and children, fully functional as a center of commerce and rule for the island. Now it was a pile of rocks, of no interest to anyone but the curious, and the chamber in which he'd slept with his wife looked like an empty eye socket in the face of his former home.

Now Alex was among the curious and wanted to tour these ruins with the Germans, Brits, and other Americans arriving on the ferry, but he had other business at hand and there was no time to dawdle. He lifted his bag to sling it over his shoulder and hurried from the ferry the instant it landed, then made his way past the cramped, white-painted dock offices, past a line of fishing boats bumping their gunnels against the seaweed-smelling dock, and on into the village that hadn't existed in his day, back when Robert the Bruce had been King of Scots.

Alex was hungry—he hadn't eaten since breakfast at the hotel in Glasgow—but he didn't stop for lunch. He looked to the sky for his bearings and found south, for it was midday and the sun was at its zenith, checked out the surrounding mountains to be sure of where he'd landed, then took a heading straight for the interior of the island. A narrow street lined with whitewashed houses led him from the village and onto a road that wound between sheep pastures. There his stride settled into a ground-eating length.

Ahead stood a wood newly reforested with Scandinavian fir trees. They struck him as odd, for he was accustomed to the gnarled Scottish pine and oak of days past.

The stand was tall and dense, and looked like a Christmas tree farm on steroids, oddly missing the twisted, mossy thickets. A man could get lost in this forest, where all the trees looked the same as every other. He sighed and kept walking, hoping the faerie ring was still where it had been. If the ring remained, so would Danu, he was certain. But if she was gone, his trip was wasted and he would have to take his search elsewhere. He had no clue where that might be, for faeries were a mystery to him and always would be. Elves, gnomes, brownies, leprechauns . . . he had to acknowledge they existed, but he didn't like them very well and knew little about them.

The walk was longer than most people would travel by foot in this time, but he knew where he was going and had run this route many times for the exercise. The road more or less followed an extremely old trail, and he knew exactly where to leave it and head into the woods. It had been densely planted and he wended his way between the trees. Frequently he looked skyward to the light, to be certain he was headed in the right direction, and in that way kept to his course. When finally the firs gave way to the familiar Scotch pine, he felt a sense of relief. Even comfort, for these trees spoke of home to him. As a fourth-generation Navy brat, he'd never had a place to call home until he'd come here. This island spoke to his soul like no other place he'd ever been. The raw rock and hardy trees, the deep, dim forest, the ocean beating its shores, all seemed part of him. Ancient oaks covered in moss. Soft grass and fungus underfoot. Smells of deadfall and earth, so thick they filled his head and made him dizzy. If it weren't for his reason for being here, returning to this might have made him happy. He'd given it up only for Lindsay's sake, and for the baby.

The cool dimness of the forest had closed around him by the time he came to the spot he knew must still be there as he'd left it. Danu and her people wouldn't have let it be taken by humans. It was as sacrosanct now as it had been since time immemorial, and the very depth of this forest was testimony to that. Unlike the rest of the island, the indigenous trees were still thick here, healthy and thriving. Danu must have protected them all this time. Certainly nothing human of any consequence had ever been allowed to intrude here.

But he found no faerie ring of toadstools. Nor any sign there ever had been one.

This must be the place, however. Alex looked around. He knew it had to be. This ground was familiar. The same slope and lay of the earth, if not exactly the same trees and brush. Not as much had changed here as elsewhere. There was a slight mound in the grassy middle; he remembered it from when he'd spoken to the faerie queen. There had been a log of a fallen tree before, but that had surely long since rotted to dust and new trees had grown up in place of dead ones.

But the faerie ring was gone. He sighed and cursed, and let his bag fall to the ragged grass with a thump. *Now what?* He looked around for some sign that Danu was nearby, but found nothing. No sign Lindsay had been here either, but that didn't mean much. If Lindsay was looking for Nemed, she might know where to find him and have gone straight there. A knot tied his gut as he wondered if the elfin bastard had even escorted her from London.

Again the image of those two together came, and this time he shook it from his head. That was no way to think; Lindsay had as much reason as he did to hate Nemed. Thinking they could be together was silly. Irrational. Now that he'd calmed down, he realized it. She'd gone after the baby, nothing more. He had to believe that. She'd been crying, James had said. If she was crying, it must be because Nemed had taken the baby from her. There had to be an explanation for this mess. For the photograph. There must be something beyond the obvious, which would vindicate Lindsay. With a deep sigh, he looked around some more. For something. Anything.

A hole in the ground caught his eye. Beside an outcrop of rock sticking up from the grass, it wasn't large and didn't seem like much. Nothing more than a bit of grass drooped over a dark hollow in the ground, like eyelashes

over an empty eye socket. But he knew some of the wee
folk were called "wee" for a reason, and they lived underground. Inside knolls and such. Funny, he hadn't ever noticed that hole before. Not ever. He went toward the
opening. It was small; it could have been there for a long
time and still not have existed last time he'd been here. For
a moment he thought he saw a light. Just a flash, then gone.
Huh. Peering into the hole, he went closer. Was that another flash, or did he imagine it? He knelt beside the thing
to look in. Darkness.

Then a force, like both wind and suction, but ultimately
neither, shoved him and pulled him. With a helpless cry, he
found himself thrust into the hole. His shoulders barely fit,
and for a second it seemed he would be stuck. He struggled
to back out. His fists grabbed at the grass nearby, but it tore
from the ground. The force moving him shoved and pulled
harder, and he squeezed on through.

He tumbled in darkness, then landed on his back with a
thud. For a few moments he thought only of breathing,
gasping for dank, earth-smelling air. When the colored dots
swimming before his eyes slowed, then stopped, he groaned
and looked around. Tree roots. Of course. He'd once been
inside a faerie knoll, and he knew how these folk loved their
trees and sheltered among the twisted, labyrinthine root
systems.

Voices twittered and giggled in the distance. Yeah, there
were faeries here, all right. Alex sat up and peered around
at the dimness as his eyes adjusted. There were fires here
and there in the cavern, and he could see corridors off of
it, lit with torches. The tree roots intruded everywhere,
some thick like pillars that seemed to hold up the ceiling,
and others in twisted, convoluted masses here and there
like decoration. Celtic knots, a few of them even stripped
of bark and lovingly polished. These bore carvings, sculpture on natural sculpture. Writing of a type he'd never seen
before.

This place wasn't much like the knoll where he'd met
Nemed. That had been an empty hole in the ground, dark

and deserted, and not decorated at all. This was someone's home, lovingly furnished with cushions and pillows, and hung with tapestries of rich color. And there were people lounging about. Little people, but not of Danu's tribe. The queen of the *Tuatha Dé Danann* looked nearly human, and these were the smaller folk he'd seen only once before. Thin, poorly dressed, but lively with humor of the rude, irreverent, out-of-control variety. The one he'd met before had been an irritant. These faeries laughed entirely too much, and they were laughing now. Surely at him. Some of them were standing, moving closer to have a better look at him. He stood, and found his head came just short of the ceiling. He ducked under a gnarled root to find space for himself.

"Who might you be?" said one of the faeries who had sauntered over, chin high and chest thrust out in a posture of challenge. He was larger than the rest but still only stood to Alex's rib cage. Spindly arms and legs were clad in a ragged tunic and trews, the tunic little better than a length of cloth with a hole at the center tied at the waist with a rope. But it was a golden rope that glinted in the flickering firelight. The faerie stood hipshot, arms crossed over his narrow chest, a bright look in his eye that spelled either antagonism or mischief. Alex couldn't tell which, and knew enough about the fey creatures of this country to understand that neither was good.

"I'm Alex . . ." Alex hesitated, then decided if he was going to search down one of the fey he would need all the influence over this guy he could get. He reached back to the far distant past for his best bet. "I'm Sir Alasdair an Dubhar MacNeil, Laird of Eilean Aonarach and Knight of the Realm of King Robert."

"Which Robert?"

"Robert I. Robert the Bruce, leader of the Wars of Independence."

"A mite out of your time, don't ye think?"

Alex ignored the obvious and unproductive comment, and continued. "I'm looking for an elf."

A voice from the rear said, "I'm looking for one meself; let me know if ye find a source."

A round of twittering took the gathering, and a light of excitement brightened every eye. The faerie with the golden belt said, "An elf, ye say. Might we know him?"

"You should. I'm looking for King Nemed."

The faerie leader laughed loud and long at that, accompanied by the voices of his kindred. When he recovered himself, he said, "Indeed. Nemed. I'm Brochan of the Clann Bhrochan, and I will have naught to do with the Elfin Lord, nor anyone who would have aught to do with him, neither. Just what is it you wish of him?"

"I want to kill him."

That brought forth a huge grin so infectious, Alex had to stifle one of his own. "Och! Then, by all means, welcome to our home!" Brochan threw up his hands and waved Alex in toward the fire. "Come! Sit with us, Sir Alasdair of Eilean Aonarach! And just where is this island of which you speak?"

Alex followed the faerie as the others gathered around him and came as well. "Up th . . ." He looked up and gestured toward the hole from which he'd come, but found no opening. Dim as it might be here, there should have been sunlight shining down from above, but the ceiling was quite solid with earth and tree roots. Alex stared, and disquiet stole over him. He said as he proceeded toward the fire, "Eilean Aonarach. Not far from Barra. It was part of my award from Robert after Bannockburn."

"Robert who?" Brochan gestured to a cluster of his people, who leapt to comply and scurried away. Then the leader of the faeries gestured to Alex for him to sit. "Rest yourself a spell. Robert who, then?"

"Robert the Bruce, as I said."

"I've heard of no Robert the Bruce."

"But you said—"

Another faerie spoke up. This one was older, with a grizzled beard and unkempt, long hair. But his voice was one of reason. "He means the Robert that will be, Brochan."

The light of understanding came to the leader's eyes. "Oh, aye. That Robert. King of Scotland."

"The first Robert."

"Aye." Brochan nodded.

Alex looked from one to the other, then around at the folks who had gone back to their lounging and eating, carrying on with what they'd been doing before his arrival. He seemed less of a curiosity now, and irrationally he felt ignored in a way that made him uncomfortable. His stomach growled. To Brochan he said, "A minute ago you knew who he was."

"But that was no minute, and it wasnae 'ago.' "

That made so little sense, Alex couldn't even formulate a query that would help it make any. Hairs all over his body stood up in alarm. He had a very bad feeling about these creatures, and the fact that the hole he'd come down was no longer there gave him a claustrophobic feeling he didn't care for. His route of retreat, if there ever had been one, was gone, and the only course for him now was forward. He said, "I want to return to my island and the time in which I was laird there." Danu would be there. She would make more sense than these nitwits.

"You were laird more than once?"

"No. I mean, the time period. The year."

Understanding lit Brochan's eyes. "Ah, that. And you think we can help you?"

"I think either you can, or you know someone who can." He hated being forced to even speak of this to these nutcase types. Danu was a queen. God knew what this guy's function was in the world. But he pressed on. "I know there is a spell that can return me to the past."

"Because you've done it before."

"Right."

"And you want us to do the same? Or do you want us to tender your request to Nemed that he oblige you once again? Before you kill him, that is."

Alex's eyes narrowed. "How did you know it was Nemed who brought me here? Sent me there, I mean."

"I did not, until you just told me." Twittering laughter riffled about the room. Alex realized the entire clan was listening in. His ears warmed.

Again, he pressed the faerie. "Can you send me back? Do you have that ability? Or should I look elsewhere?"

As if Brochan hadn't heard the question, he rose up from his pillows and shouted out across the room, "Some wine for my friend! In haste, if you please!"

Friend?

Then the faerie lay back once again and addressed Alex. "You'll pardon my rudeness, Sir Alasdair. We'll have your wine to you in but a moment."

Alex didn't want any wine but was loath to alienate this guy by refusing his hospitality. So he nodded, and leaned an elbow back against a knotted rise in a tree root beside him. The curve of the thing was smooth with the polish of many elbows before his, the top of it a glossy, jet black.

A drinking bowl was brought, what Alex knew to be a *cuach*, flat and with knobby handles on either side. He'd seen them often while on Barra, back in the far distant past, last year. This one was of gold, the handles wrought with knotted bears and the lip etched in a delicate design. Alex lifted it to his mouth to taste the drink. It turned out to be honey wine. Mead. This stuff was spiced, and quite tasty. Alex remembered he was hungry, and took an injudicious draught. It hit his empty stomach like a small nuke, spreading and roiling heat throughout his body, all the way out to his fingers. The effect was far out of proportion to how smoothly the mead had gone down. He instantly felt better and took another drink before passing the cup to his host. The stuff was good; he had to hand it to these guys for their mead at least.

Brochan took the cup and drank. "So, tell us all the story of how Nemed has crossed you." He gestured to his kinsmen. "We all love a good story, aye?"

The faeries listening nearby all nodded and murmured their agreement.

Alex shrugged. He didn't want to blurt all that had gone

on between himself and Nemed. But Brochan waved him
onward, insisting. Then he thrust the *cuach* back at him for
another drink. Alex took it and emptied the bowl, then
cleared his throat. He was stuck. He took a pause while the
mead warmed him, and his mood improved. Then he
spoke. Carefully, for the drink had also seeped into his
head and was making his thoughts dance. "Well, it was a
couple of years ago."

"You said it was centuries past."

Smartass little prick. "Okay, a couple of years have
passed for me since this story began."

Brochan's face brightened. "Oh, aye! I'm beginning to
see! When ye use terms I can understand, you make it so
very plain!"

There was no telling what the guy meant by that. Alex
gazed at him for a moment, once more at a loss, but then he
went on. "Well. All right then. So, there was myself and
Lindsay—"

"And who would this Lindsay be?"

"My wife." A sudden urge to weep rose in him, and took
him by surprise. Never before had he lost control like this
in public. Panic he would embarrass himself in front of this
guy quarreled with his grief over losing Lindsay. He fought
back both emotions, and wondered why he was losing it
now. For a moment his throat closed and it was impossible
to speak, but Brochan only gazed at him with expectation
that he should continue his story. Alex swallowed hard,
then choked out more words. "But not at the time. She was
a reporter for the *London Times* and I was flying her from
my ship to Scotland." God, he missed Lindsay! Just then
he wanted nothing more than to have her back. Nothing
mattered but that she would be safe again, and his again.

Brochan became quite excited and leapt to his feet,
hands fluttering and his entire body aquiver. "Flying? In
the air? You have flown?"

His job seemed distant now. An eternity ago. "Aye. I
was a pilot by profession." Was. Would he be again? He'd
left London without telling anyone where he was going.

Bad lieutenant. But he figured he'd be back from the past as soon as he'd found Lindsay and the baby, and return to the moment he'd left. Nobody would know he'd ever gone, just as before, no matter how long it took.

Brochan did a little dance, like a leprechaun in a cereal commercial, then plunked back down on his cushion to lean toward Alex with wide eyes and an eager look of hope on his face. "Och! Tell me what it is to fly! Please! I so envy those with wings!" He nodded as if to affirm his own words and waved Alex on to hear what his guest would say about being a pilot. More mead came, and Alex found himself expounding at length on the sensation of zooming about the sky and what it was like to be shot from the catapult on an aircraft carrier. The faerie wanted to know what an aircraft carrier was, and Alex was unable to resist talking about them. He let his troubles slip to the back of his mind.

Then there came some food. A roast bird that smelled heavenly and tasted so good he might have died then and been happy. The hospitality here pleased him, and Alex began to relax. After a while he was reminded of the story he'd been asked to tell, and went back to it.

"Oh. Right. The flight. Lindsay and I were going to northern Scotland, and we flew through this space where ol' Nemed was casting a spell. Only he was doing it from back then."

"He will. Or is."

Alex ignored Brochan's interruption, for it made his head hurt to puzzle out what the faerie had meant. "Whatever." He waved a hand of dismissal. "In any case, we bailed—"

"You threw water from your ship?"

After a moment of mead-induced mental confusion, Alex worked out that Brochan meant bailing water from the bottom of a sailing ship. "No, we threw ourselves from the plane. It broke when it went through the portal, and we came down in a parachute."

"Ah." The faeries seemed to know what a parachute was, and that was odd.

"We ran into Robert right after that. On his way to the coronation, he knighted me—"

"Just like that, you were a knight? I was unaware the humans allowed commoners into the knighthood."

Alex grunted. "Sure they do. All the time. Not back then, I guess, but eventually all you had to be was rich and famous. And British, I suppose. In any case, Robert was pretty hard up for fighting men, and he'd just seen me fight. I'd killed a guy who was out to kill him. It's not like he took too close a look at my pedigree."

"I see. And I suppose if it walks like a duck and talks like a duck—"

"Then I was as good as a noble and might as well be put to use."

Alex's stomach heaved of a sudden, and for a scary moment he thought he would lose his lunch. In a hot sweat he leaned over the polished root at his elbow, hauled in deep breaths, then the sensation passed as quickly as it had come. A moment later it was as if he'd never felt sick, and the sense of well-being returned. Increased, perhaps. He smiled at Brochan as the faerie continued the conversation as if he'd not just watched Alex nearly vomit.

"I suppose it's to your unending credit that nobody has attempted to attack you by searching out a flaw in your claim. Even the most entrenched laird might find himself subject to such trouble, were he a stranger."

Alex shook his head and grinned. "Nah, you see, I've got the laird of the MacNeils backing me up. Good old Hector, of Barra."

"Do ye indeed? And how did you manage that wondrous coup?"

Alex chuckled, amused by the memory of how that had worked out. "I didn't even have to make up the story; it just sort of all fell into place because everyone assumed I was his father's illegitimate son. Apparently the old man was a horndog of some sort and littered the landscape with kids. All Robert needed was to hear my name, and he assumed I was one of those sons."

Brochan erupted with uproarious laughter, and Alex wondered what was so funny about that, but continued. "Eventually I was forced to tell Hector the truth. That I'm from the future."

"Or the past."

Alex frowned, but went on. "He found out Lindsay was a woman—"

"He learnt you were banging your squire, and ye did not want him thinking she was a man."

Alex shrugged. "In short. So I ended up telling him the whole truth. He came to know that I'm descended from his own people and has kept my secret. He's my friend and still thinks of me as his brother. He'll back me up if anyone tries to give me guff."

Brochan adjusted his seat and leaned forward again with great interest. "So tell me, Sir Alasdair an Dubhar MacNeil of Eilean Aonarach, if 'twas yourself who ruined Nemed's spell, why is it you're the one wanting to kill him and not the other way around?"

Alex's eyes narrowed. He hadn't told that part yet. "How did you know I ruined the spell?"

"By flying through it, ye sumph. It couldn't have been good, and such a spell must have taken a great deal of power to knock out your engines."

This faerie was finally making sense, but he did seem to be entirely too cognizant of specifics Alex hadn't mentioned. "Yeah. The engines." He fell silent and let a long pause string out. Glancing around, he noticed the crowd in the room had dwindled. Many who remained were fast asleep, snoring little faerie snores in the dimness of fires reduced to coals. How long had he been there? It seemed only moments, but at the same time it felt like forever. Days, maybe. How many times had he eaten since sitting down? Had he needed to pee? He couldn't remember. Surely he must have.

An overwhelming sleepiness descended on him as quickly as had the urge to vomit. Alex leaned back against the cushions behind him, just to rest for a moment.

But when he opened his eyes again the room was lively with people. Instead of feeling refreshed by his sleep, he was groggy as hell. He blinked through a haze thick enough to have been smoke from the fires, but it was only in his head. A *cuach* was thrust into his hands, and he drank deeply, thirsty and hungry. He ate from a plate of food someone gave him, and looked around for Brochan. The faerie with the gold belt appeared immediately, in a hurry from another part of the complex of burrows.

"So! Continue!"

Alex plundered his brain to remember where he'd left off in his story, but everything in his head was as fuzzy as the air seemed to be. He'd slept, he was certain, but had no idea for how long, and he didn't feel rested at all. He felt as if he could go unconscious again at any moment. He leaned heavily on the polished tree root beside him and struggled to stay upright.

Finally Brochan seemed to notice there was something wrong with him. He lowered his chin and peered into Alex's face. "Are ye not feeling well, Sir Alasdair?"

Alex opened his mouth to speak, but no comment would come.

Brochan shrugged as if this were of no consequence, and waved a hand. "Och, I ken what ye're needing! I see how tense ye've become, and that must be remedied!" Brochan called out, "Come! Fiona! We've a man here who needs to be put at his ease!"

A faerie woman rose from a cluster of folk near the large fire and made her way toward him. Weaving between the lounging people, she gazed at Alex with deep, intense blue eyes and a big smile on her face that told him she was thrilled to have been called on. She fairly danced as she came, and the swell and bounce of her very healthy breasts was barely disguised by the thin drape of ragged tunic. Clarity descended on Alex, and at that moment he thought she was the most gorgeous creature he'd ever glimpsed. He feasted his eyes, and all that mead he'd just sucked down went straight to his groin while his neck went boneless. His head wanted to fall back with the pleasure of this vision, and he barely managed to hold it up at a tilt to follow her progress toward him.

The tiny woman slipped behind him and knelt to take his shoulders in her hands. They were hands far stronger than he might have thought, and the fey creature kneaded the tight shoulder muscles expertly so that Alex's eyes drooped nearly shut.

A groan of deep satisfaction rose from him. The world spun and colors danced before his eyes. A *cuach* was thrust into his hands again, and he drank deeply. Again the sensation of well-being surged through him. Hands on his shoulders continued, then became breasts against his back and the hands moved to his arms. More hands reached to lift the T-shirt he wore, and he let them pull it over his head. The massage continued, and he was encouraged to lean back against the woman behind him so that he lay in her lap. Looking up, he could see she'd removed her tunic and her chest was directly over his face. He stared. The blood raced in him, but none of it through his brain. The curve of flesh, smooth and swaying with the movement of her hands, invited him to touch. To feel the skin, and the softness beneath. His jeans were tight against his crotch, and he wished for his old tunic to cover what he knew must be an enormous bulge though he wouldn't look to see.

But Brochan's voice intruded. "And so the spell was ruined and you were knighted by the king . . ."

Alex's voice was weak and distant, but he resumed his story, picking up the slender thread he was offered. "Yeah. I was a knight, and Lindsay disguised herself as a boy and became my squire."

"Strong woman."

"Aye. She was." Breathing became difficult. Thinking was nearly impossible, but he forged ahead. "She distinguished herself in battle and became a knight herself. When I was awarded Eilean Aonarach, she became my wife." Wife. Lindsay was his wife. They were married. He shouldn't be lying in the lap of another woman. But

Lindsay had left. She was gone. "I'd thought we were going to settle down, have a family, and run the island." The room spun out of control, and his story echoed in the far recesses of his mind. He struggled to tell it, as if the telling were the only thing keeping him on the earth. Or in the earth. Where was he, anyway? *When* was he? He had no idea anymore. "And there was a baby." His own voice faded into the distance, and he had to shout to hear himself, though it only seemed to make his voice harder to hear. "The baby was coming. We had to leave. So he would be safe. To go back to the future. The present . . . We made Nemed . . . We returned . . ."

Finally he succumbed to the pleasure of hands on him. With a sigh he stopped talking, relaxed, and the last thing he remembered was some various hands plucking at his belt and fly, and starting to slip his jeans and skivvies from his hips.

CHAPTER 3

Lindsay MacNeil stood before the faerie knoll near Scone Palace, staring up at the pointed top that was just a little too pointed to be entirely natural, then turned her focus to the little, bitty door halfway up. A depression like a navel, nearly grown over with bracken. She and Alex had gone through that door once, and had regretted it mightily. Another such regret would more than likely come her way soon, but there was nothing for it. Nemed had her son she was sure, and by God she was going to get the boy back.

She hitched up the carrying strap of her oblong athletic bag higher on her shoulder, then started up the switchback trace that looked like a cow trail except that it led directly to the entrance. There she regarded the weather-worn little door, framed by rough wood and intricately carved as it seemed everything had been back in the days when she'd seen this last. Carved or painted. The wood now was cracked and gray with age, and it looked as if it might fall to pieces if she touched it. But she knew it wouldn't, even if it were entirely dust held together with magic. Nemed wouldn't let

it fall apart. He probably wouldn't even let her through if
he didn't want her to come.

As she watched, the latch snicked and the door eased
open a couple of inches on squeaky hinges. There it was.
The gesture. Nemed surely had the baby, and now he was
inviting her to come on in. A bluff? The thought made her
grimace. Right. Like that elfin king could ever be afraid of
any human. Last time she'd seen him he was ready to set
her on fire and watch her burn. Herself and the child. She
knew he would have done it without so much as a blink or
a sweat. Even when Alex had a sword to his throat, the
pointy-eared devil had shown no fear.

Neither would she, anymore. Loathing surged in her,
and she pushed the door the rest of the way open. She was
going to kill the bastard, but first he was going to tell her
where her son was.

Inside the knoll was the chamber she remembered from
before, but it was empty. Not like before, when there had
been a fire and food. Today she wasn't hungry. She looked
around for Nemed. There was nobody there, so she moved
onward and into the tunnels.

As before, there was no discernible light source in the
tunnels though she could see perfectly well. Odd to be able
to see in the dark. The curves and bulges of the burrow
walls seemed flattened. Undefined by light, but sensed by
Lindsay's mind. All was shades of dark gray. She peered
into spaces, unable to see how deep they went. But she
could see no shapes to suggest the presence of anything
living. Nor even anything dead. Just earth. And tree roots.
Tendrils and taproots growing into and out of the spaces
within the knoll. The burrow led her on. Her booted footsteps were dull thuds against the packed earth beneath, and
she ducked under and between bulges of root and earth
overhead. Lindsay didn't worry about where she was going. Finding her way back wouldn't be an issue until she
found her child. Once she found her child, then she would
worry about returning with him.

The urge to weep came over her again, and she paused

in her search to squeeze her eyes shut and hold her breath against the tears. They hadn't even named him, what with the bad connection from Alex's ship. He was only Baby Boy MacNeil, and she'd known him for just three days. Held him and nursed him but a few times. In hospital she hadn't been with him long enough to even notice the ears under his little blue baby cap. Hadn't seen what everyone else in the delivery room had gone quiet over. In hospital she'd been so joyful to have her son, and to know how pleased Alex would be when he heard, she hadn't noticed the ears.

Then at home she'd seen them and was horrified. With his cap off, the shape of his ears let her know she was not yet finished with Nemed. He'd done something to the child. She didn't know what, but those ears were surely a trick of some sort. For hours she'd sat with him, examining him, touching a finger to those tiny points and struggling to know what had happened. Aside from that one feature he seemed perfectly human. A perfectly normal baby, big and healthy and entirely intact. Mum had come to see him, and with the cap on she couldn't tell anything was amiss. Lindsay's mother would have known if anything was wrong with the baby, but she'd said nothing and gone home as happy about the birth as when she'd arrived.

But then when the changeling had come . . .

It was a little faerie man. Or an elf. Leprechaun or brownie, perhaps; it was hard to tell sometimes with those folk. Filthy and evil, and lying there in the crib with a terrible grin on his face as if it were a huge joke on her. She'd caught the creature by the throat where he lay and shook him. His eyes bugged out with fear, and that fed her anger. She demanded to know where her son was, and the thing in her hands pointed to his throat. He was choking. She let up just enough for him to gasp for air, and growled at him that he should comply with her request or be strangled.

He said, "Search the past, for he has died there. In the place of his conception. He's returned home."

"Why?" *Died? In the past?* "When? Who killed him?"
She could go there and stop it.

" 'Twas his fate." The faerie in her hands grinned. "And
yours." Then he laughed. Shrill and manic, his laughter cut
to her core.

Outraged, she strangled the creature, throwing the dust
of death every which way and leaving her with nothing but
an empty crib and a photograph of the child with deformed
ears. Perhaps it had been a bad idea not to take him prisoner and bring him with her, but to see that . . . *thing* where
her baby should have been was too horrifying. Too evil.
She'd not been able to countenance letting him live in
place of her baby for even a moment.

After that, memory grew a little fuzzy. All she could
think of in her rage and grief was that she must find Nemed
and make him give back her child, then kill him so the boy
would be safe. Now she was close to her goal. Nemed was
here somewhere. She would find him, make him give back
her son, then kill the elf.

Now she opened her eyes to continue her search and
thought of how upset Alex would be when he learned of
the ears. Those ears. God knew where they'd come from.
A spell? What had Nemed done? Was the child even
Alex's genetically? And if not, then how had she conceived? She was not conversant with the ins and outs of fey
magic; she imagined anything was possible. If Nemed did
this to her—destroyed her marriage to Alex—for that
alone he should die. He certainly would once she caught
up with him.

Finally she found herself in the room she sought. This
was the place; she was sure. But no Nemed. It figured. Cowardly wanker. She set her bag on the dirt floor that sloped
to the middle like most earthen floors packed hard by the
feet of occupants. Off in the corner was the secluded spot
where they'd seen Nemed before, but though she peered
into it she couldn't discern any presence. That meant little,
for she knew the lack of light made for deceptions she
couldn't penetrate.

She pulled open the zipper of her bag and took the rolled elastic bandage from it. Quickly she unbuttoned her blouse and removed it, pulled off her bra, then wrapped the wide bandage around her breasts to press them flat. Or, at least, as flat as she could get them just then. Her teeth clamped to her lower lip at the pain of binding breasts filled with milk, and her heart broke that it would go away soon unless she could find her son very quickly. It was already dwindling; her breasts had been rock hard at first but now seemed only heavy. The milk would keep coming if she expressed it, but that wouldn't be possible, nor even a good idea, where she was going. Anyone there who saw she was lactating would expect her to hire out as a wet nurse, and as a woman there would be no freedom of movement to look for the elf. No, she had to return to the guise of Sir Lindsay Pawlowski, in search of his nephew, the child of Sir Alasdair and Marilyn MacNeil of Eilean Aonarach. Lindsay Pawlowski was supposedly dead, but it would be a simple story to resurrect the brave young man who had fallen down a mountainside in a struggle against a bandit, for the body had never been recovered.

When she finished, the bandage was tight and bulged more than she liked, but the tunic and mail hauberk she'd brought went over it and hung well enough to disguise her gender. She looked like a barrel-chested man. A pouch she attached to her belt contained a large packet of the thinnest, most compact, yet maximally absorbent sanitary towels on the market. The postpartum bleeding would continue for a while yet. In the past she'd used pieces of linen for her periods, which she'd then burned or buried to keep her secret, but though the sanitary towels would cause questions if discovered, it would be worth the risk not to have to carry so much bulk. One of these would last so much longer and protect so much better than a plain piece of cloth.

It was a tightrope she was about to walk. A dangerous game of deception, to present herself as a man in a world where she could be killed for it if discovered. But she had experience moving like a man, walking, talking, and behaving like one. Her shoulders shrugged, and the chain mail settled over them. The garb felt heavy, but familiar. The gauntlets that had also been Alex's were a bit large on her, and the spikes riveted to the knuckles would probably not be terribly effective because of that, but there was nothing for it. A weird nostalgia for the days when she rode with Bruce's army against Edward of England made inroads beneath her hatred for Nemed, and it made her feel stronger than she knew she was.

She reached into the bag again and brought out the sword. It was an authentic reproduction of a real medieval weapon; she'd bought it in London. Nearly a museum piece in its own right, it was not a toy or sport piece like those favored by people who attended historical reenactments and such. This was a real weapon. Made of genuine tempered steel, it bore an edge and balance worthy of the knight she would have to become on the other side of this wall. The hilt was not solid silver as it appeared, but nobody would know that. The grip, however, was wrapped in silver wire and would tarnish normally enough not to raise eyebrows. She knew how to use this weapon, as well as the dagger she'd also bought. She hung them both in scabbards, on a leather belt she then slung about her hips over her surcoat and mail, then donned the mail coif and addressed the walls.

"Coward. Show yourself!"

The voice then came. "You're serious, I can see." It sent a frisson of fear down her back and out to her fingers, but she clenched her jaw and kept the emotion to herself. Nemed was there, as she'd expected.

"You have my son."

"I have no such thing. Go away. Leave me alone, and tell that idiot American you've married to do likewise. I've finished with the both of you."

"Where are you?" If she could get him to show himself,

she thought she might be able to fight him right there and have done with the whole issue. But his reply was a disappointment.

"Not here, I assure you. That husband of yours nearly killed me with his demand I send you both home. I barely exist anywhere anymore."

"Liar."

There was a great heaving sigh, then, "If you say so, but in any case I'm neither where nor when you are currently. I really don't care to discuss it."

"Where is my son?"

"I've no idea. Now go away."

"I want my child back."

"And I can't help you. Not even were I so inclined, which I decidedly am not. I've no idea where your cursed brat might be."

"But you know where I am."

Impatience tinged the voice. "Were he lurking about my burrows, I expect I might also know where the little monster was. But he is not, and therefore I couldn't tell you where you might find him."

Lindsay's throat tightened with frustration, and now she was more afraid of having to give up and leave the way she'd come than she was of anything Nemed might do. She said, "Then allow me to search for him myself. If you don't have him, then someone does. I want to go looking."

"By your costume I assume you mean to search a century other than your own. What makes you think you can find your offspring there?"

Because I know you have him. But Lindsay didn't say it out loud. "The changeling. There was a changeling, and he told me the baby had been taken to the past. Back to where he'd been conceived."

"To Eilean Aonarach. Fourteenth century."

"Right." 1315.

"And you need my help in this because . . . ?"

"You can send me back."

"I can?"

"You've moved me through time before. You can do it again."

"At what cost do you think I did that? You think it such a simple thing to send a being back and forth in time? Surely you know better than that."

"Alex and I both once traveled seven years and a number of miles in this very knoll. It seemed simple enough for you at the time."

"It was. And it was random. What you ask is not the same thing."

"It's not? How? What's the difference between that and what you've already done on a whim?"

A great exhausted sigh came from nowhere. "Och, that I would be saved from impertinent mortals." Then the elf said, "How might I explain this so your tiny, modern human mind might grasp it?" There were some more sighs and mutterings, then, "Take, for example, a boat on the ocean. The boat drifts. It moves. It travels from one spot to another without any effort on the part of its passengers. No cost."

"All right, then, a boat on the ocean."

"It travels neither fast nor far."

"Right."

"Now compare that to travel to the moon. Nobody arrives on the moon accidentally, nor without a great deal of effort."

"Fast and far."

"Indeed. Not to mention costly."

"So, what happened to Alex and myself in this knoll was like drifting. Accidental. Even though it was you who sent us there."

"I tossed you through the wall only. What awaited you was there without my influence."

"And now what I need is influence, such as what got us home. Such as what sent us to the past to begin with."

"Such as what has made me but a ghost of my former self. Your vile husband has nearly destroyed me. Twice."

"And for that you've taken our son?"

"I've nothing to do with your brat!" The outburst was loud, and assailed Lindsay's eardrums to the point of pain. She knelt, gasping, her hands covering her ears, until she thought she could stand sound again. For all the elf 's complaints of weakness, his voice was powerful. Then she looked up, drew a deep breath, and made an offer.

"Let me bear the cost. Take from me what is necessary to get me there." *Just don't kill me doing it.*

"I could, you know. Kill you by doing that. That is to say, you could die in the attempt."

Lindsay squeezed her eyes shut. The wanker was reading her mind. She knew Nemed couldn't kill by magic. Nor could any fey being, but she also knew accidents could happen. The spell he'd fashioned, the one ruined by Alex's plane, had killed thirty Nemedians who had been the last of their kind.

"I can't read your mind. Not well, in any case. Some things are just obvious."

"Allow me to search for my son." What she really wanted was to go where the elfin bastard was and kill him. She guessed—hoped—the path to the past of least resistance would be within Nemed's natural lifetime. If he sent her anywhere, it would be there.

"I told you, I have no idea where you might find him."

"Then let me search where I think he might be. That Danu. Perhaps she would have an idea of where to look." Danu had once given her a book of psalms, a gift Lindsay had puzzled over and had never understood why it had been given.

"What do you know of the faerie queen?"

"Only that Alex has spoken to her. That she took an interest in him and our situation. He used to talk about having met her in the forest on Eilean Aonarach. They had chats."

There was a long silence. Nemed was thinking about that. Lindsay looked around at the flat, gray room, and for a second thought she might have glimpsed the elfin king lurking against a wall. Two red eyes against a gray background. But it was only a glimpse, then it was gone.

She addressed that space. "Send me back to where I can find her, then I'll be out of your hair and will seek my son with her help."

His silence continued until she thought he'd gone for good and she would be forced to either press farther into the burrow or retreat empty-handed to the century from which she'd come. But then he said, "Go. The way you went before."

"Seriously?"

"Just go, before I come to my senses. But be warned. You won't find what you seek. I guarantee it."

Says you. It was with a deep relief Lindsay reached toward the earthen wall through which she and Alex had been thrust the last time. Her hand went into it, and it hurt. A burning sensation that worsened as she pressed on.

"Ow." She retrieved her hand.

"I told you there would be a price. If you shrink from that little pain, you've no hope of making it to where you wish to go."

Asshole. She touched the wall again, and the burning came again. Her hand jerked back.

"Who's the coward now, eh, Sir Lindsay?" His voice was thick with derision.

Disgusted with the scheming creature, she glanced around for him and wished he were there so she could take his head with her sword, watch it roll across the floor, then piss down his neck. But that wasn't yet an option for her, so she turned back to the wall. Deep breath. Let it out. Another deep breath, then she leapt at the wall.

As hard as she threw herself, it still wasn't enough force to put her all the way through. Agony of burning took her. It began to consume her. She thrashed and struggled against the substance that held her, stuck in that place between centuries. A wail of pain wrenched her. She kicked, and swam through, burning all the while. Thoughts of fire and brimstone filled her head, and despair accompanied it. She had to kick harder, and somehow she found the strength to do it. Finally she was through, and collapsed. One hand gripping the hilt of her sword, she then fell mercifully unconscious.

CHAPTER 4

The cold was at Alex's core, and he was shivering. Shaking so hard his joints rattled. As he regained consciousness, the pain he felt was monstrous. Every inch of flesh, every nerve, each joint was in such screaming pain that he tried to return to blissful oblivion, though through the haze of semiconsciousness he knew he might die if he didn't get warm soon. But then, it also seemed he might die if he became fully conscious of his agony.

He wasn't that lucky. Against his will he came to and found himself facedown in the rain, on grassy ground with his face pressed against a hard, black fungus. The drizzle was light but insistent, and rivulets ran from him here and there over his body. The realization he was naked seeped into his brain, and it made him feel even colder. When he tried to move, his stomach heaved. It hitched and rolled, and he swallowed hard to keep the bile down, but in the end was forced to raise his head and vomit on the grass. That made him sicker, dizzy as well, and he rose up on his hands to vomit again. Gummy strings dangled from his mouth to the ground as his stomach continued to heave and jerk.

Now he was glad for the rain, and he wiped his face with his wet fingers. He spat as he struggled to keep from throwing up a third time, and turned away from the steaming puddle before him.

There would be no standing up for him. Not for a while. Elbows trembled under his partial weight. He continued to shiver and his stomach hitched in an effort to rid itself of whatever might be left in it. This time he was able to keep the heaving under control, but knew it was probably because there was nothing left to hurl. Rain ran from his hair down his face, down his back, down his arms. It sprayed from his lips with each shivering gasp and dribbled from his chin to his chest.

He looked around. It was a small clearing, and it appeared familiar. He'd been here before. Grass mingled with black fungus patches and a line of toadstools.

Toadstools. The familiarity of this place clicked, and he looked around to find the toadstools surrounded him. He was in the middle of a faerie ring, one he'd seen before. And off to his right was the log. The one eaten up with moss, that had graced Danu's place on Eilean Aonarach. Not only was this his island, it was also his time. Or near to it, in any case. Within a few decades.

Excitement surged in him, causing his stomach to hitch again, and he choked up dregs from his gut. Nothing there to speak of, and he spat mucus onto the grass in front of him. Then he sat up. Hunched over to keep the rain from his eyes, he thought he might yet collapse back onto the ground. Deep breaths seemed to help the pain, and he took several long moments to settle his stomach. But the cold was monstrous and the shivering uncontrollable. He needed help.

"Danu?" His voice was hoarse, and he coughed to clear it.

His query was met only with silence. He tried again.

"Queen Danu? Are you there?" He hated the pathetic sound of need in his voice, but he couldn't help it. He needed her. But she wasn't responding.

"Bitch."

Neither did that bring her from hiding. So he looked around in hopes of finding his clothes, but those damned faeries had left him nothing. Not even his tote bag with the medieval clothing, which was probably still in the twenty-first century. They'd thrust him into this time, more than likely almost killing him, with not so much as a swatch to cover himself. And if he didn't get to shelter soon, he might end up dead in any case. Painfully, the shivering voiced with each breath, he began to pull himself together and rise to his feet.

His knees buckled, and he knelt in the soggy grass. The rain had increased and now was beating his back rather than just dropping on it. A steady stream came off his chin, a smaller one from his nose, and he gasped for air as he watched the water dribble to the ground. It was miles to the castle, and he had no guarantee there would be anyone there. An equal distance in the other direction would be a farmhouse, but without knowing the year he couldn't say whether it was occupied either. No telling what the year was. He recalled that before he'd taken possession of his award there had been a long-running feud over the island between the MacDonalds and the MacLeods. God knew who was in control just then, and he wouldn't put it past that crazy little freak Brochan to have set him in the midst of a war in this condition.

But Alex wasn't getting any stronger just sitting there. He had to do something—go somewhere—and dear sweetheart Danu obviously was not going to be of any help. So he pulled himself together once more and rose to his feet. This time he was able to stand without collapsing, feet splayed like a colt, his concentration on keeping himself off the ground. Then, though he knew it was risky, he took a step. The leg failed, and he went to one knee. Okay, it was going to be harder than he'd thought. Once more he struggled to both feet, then took another step. This time he was able to keep from falling. Another step, and again he didn't fall.

It was going to be a long walk at this rate. But he took another step, knowing if he didn't the alternative was to lie on the grass and die of the cold. He kept going.

The rain was relentless, leaching from him the little heat his body was able to produce. He stuffed his hands into his armpits and huddled his arms against himself, but it made little difference, as exposed as he was. He followed his old running trail toward the castle, and it heartened him that it seemed unchanged from the last time he'd come through here, in 1315.

Hours passed. A couple of times he knelt to rest, but the cold at his core encouraged him to press onward. Mud at his feet became slippery, and that made his progress more difficult. His concentration focused on putting one foot in front of the other. His entire existence narrowed to the single task. Soon it seemed he'd never done anything else but this and would never do anything else again as long as he lived. But he hoped that would be longer than just today.

A glance at the dimming sky told him the afternoon was nearly over, and soon it would be dark. He stepped up his pace.

Finally, just as the darkness was about to swallow Eilean Aonarach, he emerged from the forest and onto the plain that lay before the inland gate of his castle. Almost immediately there was a shout from the crenellated battlement ahead. The castle was occupied. On one hand that might be good, but on the other it could mean his death. Painfully he made his way across the field, hoping that if they killed him it would be quickly. Just then hell sounded toasty warm and inviting.

By the time he reached the portcullis, a line of silhouettes in the dusk had gathered along the battlement, most of them bearing crossbows. None of them were pointed at him yet, and Alex figured he wasn't such a threat in his state of dress. The gathering was probably more curious than alarmed at a naked man wandering about in the rain. He halted at a distance and eyed them carefully, but knew if he was close enough to be heard he was close enough to be shot. The men up high waited, letting him make the first hail. He obliged right away, for there was little time for him to be fooling around.

He ventured in Middle English, "Ho! Castle!"

"Who goes there?"

Alex might have just blurted his name, but wanted first to know how it would be received. With all the strength he had left, he stood as straight and confident as he could. His vulnerability was obvious; bluff was his only option. He didn't even bother to put a hand over his crotch, but stood as if he had no need for the clothing he so plainly lacked. He responded in a voice that rattled with shivering, "Give me your name, guard, so I can praise you to your master for your alertness. You saw me the very moment I came from the forest." His eyes shut against the rain and against his own exhaustion, then he looked up again to the dark shapes above.

The guard had a nonplussed moment. Alex saw he was scanning the forest edge, more than likely in search of any indication this stranger was a decoy bringing invaders to attack if the gate should be opened. But then the watch shouted, "Sir Henry Ellot, stranger. And, as my master is away, I think you'll tell him naught."

Relief washed over Alex and he nearly collapsed for it. Ellot was one of his own household guard, from the Lowlands and brought to the island by himself after Bannockburn. He nearly laughed. Those blasted faeries had come through, in their own, weird way. He swayed as he shouted, "Open the gate, Sir Henry! Your master has returned!"

Alex's bluff quite left him, now that he knew they would not kill him, and his strength failed completely. As he collapsed to the muddy ground and his mind faded to haze, he heard a shocked cry. "MacNeil!"

He remained conscious enough to be aware of further shouting and the chain clatter of the gate being raised. Dimly he knew there were hands lifting him, then carrying him into the bailey and on up the winding path between the various castle structures, then finally there was warmth. Good heat from the fire in the great hall, where a call for clothing and plaids and cushions went up and was repeated at full voice throughout the keep. He half lay over the side of the long fire pit that ran much of the length of the room, where an enormous pile of burning logs kept the large hall heated and often fed the troops with roasted meat. Alex lay his face against warm stone and groaned. His skin felt on fire with the heat, and it was a welcome pain.

Servants gathered, shocked. There was much talk in Gaelic, which Alex understood in a rudimentary way, but just then he was too sick to figure out what they were saying. Soon a cup was put to his lips, and he tasted mead. Hair of the dog that it might be, he turned his head away as his stomach heaved and he choked. "Broth. Bring some broth." There would be some in the kitchen, the building just down the slope.

Someone was sent to get it. Someone else was dispatched to ready the laird's chamber.

Alex's shivering grew more violent. His pulse picked up, and he was in a misery of uncontrollable shaking. Like a grand mal fit. The warmth felt like burning, as if he were flaming and freezing at once, on fire but shivering for it like fever. If only he could fall unconscious again. It would be so sweet to pass out. He was wrapped in wool blankets, nearly like a mummy, and he gathered them in to himself. No matter how bundled he became, the cold seemed to radiate from inside him. The shaking continued.

Soon another cup was put to his lips, and he tasted beef soup. Much of it spilled as they tried to get it down him, but enough of it made it into his mouth that he could swallow. It made a heat trail down his throat and into his gut, which heaved at the outrage. He held his breath and made it stay down. Then he took some more. Warmth. The soup tasted like pure heat, and it was delicious.

Once the soup was in him, the shivering calmed to a bearable trembling that only made his breathing stutter. His eyes closed, he lay at the side of the hearth and let the warmth seep into him. When he finally felt something other than cold, it was exhaustion. From somewhere in the incomprehensible distance the announcement came his chamber and bed were ready for him. Hands lifted him in his bundle and carried him down the stairs from the hall to the laird's apartments. They unwrapped him from the plaid and laid him in the elaborately carved bed, on silken sheets, beneath a thick comforter stuffed with goose down. The shivering calmed some more. The fire in the hearth was high and bright. The wall of living rock at one side of the room ran with water from the rain outside, making a trickling sound that brought to mind the nights he'd shared this bed with Lindsay. It soothed and warmed him, and he fell into oblivion.

When he came to again, it was in a red haze of fever. Shivering took him again, this time in a rage of heat. Faces hovered before his eyes, and he thought he recognized them but the names escaped his pain-wracked mind. One was a priest—Alex knew by the tonsure—dabbing oil on his forehead and muttering in Latin. Father Patrick. It was Father Patrick, the young guy from the castle chapel. There was a boy. A blond kid. Another man stood at a distance. Short and bearded, Alex felt he should know who that man was. But the struggle to remember brought more pain.

"He's still with us," said the man with the beard. Then it came to Alex who he was. Hector. This was Hector MacNeil, Laird of Barra. The one who owned him as half brother, though he knew Alex was a distant descendant from the future. Alex tried to sit up, and the boy stepped back. The blond kid, seven or eight years old. Gregor. Alex remembered now. Gregor MacNeil. Hector's nephew, the son of Hector's deceased brother, and Alex's foster son. His page. The boy's eyes were wide, and he looked as if he were about to cry. People around here thought it was okay for guys to cry. Alex had never been able to figure that out, but just then he didn't give a damn whether Gregor bawled himself red in the face or laughed and danced a jig.

The room spun, and Alex groaned. A woman came to press him back onto the bed. His wife's maid, Mary. "Lie back down, sir. Ye're in no condition to be sitting up."

The room was sweltering. The high fire threw light to the most distant corners. Alex shoved the bedcovers from himself, then lay back, panting. Every inch of his body ached to his bones. He wished he could slip back into the darkness from which he'd just come and stay there, even if it meant never coming back. "Somebody kill me," he said, and he wasn't sure whether he was speaking modern English, Middle English, or Gaelic. A hard shudder took him, then stopped, then for a moment there was respite before the shivering began anew. Mary tried to restore his blankets, but he pushed them away until she compromised with only the silk sheet.

Then he must have gone unconscious, for the next thing he knew someone was offering a spoon to his mouth. A drop of something warm touched his lips, then spread along the line between them. He licked them and tasted soup. "Here, eat," came the female voice he assumed was Mary. But when he opened his eyes it was another maid. One he didn't know, who was younger than Mary. The daughter of someone, he thought. Surely someone's daughter, but he couldn't think whose. She touched the pewter spoon to his lips again and he sipped the broth. Suddenly he was hungry, and he struggled to sit up so he could take more soup. The girl sat at the edge of his bed and patiently fed it to him. The room seemed cooler now, and his sheets were soaked with sweat. The damp, clammy silk stuck to his skin uncomfortably.

"Where's Hector?"

"Above, in the Great Hall, sir. Shall I have him summoned?"

A wan smile came to him at the thought of anyone ordering Hector around. Alex took with his teeth a bit of meat on the spoon, and chewed. "Let him know I've awakened and am well enough to receive him if he would care to visit."

"Are ye certain you're well enough?"

"No, but if I die I'd hate to miss him."

Alarm struck the maid's face. "Die, sir?"

"Go get Hector, girl." The talk was wearing him out.

She set the bowl and spoon on a nearby table, picked up her skirts, and hurried from the room.

Alex lay back and rested his eyes as he waited, and presently Hector entered. The maid hadn't returned with him, so the Laird of Barra took the bowl of broth from the table and came to offer some more to Alex.

"Tell me what happened, brother, when you met the elfin king."

"I won," Alex said, and sighed.

Hector's bushy eyebrows rose. "Your opponent must be dead, then." The last Hector had seen of Alex was when he'd left Eilean Aonarach to confront Nemed and make him send himself and Lindsay to the twenty-first century. He'd told Hector he wouldn't return.

"You've not brought Herself back with you. I fear to ask what has become of her."

Alex's heart clenched. "She's gone missing. I don't know where she is; that's why I'm here, to find her. How long was I gone?"

"Half a year. 'Tis nearly Beltane." A light of confusion at the question told Alex Hector was still having trouble with the truth of Alex's origins. He'd accepted that Alex was a descendant, but wrapping his mind around the idea of moving backward and forward through time was a strain on him.

Beltane. Alex remembered it was the first of May. Nearly Beltane would make this April of 1316. He said, "I was in the future four months, Hector. I made him send me back to where I came from, and my son was born there."

Hector grinned. "A son, ye say? And healthy? Praises to God!"

Pain curdled the joy Alex should have felt, for he wished he could believe the boy was his. But he said, "And as soon as he was born, he was taken. Someone abducted him from his mother. She's chasing after him, I think. I don't know where either of them are."

"Och," said Hector, more softly than Alex had ever heard him speak. "But you think they may have come here?"

"I'm certain she has. She's taken my armor. I think she came back because this is where I can find people who might help me." But he wasn't finding Danu, and Hector would be no help, either. "I need to take my men and search for her. I think she's come to this century. She's got my hauberk and gauntlets, which aren't much use in future times."

Hector gave a thoughtful sigh and fed Alex some more soup, then said, "'Tis a rather large century. A man's life is nae so large." Meaning, Alex could live his whole life and possibly never live in the year to which Lindsay had returned.

"I know. But there weren't any other choices. The wee folk were my only hope."

A small, disgusted noise rasped in the back of Hector's throat. "Then hope is lost, for the faeries are dangerous and not to be trusted."

How well Alex knew that! But he said, "They sent me here, and nailed the date pretty well, considering."

"And nearly killed ye in the nailing."

"In any case, I'm here. And I must find my wife."

"Aye. But not today."

Alex sighed. "No. Not today." He closed his eyes and tried to rest, but images of what the future might hold buzzed through his brain. Adrift in the grief of the past days, he made his plans to take men to the mainland in search of his wife and her child. And he wouldn't give up until they were both found.

For several days he slept and ate, gaining strength. Whatever that Brochan guy had done to him turned out to be the worst illness of his life. Even the stabbing he'd taken while on Barra a year and a half ago had not laid him out this badly. He'd never been this sick before and hoped he'd never be this bad off again. A quick death for him would be his preference.

Finally he recovered enough to rise from his bed and
dress. It was to his disappointment he wasn't yet strong
enough to don chain mail and ride off on his search, and so
he wore his domestic robes to present himself in the Great
Hall for breakfast. Deep red to reflect his livery of red,
black, and gold, his garb was cinched with a wide, black
belt. He wore black trews beneath and black leather boots
with unfashionably blunt toes. Pointed shoes irked him. He
found it difficult to take seriously men who dressed like
munchkins, no matter that it was all the rage among the nobility to have long points that sometimes curled up and
over. Every time he saw the truly ridiculous ones, the ones
that curled so high the tips wiggled with each step, the Lol-
lipop Guild song leapt into his head and sometimes he
found himself humming it to himself the rest of the day.

With as much dignity as he could summon, Alex made
his way to the table at the head of the long hearth and
presided over the meal among his men. There seemed to
be an air of relief in the room that the master was recovered. Men ate heartily and occasionally stood to make
short speeches of their joy at his return and improving
health. The musician playing small bagpipes kept to lively
music, and Alex smiled as brightly as he could. It was going to be a long, expensive campaign to find Lindsay, and
he wanted his troops to maintain their enthusiasm to find
his wife. They seemed cheered to have him back, but
there was an underlying concern about the mistress of the
castle.

A cry went up from the bottom of the bailey, and a
trumpet sounded. An approach of strangers. Every ear in
the Great Hall perked to hear the call again, to determine
whether it was from land or sea. When the call came from
the land side, alarm struck and the knights present rose to
their feet to hurry into the bailey and down the slope.

Alex also rose, but dizziness made him sit back down
for a moment. Then he rose again, slowly, and followed his
men out to the lower curtain. Gregor came to aid him, but
he declined the offered arm and only rested his hand on the

boy's shoulder as they walked together down the winding path to the gate.

As he reached the stairway to the parapet over the portcullis, his knights prepared to sally forth and meet their visitors if they proved to be enemies. Horses milled and snorted, and men spoke excitedly of action. Alex's squire, Colin, had his horse saddled and was holding it for him, but he gave instructions to wait. Feeling like an old man, sore of joint and out of shape, he climbed to the parapet and moved past the guard to lean against the stone battlement. He looked out over the field that lay before the castle.

A cluster of mounted men stood dead center of the pasture. They flew no banner. Not good. That suggested a wariness or subterfuge that usually equaled threat. At the very least it lent itself to misunderstanding, which was nearly as dangerous. He instructed the guard to call out a challenge, and was obeyed, but no reply came from the intruders. Instead, the one at the front reached behind him to be handed off what looked like a long pole.

A banner, perhaps. Good. This would tell Alex what he needed to know about these clowns, and then they could talk. Or not.

But as the cloth unfurled from the pole, Alex's heart stopped. Then it began to pound with an insistence that made him nearly choke. His mouth dropped open.

The flag raised by the leader of these men was of red and white stripes, and stars on a field of blue. Flapping lazily in the breeze outside his castle in April of 1316 was the flag of the United States of America.

CHAPTER 5

Lindsay's skin felt burned. As she regained consciousness, she knew there must be blisters all over her face
and hands. She groaned, and her throat rasped in raging
pain. But when she ventured to touch her fingertips gently
to her forehead, there were no blisters. Her skin was smooth,
though it flinched at the touch. She looked at her hands. No
discoloring. Only the pain. She looked around without
moving her head, for even the turning of her eyeballs was a
tender thing. She lay there, drawing slow, careful breaths,
hoping the pain would diminish enough for her to raise her
head.

From here she could see she was still near Perth, in
Scone. The knoll rose above her, but not as it had been in
the twenty-first century. The door was cleared of bracken
and appeared sturdy. Almost new. She'd gone back in time,
and could only hope it was far enough. Drifting on the cur-
rents of fate wouldn't cut it this time.

After a few minutes, she tried again to move and found
the pain had subsided. She could raise her head without
feeling as if her skin would split open, and found the places

her clothing bound weren't as excruciating as they had been. She sat up.

It was nearing dark. The weather was cool and overcast, so she guessed the month to be May. June at the latest. The year could be nearly any. Not that it mattered all that much. It was Nemed she was after, and so long as he'd deposited her where she could find him physically, she could have what she was after. Alex had once forced him to send them home; she figured she could make him give back her son. Or else she'd kill him. Just then, in her pain, the prospect of killing him anyway was oh, so tempting.

As the burning faded to become tolerable, she climbed to her knees, then to her feet. Hard to tell where the sun was. By her memory of the knoll, she knew the river was beyond the stand of trees in front of her. The town would be just south of her. She began walking. The clothing chafed against her skin, and each step brought new pain.

Soon she came upon a cluster of buildings, along a dirt track pitted with deep hoofprints left from the last heavy rain. Not many wheeled conveyances came through here, and Lindsay's heart stilled with fear she might have gone back too many centuries. Torches and candles were being lit here and there in the village. She thought Scone would have been bigger than this.

One building was lit up more brightly than the others, and before it stood several mounts held by two squires chatting with each other in low voices. She guessed the place was a public house of some sort, the operative word being "house," since it was apparently someone's abode made available for travelers and locals to refresh themselves with food and drink. She made her way toward it, nodded perfunctory greeting to the bored squires, and took a deep breath to ready herself for the bluff. From experience she knew that in being convincing as a man the best defense was a good offense. Timidity of any sort would get her nothing but picked on, particularly in a time when even a modern man complete with penis and Y chromosome would be thought a shy coward of the worst sort.

Except Alex. Alex had impressed them from the very
start. She missed him horribly. Her heart ached at what he
would believe of her if she were unsuccessful, and she re-
solved that she would bring him Nemed's head, or die in
the attempt.

Lindsay ducked through the door to the public house
and went inside to learn what she could.

A large hearth at one end lit the room with a bright,
merry fire, and near it stood a counter of sorts. Unattended,
it was little more than a high, narrow table of rough wood.
Under it was a shelf that bore a single jug and some
wooden cups. The room was small enough the one round
table surrounded with chairs filled half of it. Most of the
chairs were taken by knights, more than likely the men
whose horses and squires awaited outside. A single door-
way containing no door led to a back room, from which
low voices of a woman and children emanated. The building was a single story, and Lindsay guessed the two rooms
were all there was to the place: the public room, and the
back room for the merchant and his family. Maybe there
was an outbuilding of some sort, for storage.

The men lounging around the table were plainly knights
by their swords, as she would also be identified as a knight
by hers. One squire stood off to the side, alert to his master's bidding but taking glances at Lindsay the newcomer.
The knights sitting casually in their chairs all stared at her,
their talk having been suspended on her entrance.

By their chain mail, and their lack of plate armor besides, she saw she had indeed come at least as far back as
she wished. By the style of their tunics and shoes, she was
relieved to note she'd probably come no farther back than
that. The appearance of these men was as she would expect
for the span of years she had aimed for, and that brought a
measure of relief. Her confidence rose, and she made certain it showed in her demeanor. She coughed to clear her
throat and relax her vocal chords so her voice could go as
low as possible without straining or softening. She would
never sound like anything but a teenage boy, and every bit

of pitch advantage helped. She said to them, "Is this a place for a thirsty man to find refreshment?"

One of the knights nodded toward the counter, and said with a voice of authority that suggested he was in charge of the group, "There. You'll find a jug and a *cuach*. Leave a penny for the jug, if you would have it all." The men seemed fairly scruffy, even for guys that were probably out on campaign. They looked like mercenaries. This one wore his hair long, to his shoulders, and though he had a beard along his jaw, chin, and lip in the English fashion, he also had heavy stubble where he hadn't shaved elsewhere in what appeared to be at least a week. Such a hairy face wasn't the way among Scottish nobility. The others were less scraggly, but not by much.

"And for just the cup?"

"Leave nothing, and Himself will come to you once you've had enough."

Lindsay figured she'd end up paying the entire penny that way in any case, so she went to the counter for the clay jug and wooden cup, and dug a silver penny from the pouch tied at her waist. One of the other knights kicked out an empty chair for her to sit, an amiable gesture, even if it was the only chair left in the room and she would have sat in it in any case. She brought the jug and sat, leaning back like the others in the rickety wooden furniture. Her skin was still sore, and she couldn't get over the concern she might have a reddish color they would see. But her hands showed nothing, and the fire made everything in the room orange regardless, so she put it from her mind. The heat from the fire heightened the pain just a notch, like wearing a hair shirt.

She poured from the jug and took a draught from the cup. Grape wine. English. Her nose wanted to wrinkle at it, but she kept a straight face. Even mead, made from honey and gagging her with its sweetness, would have been better than this. She was certain there were very good reasons French imports would one day kill the production of English wine. She drank it anyway, for it was all there was.

Then she cleared her throat and took a chance to introduce herself.

"I'm Sir Lindsay Pawlowski from distant Hungary, until recently household knight to Sir Alasdair an Dubhar MacNeil of Eilean Aonarach, near Barra."

"Should we have heard of ye?"

Good question. She had no idea what year this was, whether Bannockburn had been fought yet, or if the battle was so far in the past she couldn't possibly have fought there. But the mention of Alex and his island didn't seem to give them any trouble, so she ventured, "King Robert knows my name, for I was knighted by him."

That brought grins to the knights and relief to Lindsay when another of them said, "And we all ken the name of Robert, now that he's stood against the English crown and prevailed."

Oh, good. After Bannockburn. Not too long after, either, by the use of present tense in the comment. It was beginning to look as if she'd been returned to a time very close to when she'd left. The knight continued. "We still fight for Scotland and Robert. How do you do yourself?"

"I'm pledged to nobody. One fight is as good as another for me. I'm in search of a situation in need of a paid sword, for I've no use for land and taxes. Give me a bedroll for sleeping, a good fight on waking, and some mead afterward to wash down the blood and return me to the sleeping."

That brought a laugh and some nods of agreement. Tension in the room dissipated, and a platter of meat was shoved across the table in her direction. Chunks of beef lay beside pieces of roast fowl, and she took a greasy bit of bird. Not that she felt hungry, but she should be and knew it was best she ate. Food in these times was often hard to find even when one was blessed with a pocketful of cash, which she was not. The few coins she'd brought with her, left over from her last stay in this century, would cover her for a short while, but she would need gainful employment to survive long. It was good she was being questioned by these guys, for in the questions she smelled a job offer.

To nurture it, she said, "I've tired of living on so remote an island as Eilean Aonarach, and wish to find a more interesting life among those who harass England." She knew, if the year was anywhere near 1314, there were still Scottish men at arms making forays across the border into England. Noblemen, most notably James Douglas, First Earl of Douglas, took raiding parties south in an effort to convince England's Edward II he had no business north of the Tweed.

One of the men at the table, the first one who had spoken, sat up in his chair and leaned forward to lay his palms on the table and look her straight in the face. "Would you take plunder for your only pay?"

"No. I would take what I find, and three loaves of bread a day besides. And mead." Working on straight commission was a bad idea in any century, and she didn't intend to starve while waiting for the next raid. Surely these guys were being fed by their master during downtimes, and she didn't care to let herself be shorted.

The knight grunted. "And are we to trust you're worth your keep? Can ye fight?"

Lindsay snorted. "If not, I'll be dead in the next foray and no longer a bother to you. The sooner we ride into England, the less stake my master will have in my success."

The men looked to their leader, who considered her words then nodded. "Aye. If you can fight, we'll be glad to have you."

"I'll need to borrow a horse until I can reive one of my own."

The knight sat back. "You've no horse? Nor arms? No squire?"

"Only what you see before you." It suddenly occurred to her she hadn't brought a bedroll, and she mentally kicked herself. "Stake me for the first raid, and I'll reward the favor."

Clearly the guy didn't care for this development, and he frowned and grumbled. "Did your master at Eilean Aonarach not pay you sufficiently?"

Lindsay grunted and made herself lie. "My master is a close man and that is why I broke alliance with him. In my service to him, as squire and knight, I'm left with naught but my sword and mail. I've fought well and hard, and have not been properly rewarded. That's why I seek better fortune elsewhere."

The knight gave that hard consideration. But finally he shifted in his seat and said with some reluctance, "Very well, then. You'll have one of my horses until the next raid. Then you'll either have your own or you'll be on foot. Again." The disparagement was thick in his voice, for a knight on foot was not really a knight at all.

Lindsay let the insult slide, lifted her cup in agreement to the deal, and drank. Again she resisted a grimace at the dreadfully sweet wine. The men introduced themselves, and the unkempt, dark-haired one in charge turned out to be called Jenkins. His accent seemed from all over, and by his dress and demeanor she guessed his origins—and possibly his loyalties—were as diffuse. She pegged him for a hard-core mercenary, the sort she hoped they thought she was.

The men drank and talked for a while longer, then made their way to their camp. It was not far from Scone, tucked into a small hollow among a stand of oak and pine. One of the men loaned Lindsay a blanket for the night. After a trip into the woods to relieve herself and to change and bury her blood-soaked towel in private, she rolled herself up in the borrowed blanket on the hard ground near one of the fires and dropped into a not particularly restful sleep. Images of Nemed came, and in her imagination she fought and killed the slanty-eyed, pointy-eared monster. Over and over.

The following morning she was introduced to the commander of the company. He was a big blond guy, and called himself An Reubair, which she recognized as a nickname in Gaelic. *The Robber*. He had a look about him that struck her as odd. Something about him wasn't quite right. Like the one who had recruited her, the commander was extra scruffy and had very long, thick hair, and that was expected. His dress was rich but not fancy; at his throat he wore a leather thong from which dangled a silver crucifix, and that was his only ornamentation. Knights these days were fighting men first and nobility second, and even those among the peerage were rough by modern standards. These guys even more so, for they were definitely not ruling class. Nor did many of them even seem Norman. It was a motley assemblage making its way south to fight, but Lindsay couldn't quite put her finger on why their leader was unusual. An Reubair's eyes were narrow and seemed wary, but wariness was also to be expected on campaign, especially in the presence of a stranger. No, the oddness about him was something even more subtle than that. A look in his eye, perhaps, that bespoke secret knowledge. Lindsay had a distinct feeling he knew something she did not, and that was unsettling in spite of its unlikelihood. Probably it was a control technique he'd cultivated as the leader of this ragged crew. She shrugged one shoulder and focused on what her new boss was saying in response to her explanation of herself.

"An Dubhar MacNeil, ye say? I've heard of him."

Lindsay's heart flopped, then began pounding. "And what have you heard?"

"Only that he killed nearly twenty men at the battle near Stirling summer before last."

Two summers ago. This was 1316, then, if spring, and only a few months after she and Alex had left this century to return home. Only a few months difference. For a moment she stuttered at her incredible good luck, then recovered and replied to the comment. "The number was more like ten or twelve, but it's true he's a formidable opponent." Her chest tightened at the memory of Alex standing over her with his claymore, slaying all who challenged him. She wondered whether she would see him again, ever.

"Have you ever tried him yourself?"

Her chin raised, indignant, she said, "He is my foster brother. We were raised together in Hungary." *He is my husband, and the father of my son. I love him more than my life.*

"And so your allegiance is still with him?"

"When I pledged to him, it was to him. My pledge now is to you." *I will always love him, and no man will ever come before him.*

"You would fight him if necessary?"

"Of course." *Never.*

But now Lindsay smelled something not quite right. She frowned and gave him a slanted look. "Alasdair is a royal vassal of King Robert, and by the account of your man Jenkins we are also pledged to Robert. How would it ever be necessary to fight An Dubhar MacNeil?"

An Reubair snorted. "Jenkins has given a false impression, I think. We're pledged to nobody but ourselves, and we foray into England because that is where we find the fight most profitable. If Robert and his nobles appreciate our efforts, they are welcome to it, and that is the whole of our allegiance to him."

Jenkins, who was kicked back in a chair in a dark corner of the commander's tent, snorted and chuckled. "'Tis not as if His Majesty were stumbling over himself to elevate us to the peerage for our efforts, is it? Nor even reward us with land."

An Reubair shrugged. "'Tis better for us if he doesn't even know our names. Too many men have lost their lands, and often their heads, for being too close to the crown. I like it here in the shadows, and I like my wealth portable."

Jenkins only grunted, and returned to his quiet watchfulness. An Reubair returned his attention to Lindsay. "So, take warning, then. Your allegiance is to me, and to nobody else, until we are agreed you are released. On your life."

Lindsay nodded readily, for hesitation would be taken as the misgiving it was. "Aye. I'm a man of my word."

The interview accomplished, she was told who to see about rations and equipment, then dismissed. With little comment she accepted her day's rations from the company's equivalent of a quartermaster, then went to take possession of the horse and trappings placed on loan to her.

It was a sorry animal. Ribs poked out under a dry coat,

and the spine was so prominent the saddle almost wouldn't stay on. The dull look in its eye told her she shouldn't ride it too hard lest it drop dead under her. Seated on this creature, she was going to look like Don Quixote de La Mancha. Not very sporting of her employer to expect her to prove herself on this mount, but she would make the best of it. She would feed it well and hope it would carry her long enough for her to buy or steal a more appropriate steed. She even borrowed a brush to clean the animal's matted coat, though it was a hopeless effort to make it presentable. This might be a rickety old beast, but for now it was *her* rickety old beast.

That day they headed south, which was no surprise. Though it didn't seem that information concerning their prospects for action was ordinarily forthcoming from An Reubair, it stood to reason they would head for the West March, where the pickings would be good and there was convenient retreat to the mountainous western territory held by Robert. Even Lindsay knew Scone was too far north for any action that wouldn't attract the ire of the Scottish king. It was the Borderlands where the fighting was hot and sanctioned by Robert, and there was plunder to be had from the English who strayed too far into Scotland.

Along the way, it didn't take long for someone among the raiders to challenge Lindsay to a fight. She'd seen it before and knew it was inevitable. One morning as they neared England, one of the knights she rode with shoved her when she knelt by a stream for some water to wash down her breakfast bread. She held her ground.

"Out of my way, Pawlowski." Simon shoved her again, and she landed in the grass on her rump. He was not the largest guy in the company, but he was the most arrogant ass. He bore more scars than anyone else, and his nose had once been caved in so it lay flat and squat on his face. From his boasting around the fires at night it was plain he wore his scars like badges of honor, but Lindsay knew they were the mark of a man who had lost many fights. The bank of this stream was open and there was plenty of room, so it was plain this guy intended to challenge.

She sighed. Fighting was her least favorite thing, and she was more annoyed that she was now going to have to clobber him than that she would have to wait to get her drink. She stood and turned to him. He faced off against her, not kneeling to get his own drink, and they both knew that was not his purpose here. A grimace of disgust twisted her mouth. Men could be so stupid. Why this guy wanted to fight her was a mystery, though she accepted on an intellectual level that this was a test she needed to pass. He needed to put her in her place to determine what his own place was, and now she was going to have to beat him up to show him how worthy she was of his company. As if she cared how worthy she might be to be graced with the company of this clod. Cutting right to the chase, she dispensed with the ritual belligerent talk and shoved him right back.

He tried to backhand her, but she stepped deftly out of his way and kicked him sideways. Long ago she'd learned her disadvantage of upper body strength could be mitigated by her unusually long legs and hip strength. Kicking was admired less than punching, but anything that was effective seemed fair to her. She turned and kicked him again before he could recover his balance. Her boots were heavy, modern leather, with arch support, and fit her better than Simon's did him. He staggered sideways with a yelp. She followed him and hauled back to punch him hard in the face. He went over entirely and splashed into the stream.

"Are you finished?" she asked. "If you're done, I'll let you out of there, but if you want to fight some more I'll keep you in there until you're good and cold and you've gone all wrinkly. So . . . are you done?"

He hauled himself to his feet, knee-deep in the water and looking sheepish. "Aye. Have your drink. I'll take mine here." And he bent to scoop a handful of water to his mouth.

Some onlookers chuckled, then went along about their business. Lindsay took her drink, then reached to help Simon from the stream. Though he wasn't pleased to have lost the fight, he didn't seem to bear any animosity from it, and that was good. Simon was a loser, but he was a good loser.

The company proceeded into England, where Lindsay knew she would face her first real challenge, in battle.

CHAPTER 6

Without a word, Alex turned to make his way from the parapet to the bailey, where he mounted his horse among the cluster of his fidgeting knights. Colin handed up his sword and dirk, which Alex belted around his waist. With a couple of gestures he indicated only five other men who would ride out with him. He wore no armor, not even his helmet, but the knights with him were fully equipped, and he was in no shape to fight in any case. This was a parlay; it wouldn't do to approach it with more than necessary arms.

He rode from the bailey and onto the field at a trot, and stopped in the middle, a fair distance from the group. Their leader spurred his horse, and five of his men, half by Alex's count, accompanied him to the middle of the field with the United States flag flapping in the breeze.

As the strangers approached, Alex eyed their leader, whose armament was excellent. New and shiny, and with more plate than was common this far north. The helmet, left under the arm of one of the men who stayed behind, was of an uncommon design. Italian, perhaps, or French.

Or as if it had been made in a different period, like a movie anachronism. Alex himself owned very little plate, for it was expensive on a level real ivory and python skin would achieve in the late twentieth century. The horses were also fine animals. This guy had money.

When that leader came close enough to see his face, Alex's heart leapt. It was his brother's face. He looked just like Carl, and Alex smiled and took a breath for a joyous welcome.

But it died on his lips, for it wasn't Carl. The shaggy hair tossed about his head was way too dark, and the lips too thin. Too red. This man was older than his brother. Now Alex peered hard at the guy, who trotted to a halt before him and gave him a hard stare. It was eerie. Even close up, this man, slightly younger than himself, looked so much like him but wasn't. Same jawline, same nose.

"Who are you?"

"You can't tell?" Modern English, and the accent was American. Southern U.S., just like Mom, who was from Kentucky. That was why he and his brothers all sounded Southern, though they weren't. Alex blinked in confusion. This guy even talked a little like Carl. Same speech. Same voice, and it sent a shiver up his spine.

"No. I can't," Alex replied. An ancestor? But with that accent? A cousin on Mom's side? "Stop screwing off and tell me who you are."

"They named me Trefor. I'm Trefor Alasdair MacNeil. I'm your son." There was a bright heat of anger in his eyes, and he raised his chin as if to challenge Alex to deny it. His horse picked up the tension in his voice or in his knees, and pranced as if ready to bolt. The man could ride, and held in his restive mount.

No words came, of denial or acceptance. Struck dumb, Alex could only stare. Of course it wasn't possible. This man was no more than a couple of years younger than himself. And his son was still a baby.

Then realization came. His son had been born in 2005. This was 1316. Since he could have come to the past at any

moment during his lifetime, all timeline bets were off and
relative age was meaningless. It could be true.

He reached out to brush aside the hair covering the
stranger's ears, who ducked away and reined his horse to
the side. But not before Alex caught a glimpse of one elfin,
pointed ear. Those ears. Nevertheless, the guy still looked
like a MacNeil. Not like Nemed at all. Surprise overlaid
shock, and Alex stared hard, still speechless.

"So, Dad, what do you think?" The glint in Trefor's eyes
caught Alex's attention, and he saw they were green. Just
like his own, the crystalline green that was so rare, and
unique to himself within his own family.

Alex finally found his voice and said, "How?"

Trefor's mouth pressed closed and he glanced off to the
side for a moment. "Well, you see, when a man and a
woman fall in love they want to be close—"

"How did you get here? What happened?"

"I was kidnapped."

"I know that."

"By faeries."

Alex's jaw dropped open. "Faeries?"

"Yeah. You know, the wee folk. Leprechauns and all
that."

"Well, who was it? Faeries, leprechauns, elves, what?"

"How the fuck should I know? They dumped me on a
doorstep in Tennessee and left me there until about a year
ago." The barely controlled anger began to sputter from him,
and his voice rose. Alex's men didn't understand modern English, but they understood rage, and the five of them reached
for their swords. Alex put back a palm to stay them, and they
stood down. Swords snicked back into their scabbards. Trefor
continued. "I lived in foster homes my whole life."

"What, they just took you, got you out of the country
and all the way to the U.S., then left you? Why?"

"Why do they do anything? I think it was just one big
joke to them. Like, 'Haha, let's see if ol' Alasdair an Dubhar is as powerful as he thinks he is. Let's put the guy to the

test.' Or something. I never got what they were after; all I got was dumped on."

"And what are you after?" This man couldn't be his son. His son was a baby. His baby was only a few days old. Alex wasn't old enough to be this guy's father.

Trefor's jaw clenched. "I wanted to meet my father."

"Now you have." Probably. Alex wanted to deny but was faced with a resemblance that was far too strong for that. Trefor was a MacNeil, and closely related, by those eyes. He looked up at the flag drifting back and forth on the pole. There was no denying he was from the future.

"And I want to join your household knights. Me and my men."

"Who do you think I am, Trefor? What is it you want?"

"I think you're a knight on the fast track to the peerage. I want my birthright as your son."

"Are you nuts? You want to be my son here?"

"I was denied it my whole life. I want it now."

"How old are you? Twenty-eight? Thirty?"

"Twenty-seven."

"I'm only five years older than you. Who's going to believe I'm your father?" Alex's heart sank that once again he would be stuck pretending his son was not his own.

"Call me your brother."

"I can't. Everyone here already knows me as having no brothers except MacNeil of Barra. The closest relative you could be is a cousin on my mother's side. A Pawlowski. You couldn't even call yourself MacNeil here. No relation in the male line, no birthright. That's how it works." Alex realized he wanted this guy to go away. He wanted to get rid of the man, and return to searching for his baby son. The reality of this faded for him, and suddenly he wished to push the "reset" button and go back to when his son was still missing and still a child.

"You can't get rid of me."

"I don't want that." It was a lie, and Alex was ashamed of it.

"Then call me your cousin, if that's all you have to offer. But I'm not leaving."

Alex thought that over hard. Trefor looked him straight in the eyes, and he returned it. This was too weird. Incomprehensible. He wished Lindsay were here to take some of this pressure. And blame. He was faced with only one honorable choice. Finally he said, "All right. Join my household. We'll figure this out."

Trefor nodded, gestured to his men, and followed Alex and his escort to the castle at a walk. As they rode, they stared at each other hard, until Alex finally looked away and focused on the gate as they approached. Hector wasn't going to bloody believe this.

They climbed the path to the Great Hall and dismounted outside the entrance. Standing once again, Alex's aching body reminded him how deathly ill he'd been and how weak he still was. But now he didn't reach for Gregor's shoulder. Damned if he was going to let this Trefor guy know how vulnerable he was. So without a word to his newest knight he went into the stone building and strode on his own to his chair at the head of the room to resume his interrupted breakfast. At that end of the long, narrow hearth down the center of the floor, the fire was well lit and warming. Alex sagged into his heavy chair and took a lounging attitude to watch Trefor and his men enter. The flag stayed outside with the horses, and he was glad for that, for he had no clue where or how he might have displayed it among his own banners and his men's shields. Just as well not to have to decide. Trefor's contingent hung their weapons on the pegs provided at that end of the room, and looked around at their new post. There were ten besides Trefor, and Alex wondered who they all were. Locals or Americans? He had quite a few questions for this guy.

"Trefor!" The dark-haired, pointy-eared stranger looked across the room to him, and Alex gestured to the chair next to himself. The one Lindsay would have used, had she been there, he couldn't help thinking. "Come sit, and eat."

"What about my men?" Trefor shouted from where he

stood, and the sound echoed among the timber rafters above.

"Let them find seats and they'll be served."

Trefor nodded, then turned to speak to his cluster of guys. Alex watched closely and saw that most of them seemed to know this drill. Probably locals—genuine fourteenth-century knights. But there was one who kept looking around, staring at the shields and weapons hung on the wall pegs, up at the heavy wooden beams holding up the roof, peering at the windows glazed with thick, wavy glass. His hair was shorter than the others', even shorter than Trefor's, and he moved with an unwariness Alex had learned was peculiar to Americans. Alex guessed this was someone from the future. He recognized a tourist when he saw one.

That assessment turned out to be accurate, when the gawker followed Trefor to the head table and the others found seats at the lower tables. Alex watched the two approach and decided he didn't like the look of this other guy. It was nothing he could put his finger on, but there was a distasteful sense about him that made Alex think of a newly deployed seaman who was unlikely to last out the cruise. He could almost smell it.

Trefor came, sat in Lindsay's chair—his mother's chair— and gestured to his friend to pull up another from one of the lower tables.

"No. He'll sit with the men."

Trefor frowned. "Why?"

Alex leaned forward. "Because that's the way we do things here, and I'm the laird. This is my castle. My hall. My table. It matters who sits at the head table, and I get to say."

Anger flashed in Trefor's eyes, so eerily like Alex's own, and he said to his friend, "Go sit with the other guys, Mike. I think my dad and I got some private talk to do."

Mike looked from Trefor to Alex, then back again, as if to suggest he didn't approve of the way Trefor had caved on the issue. His teeth were too small for his head, giving his square face a loose-lipped appearance of toothlessness, and that mouth twisted in a grimace. But then he nodded and complied without speaking. A servant woman came with a plate stacked with pieces of beef to place in front of the master's guest.

Alex watched Mike go, then sat back and said to Trefor, "He's from the States?"

"My best friend. I've known him since my last foster home, ten years ago."

"What about the others?"

Trefor shrugged. "Hired swords. Lots of out-of-work knights hanging out in Edinburgh these days. Every man in Scotland under the age of sixty fought at Bannockburn, don't you know. Most of them came within a hair of capturing King Edward single-handedly. It would appear the whole Scottish army followed him across the battlefield when he escaped. Must have been quite a sight."

"You brought a lot of money with you."

"I'm comfortable. Fake jewelry is indistinguishable from the real thing here, what with there being no magnifying glass yet, and I figure if nobody can tell it's not real, then it might as well be. Even the real stuff is worth more in trade value here than it is where we come from. Like bringing Cuban cigars into the U.S."

"A treasure chest full of cubic zirconia?"

"Pretty much."

Alex refrained from saying he didn't think much of that sleazy solution to the problem of finances, for he remembered his first stake in these times had been a pouch full of coins and jewels he'd taken from a man he'd just shot to death. Instead, he said, "Can you fight?"

"I've had my scuffles."

"I mean, with a sword. You know anything about how to fight in a battle?"

"I took riding and fencing lessons before coming here."

Alex grunted. "Fencing. Like, with a foil? That'll do you diddly for good here. Forget everything you learned in your classes. I'll have to teach you how to swing a broadsword."

"It can't be so different."

"Trust me, it is. I'll teach you."

"I can figure it out for myself." The fire rose higher in Trefor's eyes.

"*I'll teach you.* If you're going to fight under my command, you're going to learn how to handle your weapon without getting yourself killed. Try to fight with a broadsword as if it were a foil, and you won't last one battle. Hell, you won't last past the charge."

"I didn't come here to—"

"To what? To fight? Or to take orders from me?"

Trefor fell silent for a moment.

Alex continued. "If you're going to hang out here—become one of my household knights—you're going to have to follow orders. You're not a knight. You're just a guy with enough money to buy a lot of shiny iron plate and a horse. I don't know how you fooled those guys sitting over there into thinking you were a nobleman and a knight like them—"

"Same as you. You aren't—"

"I was knighted." Alex leaned forward and into Trefor's space. To his credit, the younger man did not lean back from him. "I was dubbed by the king himself, and later made knight banneret, also by the hand of Robert. That is why I am entitled to ride around Scotland with my own men under my own banner, without attaching myself to another unit or asking for a by-your-leave from every landholder in the country. It's why I'm going to be able to go in search of your mother with my contingent without annoying the crown and making the current administration think I'm out to work against him."

"You won't find her."

Alex leaned back but otherwise didn't betray his alarm. Trefor was from the future and might know something. Alex hoped he didn't. "I will."

"You won't. I know you won't."

"How could you know?"

"You didn't find me. I don't think you even went looking

for me. I know you won't find her, because you didn't."

Alex didn't want to ask the next question, but he had to. "Did you read it somewhere?"

Trefor snorted and took a large bite of his meat. He said past the wad in his cheek, "Don't think all history got written down. And you were never important enough for anyone to write about. It's not like you were a king or anything."

Alex knew that. But he would have liked to know about Lindsay. Or maybe even if he would ever be an earl. Trefor thought he would be, and had said as much. "How do you know, then?"

"They told me. The faeries."

Alex snorted. "Right. Like they're the epitome of honesty."

"They told me where to find you."

"Because they wanted you to find me. Like you said, it's all one big joke to them. Stirring the pot to see what happens."

Trefor just grunted and fell silent. It was plain he had no answers. Alex said, "I'll find your mother, and you can tag along or not, as you please."

Trefor's eyes flashed again with a glance toward Alex, but then focused on his plate.

Hector's loud voice cut through the ambient noise of breakfasting knights. "Introduce me to your guest, brother! And curse me for a blind man if he isn't a relation from your Hungary!" The Barra laird, wearing little more than tunic, trews, and a long, ugly brown plaid draped over his shoulder, strode up the room, snagged a chair from one of the lower tables, and set it behind Alex and Trefor. Then he leaned between them, took a slab of meat from Trefor's plate, and sat back on the chair to eat. Trefor stared at him with an evil look in his eye that Alex wanted to slap from his face. Hector was a good friend, and if not an actual brother, nevertheless behaved as much of one as Pete or Carl.

"Hector MacNeil of Barra, this is my cousin from Hungary, Trefor Pawlowski."

Hector laughed out loud, then lowered his voice and said, "Why the story? Who is he in actuality?"

Alex also lowered his voice. "He's my son."

Now Hector's face fell. "Truth to tell? Ye wouldnae lie to me, brother?"

"Never. He's my stolen son, all grown up. Faeries did it."

Alarm crossed Hector's face at the mention of faeries, and he eyed Trefor. "And why is he here?"

Trefor said, a testy edge to his voice, "You don't have to talk like I'm not here." He spoke Middle English. A bit stiffly, but it was understandable.

Alex gazed at him. *Huh.* What else about Trefor did he still need to know? "Where'd you learn to speak the language?" Alex continued in the archaic tongue, for the benefit of Hector, who had English, Gaelic, and a little Latin.

"I have a gift for languages. I know all the major modern European ones, some minor ones, a little Chinese and Japanese. I'm a wiz with Farsi, and I speak fluent Klingon. Picking up Middle English in preparation for this trip was like falling off a log."

"Gaelic?"

"Modern Scottish Gaelic and medieval Gaelic. I was lucky enough to find an instructor who knew both."

Alex grunted once and considered that, then turned to Hector. "He came to claim his birthright. I've explained to him there is none, but he wants to stay anyway and help me look for my wife."

"My mother. And you're not going to find her."

"But we're going to go looking anyway."

"Pissing up a rope."

"It's my rope. My piss."

Hector butted in loudly. "Very well, then! It's a search we'll have. A hunt for the fair Lady Marilyn Pawlowski MacNeil."

Trefor peered at Alex and frowned. "You let them think you married your cousin?"

"Distant cousin. It's really the foster sister thing that is stickier here. No actual law, but it's frowned upon."

"Ick."

"It's not like—"

"The two of you put your heads together, you'll find the woman." Hector leaned forward to grab another piece of meat from Trefor's plate, then sat back to eat it. His cheeks stuffed with food, he said, "I see he's a MacNeil to the core, Ailig."

Alex gave Hector only a bland stare, then said to Trefor, "Show him your ears."

"No."

"I said, show him." The threat in his voice was to let Trefor know he would draw blood if Trefor didn't comply.

Slowly the younger man raised a hand to draw aside the hair covering one ear.

"Och," said Hector.

"If he's a MacNeil—if he didn't get those from me— where did they come from?"

"Faeries. 'Tis a mark of faeries. Had he been left instead of stolen, I'd be calling him changeling."

"What's a changeling?"

"When a child is stolen, the faeries leave behind one of their own. Sometimes identical to the child but weak and failing, sometimes a creature plainly not human at all."

Alex remembered the crib splattered with dust. Slowly he said, "And . . . if one were to kill such a creature, would it turn to dust then and there?"

Hector nodded. "I've heard of it." He leaned toward Trefor, his eyes wide, gawking at the faerie man before him. He leaned to see, but Trefor brushed his hair over his ears and made sure they were covered.

Alex said, "Faerie blood you say? You mean those goofy little folks who are all mad as hatters?" He'd almost rather it had been that elf, Nemed.

Hector shook his head. "I cannae say. But if he's your son and your wife's, one of you has given him the blood.

And I can see he's your son. There cannae be any doubt about that."

Alex made a disparaging noise in the back of his throat. "My kingdom for a DNA test kit."

Only Trefor snorted at that, for half the sentence was necessarily in modern English and the reference was to a play that wouldn't be written for another two and a half centuries.

Trefor asked, "What does *An Dubhar* mean? Your nickname?"

Now Alex's bland gaze fell on his son. "I thought you knew Gaelic."

"I'm fluent, not a scholar. This particular word has escaped me until now."

"It means The Darkness. Shadow of Death."

Trefor grunted. "Yea, though I walk through the valley of the shadow of death, I shall fear no evil." He grinned, then continued. "For I am the meanest sonofabitch in the valley."

Alex stifled a groan.

CHAPTER 7

A small town not far from Carlisle lay unsuspecting in the path of the company led by An Reubair. Lindsay looked down the slope at the cluster of wooden buildings set around what passed for a town square, thin trails of smoke from cook fires drifting skyward through holes in dusty gray thatching. Her gut tightened to a knot. No fear of dying; she knew how to deal with that particular terror. It was the knowledge she would have to kill someone today in order not to die herself that made her jaw grind shut and her hands grip the reins too tightly. As refuge from the guilt, she told herself she was on the right side, that Scottish freedom from Edward was a worthy fight. If she could convince herself this was no different from the battle she'd fought at Bannockburn, perhaps her heart would carry her through this raid. She'd fought willingly under Robert, and not just because she'd known the Scots would win. She truly believed the attempt of Edward I to usurp the Scottish crown was not in the best interest of the Scots. It was a valid fight. She had to believe that.

But this raid was different. These were not combatant

knights they would attack; they were farmers and townsfolk. Never mind that they paid tribute to the English
crown; they didn't deserve what was about to happen to
them. Gazing down at the small buildings clustered around
a proud stone church, she drew deep, steady breaths and
prepared herself for what she must do, though she hated it.

Horses approached from the flank. Two of them, and
Lindsay looked over to see An Reubair and someone else.
The other figure rode a fine steed with a glossy coat and a
rich, flowing bard. The stranger wore no armor and didn't
appear equipped to ride along on the raid. Something about
him caught her interest, and she stared hard. He was too far
away to see clearly, but the way he moved, the shape of his
frame and the long, long hair that lifted in the breeze made
her stare to know who he was. His identity eluded her, and
she began to think she was imagining the familiarity. When
An Reubair raised his hand in farewell to the man and rode
toward his gathered men, she shook off the curiosity and
attended to the job at hand. Distraction would get her
killed; Alex had told her that often enough, and she trusted
him in all things martial. So she focused, steadied her
breath, and waited for the signal to charge.

An Reubair said only, "Go."

The hundred or so men and Lindsay kicked their horses
to a gallop, and when they were in earshot of the town a
roar went up from them to put fear into the hearts of their
targets. Men ran from houses, bearing whatever weapon or
farm tool was at hand. Women screamed to their children.
Children stood and stared at the oncoming riders.

Lindsay chose an opponent and rode down on him, but
one of her compatriots beat her to him and engaged the local man with his sword. Lindsay swerved off to pick out
another defender, and hauled back her sword to lay on. The
man was on foot and defended with a sickle. He was sur-
prisingly deft with it and knew how to catch her sword with
the curve of his blade. Crowding him with her horse only
got her mount stabbed in the haunch, so she wheeled to
take advantage of her longer weapon. She swung hard and

beat him back. Then another quick swing and she caught his
face hard with the tip of her blade. His head jerked backward and blood flew. He dropped his sickle and grabbed his
bleeding wound, screaming. His eye was gone and a deep
gash split his face from ear to forehead. She moved onward, knowing that though this guy might live, he wasn't
going to fight any more that day. Hope rose that she might
yet prove herself to her employer without having to kill
anyone for now.

A woman came at her with a rod of some kind, and
Lindsay swung her blade at it. "Get away!" she shouted at
the fool. It was a piece of wood. The nitwit woman was going to get herself killed. "Go! Hide!"

But the woman screamed at her and tried to whack her
with the pole again. Lindsay wheeled her horse to crowd
her. "Get away, you idiot!" But the woman wouldn't. Lindsay's horse, trained to battle, reared to strike at the combatant on foot. The woman went down, and the horse trampled
her. Lindsay reined off to the side and rode away. There
was no point in looking back to see if the woman would get
up; Lindsay had other more important business to handle.
A man with a bow was shooting into the fray, and she went
after him.

It was a small hunting bow, not the longbows used in
battle, but it was putting a dent in the attackers. In a fury,
Lindsay rode down on him from behind and took a long,
leisurely swing at the back of his head as she passed. He
went down like a bag of rocks, and the bow clattered to the
ground beside him.

Lindsay knew the man was dead. No point in thinking
about that now; she needed to stay alive herself. Several of
the raiders were on foot now, engaged with local swords-
men. Lindsay picked out one of the defenders and rode
past to knock him on his helmet. Her blow didn't kill him,
but it dazed him enough for her compatriot to finish him
off easily. She wheeled and rode back to the fray, this time
choosing another defender. Again she enabled her fellow
raider to prevail. Twice more she did that, and about that

time the fighting began to dwindle. The clash of weapons stilled, and soon only the sounds of weeping women and crying children were left. Some survivors ran from the village, across tilled fields, and into a forest to the south. The men of An Reubair began the job of gathering the spoils.

Lindsay dismounted to help gather the livestock from pens and barns. Others would deal with the surrendered people; she didn't want to see them. They were English, as she was, and she had no desire to think too hard on how she felt about that. These days she didn't really want to think too hard about anything beyond her purpose, which was to find Nemed and her son.

Ankle-deep in the mud near a sheep pen, struggling with a ewe who objected to being taken from her home, Lindsay looked up to see that stranger talking to An Reubair again. Nearer to him this time, Lindsay stared hard and a tingling stole up her spine. Now she recognized the man in such close conversation with her boss.

God help her, it was Nemed.

She muttered a curse under her breath that might have gotten her burned at the stake had anyone heard who cared, and dropped the ewe. The animal went scrambling, then slowed to a nonchalant walk toward her fellows. *Nemed.* A thrill coursed through Lindsay at her excellent good luck, and she reached for her dagger. He was right there, talking to An Reubair, and without further thought she drew her weapon and headed toward him.

But the elfin king chose that moment to rein his horse around and ride away in the other direction, leaving her on foot with her impotent dagger in her fist. An Reubair also wheeled to ride to the village. Lindsay missed her chance and muttered a four-letter Anglo-Saxon vulgarism that would not have been understood had it been heard, for it was only vulgar in modern English. She scabbarded her dagger and returned to her work. But then she turned again, looking after the retreating rider on his splendid horse.

What was Nemed doing there? What involvement did he have with An Reubair?

She slapped the arm of Simon, who was passing with a lamb in his arms, and said, "Who is that?" She nodded at Nemed in the distance. "He was talking to An Reubair just now, and I saw him before the attack."

Simon looked. "Aye, that there would be the elf king, Nemed." He said it as if elves were the most ordinary thing in the world, and not the fey, elusive, and rare beings Lindsay knew them to be. In fact, Nemed was the only one left of his kind.

"You know him? An Reubair knows him, too?"

Simon looked at her as if she'd just said something incredibly stupid. "Of course. Did you not know we are under his banner?"

Whatever banner Simon might be talking about, Lindsay hadn't seen it. Their group traveled like pirates, without identification of any kind and alert to elude anyone who might smack of authority. This news was dumbfounding. "We work for him? Nemed?"

"Indeed. Fully a third of what we bring back to Scotland goes to his pockets." He held up the lamb and grinned. "Except this. Tonight we eat well, and in England." A sly laugh burbled from him.

"You know he's an elf?"

"Of course I do. Just as I know An Reubair is a faerie. One of the *Tuatha Dé Danann*. Can you not see it yourself?"

Now Lindsay was truly stunned, and she looked off toward An Reubair, who was now in conference with Jenkins near a burned house that was falling to ashes and throwing showers of sparks to the wind.

Simon continued. "How could you not know? The fey can nearly always be picked out by the way they keep their ears covered with their hair. The longer and more carefully arranged a man's locks are, the more likely he is to be hiding the mark. There are many in our company who are exiled Danann."

Lindsay looked back at Simon. The lamb was restless in his arms, and he fought to keep it under control. She said, feeling stupid, "But he's a Christian."

Simon shrugged and gave her a look so blank she didn't know how to even approach the question of a Christian faerie.

So she dropped it and asked, "What is their purpose here?"

"Plunder." Of course. It was why they all were here. He looked at her as if to add, *Duh.*

"Nemed is an elf. If An Reubair is Danann, he's also a magical man. Why are they here? Why do they need to fight?"

Now Simon shrugged and his brow furrowed with his hard thinking. "The powers can come and go, as I understand it. And I hear the magic is costly to life. Were it a simple or easy way to amass riches, I'm certain all kings would be fey and wars would be fought in the sky with lightning bolts."

Lindsay's head shook from side to side, and she looked off in the direction Nemed had taken. Her dismay then began to turn to hope. This might be a good thing. If she stuck around, Nemed was sure to be back eventually. All she had to do was wait until he would return. And then she could kill him once she'd made him give back her son. A tiny smile curved the corners of her mouth, and she returned her attention to the sheep and went back to work gathering livestock for herding to Scotland.

So . . . An Reubair was a faerie. One of the *Tuatha Dé Danann*, like Danu. Lindsay couldn't figure it. She'd met Danu once. The woman was graceful, polite, and regal. Everything An Reubair was not. But An Reubair was a bandit, associated with an elfin king who had no followers, without a place among the people of Danu. Surely he was an outcast.

Lindsay began to look for faeries among the other knights and noticed several of her compatriots kept their ears covered. Not Simon, nor Jenkins, but two others for a certainty—she glimpsed their ears—and possibly one other who tied back his long hair in an unfashionable queue, tight over the tips of his ears. Now that this had been pointed out to her, it seemed obvious and she wondered how she'd missed it.

She considered her baby. The tiny points at the tops of his ears had horrified her. At first she'd thought it was an indication of a birth defect of some sort, and she feared for his health. But then she realized it was the elf. He'd done something. No telling what, but only magic could have given her and Alex's child those ears. The sign of the fey. Her heart felt sick and she wondered what else was happening to her child.

That night was spent in celebration of their success that day. Fires dotted the field where they made camp, and sheep carcasses on spits threw delicious smells into the breeze. Several knights played instruments or sang ballads, some of them extempore, about that day's adventure, and hilarity ran high. Working off the adrenaline from the day's fight, Lindsay shared the mood. Glad to be one of the ones left alive, she drank more than her share of mead, for though she considered it a drink fit only for crude, classless, immature cretins, it was all there was to be had that would take the edge off the world for a while.

Women came to share in the food and festivity. The poorest from the destroyed village, they were happy to gather coins and eat whatever they could stuff into their mouths in exchange for giving comfort to those who had taken those things from fellow townsfolk. Like hookers of the future, the whores hung onto the men and jockeyed for the ones who seemed wealthiest. Lindsay, leaning against a tree just slightly beyond the light of one fire, slugged down a *cuach* of mead and watched the pageant of human reproductive behavior and social dominance with idle interest.

Simon had a likely bird in hand and was groping her through her skirts. The woman played coy and backed up, laughing so he would know she was only playing and would soon succumb to his obvious charm. He kept coming until she was backed up against the fire and her skirts caught. Then followed a bit of panicky stamping out of her skirts, but it was a momentary distraction and the two were quickly back on track with fondling each other. Lindsay smiled to herself, for she'd seen Jenkins already have his way with this particular woman earlier in the evening, and knew Simon was seducing someone else's mess. And spending an awful lot of energy to get it, all things considered. Since there were only seven or eight visitors that night among thirty or so of An Reubair's men, it was certain the women would all be well used by morning, and their pockets and stomachs would be well filled.

Jenkins, with his fine clothing and gleaming weapons, had moved on and now enjoyed the company of two other women. Or thought they were enjoying his, because he had his arms around both and was telling them of his exploits in battle. Their attention was rapt as they chewed on pieces of meat. Lindsay had thought he was finished for the night, but damned if he didn't take them both and move off into the darkness again. Lindsay blinked, and wondered whether he was just showing off or if he really had it in him.

A hand at the bottom of her hauberk startled her, and she hauled off to backhand whoever it was, but turned to find one of the whores there with a sweet smile on her face. Stupidly Lindsay realized she'd forgotten this aspect of her disguise, and she switched gears as quickly as she could. Rather than hit the woman, she grabbed the intruding hand and put it over her shoulder. Then she kissed her as roughly and as quickly as she could manage without hurting her or disgusting herself too much. The visitor was a small woman, much smaller than Lindsay, and seemed frail. Had Lindsay been a man, she might have found her attractive, but since her orientation was for partners larger, stronger, and harder than herself, her distaste went beyond just her preference for male anatomy. She hoped the kiss was convincing, but didn't see how it could be.

Before the woman could say anything, and especially before she could get her hands under the hauberk again, Lindsay began to pull up the skirts on her visitor. "My, but you're a pretty one," she said. She was drunk enough not to have to fake inebriation, and was glad for it just then. Her

voice was husky and her diction slurred, just like the other
guys. "How about we go off over there for a spell? I've got
no money, but I can show you a good—"

"Och," said the whore. "My sister over there needs me,
I think." With that, she yanked her skirts from Lindsay's
hand and picked them up in her fists to hurry away. Whether
to her sister, or to a man with money, Lindsay neither knew
nor cared. She took her empty *cuach* and went in search of
more mead. With luck, her performance was observed by
the guys and wouldn't be wasted. She spent the rest of the
evening making herself as drunk as possible, threw up in a
cluster of bracken like everyone else, then found a spot to
roll herself into her plaid and slept.

The raiders plundered two more villages before they retreated across the border to shelter in a small, ruined keep
near Lochmaben. Little more than a single tower to begin
with, it had been reduced to only two intact levels containing a total of three rooms, all of them leaky in the rain and
alive with mold and vermin of all kinds. Lindsay claimed
space as near as she could get to the small hearth on the
ground floor. Without a squire to serve her like the other
knights, she'd had to tend her wounded horse. The others
had all claimed their spaces before she'd been free to claim
hers, so her spot was not close to the fire at all. It was going
to be a cold stay.

She looked around at her new home. It was a dump,
even nastier, dirtier, and more overgrown with moss and
weeds than Eilean Aonarach had been when taken over by
Alex. Cracks between the stones ran from ceiling to floor,
and it seemed a wonder it gave any shelter at all. In her
own time, if this place might still be standing, tourists
would wander through it and gawk, declaring it to be wondrous. And it would be, to have survived so long. Never
mind the encroachment of increasing population in the
next several centuries, King Robert had more than likely
been the one to order the destruction of this little fort, to
keep Edward from manning it himself. So now, unfit for
English occupation, it suited Nemed's rogues.

Lindsay lay on her bedroll, newly purchased though aged and worn. Her participation in the three raids had enabled her to claim from the spoils a good horse and accoutrements, as well as a coif of mail to accompany her hauberk and gauntlets. No cuisses for her thighs nor poleyns for her knees, nor even greaves for her shins, though. She wished she had them, for her legs were vulnerable in raids on horseback against defenders on foot, and so far she'd been lucky to have avoided bad wounds. She hated being so poor. Most of the other knights had squires or common servants to maintain their animals and equipment, and it was humiliating that she was forced to do for herself.

Her apparent youth, evident by her lack of beard, had worked well for her before. She'd done for Alex as his teenage squire when they'd first come here, and now it annoyed her she was so alone. He should be there; they should be together. Her eyes closed and two tears squeezed from them to roll into her ears. It had been a mistake to leave London without him. She should have waited. She'd left in too big a rush to find the baby, too intent on chasing down Nemed and her son. Too angry. Perhaps even overly confident of finding them and returning to the twenty-first century before Alex would know she'd gone. Now she realized what she was up against and saw it wasn't going to be so easy. Even if she found the baby, there was no way to be certain of ever finding a way back. She cursed herself for an idiot.

Snores began to rise from the men around her. She rolled over to cradle her face in her arms and pulled her plaid around herself. All there was to do now, she decided, was to press onward and see what would happen. Maybe there was a way. Perhaps she would succeed and return to London to greet Alex when he arrived from his ship. But hope wouldn't come. Her sense of the rightness in the world had bled from her until there was nothing left but raw need. Desperation. Stripped of hope, all she could do was resort to irrational expectation. The thing she needed would happen. It must happen. It would simply be so, because the alternative was unthinkable.

The next morning she rose before the other knights were awake, to care for her horses. Better not to be seen working, even if everyone knew she had no squire. The men slept like rocks that morning, unlike while on the move when they would be alert at the slightest noise near camp. Lindsay had not slept so well as they. Even in her travels as a reporter she'd never rested easily away from home. Only at Eilean Aonarach, and only when Alex was there, could she truly relax. Only he ever made a strange bed home for her. She sighed and took a brush to her new property.

A voice made her blood go cold and the hair on her arms stand up. "Persistent woman." *Nemed.* No presence, only his voice coming from somewhere else. The disembodied voice had an echolike quality, ever so slight but distinctive. As if she were hearing it only in her head, and her head were the size of a school gymnasium. Lindsay resisted the urge to turn, and continued grooming her horse, ignoring the elf.

"What do you expect to accomplish?"

She didn't reply and pretended she couldn't hear him. Bristles from the decrepit brush came off on the horse's coat, and she picked them off.

"Do you imagine you have them all fooled?"

Finally she said, "Yes." That much she knew for a certainty. She'd exhibited enough manhood in her fighting and her whoring to allay any suspicion she might be a woman. Or even a weak man. She was one of the guys, and she knew it.

But Nemed said, "I cannot see how. They all must be blind. I find you most alluring."

Lindsay rolled her eyes, and the strokes of her brush became harder in her irritation until the horse stamped its foot in protest.

"I think it's but a matter of time before one of them catches the scent of you and comes to attention for it. I certainly have. Something about the presence of a woman. It changes everything in the men around her, whether she or they want it to or not.

"Not my problem."

"It would be, were you discovered."

Her brushing slowed. "I suppose you'll be the one to tattle."

"Oh, no. Not I. I don't expect I'll need to." The quality and direction of the sound of the voice changed, and a hooded figure stepped from behind a stack of straw near a low, ruined stone wall. Lindsay stopped her work and turned her back to her horse so it wouldn't be to him. "I think you'll betray yourself."

"I never did before. Not in over a year of being Alex's squire."

"You never rode with the fey before. Trust me, there are men here already wondering what it is about you that makes them think about you at odd moments. Men like me." His voice went all husky, and he tried to get her to look him straight in the eye. But though he ducked his head to address her eyes with his, she avoided them and went around to the other side of her horse. If he thought she was going to go all wobbly kneed because he thought she was attractive, he was mad.

In fact, she'd long thought Nemed was certifiably insane by human standards. He was, after all, a different tribe altogether. Maybe he did think he was seducing her. Perhaps sliminess was a standard elfin come-on. Her mouth twisted in a wry expression not much resembling a smile.

"You don't find that intriguing?"

"Not in the least."

"Oh, come." This seemed to amuse the elf. "Surely you've wondered what it might be like to be bedded by one of us."

"Never." Since Alex, she hadn't even thought much about other human men. Now the thought of him brought a longing that made her eyes sting. She returned to her work and continued down the flank of her horse, wishing she had a knife in her hand. "Where's my son?"

Nemed feigned shock and laid a theatrical hand over his chest. "You haven't found him yet? I thought that was why you came here. What are you doing riding around the countryside, burning people's homes and taking their belongings, then? Why aren't you out searching for your offspring?"

Lindsay ignored the question, which was meant only to anger her, and said, "Why I am here is an excellent question. Why *am* I here? Why did you send me to that particular day, when Jenkins and his contingent were passing through Scone?"

"I didn't. I had no idea they would be there. You meeting up with Jenkins and An Reubair can honestly be chalked up to the vagaries of fate. The whims of forces over which no earthly creature has control. In fact, I did my best to make certain you weren't sent anywhere. Not alive, in any case."

She looked over at him, and a frown knotted her brow. Not alive?

"Awfully trusting of you to come to me and expect me to send you back in time. This is the precise time you wanted, yes? Had I known you would survive the trip, I would not have obliged so well."

"You tried to kill me?"

"Of course I did, you stupid cunt." He made a noise in the back of his throat and looked away. Then he turned back and said, anger flashing in his eyes, "For someone of your heritage, you are singularly dull witted."

"My heritage is Polish and English."

"And faerie. How can you be what you are and not know it? Nor know much of anything else?"

"I'm no faerie."

"You must be. I should have killed you, but here you are. You are not entirely human, Lindsay Pawlowski. There's fey blood in you, and by the look of you I would call you a daughter of Danu. Tell me, are there any ancestors in your human tree who were born on the wrong side of the blanket?"

Lindsay blinked away her confusion. Nemed was lying,

as he always did. "Undoubtedly. Everyone does if they look back far enough. The Queen of England, for instance."

"Within the two centuries preceding your birth."

"Go away, elf. King or not, you're full of crap and I don't care to listen to it."

"I want to know, Ms. Pawlowski. I wish to understand how it came to be that I've been saddled with your presence, your expectations, and your conviction that I've taken your brat. I'm quite fed up with you. It would please me to lay you at the doorstep of the great faerie queen, Danu. There's no doubt in my mind that she is your ancestor. Perhaps even she herself was the one who seduced the mortal you call . . . what? Grandfather? Great-grandfather?"

The duke. As she was fond of pointing out to anyone who asked, Lindsay had nobility in her ancestry, but the duke's daughter had been illegitimate. How did Nemed know she had an illegitimate ancestor? And why was he so sure . . .

The ears. Those little points at the tops of her son's ears. The horrible realization made her go still. The ears could have come from her, her son a throwback to one of the Danann who had seduced a human. The ears could be her own fault.

Nemed said, "I can see by your sullen silence I've touched on something. You know I'm telling the truth."

"Get out of here."

He laughed. "You work for me. Everyone here works for me. I doubt I'll be going anywhere."

"Leave me alone."

"You don't want to be alone. I know you don't." Now his voice was softening. Seductive. Almost convincing, but she shrugged a shoulder and refused to listen. He continued, and she found it impossible not to listen. "You know, the question that occurs to me is why—if the man was seduced by Danu—then why was the resulting child raised as human and not fey? How did you lose your heritage?"

Heritage. Lindsay's head swam with the implications of

what Nemed was saying. That she belonged to a tribe of
faeries, and that her ancestry had caused the deformity in
her son that had made it impossible to face the boy's father.
"Get away from me."

Nemed wasn't going to budge, so she covered her horse
with its quilted bard and went to return the borrowed brush
to Simon's squire. The elf didn't follow her, and she ducked
back into the tower to see if there was meat to be had.
Mead, at least. She needed a drink badly.

Good luck for her there was a haunch on the fire, which
she bought into and sat down to wait for it to be ready. Talk
was lively around the fire, men lounging on their bedrolls
with nothing to do but chat while their squires and servants
looked after things outside. She listened to some of the
guys bragging about their time under Robert, a source of
much glory during the past couple of years. The king had
been desperate for men before Bannockburn, and every
Scot with a horse, a weapon, and a grievance against the
English had been recruited to fight. Now, having won, they
were all heroes and heroism was thin on the ground among
rogues such as these. They made the most of their boon.

Lindsay talked of her own experiences among Bruce's
army, having ridden with Alex's patrol company under King
Robert's brother, Edward Bruce, and of the wound she'd
taken at Bannockburn that had almost killed her. It was skat-
ing on the edge of discovery, though, for she was not in a position to pull off her hauberk, tunic, and sark to show them
the scar across her rib cage. Over the past few weeks she'd
satisfied the scar requirement by showing off at every opportunity the one on her arm she'd acquired in her first battle
under Alex. Nobody asked to see the one on her torso.

The meat came ready and was portioned out. Lindsay
ate with an appetite and thought she might like to roll into
her plaid for a nap afterward. It was going to be a lazy few
days, and they all wanted to get their rest before heading
back south again.

A warmth spread at her crotch. Lindsay stopped chewing, but showed no other sign of alarm as she smoothly

shifted from sitting cross-legged to sitting with her knees together. Alarm, however, sang through her body. Something was very wrong. She was bleeding, and heavily enough to soak through her trews in seconds. And now she didn't know whether she could make it away from the fire and the men without having it run down her legs. She had to move quickly, or she would be trapped. Even worse, if bleeding this copious didn't stop on its own she would certainly be dead before long.

Just as she was about to rise, one of the faerie knights—Iain was his name—frowned and looked over at her. There were no words, but he didn't need them. His nostrils flared, and he peered at her in curiosity. A look of puzzlement, then realization came over his face.

He knew. He could smell it.

CHAPTER 8

Alex ordered that Trefor and his American friend should occupy the large, windowless room among the laird's apartments below the Great Hall, off the meeting room. Close enough to keep him in sight, but not so close as to let him into Alex's very inner sanctum. Hector and his gillies had the extra room off the anteroom to Alex's bedchamber. Trefor and his buddy wouldn't have access to Alex's private chambers, and the quality of the accommodations wouldn't let them overestimate their status within the household. Not that they were going to be there very long; Alex determined he would take his knights to the mainland as soon as possible to begin the search for Lindsay.

He was not nearly recovered enough from his illness to travel, but he had no choice. With Trefor watching him, eyeing him whenever he was in the room, needling him whenever they spoke, Alex had no desire to let on he'd even been sick, let alone that he was still nearly incapacitated. So he gave orders to ready the boats for hurried departure. Then he went to his bedchamber to rest again while Trefor and Mike settled into their room and Hector and Henry Ellot supervised the preparations. Gregor attended to Alex, who slept through the day and rose again in the late afternoon to make his way to the roof of the Great Hall for a look at the progress.

At the quay to the seaside of the castle stood two large boats, their furled sails red, black, and gold with the arms of Sir Alasdair an Dubhar MacNeil. Crates stood ready to load, and horses had been lowered to the bailey to be held in pens until just before departure. Alex observed the bustle of castle servants, pages, and squires, and saw things were going as smoothly as could be expected.

"Rinky-dink boats." Trefor's voice came from right behind Alex, who jumped slightly. There had been no noise, not even a sense of anyone being there. Trefor surely had seen the jerk of Alex's frame, an embarrassment.

The Laird of Eilean Aonarach cleared his throat, tugged his plaid more snug, and faced forward, looking out over the quay. He said, "Only the king's boats are bigger." The king's were quite a bit bigger, and far more numerous because he could commandeer merchantships, but that was neither here nor there.

"I expect he's got a lot more of them, too. Teeny as they are. Everything in this place is smaller than I'd thought it would be."

"Kinda like the Washington Monument."

Trefor chuckled at that. "I suppose, though I've never seen the Washington Monument up close." After a bit of silence, he pointed with his chin to the banner flapping over the portcullis on the quay and said, "Your arms. That bird is a bald eagle."

"It is."

"Mythical beast in the here and now?"

"I let them think that."

"You sly boots." Trefor's voice carried no humor, and Alex took the comment as sarcasm. A dig. Trefor continued. "You put a lot past these people. I bet you get away with all sorts of things."

Alex opened his mouth to deny, but closed it when he

thought of the gun he'd emptied into the enemy at Bannockburn, which had earned him this lairdship, the story he'd let people believe about being from Hungary, the lies he'd told to convince the people of Eilean Aonarach that Lindsay was her own sister so he could marry her. After some thought he said, "I do. I might burn in hell for it, but at least I won't be burned and sent there for telling the truth. Folks around here will tie you to a stake at the drop of a hat."

"It's no wonder you wanted to come back here. Lots of power. Lots of money."

Now Alex turned to look at his son and wondered what he'd meant by that. "Shouldn't I have?"

Trefor shrugged. "Search me. I was just saying."

Alex grunted and looked over the battlement, down at the loading again. The sun was settling over the hilly island horizon, and long shadows of cliffs to the west had swallowed the boats below. The night would be clear, but Alex could see a gathering of clouds low on the horizon that threatened a difficult departure within the next few days. He gave a low groan. "Looks like the weather is going to screw us. We might not get out of here soon. If that storm comes any closer, I'll have to hold off loading the boats."

"Bad luck for us."

"You don't sound like you care much." It seemed Trefor would have liked to see Alex fail.

"I care more than you think."

Again Alex grunted and stared off toward the line of clouds. "This is going to cost us in time. Possibly equipment." Damage to the boats was a danger.

"Maybe the storm will pass us by."

"The wind is pushing it straight this way. And they've already got the animals and some supplies in the lower bailey. If it hits us hard enough, it's not going to matter much that we haven't set sail. If it hasn't turned or petered out by morning, I'll have to have all that stuff moved back into shelter."

There was only silence from Trefor, until Alex tired of

waiting for a reply and looked over to find Trefor with his head bowed and his fingers at the back of his head, beneath his hair. He looked as if he were massaging his own neck, fingering the base of his skull, his shoulders tensed and elbows out. Alex wanted to ask what he was doing, but sensed he wouldn't get a reply. Not a rational one, anyway. Trefor continued that for a bit, then stood straight again and looked out over the water to the approaching storm. In the dusk, his face had paled and there was a sheen of sweat on him. His breathing was noticeably ragged, then he drew a huge sigh and let it out slowly. He whispered to himself, "There."

"What?"

Trefor glanced at him and said, "Nothing. Just maybe we could be luckier than we think we are." He said it as if he knew a joke on Alex. His eyes drooped shut, and for a moment he looked as if he might faint. Then he collected himself and sighed.

Alex wondered what he meant by that, but would wait to see what happened with the storm before asking.

Sure enough, Trefor was right. By morning the storm was closer, but the wind had shifted just enough that it appeared the worst of it would miss the island. Alex let the loading continue as they watched the progress. That night the edges of the storm barely brushed the tip of Eilean Aonarach, far from the castle and its boats. A couple of fishing vessels belonging to one of the MacConnells took some damage by banging into each other in the high swells, but that was all the effect the weather had on the island. The loading of boats continued without interruption while the storm beat hell out of the empty expanse of water to the west.

Alex looked to Trefor, who spent the day with the corners of his mouth curled in a private smile. He and his buddy hung out in the Great Hall with Trefor's mercenaries, and it was plain none of them thought the good luck weather was remarkable.

Alex wondered what had really happened on the roof of the Great Hall last night. It occurred to him that he knew

very little about the wee folk and their magic. Trefor looked
like one of them. Was it possible he had powers like theirs?
Alex didn't even know what that meant in a full-blooded
fey. What could it mean with regard to Trefor? Danu had
never given him a clue as to what she might have accomplished or how. He knew Nemed had once been powerful,
but was no longer. The Bhrochan had wiles and ways, but
Alex didn't really know what those truly entailed, beyond
that they could make him very, very sick. Now he looked at
Trefor and wondered. He was far more human than not.
Lindsay had certainly never shown any sign of magical
powers. Nor even an affinity for the Danann, in spite of favor from Danu. If Trefor was his son and not Nemed's,
then how closely related could he be to the fey?

The preparations to leave were completed that day.
They would depart for the mainland in the morning.

During the night, Alex was hard put to sleep. His brain
buzzed with thoughts of Trefor, for there was no denying
he was related to Alex, and no reason to believe he was
not the son who had been stolen just a couple of weeks
ago. Those faeries were all nuts and certainly could have
done what Trefor had said. But Alex's brain didn't want to
wrap itself around this mess. He didn't want to believe he
was the father of a twenty-seven-year-old man, particularly one who seemed to hate him so well and for so little
reason.

Frustration tightened his chest, and he sat up on the
edge of his bed to gulp air. The night chill of his bedchamber felt good on his hot skin. The dying fire in the hearth
crumbled into its own ashes, sending a sprinkle of sparks
toward the chimney. The single glazed window was a small
square of lighter black against the far wall, its frames forming a cross at the center. This room was sanctuary, deep
within the thick stone of his keep and with access from
only one door. Outside that door, three chambers away, lay
a man who should be his heir and his closest kin, but instead was more than likely an enemy. There was nothing he

could do to change it, but acceptance wouldn't come. He didn't want this. Couldn't acquiesce to the idea of letting this man into his household and his life, and couldn't countenance sending him away.

Alex rose from his bed, took his silk dressing robe from the foot of his bed to don it, and padded in bare feet from his chamber, through the anteroom, and to the meeting hall beyond his apartments. There he paused before the door to the guest chamber where Trefor and his friend were sleeping. He wanted to ease open that door and look inside. He wanted to gaze on his son as he slept, to watch him and examine him, and to know him as a father.

But he knew if he opened that door he would not find what he was looking for. In that bedchamber he would find only annoyance. Trouble. A man who hated him for something he hadn't even done. Yet. The confusion and longing choked him. He stood frozen, unable to decide what to do. Finally, at a loss to know how to feel or what to think, he retreated from the door and returned to his bed, then lay there awake until the square of lighter black on the wall of his chamber had turned to the light purple of sunrise.

The company of An Dubhar set sail for Oban shortly after.

Once on the mainland, Alex's forty knights, plus Trefor's ten, lined up in a column and set out on the route Alex had taken on his last venture here. He was headed for Edinburgh, a journey of several days. Alex was recovering from his illness, but the long hours in the saddle wore him out. Each night he stripped himself of his chain mail and woolens, fell exhausted onto the pallet in his tent, and reflected on the days when he could have made this trip in minutes by air.

Halfway there, as they descended from the Highlands, Hector came to speak to him in private, out of earshot of Trefor and his crew. "Why Edinburgh?"

"Why not? It's the last place I saw Nemed, and I figure it'll be the first place Lindsay will go. Or did go, when she got here. We're grasping at straws. There's no way to know what's the most likely place to start looking." The hopelessness of their situation sank in further as he spoke. Alex took deep breaths to dispel the gathering despair. Trefor could be right. Finding Lindsay might be impossible. Alex didn't want Trefor to be right about anything, let alone this. "We'll find her," he said, and nodded once to affirm his words.

"Who do ye figure we're looking for, then? Man or woman?"

That was easy enough to answer. "Man. She took my hauberk, so she's more than likely wearing it. She knows how to pass and knows she won't get anywhere as a woman without me around. I figure we're looking for Sir Lindsay Pawlowski, my brother-in-law who was separated from the group escorting his sister to Eilean Aonarach last year. Thought to be dead, but somehow survived the fall he took in his fight with the robber."

"And we assume she has come to this very time, and is in search of her child. We assume she did not learn where Trefor was and follow him there."

Alex looked over at Hector, and the hopelessness tightened his chest. But he said, "If she knew where he was, she never went there. He's attested to that." Alex indicated Trefor with a tilt of his head to the rear. "I figure when she saw those ears she thought the same thing I did. That Nemed had a hand in it and had something to do with the baby's disappearance." Alex kept to himself his previous thoughts of cuckoldry, for he was ashamed of them. "She's probably gone looking for him. She doesn't know Nemed doesn't have him." Whether Nemed had anything to do with Trefor's appearance was still at question, but it was certain the elf hadn't stolen the baby.

Hector grunted and nodded.

Then Alex continued, with trepidation Hector might react badly to what he would say next and accuse him of sorcery. "Besides, I think she's here. I can feel it."

"Truly, or do ye only wish it?"

"Truly." Alex wished it, but something in his gut made him believe.

"Given to augury, then, are ye?"

Alex shook his head. "That touchy-feely stuff isn't for me. But on this I just know. With Lindsay, it's different. I just . . . well, know."

Again Hector nodded. "Well, then, if your heart tells you, it might be so."

Alex only wished his heart were that trustworthy.

Several days later they made camp just outside the gates of Edinburgh. It was late afternoon, but without waiting till morning Alex set off alone to climb the rocky hill to the ruined castle. Atop the hill, his horse picked its way among the fallen chunks of mortared stone lying about, and snorted restlessly. Alex had his best horses with him on this expedition, and today was mounted on his favorite, the dark bay with the thickly feathered fetlocks. The wind off the firth blustered the stallion's mane this way and that, and wide nostrils expanded to catch every scent on the breeze. After a few moments the animal calmed and reached for a bit of grass by the side of the track.

The ruins of the castle stuck up like broken teeth all around. Wind batted at Alex, and the silence seemed eternal. It hadn't been long since he was here last, but he noticed there were far fewer pieces of broken wall than there had been last fall. Probably they'd been taken by the town's inhabitants, and by farmers in the surrounding countryside, for construction material. The smaller pieces were probably now piled onto dikes and mortared into walls of houses and shops along the granite ridge behind him. Nothing ever went to waste in this country.

Last time he was here, he'd fought Nemed and forced the elfin king to send Alex and Lindsay back to the twenty-first century. Now he wished he'd simply killed the guy and had done with it. He'd not wanted to return to the future. He liked it here and had wanted to carve a future for himself and his family from the niche he'd found in history. It had been Lindsay who wanted their child to be born modern.

Lindsay and Danu. He looked down at the camp where Trefor and his men lounged, waiting, and wondered what his wife would think of how the kid had turned out.

Kid. There was only a year's difference in age between Trefor and his mother. The weirdness of that was appalling, and Alex wondered how this guy might act around a woman his own age, mother or not. Alex certainly didn't feel like a father. He'd been one for less than a month. He'd never held his son, never watched him grow up, never taught him anything. Never learned anything from him. The grief of that loss was a tight knot at his solar plexus he knew would never unravel.

"Lonely at the top, ain't it, Dad?"

Alex jumped and turned. "How did you get up here?" What he really meant was *How did you get up here without me hearing you?* Even Alex's horse hadn't given an indication of anyone following.

Trefor shrugged. "You were deep in thought. Trying to figure something out. I could have been driving a trolley car and ringing a bell and you wouldn't have heard me."

Unlikely, but Alex let it go. He said, "I'm trying to figure out how come Nemed wanted me on this spot when he was threatening Lindsay." *Your mother.* He couldn't say the words.

Trefor shrugged. "Simple enough. This is a thin place."

"A what?"

"Thin place." Trefor spoke carefully, enunciating clearly as if speaking to a particularly stupid child. "Can't you feel it?"

Alex blinked and had to admit, "No."

"All kinds of energy here." He nudged his horse to move around Alex, and gained another rise to turn and look around. He took a deep breath and gazed off over the firth. His long, dark hair tossed in the wind, revealing his ears for the world and Alex to see. "I bet he comes and goes from this spot all the time." He had the contemplative air of someone sniffing the wind, but Alex didn't think it was a scent he was picking up.

Alex gazed across at the town of Edinburgh crouching along the summit of rock that overlooked the countryside. He could bivouac here and wait, or set off in a random direction in search. The odds of finding Lindsay weren't pleasing for either choice. "You're sure about this?"

Trefor shrugged. "If you're asking for a guarantee, I can't give you one. I just know this is the sort of place that is attractive to those who deal in that sort of power." He nodded at the ruins of the king's residence and added, "Over the centuries it's certainly been attractive to those humans who wield the more mundane forms of it."

Alex grunted. He knew little about magic and didn't much like that Trefor seemed mixed up in it. "All right, then. We'll wait here for Nemed to show himself." Having decided, he turned back toward the camp and let Trefor follow as he would. Or not.

The ordinary knights stayed encamped where they were, with Sir Henry Ellot in command and a rotating watch set on the castle ruins. Alex, Hector, Trefor, and Mike took a room in town. Alex had never seen modern Edinburgh, but Trefor assured him not one stick of the existing tiny cluster of wood and stone structures would survive to the twenty-first century. Though the town was what passed for cosmopolitan these days, it wasn't what Alex would have called "bustling." There were a few shops selling wares of the artisans who lived behind them, and there was a tavern sort of place with rooms in the back for travelers. All very up-to-date and big city in these times, particularly for Scotland, for most towns had neither.

Only one of the rooms in the public house was available, so the four men crowded into it to deposit their weapons and bedrolls. Alex and Hector claimed the bed together, and Trefor and Mike would sleep on the floor before the small hearth. Food was to be had out front in the public room, so the four of them sat around the table there to buy and eat their supper. The only food available was a sorry, watery stew of mutton and turnips—mostly turnips—and Alex made a mental note to have a chat with the proprietor about making better food available since they would be there a while.

Loud, raucous voices approached from up the high street, and presently three men ducked through the little door of the tavern. Alex looked up and was both pleased and dismayed to see the tall, lanky James Douglas. The Earl of Douglas was in an excellent mood, laughing with his companions, who turned out to be his second knight and his favorite squire, over a joke one of them had just told. Probably James, for he was fond of his own jokes and always laughed uproariously when he thought he was funny.

"James!" Alex rose to greet his erstwhile commander. He'd ridden with James the summer before, making raids on the Borderlands after Bannockburn.

The earl stopped laughing to peer at Alex in the dim light of the cook fire, then recognized him. "Alasdair an Dubhar!" He threw his arms wide and embraced Alex, whom he considered a friend. Alex wasn't so sure, but didn't care to disabuse James of the notion they were buddies. The earl was King Robert's closest friend, and had been since James was a skinny boy squire, so friendship with James was generally considered to be a very good thing and other men jockeyed for the favor Alex had gained without effort, or even intent. "Ailig! What brings you to Edinburgh?"

"The usual." Alex wasn't about to go into details of his interest in elves and faeries. "Looking for action. We just arrived, and so haven't found any yet." He gestured to the table for the earl to sit, but there was only one chair free. Alex pointed to Mike and jerked his thumb to indicate he should give up his seat to James' second, who outranked the American on so many levels there was no question as to who should stand.

Mike, lounging in the chair with one arm over the back of it, threw him a cross look, then glanced at Trefor. Trefor, for his part, didn't raise an objection though he did have a cross glance for Alex. Then he indicated with a nod to

Mike that Alex should be obeyed. Mike rolled his eyes like a teenager, rose slowly, and went to stand with James' squire while the earl and his second in command took their seats around the table. James and the other knight ignored Mike's insolence, and Alex gave Trefor a hard glance to make clear he would address the issue later.

"Looking for a fight, ye say?" James gestured to his squire to bring refreshment, and the teenager hurried off to comply.

"Aye. The men are restless. Too many winter months twiddling their thumbs, and pretty soon they're going to be raiding my own villages. Can't have that."

James laughed. "Thumb twiddling. You've a way with words, my friend, even for an Irishman."

Alex chuckled. If James only knew.

"How many men have ye brought?"

"Forty of my own, plus five pages and a number of squires, and ten knights pledged by my cousin here." He nodded toward Trefor. James looked over at him, appraising.

"Another MacNeil I haven't heard of?" He addressed both Alex and Hector.

"Pawlowski. My mother's cousin, Trefor Pawlowski."

Trefor's eyes narrowed, but he said nothing.

Then the earl said to Alex, "Well, then, if it's a fight you want, come with us. I've spent the winter up north with Edward Bruce's father-in-law and now am gathering forces to take into the Marches."

"Rounding up your Highland infantries again?"

James shook his head. "Nay. Such men were needed for the fight here in Lothian, but when in the south we need the sort of speed in attack and avoidance that can only be had on horseback. No, no matter what they say about the successful hordes at Bannockburn, the knights of Scotland will win the day and purge the Scottish Lowlands of English interference. Come ride with us. While Robert and his brother are in Ireland, 'tis left to us." He leaned close, and his voice took on a pointed note. "And the king appreciates those who lend their support."

Meaning that, because Alex had already come to the attention of His Majesty, he could benefit greatly by taking his men into the Borderlands. There had already been soft, scattered whispers of an earldom for Alex, and they both knew such a venture could clinch it. The proposal was attractive.

Alex looked over at Trefor, who had a sour look on his face, sucking on the inside of his lower lip as if it were a lemon and the taste was making him squint. They both knew what James suggested meant giving up on finding Lindsay. What Trefor didn't understand was that James hadn't made so much a request as a demand. If Alex were to decline, however gracefully, it could—and by James most likely would—be construed as waffling in support of the king. A dodgy thing under the most forgiving of circumstances, and this was not such a circumstance. James' own support of his friend and mentor Robert was absolute. It was widely known that he considered anything less in other men tantamount to treason. Alex was now stuck in a position of incurring the ire of the second most powerful man in Scotland if he stuck to his search for his wife. He gave a slight frown in Trefor's direction, then addressed James with a nod and a grin.

"That sounds like a fine plan, friend. Exactly what I'd hoped for. When do we depart Edinburgh?" He hoped it would be a while, for if Nemed were to show himself in the meantime, Alex could send his men on with James while he took care of business and caught up later. But he was disappointed.

"Tomorrow," said James. "The town is empty of uncommitted fighting men these days, all of them having dispersed to wars elsewhere, and so we'll ride to Stirling to rejoin my army encamped there, and gather whatever men can be spared in the town. That castle has been razed as fully as the one here, and so there's no need for a garrison."

"A fine plan indeed." Alex's heart sank, and the disapproval from Trevor made him annoyed at everyone present. He told himself he had no assurance Nemed would ever

show himself while his men were camped outside Edinburgh, and so leaving with James would not affect their
chances of ever finding Lindsay. Trefor obviously thought
otherwise, but Alex had to shrug that off. They were to go
with James' company, and that would be that.

The knights ate, drank, and talked late into the night, the
conversation wandering this way and that from raid and
droving strategies to the prospects of livestock to be found
this time of year, to the women also to be found among the
Marches who might be welcoming. Or at least vulnerable.
Each had a tale to tell of conquest, of beauties who swooned
for such champions of prowess and strength as the men
gathered around this table plainly were. It was in the very
small hours that the well-met company of knights finally
moved to their rooms in the back to sleep off the gallons of
mead they'd consumed.

Trefor had spent the evening in silence, sulking at
Alex's decision to suspend the quest for Lindsay. Mike had
said nothing, for he didn't speak Middle English and hadn't
understood anything said that evening. But as they stripped
themselves of chain mail before the peat coals in their bedchamber, readying to sleep, Trefor's friend muttered half to
himself, "I didn't come here to be jerked around. This is
bullshit."

Hector didn't understand modern English, but Mike's
petulant tone was obvious, and the Laird of Barra paused in
removing his hauberk, looked to Alex, then to Mike again,
in surprise that An Dubhar would tolerate such insolence
from an inferior.

Alex, having removed his own hauberk, said without a
glance at anyone else as he shook out the mail with great
care and folded the metal garment to set it on the floor by
the bed, "Trefor, tell your friend to shut the fuck up. I don't
know what you told him to get him to come with you, or
what he thinks being a knight is all about, but you can in-
form him now that he's attached himself to a military contingent and from here on out he's to obey orders and
understand there is a hierarchy and chain of command he

will respect. He will deport himself as a soldier, he will obey his superiors, he will *not* mutter to himself and whine and complain like a chickenshit little brat"— Alex now turned to thrust his face into Mike's and back him against the wall by the door—"*or I will have him hung from the nearest fucking tree and leave his rotting carcass for the buzzards to pick into little . . . bitty . . . pieces.*"

Mike was wide-eyed and cringing against the wall, staring at Alex, whose voice was hard and his eyes aflame. An Dubhar's rage was a palpable thing in the room, and the other three men kept a careful silence, waiting for what would happen next, not entirely certain Alex wouldn't do damage to Mike to show him who was boss.

Alex allowed a moment for that to sink in, then said, "Am I coming in loud and clear, soldier?"

Trefor's friend didn't seem certain he was expected to reply to that, but Alex waited. Finally Mike said, "Yes."

"Yes, what?"

"Yes, sir."

"Very well. We will allow you to ride with us, and we won't hang you from the nearest tree and leave you for the buzzards. Today."

"Yes, sir."

Alex turned to sit on the bed and remove his boots and trews. He would leave on the rest of his clothing for warmth, but the trews had feet in them and in the cold the sweat would chill his feet. So he hung the trews to dry from a nail he found in the wall near the hearth, and set his boots on the floor also to dry. His linens were due for an airing, but he would do that once they were on the road with James' army and he could hang them in the sunshine.

Trefor said, "We can't leave with Douglas."

"We have to."

Hector got into the bed, still not understanding the conversation but watching the exchange for behavior clues.

"What happened to the search? Giving up already? You said you wanted to find my mother."

Alex's blood curdled at those words. Trefor's mother.

He sat on the edge of the bed and said, "We have no choice. James has requested our support. He's an earl. Not just an earl, but Robert's favorite. That guy outranks pretty much everyone in the country right now, and he's not the happy-go-lucky sort he appears. Dude's the poster child for OCD when it comes to kicking English butt. Cross him, and you take your life into your hands."

"You don't think he would understand if you told him you were looking for your wife?"

Alex snorted. "No. He wouldn't even begin to understand. Not even if I made up a convincing story that left out the faeries and elves. Not even if I laid out my heart and told him I just can't live without my wife, oh-woe-is-me. If I did that, he'd laugh himself sick and then call me a coward. Or worse, a traitor. Throwing over support for the king for the sake of a woman, even a wife, just doesn't compute for these guys."

Trefor began to wriggle out of his hauberk. Mike was still sulking by the fire. "Aren't they married, too? Isn't Douglas married?"

"Yeah."

"And he doesn't give a damn about his wife?" Trefor's voice was thick with disgust.

"No. Not the least bit."

"Why'd he marry her?"

"Money. Status. An heir. That's the norm here. They all think I'm a schmuck because I married a woman who brought me neither money nor status."

An edge came to Trefor's voice. "Nor an heir."

Alex threw him a cross look, then turned and slipped under the blankets on the narrow bed next to Hector. Without another word he blew out the single candle on the table next to the bed and lay back on the straw mattress. Hector was taking more than his share of it, so Alex nudged him over and made him give way. The Laird of Barra complied with a grunt. Trefor and Mike wrapped themselves in their plaids and lay on the floor near the fire.

Alex noted they lay as far apart as possible without

moving too far from the hearth. They would get over that
before long, he knew. He'd learned long ago that the
warmth from another body trumped any discomfort of
having to sleep next to another man. In fact, men were better than women for that, for they gave off more heat. He
backed against Hector and knew he would be more comfortable when he awoke than Trefor and Mike would be
over by the dying fire.

In the darkness, Alex said, "We're going to join Douglas, and I don't want to hear any more about it. If you
can't follow orders and behave like a knight, then you can
take your men, go your own way, and stay the hell away
from my castle. But if you do that, be advised that the next
time I see you I'll kill you. Break your allegiance to me,
and I'll hang you as a traitor. Am I clear?"

There was a pause, then Trefor said, "Yes, sir, yes, sir,
three bags full."

Once the silence had come over the room like a woolen
blanket, Hector said to Alex in Gaelic, "Has all been settled, then?"

Alex replied, "Aye." Then he rolled over to sleep.

The next day Alex, Trefor, and their knights set out for
Stirling, not terribly far from Edinburgh, to meet up with
James' army. It was this sort of travel that Alex found so
frustrating when he compared this century to his life in the
future. The steady walk of a horse felt like a snail's pace
because Alex knew this entire day's ride would one day be
possible to accomplish in seconds. They plodded along for
hours on end, not even going to a trot. Alex was bored stiff,
and impatient.

Trefor and Mike were chatting to the rear of Alex, just
at the front of the column of knights, too far back for Alex
to hear what they were saying. They all knew Alex was the
only man present who would have understood the language
everyone except Hector thought was Hungarian, had he
been able to hear. Alex didn't much like the fact that they
were talking, let alone that they were talking out of earshot.
He fell back, even with them, and they fell silent.

Not good. He made like he wanted to converse with Trefor. "Hey, Beavis," he said to Mike. "Beat it." He nodded toward the front to indicate Mike should spur his horse and hang with Hector. Mike gave a sullen stare but obeyed, and Alex then addressed Trefor.

"What's the deal with you and the faeries?"

Trefor looked toward the front and not at Alex. "I don't know what you mean."

"How do you know that Edinburgh castle is built on what you call a 'thin place'? And what was that thing with the weather a while back?"

Trefor shrugged. "Nothing."

"Like hell."

Alex's son chuckled. "If you say so."

"You said the faeries took you and left you until a year ago. What happened a year ago?"

"They came and got me."

"Why?"

"Dunno. They just came and told me who I am. Who my parents are. They told me how you took off for Scotland the instant I was born and left me with them to raise."

"I did what?"

"You deny it, and yet here you are."

"I came to find you."

"Like you came here to find Mom."

"I will find Lindsay."

"Someday, maybe. Meanwhile, she's God knows where, and I got left in the future, stuck in the Tennessee foster care system. A fate worse than death, I assure you."

"Don't be melodramatic."

"Do it yourself sometime, and see what you think. Until then, let me tell it how I saw it. It was a fucking nightmare. I got out when I turned eighteen, and took Mike with me even though he still had a few months before he would be old enough to go. Nobody ever came looking for him."

Alex glanced at Mike. "I wouldn't have."

"Fuck you." Trefor looked at him sideways with an angry glance that made Alex think of Lindsay. Alex looked away,

for it was too terrible to see her in him. Bad enough to have
to deal with the green eyes that were undeniably his own, but
the glimpses of Trefor's mother cut to Alex's heart.

"So what did the wee folk tell you when they came to
you a year ago?"

"They told me all about how you had never wanted to
leave the Middle Ages because you were all hot to become
the Earl of East Jesus Deserted Island or somesuch—"

"Lonely island."

"Huh?"

"Eilean Aonarach means 'lonely island' in Gaelic."

"Yeah, I know. Whatever. They said you thought you
were on your way to the peerage and I was an obstacle."

"So I told them to come get you so I could go back to
the past?"

"So you said nothing and just went."

"And your mother?"

"You were following her."

"Did they have a story for why she left?"

"Did they need one? I don't know why she left. Maybe
she couldn't stand living with you anymore."

That cut Alex in places he'd never known he had. In
backlash without thinking, he said, "Maybe she was horrified she'd given birth to a pointy-eared freak."

For one suspended moment it seemed Trefor would leap
from his horse to tackle his father. If they hadn't both been
mounted at the time, he probably would have hauled off to
clobber Alex. But instead he fell silent and looked out
across the countryside through which they moved so slowly.

They rode that way for a long time, the only sound the
dull thudding of hooves on the dirt track. Alex's eyes were
on James and Hector who rode ahead, but his attention was
on his son. He wanted to take back what he'd said, but
didn't have the words for it and didn't want whatever
words he might say to be thrown back in his face. So he
didn't speak and wished Trefor would.

Finally Trefor did open his mouth. He said, "They
taught me how to be lucky."

Alex looked over at him. "What does that mean?"

Trefor shrugged. "I don't know. Except that if I concentrate hard enough I can make luck happen."

"How?"

A sharp glance at Alex, then, "You can't do it yourself."

"Why not?"

"Just, trust me, you can't."

"So tell me why."

"Because you're not a pointy-eared freak."

Alex pressed his lips together to hold back the remark that came to mind, and stared off to the side of the road. Then he said, "You're saying that you're one of them?"

"I'm saying my mother is one of them."

Alex turned to gawk at him, but realized he shouldn't be surprised. Trefor was plainly his and Lindsay's son, and those ears had come from somewhere. Now he had to ask, "Does she know?"

"You tell me. I've never met the woman. But the wee folk who approached me a year ago say I'm descended directly from someone named Danu, through the female line. Apparently that's some sort of big deal, and they were disappointed I was a boy. They say I would have been more powerful if I'd been female."

Danu? Alex stared at Trefor, trying to see her in him, but couldn't. Himself and Lindsay, but not Queen Danu. Except, of course, for those blasted ears.

Trefor saw the look on his face and said, "What?"

"Danu. They told you she was your ancestor? Lindsay's ancestor?"

Trefor nodded.

"Huh. That would explain a few things." Like the book of psalms. Now he realized he should have been more curious about Danu's interest in Lindsay. Her insistence the baby be born in the future. But it raised other questions. Alex thought back over each exchange he'd had with the faerie queen in this new light, but it was all a muddle of partial memory and unclear motives. He would need to think this out carefully.

And Lindsay was a descendant of the faerie. That certainly knocked him sideways. Had she known? Had she been hiding her true nature from him the same way she'd been hiding her gender from the world those years they'd been together? Could he trust her if he saw her again?

CHAPTER 9

They reached Stirling late that evening, and like everything else in the military, their situation was a case of
hurry-up-and-wait. The MacNeils encamped alongside the
Douglases on the flatland near the Bannock Burn, which
had of late been the battlefield where Robert's foot soldiers stymied all the best knights of Edward II of England.
James Douglas took his highest-ranking men, including
Alex and Hector, into the town below the ruined castle to
wring it of as many uncommitted fighting men as they
could find and hire. For several days they talked and drank
with the locals. Sometimes Trefor sat with them, but was
mostly silent when he did. Mike stayed away, and for that
Alex was glad.

One morning Alex, standing in the muddy, stony street
at the foot of the hill, looked up toward the ruins and saw
Trefor perched on a pile of stones, staring out across the
countryside. Alex started up the hill to talk and hoped Trefor would stay until he got there. Trefor watched him climb
the slope, saying nothing as he approached but only shred-
ding a bit of grass he'd plucked from beside his feet, and

when Alex reached the tumble of rocks, he looked up at Trefor and said, "Is this a thin place, too?"

"Relative to what?"

"Edinburgh, what else?"

Trefor shrugged and glanced about. "The whole country is more tuned to the realms than other places, but relative to Edinburgh, no. Stirling is no closer to the other side than anywhere else in Scotland. Not that I can tell, anyway. Edinburgh is . . . sort of like an orifice." He grinned. "Like the asshole of the faerie realms."

"Oh." Alex had to chuckle at that. He climbed some more and took a seat near Trefor's on the chunk of fallen wall. Below, the closely packed buildings of the town seemed tumbled atop each other and clinging to the granite slope like barnacles. Off in the distance was the wood that covered the rise from which Robert had launched his warriors in the recent battle, the Bannock Burn wending its way around it. Not far, on the other side of the burn, was the field where William Wallace had also clobbered the English a couple of decades ago. Today some people wandered here and there, going about their business in peace. The hilltop was quiet. There was no wind today. Alex sat in silence with his son.

Then Trefor said, as if continuing a conversation in progress, "They named me Trefor Andrews."

"Who did?"

"The people who found me in the Dumpster."

Dumpster? Alex's face warmed with anger at the people who had done that, and at himself for failing to prevent it. He looked over at Trefor's impassive face. More than impassive, it was blank beyond lack of expression. There was a dreaminess about it as he gazed out across the land where less than two years ago his parents had faced the army of King Edward II and his mother had nearly died. "How did you end up in a Dumpster? Those faeries took you, and then just threw you away?"

Trefor shrugged. "I guess. That's where the authorities found me. A Dumpster in a place called Carthage,

Tennessee. They say I was nearly dead, lying among the garbage for a day or so, dehydrated and all. A couple of weeks old, so the ones who kidnapped me had kept me for a while, I guess. It's probably why I survived."

"Long enough to get you from London to the U.S."

"I think that wouldn't have been much trouble for them. I found out a year ago it was the Bhrochan who did it. They came to me to let me know what they'd done."

Alex made a rasping, disgusted noise. "Bragging?"

Trefor shrugged again. "Maybe. Maybe not. I don't think it was the same particular people who came to me. One was an old lady who was part human, and she told me everything."

"No, she didn't. She told you lies."

Trefor bristled. "She told it to me as she saw it." Alex wondered how come Trefor was so touchy on the subject of these Bhrochan. The faeries were crazy; if he had met some of them he should know that. "She knew who my parents were and where to find you."

"And you just believed her?"

Trefor peered at him. "I found you, didn't I?"

Alex had to admit he had a point. He asked, "What was her interest in you?"

Trefor chewed on the inside of his cheek, almost like a cow chewing cud, and for a while it seemed Alex wouldn't get a reply. But then Trefor said, "Fate, she said. It was . . . *she* was my fate. And I think I agree with her." An odd note had slipped into his voice.

"Ending up in a Dumpster was your fate?"

Trefor gave a wry laugh. "Apparently."

"So she told you your name was MacNeil and then, poof, sent you to my island?"

"No. First she told me my destiny was here, and then taught me to speak the language and to be lucky."

"And you just bought that and bailed from your life?"

"What life? I was a cook in a greasy spoon. One of those nasty hole-in-the-wall places that open for the locals for breakfast in the middle of the night and shut down right

after lunch. I spent my mostly predawn days frying eggs
and hash browns and flipping hamburgers. Restaurants. Always restaurants."

"You didn't think you could do better than being a
short-order cook?"

Trefor shook his head. "I had to fight to get that. On my
eighteenth birthday the system turned me loose and that
was that. No driver's license, no high school diploma, no
place to live, nothing. Even the army didn't want me."

"You're a wiz with Farsi and the army didn't want you?"

Trefor tensed and gave him a blank look. Alex knew he
was sounding critical and knew he should back off. Trefor
then said, "No foreign languages for me in high school; I
sure wasn't going to college. Everyone knows as much
Farsi as I knew back then. The army was full up with guys
more fluent than I was."

Alex blinked and frowned. "*Farsi?* Nobody—"

"Twenty years later, man. It was twenty years after you
left."

"Oh." Alex nodded. "Oh, yeah." Twenty years. He realized he'd been thinking of Trefor as a month-old adult.

Trefor continued. "It wasn't until I started working in
restaurants a few years ago that I discovered I could learn
languages. I thought about trying to be an interpreter, but
nobody wants to communicate through a guy who never
graduated high school, who wears his hair long to cover his
deformed ears, and who smells like a slum apartment. See,
the foster folk and social workers taught me nothing and
told me nothing. I didn't even know how much I didn't
know. I didn't know how to fill out a job application. I
didn't know how to write out a check, which wasn't an issue for a while because it was years before I had money for
a checking account. I'm still not good with them, and I
kinda like the barter system they've got here."

Alex couldn't imagine not knowing those things and
couldn't remember where he'd learned them. It boggled
him that some children weren't taught.

Trefor continued. "At first Mike and I bounced around

homeless shelters for a while, then I finally snagged a steady job by lying like a rug about just about everything on the application. Got an apartment and a rickety old car." He shook his head. "That place made your no-plumbing-or-electricity castle look like a . . . well, a castle."

Alex resisted a grin at the joke, but his mouth twitched.

"You bet your sweet ass I bailed." Trefor stuck a piece of the grass into his mouth to chew on the end.

"No, I guess I can't blame you."

"Anyway, that should answer your questions."

Alex frowned. "What questions?"

"The ones you came up here to ask. The ones that have been bugging you ever since I showed up." Trefor's face didn't give away any indication whether he was a reader of minds or just a good guesser.

Alex looked out over the medieval landscape devoid of roads and strewn with thick forests, and wondered if he'd really wanted to know the things Trefor had just told him.

In the week James spent in Stirling he managed to recruit eight more swords. Then the army of raiders headed south for the Borderlands.

While riding, there was a lot of time for Alex to think about Lindsay and the revelation Trefor had made about her. He tried to figure out all the implications, but whenever he went back over Danu's involvement, his thoughts all crumbled to nonsense. Why hadn't Lindsay told him? Why hadn't Danu told him? How did this news reflect on the question of why the Bhrochan had taken Trefor? Indeed, why had they taken him? Those creatures were all crazy; could it be the more humanlike Danann were just as bonkers, but hid it better? Alex kept looking over at his son, surreptitiously, and wondered if Trefor had inherited the faerie mentality. God forbid. The last thing he wanted was to have a flake like that guarding his back on a battlefield.

And that thought brought to mind Trefor's lack of skill with a sword. Probably Mike's as well, but Alex would just as soon that nitwit die in his first raid so they would all be rid of him. Trefor was another matter entirely. All things considered, he'd rather Trefor would live. As they approached the Marches, Alex went to him one evening and said, "You need to learn how to swing a broadsword."

Trefor was sitting at his fire and looked up at Alex with an air of offended ego. "I told you, I can handle a sword." Alex may have been his father, but there was no getting around that he was still only five years older and could not command the authority of an older and wiser parent. All he had on Trefor was the two years he'd spent in this century his son had not. But Alex didn't want to think of that.

"Right. Show me." Alex drew his sword and held it ready at his side.

Trefor considered the challenge for a moment, then stood and reached for his sword from among the pile of belongings next to his bedroll. As he straightened, Alex hauled back and swung, and Trefor parried like a fencer, misdirecting the force of the assault, and his eyes went wide at the force of Alex's sword. He stumbled back as Alex swung again. And again Trefor was forced to retreat under the fast blows of his father's sword.

The terrible thing, though, was that Alex was not trying for speed. He was telegraphing his moves in order not to damage Trefor unnecessarily. His heart tightened that his son had come to this century as poorly prepared to survive as he'd been in the twenty-first century. This was very bad. Trefor wouldn't last more than a minute in a real fight.

An Dubhar laid off and stood down after backing Trefor a few steps. The dread of losing Trefor to an English sword shocked him with its power. As thoroughly annoying as the guy was, he was still somehow more important than anything else in Alex's life, and the realization of that vulnerability nearly paralyzed him. His response was to fight the emotion, as he fought all emotions that gave him trouble, and his voice went to a snarl with it.

"Had I been a real opponent," Alex said, "you would be lying on the ground now, bleeding to death. *Death*. Do you understand what that means? I would have sliced through your mail, hacked you to bits, and you would be helpless and dying with the full knowledge that there is no surgery here, no medical attention that will put you back together once you've been laid open sufficiently." He paused to let that sink in, and his mouth pressed together with the anger that rose from his concern. Trefor was a problem that needed to be solved.

Trefor gazed at him, his eyes aflame with rage. He was probably about to tell Alex off for attacking him like that, but Alex also saw a little fear in his demeanor. Good. Fear, he'd learned, was an excellent motivator, and even if Trefor would never admit Alex was right in his assessment, then at least the guy might want to learn how to survive. It didn't matter whether Trefor liked him; it only mattered that he would live.

Alex sheathed his sword and held out his hand. "Let me see your sword."

Trefor hesitated, then handed over his weapon. Alex examined it, a long-bladed cross-hilt with a grip nearly long enough to use as a hand-and-a-half bastard sword. It was genuine, crafted in this time. "You bought it after you arrived in this century."

"Of course I did. I'm not stupid."

Alex ignored that. "It's still too heavy. You need a lighter sword. Faster. Shorter, because you're not tall enough to wield a sword this long. You and I are taller than most around here, but this thing is for someone well over six feet, and it's too heavy for anyone who wants to last more than a few minutes in a fight."

"I want a heavy sword, to cut through chain mail."

"You don't need this much weight for that. If you were bigger, then maybe you could get away with this blade. A smaller sword, wielded correctly, will do what you want. And it'll do it without wearing you out."

"I've seen your claymore. It's a monster."

Alex's eyes narrowed at him. "You'll never see me swing it while mounted, because I use both hands. I can use it one-handed if I have to, if I hook a finger over a quillon, but I prefer not to. Two hands are better. Lindsay used

to carry it on her saddle, to hand to me if I was ever unhorsed." For a moment he flashed on how he'd used it to
defend her at Bannockburn, and his chest tightened. Quickly
he took a deep breath and put her out of his mind. He continued. "And it's lighter than you think it is." He hefted Trefor's sword in his hand. "It's hardly any heavier than this
thing. Next chance you get, replace this with a lighter sword.
One that really will cut through chain mail."

"This'll be fine."

"Do what I say."

"No."

Alex wanted to smack him for this stubbornness. He
wanted to slap him around like the fool he was acting, and
make him understand that because Alex had experience he
knew best. But he also knew Trefor would never listen on
that account. Alex's authority as laird wasn't going to cut it
because Trefor hadn't been raised to respect this system.
Alex had no hold, no leverage to even make Trefor understand the importance of what he would teach.

Then Alex realized what he must do. It was a terrible
thing, but it was necessary. Trefor would never learn any
other way, and it was far better he be taught now, by someone who would not kill him, than by an opponent who
would certainly try and probably succeed. Alex tossed Trefor's weapon back to him and drew his own sword again.
"Defend yourself."

Trefor readily went *en garde* like an eighteenth-century
dandy, and Alex sighed with deep impatience. *Fencing.*
Perfunctorily, with almost no effort, he feinted to the left
and stabbed to the right. Trefor fell for it completely, and
the tip of Alex's blade went easily through Trefor's hauberk,
into his left arm, then through and partway into a back muscle. Trefor gasped and stumbled back. Alex stood down,
knowing he'd shocked Trefor enough that there would be no
reprisal. Not today, anyway.

"What the fuck did you do that for?" Trefor let his sword
drop to the ground, and he held his bleeding shoulder.

"Probably just extended your life expectancy. There's

always the possibility of infection, but you probably won't get one."

"You stabbed me!"

"I could have killed you!" Alex wiped Trefor's blood from his sword onto his trews and scabbarded the weapon, then stepped in to impress his words upon his son. "When you are fighting for real, you are defending your *life*. There are no rules. There is no such thing as honor or chivalry when you are fighting someone who wants to kill you. There is only making certain you are not the one to die that day."

Trefor's eyes took on the sullen look again that enraged Alex so terribly, and it was no longer such a puzzle why he hadn't learned anything in high school. Alex gritted his teeth and held back his hand from slapping that look from Trefor's face.

He continued. "When I tell you that you need a smaller sword, it isn't because I like hearing myself talk. Nor is it because I'm a control freak who wants everyone around me to be like me. When I say you need another sword, it's because you *need* it to stay alive. This one will get you killed, because it's too damn big, too heavy, and you don't know how to use a sword that has an edge and weighs more than a pound and a half. I don't care where you bought it, or how much it cost, or how big my own standby sword is. Yours is too . . . bloody . . . big." He glared at Trefor and let that sink in. The sullenness did not abate, but after a few seconds Alex said, "Here. Feel this." He handed over his own sword.

For a second it looked like Trefor wasn't going to comply, but then he took his hand from his wound, wiped the blood onto the thigh of his trews, and took the offered sword. It was also a cross-hilt, with a gilded pommel. Quite fancy compared to others wielded by knights of his station, and the tip of the blade was tapered to a point where Trefor's was not.

Trefor admitted with obvious reluctance, "This went through the mail like it wasn't there."

"You've got to be faster. You've handicapped yourself

by buying a sword that's too long for you. Too heavy. You think that because it's a broadsword it's supposed to be slow, but you're wrong. The guys you'll be fighting are a lot faster than you think. They're faster than I just was, and they'll be out to kill you. Also, they're not likely to ever feel it necessary to tell you to defend yourself. They'll just come after you, and they won't apologize afterward for being so rude."

Even Trefor had to give a wry smile at that.

"Do what I say, man. Get yourself a new sword." Alex took back his weapon, then gestured to Trefor's on the ground. "Pick that up, and we'll go on."

Trefor grimaced and flexed his left shoulder a little to indicate his pain. "How about we let his heal first?"

Alex snorted. "That's nothing, and if you can't handle a little pain during practice you'll be worthless on the field and I won't have you in my outfit. Pick up your sword, and we'll continue. It'll be good experience to learn to ignore a little cut like that."

"I'm still bleeding."

"It's almost stopped. Pick up your sword."

"If I faint, will you kill me?"

"Piss me off, and we'll see. Pick up the bloody sword."

Trefor finally complied, and went back to *en garde* but this time with his left arm held to his side.

"Where's your shield?"

"I don't have one."

"Why not?"

"I prefer not to use one."

"Get one. In fact, go get that one over there." He pointed with his chin to his own kite-shaped red, gold, and black shield leaning against a tree outside his tent. Then he whistled to Gregor and told him to bring Henry Ellot's shield, which stood outside the next tent.

Trefor said, "I don't need a shield. I have a dagger to use in that hand."

"Get. The shield." Alex was losing patience and would have liked to stab Trefor again just for being such a pain.

Trefor glared at him, and Alex returned it until Trefor complied. Once he'd taken the shield, he went back to his fencing stance. Alex accepted Ellot's shield from little Gregor.

"Forget *en garde*," he told Trefor.

Trefor stood down. "What's wrong with it?"

"You're not playing a game, that's what's wrong with it. This isn't sport—it isn't even a duel—and you're wielding a blade that cuts better than it stabs, and en garde isn't appropriate."

"I've done sabers."

"Big deal. You're using a shield, but by standing sideways like that you're trying to hide the unprotected part of your body as if you weren't carrying one."

"See, I don't need a shield. I—"

"*You're not going to a tea party!* You're going into battle, and if you are unhorsed you will be in the midst of a melee with blades all around you. Not just blades, but pikes, maces, axes, crossbows, and longbows. If you are not unhorsed, you will have guys coming at you with swords and lances." Why wouldn't this guy listen to him? What bug had gotten up his butt that he had to argue with everything Alex said? "Use the shield, forget *en garde*, and bloody well listen to me!"

Trefor's mouth pressed together and a white line formed around his lips. But he finally said, "All right. How do you want me to stand?"

"Like this." Alex demonstrated a more face-on stance with his sword held high and the shield covering the left side of his torso. Trefor imitated. "You can see how your best targets are going to be the head, arms, and legs. Your opponent is going to be wearing a helmet and carrying a shield, so his legs are most vulnerable. Cut him off at the knees, as they say, and he'll topple obligingly and become vulnerable elsewhere. But the good news around here is that you don't need to bother with him once you've cut his leg deep enough. Especially if you manage to cut it *off*, because he'll bleed to death, or at least be of no further use to his king with a missing leg. In any case, he won't be annoying you anymore that day."

To Alex's surprise, that seemed to sink into Trefor's thick skull.

For another hour or so he coached his son on how to handle broadsword and shield, and Trefor managed to stop giving him guff at every turn. By the time Alex saw sweat popping out on Trefor's forehead from the pain in his wounded shoulder, he was feeling more comfortable about Trefor's ability to survive in combat.

Alex hoped Trefor's improved attitude might stick with him, but in the following days around the cook fires along the way to the Marches, Trefor regained his sullen demeanor. Particularly if Hector was around. He bitched and moaned about the way people lived in this time, the lack of technology he considered basic, in modern English so Hector would wonder what he was saying.

Mike, on the other hand, didn't seem to be struggling so much with culture shock. One evening, not far from Lockerbie, they were gathered around the large common fire and Mike let loose a thundering fart.

Alex commented, "Well, that was tuneful."

Hector snorted laughter and translated to Middle English so the others could have a chuckle.

Both Alex and Trefor looked over at Hector, as stunned as parents whose child has just said its first word. Alex said, "You understood that?"

Hector shrugged. "Once I learned the language you spoke was so similar to our English, 'twas easy enough to work out what you were telling each other. 'Tis a separate matter entirely to speak in the way you do, so do not expect me to try, and I wouldnae care to go to your future . . . I mean, Hungary, and attempt to be understood, but I understand well enough what's being said. And young Mike here is indeed a resonant fellow."

"Just trying to fit in," said Mike.

Good point, though Alex had always managed not to pick up the uglier personal habits of the times.

"What I wouldn't give for a hot shower," said Trefor. It seemed ever since he'd arrived he was missing something from the future, and hot showers had become a theme with him.

Alex figured he was embarrassed at being so filthy all the time. He didn't like it either, for while on campaign sometimes rashes would appear in spots where his clothing bound, but his nose had long ago adjusted to make body odors baseline for him and he just didn't smell people anymore.

"Showers," he said with an edge of contempt. "Refrigerators. Television. MP3 players. Why did you come here if that stuff was so important to you? You had to know there was no electricity or running water here."

Trefor had no answer for that.

Hector, however, had a comment. "What might a 'shower' be, then? And 'electricity?' "

"A shower is a very small room where heated water is sprayed out of a pipe and you bathe in it. Like a hot waterfall, and you can make it flow or stop with a lever on the pipe."

Hector's eyes went wide. "Heated water ye say? From a pipe? Why would a man want such a thing? Does not the hot water weaken the body?"

"No." Trefor sounded defensive, angering in the face of Hector's attitude.

Alex said, "It can. It makes you feel drowsy sometimes. It's relaxing."

Hector shook his head. "Then I shouldn't want it. Bathing is for those as would prefer to die in bed than on the field, I think."

Trefor's eyes narrowed. "Or for those of us who like to get laid a little more often."

Hector laughed. "There is that, and if a shower of hot water would make the women come running and leaping into my bed I would certainly consider it." He addressed Alex. "Perhaps then, my brother, that would be the secret to finding your wife? Wash yourself in a shower with the hot water, and the next thing you know Lady Marilyn will emerge from the woods all bright-eyed and saying, 'Who is that smelling

so fresh and clean and odorless? I must have him, and
now!' " Then he said to Trefor, "But I've not noticed them
clamoring after you, have I? As fastidious as ye are."

Alex laughed, but Trefor did not. He fell silent and
stared into the fire.

Then he glanced up at a spot over Alex's head, and a
light came into his eyes that made Alex look around. Behind him stood a woman of copper-bright red hair, clad in
a fine woolen overdress with thickly embroidered sleeves
that covered her hands to her knuckles. Her hair was braided
carefully the length of her back. She would have appeared
of high station, except that her only ornamentation was a
scattering of spring flowers in her hair and a belt of golden
rope. It reminded Alex of the one that Brochan guy wore,
and alarm bells set off in his head. He shifted uncomfortably in his seat.

Trefor cried in a voice that alarmed Alex even more,
"Morag!" Without taking his eyes from the woman, he rose
and in two long steps went to her and took her into his arms
in a heartfelt kiss.

Alex and Hector looked at each other, and though neither spoke, Alex knew Hector was thinking the same thing
he was. How had this woman made it into camp without being challenged by a sentry? Never mind the sentries, how
did she make it through the array of tents and cook fires
without attracting anyone's attention? They both looked
around, but everyone within sight was going about his business without even a glance toward the woman who was still
locked in embrace with Trefor.

Hector returned his attention to the couple and muttered,
"Perhaps there's something to this cleanliness of his."

Alex said to Mike, "Who is she?"

Mike shrugged. "His girlfriend."

"Ya think? How about we put that right at the top of the
'duh' list? Tell me who she *is*, Mike."

"She's one of the people who sent us here. The tall one."
He said it as if Trefor had gone into detail about the relative
heights of the folk who had come to him a year ago.

Alex looked over at her and thought her remarkably short for being a "tall" one. And she'd sent Trefor and Mike through time. By magic. He shivered with apprehension and hoped he was wrong, particularly since the two were groping each other like teenagers at a drive-in and their involvement with each other was plain for the world to see.

He asked Mike, "She came with you guys from the future?"

"No."

"But you said she sent you. Through time."

Mike shook his head as if Alex were an idiot for not getting it. "No, she *will* send us. In seven centuries when she's an old lady, she'll send us back."

Sheesh. Another blasted faerie. The old lady Trefor had mentioned. Now Alex knew where Trefor had learned to speak medieval Gaelic so fluently. "Does she know this?"

"Of course she does. Why else would she send us back?"

Why else, indeed. "So, let me get this straight. In the future this old lady is going to muster up a cubic buttload of magic"—very costly magic, Alex knew, for Nemed had harped on that—"and send you guys back to this century just so her younger self can get smoochy with Trefor?"

"Yup."

Alex raised his voice to be heard by Trefor. "Hey, Trefor, how about you introduce your friend?"

Trefor seemed happier to see this Morag woman than he'd been about anything else since Alex had met him. He stepped back, gazing into her eyes, then guided her to the rocky rise against which he'd been leaning near the fire. There she sat like a queen, smiling for Trefor in response to his joy. Trefor's face was aglow with his pleasure, and he said, "This is Morag, my friend who brought me here."

"She got a last name?"

The woman said, her voice smooth and soothing, "Nae. I'm often called Red Morag, but not among my own people, who are few enough to know me from others with that name."

"Danann?"

She turned a sharp glance on him. "No. But you know of them?"

"Enough to know they exist." He wasn't going to give away his familiarity with Danu. Then he asked, "Bhrochan?"

Now she tilted her head to the side, puzzled. "How do you know of them?"

"Are you Bhrochan?"

For a long moment she considered her reply, then nodded. "Distantly."

Crap. It was true. She was one of the crazy faeries. The ones who had nearly killed him getting him here. "How distantly?"

"I dinnae see how that matters at all."

"It matters to you because I've asked. Answer my question, or I'll have you escorted from the camp."

A tiny smile at the corners of her lips let him know she figured anything he might do to keep her away would be easily circumvented, just as she'd bypassed the sentries. He knew then he would need to take her into custody and restrain her if she gave him any trouble, and even that might not do any good.

Her reply was, "My mother's mother was of the Bhrochan."

"You realize Trefor is Danann."

The smile spread across her face to become warm and affectionate. A hand reached toward Trefor's, and he grasped it, entwining his fingers with hers. She said, "Aye, but I do not hold that against him. I care for him regardless."

Trefor chuckled as if it were a joke, but Alex didn't think it was. He had a sense any love she might have for his son was in spite of Trefor's ancestry.

"Lots of crossing between the wee folk and humans, then? I wasn't aware there were so many of mixed heritage."

"We've a long history, and live a long time. I'm over a century old, myself."

Alex said to Trefor, "Got a thing for older women, then, son?"

Trefor's eyes narrowed, and his voice came angrily. "Well, I can't call my father 'the Old Man,' can I?"

"Some would think that a good thing."

"I don't see why anyone would."

Alex had no reply to that. This round to Trefor, who was now leaning in toward his girlfriend and whispering in her ear. She giggled, and he chuckled. Alex didn't like any of this. Not one bit.

CHAPTER 10

Lindsay had to get out of there. Without another glance at the suspicious knight, she licked her fingers clean of grease and as casually as possible rose from her seat. There was no helping a glance down at the stones where she'd sat, and she was immensely relieved to find no blood spot there. But she could feel it beginning to make its way down the inseams of her trews toward her knees, and she reached for her plaid to pull it around her with a mumbled complaint about the cold and what an annoyance it was there was no garderobe intact in the tower and that meant she had to go outside to pee.

"Use that there corner," said the faerie knight who had caught her scent.

She tossed a disgusted look his way. "Filthy pig." Then she hurried from the tower as if she were headed for a spot to relieve herself. When she reached the edge of the nearest thicket, she broke into a run to get as far away from the tower as she could, lest someone else happen by on the mission she only pretended.

It was dark among the trees, but she found a patch of

sunlight in a small clearing. There she stopped, her breathing heavy for the terror as well as the running. The bleeding from the birth had stopped days before, and she'd thought she was done with it. This sudden gushing flow must mean something had gone terribly wrong, and she knew no way to even address such a problem. There were no women attached to the raiding party on any sort of permanent basis, and revealing herself as female was out of the question in any case. There was nobody she could trust to ask for whatever folk medicine was to be had. She wasn't even confident modern medicine would have had an answer for something this strange.

In the clearing she stripped herself of mail and tunic, then untied her trews and dropped them to her ankles just above her boots. The crotch was soaked, and if she didn't bleed to death she was going to have to do something about that enormous stain. In all the time she'd disguised herself as Alex's squire, she'd never allowed so much as a spot on her clothing. This stain, if not cleaned completely, would betray her in an instant. If she wasn't betrayed already by the scent that faerie had caught. She groaned, and reached for her bloodied linens.

They were bright red. So copious was the blood, it shone wet on the cloth. She hadn't bled like this even the day after the baby was born. This wasn't even approaching normal; it was a hemorrhage. She reached for a handful of bracken to wipe it from herself as she swallowed tears of panic. This much blood meant she would probably end up collapsing right here in the clearing and bleeding to death where nobody would find her. Alex would never know what happened to her. She wanted to make it back to Alex. She wished to God she wouldn't die so she could see Alex again.

But when the worst of the blood was wiped away, she realized the flow had stopped. She could feel it had quit, the tightness in her belly was gone, and there was no more blood easing down her leg. There had been just enough of it to betray her, and no more. She looked around, expecting to find Nemed watching, probably laughing at her. It was a toss-up as to whether she wanted to feel relieved or angry. A practical joke from that bloody elf. Next time she saw him, never mind if she didn't have a knife at hand, she would find one and cut his throat. For now, however, she satisfied herself with stripping off her boots, trews, drawers, and tunic, and wrapping the stained pieces in the relatively clean tunic. She had no change of clothing, so burying the clothes was out of the question. She headed for the nearby burn where she could bathe quickly and make up a story to explain her sudden need to do laundry. The long tail of her sark would cover her lack of what Alex called "package," so lounging in the sun while her other clothes dried would be fairly safe. So long as she sat hunched over a bit and made certain the shape of her hips and waist didn't show. Since the baby it had been more difficult to pass as a boy, her hips having widened some from their fashion-model narrowness of before. These days she needed to take more care in how her shape was seen.

The burn was dastardly cold though the weather had been warm enough for bathing all the past week. Lindsay hurried as much as she dared, and scrubbed the clothing stains thoroughly. Not the slightest discoloration was allowed to remain, not the faintest line or shading. Then she checked her sark again for spots and found none, and draped the wet clothing over some gorse bushes in the sunshine. Unwilling to be caught lying down, where her shape would be evident under the sark and her hippy, woman's legs would be seen by anyone happening by, she sat cross-legged in the middle of the clearing and pretended to be praying, bent over clasped hands.

The pretense did segue to actual prayer once or twice, but she was there a long time and her mind wandered to many things. Alex and the baby, wondering what their futures would be. Her hope to kill Nemed and that his future would never happen. Her hope Iain would keep the blood smell to himself.

A crashing of boots through brush approached, and Lindsay tugged at the hem of her sark to make certain it covered enough. Then came two knights to the spot by the burn. She didn't look up when they stopped to stare.

"Praying, then?" It was Jenkins, accompanied by Simon, she saw by his boots. Lindsay's pulse picked up. She didn't particularly like Jenkins, and knew the feeling was mutual.

She looked up and feigned impatience that her prayer had been interrupted. "Of course. You should try it sometime."

He snorted. "God and I have naught to say to each other."

"That's your affair, but please leave me to my own conversation." Her heart was pounding now, for Jenkins and Simon both were staring hard at her legs.

"Do you always pray naked?"

"When I've got wet clothing drying in the sun." The questions were pointed and made her uncomfortable. Jenkins was suddenly far too nosy.

"I hadn't noticed them needing cleaning."

Now she unfolded her hands and gave him as disparaging a look as she could muster in her awkward position. "Not that it's any affair of yours, but I had thought I had a fart coming and was mistaken. I'm certain you know what that is like. Be glad you weren't here for the cleaning of it."

Jenkins grunted but didn't reply. He instead went to the burn for a drink, then the two left the clearing. Lindsay continued to wait for her clothes to dry, and now prayed in earnest.

The wool and linen weren't quite dry when she put them back on, but the stains were gone and she could go stand by the fire for a while to be rid of the clamminess. Her fingers trembled as she dressed, relieved to restore her protective clothing as a man. She hurried back to the tower, where she would collect her bread ration, for it was late afternoon and she was quite hungry.

When she emerged from the wood, the men busy with their masters' horses near the tower fell silent at her approach. A charge of alarm skittered up her spine, and it was an effort not to react to it. She ignored the squires and pages as they stared after her on her way to the tower.

Inside the crumbling structure, the lounging knights also fell silent and stared. She stared back, for this was too obvious to ignore. Too wrong. The universe shifted subtly around her, and suddenly all her points of reference were slightly off. Something had been said, and she needed to thwart the rumor before it became credible. "What?" she said as casually as possible, and tried on a smile in hopes of making it all a joke.

Jenkins said, "Get all the blood out, did ye?" He was lounging against a stack of someone's stuff near the fire. His place was upstairs with An Reubair, but apparently he was slumming with the lower-ranking knights this afternoon.

"Do we ever?" Certainly everyone in the room had tried to wash blood from their gloves and surcoats at one time or another.

"Not from my drawers, I never have needed to."

"I told you why I had to clean my linens." The explanation was a good one, but the very fact that she had to explain at all was an indication all was lost. Jenkins knew, and he'd told everyone. They believed, and now she was going to be asked to prove what she could not. Through her terror she sifted for ways out of this, and at the corner of her eye she saw a couple of knights, Simon and the faerie Iain, move toward the door to block it. If she didn't get out of there right away, she would be trapped. She muttered to herself as if the two knights weren't there, "Och, I've forgotten to cover my horse. Wouldn't want him to fall ill from the cold, now." She turned and tried to move past Simon and Iain, but the faerie shoved her backward and into the room. She drew her dagger.

"Let me by."

"You were at Bannockburn, Sir Lindsay?" Jenkins rose from his seat by the fire and approached her. His rowel spurs clinked as he walked.

"Aye." She kept her eyes on the men in front of her but sensed everyone here was now her enemy.

"And how many years as the squire of An Dubhar before that?"

Trick question. Now she wished mightily to know whether Jenkins knew about the seven-year gap when she and Alex had gone into the knoll and skipped from 1306 to 1313. She turned toward Jenkins, lowered her chin, and gazed at him with what she hoped was less fear and more barely controlled irritation, and gave the same explanation Alex had at the time. "I was extremely young when I was made squire and my master brought me to Scotland. Tall for my age, and stronger than most." She let an edge come into her voice on that last, in hopes Jenkins would understand her threat. She'd clobber him if he came at her.

"You've no beard."

She chuckled and rubbed her chin. "To my shame, my beard has taken its time to grow in." If he would only let it alone. The more she had to explain, the worse this became. She considered making a run for the door but figured she wouldn't get past Simon and Iain.

Jenkins leaned over to peer into her face. "Indeed, you've no beard at all. Not so much as a sprinkling at the chin and lip. Even the most callow youth should have a hair or two on his face. Shameful, indeed."

The jig was up. Lindsay took a swipe at Jenkins with her dagger, and he dodged and drew his. She turned and rushed the door, but the two guarding it snatched her by the arms. Her dagger flew from her hand and went skittering and clattering across the floor, and she was lifted from her feet. Jenkins came from behind and clouted her in a kidney.

Screaming pain shot through her, and she shouted out and went limp. Her legs would no longer hold her up, and she hung by her arms from the men who held her. They yanked her higher, and Jenkins fumbled under her tunic for the strings that held her trews. Lindsay struggled and

twisted to thwart him, but as the initial pain subsided her
captors held her tighter. Jenkins yanked down her trews,
then her linens, then he reached around to grab her crotch.
At confirmation of his suspicion, he uttered a string of
curses punctuated by vulgar epithets. Each of the men
holding her had a grab for his own confirmation, and they
were equally offended they'd been fooled by a woman who
presumed to call herself knight.

Lindsay continued to struggle, kicking as she was lifted
entirely from the floor. She bit and clawed, but with no
sword and no dagger she had no hope of having any effect
through the mail and leather these guys wore. Jenkins
grabbed her hair and pulled her head back as far as her
neck would bend, and he spat into her face. Then he said
into her ear, "Stupid woman. You should burn for this."

Her heart pounded in terror. These guys would do it, if
they got it into their heads she needed burning. But she said
nothing, for they were perverse enough that if she pled for
her life she would doom herself.

Jenkins said to the two holding her, "Take him . . . *her*
over there. Put her across the end of the step."

The two dragged her past the others in the company,
still squirming, to the stone steps that led to the upper floor.
There they bent her over the edge of one step that was
waist high. Her trews and drawers around her ankles, her
bare behind faced the room, and as Simon and Iain pinned
her arms against the damp stones she let out a long scream
and tried to kick Jenkins behind her.

"Hold still!" He smacked her on the side of her head,
but she still squirmed as much as she could. She wasn't going to make this easy for him, and hoped he would knife
her in the struggle. Far better than burning afterward.

There was a moment while Jenkins freed himself from
his own trews, then his hand was at her thighs. Another
scream erupted from her, and she tried to hold her legs together, but he rammed her from behind hard enough for
her belly to slam against the stair. It knocked the breath
from her, and once again he hit her in a kidney with his fist.

All strength bled away and she went limp again, facedown on the step. Quickly Jenkins reached around with one hand to pull her thigh aside, opened her with his other hand, and then he forced himself into her.

She screamed again, this time with no strength. More than the pain, the humiliation and invasion made her cry out. She called him names but knew they were no longer effective, as they would have been had he still thought she was a man. That particular humiliation angered her even more than the physical assault. Jenkins shoved hard as she continued to scream and struggle as best she could with her arms pinned, her kidneys aflame, and her belly slammed hard against the stone with each thrust of his hips. Her vision grew red, and in those moments all she could think of was that she wanted to kill him. Then she fell silent as she realized she now wanted to live so she could do exactly that. She stopped struggling, to let him finish in hopes he would not kill her after.

It seemed an eternity. The minutes dragged on, though they were probably very few. Lindsay squeezed her eyes shut and concentrated on not feeling the pain, just as she had when she'd been wounded in the past. Finally Jenkins emitted a roar and a grunt she figured he must have thought very manly, then he withdrew. Simon and Iain let her go, and she collapsed to the floor and leaned against the stone with her eyes still closed as tight as she could get them. She didn't want to look at Jenkins. She hauled in her breaths with great gasps in her struggle to not cry. No way would she let anyone see her cry.

"Let that be an education for you. Now you'll leave this place." A note of amusement slipped into his voice. "Unless you care to service the rest of the men as well." He gave that a moment's thought, then added, "To be sure, you're welcome to stay if you would earn your keep in a manner befitting you." He had a good chuckle at that, then walked away. The two who had held her went with him.

Tears made their way to her eyes, but she wouldn't let them come. There was only a damp line at her eyelashes before she swallowed hard and held them back. Like a lifeline,

she clung to the idea that she couldn't cry so she would not
lose herself. Alex wouldn't cry for something like this.
Only once had she ever seen him break down, and that was
when he'd thought she was about to die. This wouldn't kill
her; she would live. Alex wouldn't cry, so neither would
she. Long ago she'd lost her sense of safety; this was nothing compared to the wound she'd taken at Bannockburn.
Nothing compared to the first time she'd killed a man.
Jenkins had let her go, she would live, and all she needed
for the moment was to know Jenkins had made the mistake
of his life. All else was trivial.

It was probably several minutes that she sat there, huddled by the stairs with her clothes down around her ankles,
unable to move. But finally she decided she couldn't sit
there forever, and she opened her eyes. The other guys in
the room were still watching her, taking glances in the silence. When she shifted, they all looked away.

The pain in her kidneys began to subside, and her back
hurt less than it had. She was able to climb to her feet and
restore her drawers and trews. The smell of semen gagged
her and turned her stomach, but she ignored it. Left it there,
as if she didn't care. She wouldn't give any of those guys
the satisfaction of thinking she'd been hurt by that. Only
the pain of having been clobbered with his fists was an ac-
ceptable hurt. It was the only one they could understand.
They all knew how it felt to be socked in a kidney, but not
what it was like to be physically invaded by another person. Slowly, as if she had all the time in the world, she secured her clothing and straightened it all.

Then she looked around. Each still took sideways glances,
and it was plain many of them were hoping she would stay to
service them. Not all men were rapists, but most were dogs.
Dreamers. She lifted her head and looked them each in the
eye. They looked away.

Her dagger lay where it had landed, by the wall, and she
went to retrieve it. Then she went to the fire and cut a size-
able chunk of meat from the haunch over it, which she ate
quickly, standing up.

"Lindsay—"

"Shut up."

The man shut up.

Finished with her meal and feeling a little stronger now, she wiped her greasy hands on her trews, left the keep, and went looking for Jenkins. She didn't have to search far; he was sitting atop the ruins of a small outbuilding at the other side of what had once been the castle bailey. His back to her, he was chatting with Simon and some others, more than likely bragging of what he'd just done.

Simon spotted her coming, and he chuckled as he stepped back from Jenkins, who saw this and turned just as Lindsay reached him. She dove the last few feet with her dagger and caught his face as he dodged. He backed into the ruins and she stumbled against the low, ragged wall.

Jenkins let out an indignant cry and scattered his listeners as he drew his dagger to defend himself. Lindsay vaulted the stack of mortared stones to assault him again. She wanted to take off his balls, or at least kick them, but knew a man's genitalia was the worst target in a fight because it was the one he was invariably quickest to defend. She concentrated on his face and circled to get the sun in his eyes. He fell for it. He probably thought she was stupid, and didn't realize until he started blinking he'd screwed up.

The rest of the men left the enclosure of the ruined walls and watched in surprised silence. Jenkins smiled. "You think I can't beat a woman in a fight?"

Lindsay didn't waste her breath with speech. Her focus was on the task at hand, and she went about it as coldly as she would take a spray insecticide after a bug. Instead she feinted and slashed. Jenkins went for it, and for his trouble ended up with a red gash in his cheek. He shuffled and staggered, and a dust cloud rose from the dirt at his feet. A growl rumbled deep inside him, and his eyes went steely. Now he knew she was serious, and she would have to be careful. She waited for him to move.

He declined. Instead he tried to circle, but she wouldn't

let him. As a result, though, she found herself backed up against a wall she couldn't get over easily. He had her cornered.

But she waited. She wanted him to move. So she dropped her guard ever so slightly, and when he took the bait she deflected with her left and stepped in to stab him in the chest.

He dodged, her dagger only sliced air, and he retreated. She was able to follow him and get away from the wall to give herself room. Jenkins tried to circle again. Suddenly she wished for her old mace, for it had a longer reach than the knife and she had more fighting experience with it. And with a cold smile she relished the image of Jenkins' head smashed like a watermelon. In conscious imitation of Alex, she straightened from her guarded crouch, went loose jointed and deceptively insouciant, then pressed him and swiped her dagger at him.

Jenkins dodged again, and on his riposte she dodged backward, then stepped in to shove him around with his own momentum and stab. She caught him in the back, a good, solid stab.

A shrill cry of surprise burst from him, and he backed away. He was still standing, so she'd missed the kidney, and she cursed her bad luck. She followed him as he backed, holding his hand over the wound. She'd hit something, for it bled copiously and stank of bowel. And the pain was enough to make Jenkins go pale and stagger. Any other time she might have taken this chance to get away, having disabled him at least for a while, but she didn't want to back off. Instead she continued her attack and delivered another stab, to the chest. Pink bubbles rose to Jenkins' mouth and he coughed, but he was still standing. She hadn't reached his heart, and muttered another curse for it. He wasn't dying fast enough to suit her. But his arms were over his chest now and he was swaying, in shock, so she stabbed him in the gut. Finally he dropped to the ground, choking and gasping and holding his belly.

Lindsay's better sense told her Jenkins was doomed and

she should leave him be, but there was nothing left in her heart to make her listen to sense. No mercy, no honor, no chivalry. Jenkins had violated her in a way that called off all bets on the basis of being a woman, or even a fellow man, and now the only way to make this right was to violate him as horribly. Suddenly she was glad he was still alive and aware. She hauled off and kicked him in the side of the head. He fell to his back in a haze of semiconsciousness.

Quickly, before anyone could climb inside the ruins and stop her, she slit Jenkins' trews up the front. Then his drawers, which still reeked of sex. Without a second of hesitation she grabbed his genitals, and with two swipes of her dagger had them off in one piece. Penis and scrotum now dangled from her fist.

Jenkins screamed. And screamed. He grabbed the bloodied patch at his crotch, still screaming. Then he passed out, probably never to awaken. Not if he was lucky.

Cold, black fury still raging in her brain, Jenkins' blood smeared over her hand and his organs dangling at her side, she turned to the onlookers and said, "Anyone else care to try me?"

The silence spun out, and she let it. These guys should be entirely certain they did not want to give her any more grief, and she wanted to let that sink in. Finally it was Simon who spoke. "It was a fair fight." The rest nodded in agreement, though they said nothing. Most of them were pale and staring at the piece of Jenkins in her hand.

Lindsay also nodded, then took her trophy into the keep. The men lounging by the fire looked up as she entered, mildly curious about the outcome of the fight, then scrambled to their feet when they saw what she carried. They moved out of her way as she approached the fire, and she threw Jenkins' floppy man parts onto the peat coals. The hairs on them flared to flame and smoke rose in a stench. The pink and gray wrinkled skin began to blister and burn, now smelling like charred meat. An alarmed murmur spread about the room.

Lindsay announced to them and to those who had followed her from outside, at a shout that echoed in the stone room, "All you men, listen to me! I am Sir Lindsay Pawlowski and I am not to be trifled with!" Her rage supported the tone of command she'd learned from Alex, and she glared into the eyes of each man present as she spoke. "The next man to touch me without permission will receive the same treatment I've just given Jenkins! I will continue in this company until I choose to leave, or until I am killed in battle. I will continue to fight as one of you, and to maintain my loyalty to An Reubair, as I have always done. If there is anyone here who doubts my ability to fight as well as yourselves, speak now and I'll be happy to disabuse you of that notion."

She looked around at the silent group and saw a variety of attitudes. Some were horrified. Some seemed angry. As if to bring home the truth of what they were seeing, distant screams from across the bailey drifted to their ears as Jenkins regained consciousness. Weeping, begging for God to relieve him of his life, his voice weakened and finally went silent again, probably with his prayer answered. The men in the tower listened in silence, each one gone pale.

But some of them seemed amused. A few smiles crept to some faces, and that surprised Lindsay into letting the knot in her stomach loosen some with hope. She'd never imagined any of the men would countenance a woman in their midst, but this made it seem possible.

One of the men said, "You didn't need to kill him."

Another made a disparaging noise in the back of his throat. "Aye, she did. I would have killed him, and in just such a manner. Would you not have?"

The first shrugged, allowing that he probably would have done so.

A third said, "Speaking only for myself, my life has been spared by Sir Lindsay's help in a fight. I cannae say as I am pleased by the loss of Jenkins, but I would also not care to lose a fighter such as this one. All things considered, I prefer her to be on my side."

A voice came from the steps to the upper floor, and it was An Reubair. "She will stay. And you will treat her as a man. If she fails in her service as a knight, she will also be treated as a worthless man who cannot fight. More contemptible than a whore, in my opinion." He let them think that over for a moment, then he added, "But I believe she will prove herself. Anyone strong and determined enough to relieve the mighty Jenkins of his most prized possession is surely one to be feared and respected."

Lindsay believed she already had proven herself, but let it pass. They were going to allow her to remain, and all she had to do was fight well. She knew she could do that.

One of the men said, "I've no complaint at having a fighter such as herself at my back."

The others, though not all of them appeared to agree, offered no complaint either.

Lindsay nodded and decided to take her hubris one step further just to see what might happen. "Right. I'll be relieving Jenkins of all his possessions, I think." She glanced toward the stairs. An Reubair didn't offer an argument, but only gazed blandly at her. She looked around for Jenkins' two squires. "You'll be going home. On foot. Now. I'll find my own men to serve me and my horses." The last thing she needed was young, resentful squires handling her stuff. The two teenagers rose in glum silence and obeyed.

Lindsay looked around the room and the fight adrenaline eased. Someone poked the burning piece of flesh from the fire and tumbled it onto the floor, where it lay, smoking and sizzling. As she calmed, and the smell of charred meat, skin, and hair permeated the keep, a realization came. Jenkins, in his unthinking arrogance, had actually done her several favors. He'd given her an excuse to kill him and had provided her with badly needed money and equipment, but—most important—he'd relieved her of the secret she'd spent so much time and energy to keep. For weeks she'd had to watch everything she said, every gesture, every movement. She'd had to bind her breasts tightly enough to restrict her breathing, and had never bathed or relieved herself without a breathless, panicky rush. Now none of that would be necessary. Now she would be able to live as a knight without living in terror of discovery. A cold smile came to her face.

CHAPTER 11

I n a village along the coast north of Berwick, Alex noted that Trefor located and bartered for a sword appropriate to his height. It was the same size as Alex's, tapered like Alex's, and gilded like Alex's. The only thing distinguishing them was that on Trefor's the hilt guards were curved rather than straight. One up on Alex, and that gave him a weird feeling, but he ignored it. In the end all he wanted to care about was that it would serve Trefor well.

They continued to drill and spar in the evenings, along with the rest of the company who were preparing for the coming raid into English territory. Berwick, on the Scotland side of the Borderlands, was still held by Edward II and was the place from which the assaults to the north had been launched by him and his father for the past several decades. Taking it and holding it against English will was not a possibility; Robert didn't have the military resources to stand against an English king who demanded this bit of Scotland so close to English territory. But the harrying tactics employed by Douglas were a useful tool to make certain Edward would not attempt to march north again as he had in 1314. The Black Douglas and Alasdair an Dubhar were set to make clear to Edward he was not welcome north of the Tweed.

The night before the assault on Berwick, as the company huddled around tiny fires built small and under tree canopy for the sake of not betraying their position, Alex watched Trefor's face. They all knew they would be riding against English knights the next day, and Trefor seemed calm. Almost carefree. His girlfriend sat with him, and he spoke to the group of how eager he was to show the English the business end of a Scottish sword. Whenever the locals boasted like that, Alex knew they meant it. They all had reason to hate, especially James, who was always on about how much he would love to march to London and have Edward's head on a platter. But in Trefor the talk rang hollow. Like whistling past a graveyard. The fear was in his voice and in his eyes.

Alex didn't have to wonder what was going through Trefor's mind just then. He'd felt it himself just before his first combat flight over Kosovo a number of years before. Trefor was thinking of what it would be like to die. How much pain there would be. What lay beyond that pain. How it would be if there were nothing on the other side, and that had given Alex the willies more than anything else had. The locals— men from this century—had no doubt about what lay beyond, for they'd been taught all their lives exactly what awaited them. Obviously Trefor lacked that assurance. Alex had his own doubts, though he never dwelled on them. He'd learned to accept that he would one day die and there was nothing he could do about it. He'd long ago reconciled himself to a violent death, for given the life choices he'd made, the odds were pretty much against him living to an old age. With all the wounds he'd taken over the years he didn't give the pain much thought anymore, beyond settling his focus before a fight so he would not be distracted from the task at hand. He hoped Trefor would be able to sort himself out, but knew talking to him about it would be a waste of breath. It was something each of them had to do for himself.

Then Alex looked over at Mike, who was very quiet and pale, his mouth crumpled and thin lipped. He appeared to have a sharper fear of what tomorrow would bring than did Trefor. Alex didn't put the odds very high that Mike would survive, and knew he wouldn't consider the loss a great one.

It was shortly before dawn the next day that James Douglas's army swept down on the township. English men of war poured from the castle to clash with the Scottish cavalrymen with ringing iron, shouts of rage, and much blood. Alex dispatched a knight in quick order, then turned to another and found himself engaged with a horseman who seemed more interested in looking busy than in killing him. In a blood rage Alex bore down on the knight, who shouted, "Hold!" and began to circle. Though he was chased he kept circling, and held his sword as if to use it. Alex couldn't get near him, and every time his horse sidled in, the knight retreated just far enough to be out of reach. Alex grinned, for it struck him as funny in a Three Stooges sort of way, and he wondered what the deal was. His peripheral vision sharpened as he wondered whether his opponent was waiting for help, but everyone nearby was otherwise engaged. The man circled, sword raised, but he didn't approach Alex with it. Waiting for Alex to make a move, it seemed, and Alex considered it, for he'd come to fight and in this frame of mind it was difficult to stay his hand. But instead of attacking he circled also, to see what would happen.

"You're Irish," said the knight. His accent was Scottish, but that meant nothing. He was a noble, plainly of Norman descent and pledged to the English king.

Alex blinked at the comment. Now he wondered if the wrong reply would get him attacked of a sudden. He said, "I'm a MacNeil. Not Irish, but we come from Irish kings."

"Irish." The knight grinned and nodded to affirm his words. Then he nodded off toward the herds shifting and lowing in the excitement. "You know I don't give a damn about these cattle."

"Good, because I do want them and I'll kill you for them. I've got folks back home to feed." And a king to impress, but he didn't waste his breath stating what this guy surely already knew.

"No need. You can have the beasts, and welcome to them. I've seen too much blood of late and have sickened of it. I know you're going to have the cattle and horses in any case. In a short while, once the kine are on their way, you'll be called off and I'll give chase for a distance. But you'll ride faster than I will, and I'll find it not worth the trouble. My fellows and myself will fall back and return to our garrison and our fires, to boast of what little we can of this defeat."

"You want to lose?"

"I want to spin out my time owed to my liege and go home in a single piece. If that makes me a coward, then I'll be a live coward enjoying my children and my wife in my home."

"You're serious?"

"Would you care to try my sword and risk your own life for naught?"

It seemed reasonable, though surreal in the midst of a killing clash of men and metal. Alex considered abandoning this guy to find something real to do, but knew if he did he would be chased down and would then have to fight him in earnest. So he continued to circle, sword raised as if he were looking for an opening he knew would never come.

A shout went up in the distance, and retreat was called by the Scots. The cattle had been stampeded, and everyone was off on a merry chase away from Berwick. "Very well, then," said Alex. "Live long and prosper."

"Same to you, countryman."

With a grin, Alex whirled his sword in a flashy mulinette, wheeled his mount, and spurred away. The other knight gave a shout and pursued. It was less than a horse-race for a distance as Alex followed the rest of the Scots and their stampede of cattle and horses away from town, with the English knight not so hot on his heels.

The other knight fell back, and Alex took a glance to the rear to see if any of his own men were lagging behind. To his horror, he found Trefor still back there. He reined in to a skidding halt and turned.

But Trefor wasn't in trouble. He was riding hard in the retreat, bearing down on the slowing Englishman who was at that moment turning. Sword raised, Trefor approached from behind. The knight found himself confronted by Trefor just as Trefor swung and caught him at the neck. The knight's head toppled, a fountain of blood spray in the air, and dangled by a shred of muscle and a hank of mail from his coif. He wobbled crazily on his horse for a moment, the torso not yet knowing it was dead, then it collapsed and fell from its mount in a confusion of mail, flesh, and blood.

There was no time to think or feel. With a piercing rebel yell Trefor blew past Alex at a dead gallop, still with his sword overhead. Alex turned and spurred on after him. He would think about this later. Now, while they were being chased by men who did mean to kill them, was not the time to consider what Trefor had just done. Alex rode hard with his men and focused on getting out of there alive.

The defenders of Berwick had been well softened by the fighting and were not motivated to follow far. They fell back quickly as the Scots made their retreat. Dozens of horses had been taken, and many cattle made their way from Berwick. But they did not go north. They headed south, across the river and into England. More plunder awaited them in the rich countryside there. James Douglas and those accompanying him made camp in England that night.

Having circled the support wagons with their shields to the outside, and butchered enough of their plunder for a hearty meal paid out to everyone present, the men indulged in a party atmosphere, eating, drinking, and bragging to each other of their exploits that day. For himself, Alex didn't partake of anything but food. He straddled a tree root and leaned his back against the trunk, chewing thoughtfully on his supper, thinking hard about the knight Trefor had

killed. He listened to the story as Trefor told it, and held his
tongue when the embellishments became too wildly inac-
curate and colorful for his taste. In Trefor's telling, the
knight had been bearing down on him at full speed, ready
to take off his own head with a sword as long as a claymore. Alex supposed he might have thought that; percep-
tion in the heat of things was often dicey. Trefor may
actually have thought he was in that sort of danger. Alex
gave Trefor the benefit of the doubt and couldn't blame
him for not knowing his opponent had no intention of
killing anyone. It had been a battle, after all, any armed
man fair game in anyone's book. So Alex kept shut and let
Trefor brag.

But then the talk went in an entirely unexpected direction, and Alex's attention perked with alarm as he sucked
on a crispy bit of fat from his meat. "And you," said Trefor
in a voice dripping with disdain, "you had let him go."

"I did what?"

"I'd seen the two of you circling each other like dogs
about to mate. Made me wonder which of you was the
bitch."

There was no laughter at that. Silence fell over those
nearby. Hector and his squires, young Gregor, James, his
high-ranking men and their squires all looked at Alex to
see what he would do over this accusation. Even Mike was
quiet, as was Morag, who hovered in the periphery and
watched.

"Excuse me?" Alex stuffed the rest of his food into his
cheek and chewed slowly, but gave Trefor only a bland
look and wiped grease from his lip onto his sleeve. His
dagger was at his belt, and his sword was only a few paces
away. Trefor also had a knife, but Alex wasn't sure where
his sword was. He knew he could beat the guy in a fight,
and it looked as if there might be one. He hoped not, but he
couldn't let Trefor get away with this.

Trefor elaborated. "Are you always in the habit of letting guys go like that?"

"I don't know what you're talking about."

"Like hell. I watched you chatting with him for a while before the retreat. Then he let you go. He waited until you were away before he came after you. You were practically loping. You never even tried to take him out."

"That's a lie." Alex felt his neck and face warm, the more embarrassed for the truth of Trefor's words than that they were being said.

"I saw it. I bet I wasn't the only one." Trefor glanced around at his listeners for confirmation.

Mike narrowed his eyes at Alex and said, in the scant Middle English he'd picked up in past weeks, "I seen it. It's not a lie."

Alex threw Mike a cross look, hoping nobody had understood Mike's American accent, but it was a vain hope. The men present had heard Mike and now regarded Alex with curiosity to know what he would say to the accusation. He responded with disdain. "I expect you spent the entire time at the edges of the fray, watching the rest of us fight."

Now the listeners looked at Trefor. If anyone else had seen the exchange between Alex and the English knight, they certainly weren't going to admit it now. Alex hoped they just hadn't seen.

Trefor continued. "Well, it's true. They were chatting like big buddies." The word "buddies" mixed in with his Middle English earned blank looks all around, and he said, "I mean, great friends. Like they were catching up on old times."

James said to Alex, "Did you know the man? I often find myself confronted by men who once knew my father. More than once I've been asked for mercy by those who betrayed him."

Alex shook his head. "I was circling, looking for an opening. He was avoiding my sword. I couldn't get near enough to attempt him."

"Weren't trying very hard, as far as I could see."

"I would have been a fool to swing on him."

"Fool . . . coward . . . whatever."

"Shut up, Trefor!"

"Sir Trefor."

Alex stood over Trefor and switched to modern English. "Shut the hell up, you little shit. I'll call you what I like, and don't push your luck with me."

"Afraid I'll wreck your chances with ol' Robert?" Trefor tilted his head to address Alex, but otherwise remained lounging against his saddle.

"You don't know what you're doing. Mess with me, and I'll make you regret it. You don't know the system. You need to tread lightly."

"I know the system well enough to know you screwed up."

"You can't survive without me. I go down, you go down."

"I don't think so. I mean, it's not as if I stand to inherit, is it? Even if I were your heir, which you've made it clear I will never be, you're not old enough to beat me to the grave by enough for it to matter. Shoot, you're liable to outlive me. I should kick free of you now, and make my own way."

"Then, by all means, do so. Get the hell away from here. Try this again, and I'll kill you."

"Big talk. Just like that nonsense about finding my mother."

"I will find her."

"No, you won't. Just like you didn't find me."

Alex shifted his weight in disgust. "Oh, but you so make me want to. I'm beginning to think I'm lucky to see how my son will turn out before going to the trouble of searching you down and trying to raise you. Glad to know up front what sort of little monster you're going to turn out."

Trefor pressed his lips together, and his eyes blazed with a rage Alex rarely had ever seen in anyone but his own father. It felt like a sock in the gut as it sank in on a bone level that this was his son, the life he and Lindsay had created. His responsibility and his problem for as long as he lived. For a moment the world seemed to tilt, and he went breathless. Then Trefor said, "You're never going to find her."

Alex swallowed hard the knot that suddenly blocked his throat. "See if I don't."

"I intend to."

"Meanwhile, Mordred, shut up or I'll have to find a way to silence you. I brought you into the world, I can bloody well send you from it."

Trefor emitted a little bark of a laugh. "Maybe. But you know I'm right about what I saw. I don't think very highly of that."

"I don't give a damn what you think. Shut up, or I'll have to take you out. I'll have no other choice, and I don't think I can be too squeamish about how I will go about it. Rules of engagement are different here. I've been here longer than you have, and I've quite let go of the twenty-first century concept of fair play. Think that over real hard."

Trefor went silent. Alex returned to his seat on the tree root and asked James to share his tales of the day's battle. The earl was content to drop the subject of Alex's performance in Berwick and to do some boasting of his own exploits. Trefor shut up and for the rest of the evening shot ugly glances at his father. Morag came to whisper in Trefor's ear. Alex pretended to ignore them, but they bothered him just the same. He thought about Lindsay and wished mightily she were here.

After Berwick the raiding party plunged deep into Edward's domain. Having crossed the spot where Alex knew the modern border would be, they passed Hadrian's wall and pressed onward, traveling by stealth now. Alex knew, as James also surely knew, that the farther into England they struck, the more fear they would inspire in the king by their daring and the more he would be encouraged by his nobles to make peace with Robert.

Over the next months they raided several more towns, making their way south and west as they'd done the summer before, each time bringing away an abundance of cattle, sheep, pigs, and horses at a minimal cost of men. The Scots were as fierce as their reputations had them, and the English defenders were the quicker to surrender their livestock and goods for their terror. James Douglas cut a swath through northern England, and the MacNeils went with him.

The day after a particularly lucrative raid, when they were on the move again and the kine had been dispatched northward, Hector was riding alongside Alex and they were chatting away the boredom. At a lull in the talk, Hector nodded toward Morag, who rode between Trefor and Mike. "Do ye think she's magical?"

Alex glanced over. The woman was fey any way one looked at it. Not frail looking like some of the other creatures he'd seen, but small, and though mostly human, there was no denying she had a lot of faerie in her in spite of her round ears. Her face glowed with it, and with the magic. With her braids undone, her bright hair fairly sparked, curled around her face and flowed down her back. He said, "Aye. As magical as it gets." Magically delicious? The thought made him grin to himself. She could be called a leprechaun, though she would probably not answer to it. The woman seemed as Irish as everyone thought he was. But he knew she was magical because she was—would be—the one who would one day send Trefor to him. Or to herself, which now that he thought of it was more likely. Surely she, as an old woman, would have sent him to be with herself as a young woman, and now he wondered how many mortals she'd done that to over the centuries.

Hector said, "I don't see how you can abide the wee folk."

"They're not so bad. Some of them, anyway." He'd liked Danu and wondered where she'd got off to. Nemed he'd like to strangle, and he wasn't all that enchanted with that Brochan guy. But though the wee folk were all crazy, in the end they were still people. Apparently Lindsay was one. He was going to have to come to terms with that.

"They're evil and not to be trusted."

"You've noticed my son is one of them."

"And has he behaved as a son? Has he shown any loyalty to his father?"

Alex didn't have an answer for that beyond "No."

"Were he any other man, he wouldnae be riding with you today. You're a fool to keep such a one in your complement."

"I can't just send him away. He's my blood."

"He'll be your downfall, mark me. Gregor is a better son to you than that one."

Alex glanced over at Gregor, who rode atop the canvas covering a provisions wagon. Though short like his uncle Hector, the boy was handsome and full of energy, and as long as he'd been Alex's foster son he'd carried out his duties in earnest and with a dignity rare in children. Kids in general were different here—sometimes they seemed more like miniature adults than children—but Gregor was special even for his time. As Hector suggested, he was the son Alex wished Trefor could have been.

"Gregor's a good boy."

Hector nodded. "He's a MacNeil."

"So is Trefor."

"And one day he may prove himself as one, but until now he has not. Until he does, you should beware. And especially beware of the witch Morag. Her loyalties are entirely in question, even where Trefor is concerned."

Alex had to agree with that last. He didn't like Morag either. "I'll take this under advisement."

"I assume that means ye will think on it."

"Aye."

"And then do as I tell you."

Alex grinned. "We'll see."

Hector emitted an indignant grunt and faced forward.

Morag stayed on Alex's mind, an annoyance and a curiosity. She seemed to thrive on the rigors of travel, spending long days in the saddle without so much as a telltale crease of fatigue in her forehead. Rarely did she speak to anyone but Trefor, and didn't even seem to have much attention for Mike. It was as if she were in orbit around Trefor, or a moth flitting around his light bulb. A highly decorative moth, and Alex could see Trefor was pleased to show her off.

One evening Alex noticed her slip away from the fire. Trefor's attention was elsewhere, and he didn't seem to notice her leaving. Alex waited a few moments, then rose from his seat with his hand at the ties of his trews as if he were headed into the woods to relieve himself. For all he knew, that could be what Morag was up to, but he wanted to know for certain.

She hadn't gone far. Not far enough to lose him, in any case. A short distance into the forest, he found a small fire in the midst of a tiny clearing barely large enough to contain that fire and a dancing figure. He hung back inside the forest, hidden by the darkness.

How she'd lit the fire so quickly, he could only guess. But he had a hunch. Still as the black trees around him, he watched Morag dance naked, what the faeries called "sky-clad." The orange light from the little flame flickered across her skin, and she moved in silence, accompanied only by the crackle of burning sticks and her own breathing. Her copper red hair floated about her head and down her back, and tendrils stuck to the sweat on her face. As cool as the night was, she ran with perspiration that made trickles from her face, down her neck, and between her breasts. Distasteful as she was to him, he couldn't deny her beauty, and just then it mesmerized him fully. She moved like a snake in water, smoothly, fluidly, her frame flowing as if boneless.

Then she came to a sudden stop directly before him, panting and gazing straight at him, her breasts heaving and utterly fascinating. He held his breath, stock still. Could she see him? A tiny smile touched her mouth, then she continued dancing. If she'd seen him, she was ignoring him. He kept still, barely breathing, and continued to watch.

Soon he realized she was muttering to herself. Her lips moved in a voiceless whisper as she danced on, a little faster and a little faster. Soon she was spinning, hair flying, her chanting a silent mouthing of words. Finally she collapsed to her knees, bent over the fire, gasping for air. For one moment of madness Alex wished he could join her, to fall with her to the ground and lie with her. But then he blinked, shook his head, and the desire went away. The need stayed, but his distrust of this woman told him that to touch her would be enormous folly. Alex chose this moment to fade back into the forest as silently as possible, and he returned to the camp and to his tent. He wondered what Red Morag had been up to, and figured it couldn't be good.

The next morning when he saw her, she gave no indication she'd seen him the night before. Perhaps she hadn't. Trefor certainly hadn't noticed anything amiss, for his demeanor today was his usual sullen self. Alex put the incident from his mind and focused on what lay ahead on their march through England.

CHAPTER 12

Alex figured his future and his position were largely dependent on James Douglas, and it was James' opinion of things that mattered. It was he who reported to Robert, and as a royal vassal Alex's status was entirely contingent on what the king thought. Such dependence on a single man did not lend itself to a feeling of security, particularly since Alex had never much liked James personally. He never let on how much he didn't care for the single-mindedness and obsessive behavior, for James appeared fond of Alex and Hector. They were good fighters, and that seemed all the earl cared about, so that was how Alex stayed on his good side. After Berwick Alex took no mercy on his opponents and racked up kills he then bragged about around the fires afterward. His reputation was solid, and he knew James was impressed. Trefor was silenced for a time.

News came one day, via a Scottish rider who intercepted the raiders as they made their way across northern England, and it was the first contact they'd had from Scotland since leaving Berwick. Alex looked to the front to see the single horseman approach James at the head of his column, and watched the exchange he couldn't hear. The rider pulled a leather packet from inside his tunic and handed it over to the earl. James took it, opened the thong, broke the seal on the papers inside, and unfolded them to read as he rode. Even from where he sat, Alex could see the large, elaborate seal. Important papers. From the king? Who else would be allowed to know where to send a messenger to James? The rider was astride a fine horse and was well appointed in his dress and accoutrements, obviously of high rank. Alex's interest perked, and even more so when James paused in his reading to have a glance back at him. Something was up, and Alex had to resist the urge to spur forward to find out what. He glanced over at Hector, who raised his eyebrows as well, having been watching James himself. Alex feigned indifference but probably did not fool Hector.

They both looked behind at Trefor, who didn't seem to have noticed anything. He was deep in conversation with Morag riding beside him. Mike was gazing at the horizon, daydreaming, and also not noticing what went on up front.

It was a wonder Mike was still alive, but Alex had to admit the guy was holding his own as a fighter. At least he was still walking around, and that was better than some others of Trefor's men had managed. He'd gone quiet these days, and wasn't so mouthy as he'd once been. Alex figured that was a good thing, even though bragging rights were stock-in-trade for a knight. Shutting Mike up made him less of a loose cannon.

When they stopped to make camp that night, Alex expected to be approached by James about the day's messenger, but was disappointed. Nobody came to summon him for the earl. *Huh.* Alex supervised his men while they encamped, turning over in his mind what he'd seen earlier. Maybe he'd only imagined that glance back from James had been at him.

While supper was roasting he went to his tent. His sword needed cleaning and sharpening, and once that was done he figured he'd strip and pick off the lice and fleas he'd collected over the past few days. The wee beasties were a constant nuisance, and if he wasn't diligent about keeping them away they drove him nuts while riding.

He sat inside his tent, on the edge of the low pallet he'd acquired since his last foray with James, by the oil lamp that sat atop a folding table. Yellow light flickered over the blue fabric of the tent and the lamp threw a slightly rancid whiff into the air. He liked these quiet moments when he could think slowly, turning things over in his mind, sifting through his thoughts in search of something soothing. He found Lindsay.

She'd always been the best part of these hours that stretched into the interminable twilight of mid-summer, when they would talk quietly of their situation in a language that only they shared in this century. Back when his feelings for her had not yet been requited, he'd secretly relished the long conversations. There had never been anyone like Lindsay. She thought and spoke like no woman he'd ever known, and she seemed to understand things even the men around him couldn't grasp. Certainly she was the only person on the planet with a clue about his culture shock over medieval life. That had been important to him, and it occurred to him how odd it was to be unable to relate to Trefor and Mike that way. Especially Trefor. They should at least have that, and they didn't.

But even more than relating to Lindsay, he'd been attracted to her physically from the very start. The woman was hot. On nights like this he'd been sustained by watching her, drinking in her beauty, her grace. The way her almond-shaped eyes shone, the way her hair waved just enough to make tendrils around her face. And how that face brightened when she smiled, and darkened in a way not to be taken lightly when she did not. But he smiled at the memory of how she'd been so fascinated by the hair on his chest. Often she'd play with it as he lay on his back in bed, petting it down or smoothing it into swirls this way and that. Like doodling, she'd fiddled and tickled, and he'd grown to love it.

Now, as he ran an oiled linen cloth over his blade, his chest tightened the more he thought of his wife, and he wished for her to tickle him again. Lindsay had become his life well before she'd become Lady MacNeil, and tonight, here in the tent they'd once shared as knight and squire, he missed her horribly.

He had to cough to free up his breathing again, and forced his focus onto his sword.

This weapon was pleasing; it had stood him in good stead over the past couple of years. He'd taken it from a man he'd killed early on in his career. The opponent had been of high rank, and so the sword was more showy than those usually owned by a knight banneret not of the peerage. The gilded pommel glowed with a warmth he'd never seen in modern metal work; the gold was rich and nearly pure. Nearly red, almost as if it had been dipped in blood and bore a translucent coat of it. The wire around the grip was thick and solid. The blade was finely forged and kept a keen edge. He cleaned his weapon with the same care he took with his body.

A woman's voice came from outside. "Sir Alasdair?" *Morag.* Alex looked over at the tent flap and debated the pros and cons of not answering.

But he decided he had to eat sometime. He couldn't avoid her for more than a couple of hours, and that wouldn't be enough. So he said, "Enter."

She ducked through the flap and stood just inside with her hands folded before her. "My lord—"

Alex laughed and continued running his whetstone over his sword. "Nice try. Flattery will get you nowhere. 'Sir' will do, thank you all the same."

"Will it indeed?" She seemed unfazed.

Now he looked up at her. A tiny smile lifted the corners of her mouth and her eyes sparkled as brightly as her hair. Whatever was on her mind intrigued him, but he didn't care to pursue her down whatever weird conversational path she might have on her agenda. So he said, "What can I do for you?"

"I wish to speak to you of Trefor."

Alex returned his attention to his sword cleaning. "What of him?"

"You don't like him well."

He shrugged. "He's my son. Whether I like him or not is irrelevant. In the end, he's not all that likable. You have to admit that."

"He has had a hard life."

Alex looked up again. "I can't help that." He wanted to ask how hard Trefor's life had been, but didn't dare.

"He has, nevertheless, had a hard life."

"He was in foster care. I see kids here every day who would climb over each other for the chance to live the way he did. He didn't starve."

"You think he did not?"

"You think he did?"

Morag stepped closer, farther into the tent, and put a hand on the center pole. "Trefor has told me some things of the many homes they sent him to in your future time. Of one home where food was rationed to an extreme that some might call starvation and where he slept on the floor with a number of other children. Where babies were rarely cleaned of their own dirt until they had open sores and cried for the pain. Where the older children did injuries to the younger and were not disciplined. Where the foster parents' own children were given preference in all things and he was given nothing. He tells me of the medicines given to him and other children so they would sleep and not be a bother to their caretakers." Her voice took on a pointed note, and her eyes narrowed. "You must acknowledge that even in these times you consider 'backward' only the poorest and most wretched people do such things to their own family members, and particularly not to foster children who are often honored more than one's own. Fostering is a privilege here, but apparently not so where you come from, and I would wonder who are in fact the backward ones. Even when Trefor was quite young, he knew it was not the usual for children to be so treated. He tells me he knew from drama stories told to him by . . . what did he call it?" A hand waved and she glanced around the tent as if looking for the item she was trying to name. "A box with pictures?"

Alex looked around as if he might see the thing, too, then realized what she meant. "Television."

" 'Tis true, then? A box with pictures on the front? That move all by themselves?"

"Yeah." Alex didn't know how to explain a cathode-ray tube to someone who didn't even have the concept of an electric lamp, so he left it at that. "We have TV like you guys have bards. It tells us stories."

Morag nodded and continued. "The television stories showed him how life was for children who had parents. He spent his life knowing he'd been abandoned by his kin, another thing we primitive folk of this time and place are not prone to."

"I didn't abandon him. And I really wish you would stop telling him I did. I haven't even had a chance to abandon him."

"Yet."

"He was stolen. You bloody know it. Your people did it."

For a moment she bristled, then took a deep breath and let it out slowly. "Regardless of how you were separated, there were other things to cause him pain. His physical appearance brought much grief. The other children teased him mercilessly. Called him names."

"I bet they did. Let me guess: Mister Spock, Legolas, Bugs Bunny, Roger Rabbit. . . I expect the list was long." As a boy Alex had been the new kid in enough school yards to know how that went. Being a military brat who moved frequently with his father's transfers, he'd learned early on how to fit in quickly. Trefor would have had no hope of ever fitting in. Not with those ears.

"All that and more. He tells me that when he was finally told by the Bhrochan why he looked that way, he nearly wept for joy at finally knowing it wasn't a malformation. A defect."

Alex's heart clenched. "I can't help what happened to him."

"You were . . . *are* is father. You gave him his life and were responsible for his safety."

"I kept him as safe as I could. And his mother. I took them to the twenty-first century where he would have a better chance to survive. Faeries snatched him. Look to them for blame."

"You are nevertheless his father. In the end you are responsible for who he is."

"I'm not."

"Would you not be proud if he were more, as you say, 'likable'?"

Alex had to admit he would be, and nodded. He knew what she would say next, and sure enough she did.

"Then you should take the blame for what you do not like in him as well."

"Did you just come here to give me guff, or is there a point to this?"

"I came in hopes you will begin to consider him your son, and—"

"I do. I just wish he wasn't such a brat. Sometimes he acts like he's twelve."

"And you act as if you were just another foster parent."

"To a twenty-seven-year-old."

" 'Tis what he is."

"And I am what I am." Irritation rose, and he looked down at his sword blade, thinking. Then he addressed her again. "Tell you what. How about you let Trefor know that if he wants to talk to me he can come talk, but that he shouldn't send his girlfriend with messages."

"He doesnae know I'm here."

"Uh-huh."

"I do not do his bidding only for the sake of it." Now the anger was in her eyes.

"No, you're right. I think you have an agenda entirely your own."

"And that means exactly what?"

"If you love him, then why will you one day send him here where he'll probably get killed? And as unprepared for battle as he was when he got here? What's the deal?"

For a moment he thought he'd actually touched a nerve and asked a question with a difficult answer. She blinked a little, then said, "I cannot say." He opened his mouth for a snide reply, but she continued. "That is to say, I do not know. I won't know until I come to the juncture when I will do it. I only trust that I will have a good reason for it at the time."

"You mean your woowoo magic can't tell you what's going on with your future self?" He gestured to his head with twiddling fingers and rolled his eyes. Forced to admit magic existed, he still didn't think very much of it.

She smiled, and a sly light came to her eyes. "Magic takes an effort I think not worth what such an effort would tell me. I only am glad he is here and dinnae care why." There was a hesitation, like a computer processing a request, then she said, "I can, however, tell you to expect a visit from Himself this evening."

Alex's heart skipped a beat, but he let nothing show. He grunted, then said, "Sir James? He visits me often. The odds are good."

But the sly smile remained. She inclined her head toward him and said, "Indeed. Then I will take my leave of you now, and have a good evening, my lord." With that, she turned and left the tent.

Alex's pulse began to skip like a mad hatter. Twice she'd called him that, and pointedly enough to catch his attention. Could she know what had been in the message James had received? Alex could no longer concentrate on his sword and put it aside in its scabbard. He went outside to see how supper was coming and how soon they might eat.

James was there, approaching from his own fires with the leather portfolio in his hand and a big grin on his long, ruddy face. He hailed Alex.

"Alasdair! Come! Gather your men. I have great good news for you!"

Alex made like he was surprised though pleased to have James in his camp, neither of which would ordinarily have been true, but tonight he at least was pleased. "What is it?"

James gestured impatiently that Alex should stop asking questions and gather his men as he was told. With a whistle and a wave to Henry Ellot, Trefor, and Hector, Alex obeyed. The men came in a hurry and the ordinary knights and squires followed, most of them having witnessed the arrival of the letters that James now held. Everyone wanted to know what was going on.

Once the MacNeils were in attendance in the clearing, James held the packet over his head and announced, "I have news from the king. Our liege Robert is well pleased with the loyal service and prowess in battle of Sir Alasdair an Dubhar MacNeil. In his wisdom and grace he has determined an appropriate reward. Many times Sir Alasdair has proven himself on the field. He has shown his heart to be true and his loyalty to his liege unflagging. I hold in my hand the charter elevating Sir Alasdair to take his rightful place among his equals in nobility, chivalry, bravery, and the grace of God." There was a pleased murmur among the knights. James grinned at Alex and added, "Not to mention hatred of the English." Alex noted Trefor's face was impassive and he said nothing. The Earl of Douglas continued. "Now all pay obeisance to your lord, the Right Honorable Alasdair Joseph an Dubhar MacNeil, Earl of Cruachan."

Each in the gathering went to one knee, while James, who was the only one present who still outranked Alex, inclined his head in a bow. Looking out over the genuflecting men, an array of bent heads before him, Alex felt a surge of pleasure so boggling he could hardly keep from laughing out loud. *Earl.* Knowledge of what that meant in terms of both rights and responsibilities nearly knocked him sideways. He barely sensed James hooking an arm around his neck and telling him something about a formal ceremony when Robert returned from Ireland, as the men rose and he was guided off to James' camp for celebration. Alex was handed the message from Robert, and though he couldn't read the Latin, his eyes settled on the word "Cruachan."

He held out the parchment to Hector, though Hector couldn't read at all, let alone decipher Latin. "What's this? Cruachan?"

"'Tis an island not far from your own. Did ye not know it?"

"I've heard the word but thought it was just something they called the little, uninhabited islands, like slang. You know, a 'stack of stones.'"

"'Tis named for the cairn that holds one of our ancestors. I expect Robert has given back the land to the Mac-Neils for that reason. It was held by the MacDonalds for a while."

"A while?"

"Some centuries. Not long."

Then Alex blinked. "Wait. Given back? What given back?"

Hector chuckled. "Surely you understand this charter is not just for the title, but for the land itself. Your vassalage to the crown has just increased. Cruachan is a slightly larger island than Eilean Aonarach, and were Barra not such a large and beautiful place, I might be envious."

Alex was speechless. Another island to manage, and bigger than the one he already held. Coming up in the world this way was a heady thing and his ego swelled in spite of his better judgment. But he went with his friends to James' camp with as much dignity as he had at his command. He was an earl now. Not just nobility, but ruling class. This meant being summoned to parliament. It meant powers over his vassals alien to his American sensibilities. It was increased responsibility and debt to his king he would have to fulfill if he were to keep this position. It made him one of the more powerful men in Scotland, and therefore even more under the king's scrutiny.

To celebrate, he was going to get good and drunk.

The wine flowed freely that night, and though the supper was not the sumptuous feast they might have had if they'd been home where food and servants were more in abundance, the beef was plentiful and well seasoned from James' stores. His musicians made bright, merry tunes and some of the men danced, sloppily and with great hilarity. Within James' compound of tents the highest ranking of the raiders set to helping Alex acknowledge his good fortune and new status, welcoming him to a club that was as dangerous as it was exclusive and lucrative. Alex's head swam with more than just wine and mead that night, and he could feel the power surge within him.

Late in the evening, when talk ran down, the players packed up their fiddles, whistles, and drums, and men began moving away to sleep off the alcohol and exhaustion. Trefor came to flop down on the ground next to where Alex sat. He groaned with his full belly, then turned a bleary, sodden eye on his father.

"So, Robert's got his hooks into you good now, aye?"

Alex glanced at him, then peered into the *cuach* in his hand. "He's my king, and he holds a power over us you obviously don't understand."

"I understand he's keeping you from looking for Mom."

Alex glanced sideways at Trefor. "Have some respect."

"For her, or for you?" There was silence, then Trefor said, "When are you planning to go get her? You keep saying you'll find her, but you haven't lifted a finger so far."

"I don't know where she is."

"And you won't ever, if you don't get off your ass."

There was very little on earth Alex wanted more than to find Lindsay. But he had duties and wouldn't be allowed much of anything once he found her if he didn't live up to his obligations to Robert.

Trefor continued. "Now, I can see where you wouldn't want to come after me, since I'm so unlikable and all." Alex gave another sideways glance. That blasted Morag and her big mouth. "But I'd think you would be pretty hot to have your wife back. I don't think you've been laid once since I got here. Not like James and his bunch, who pick up on whatever girls bat their eyelashes at them."

"Or you and that Bhrochan chick."

Fire flashed in Trefor's eyes, and Alex wasn't sure whether it was because of his disparaging tone regarding faeries or that he'd spoken of Morag. Other than that, the comment went ignored. Trefor continued as if he hadn't heard. "You must be pretty horny by now."

"I'll live."

"Man, I wouldn't. Ain't nobody that good I would wait for them like that. Especially since it looks like it's going to be a good long time before you even start the search."

"I'm going to find her."

"Then you'll need some help."

Alex regarded him with curiosity now, knowing Trefor had an ability he did not. "What sort of help?"

"Not me. Morag."

That brought a grunt of disgust. "Morag." That nitwit was going to have to keep her mouth shut if he was ever going to address her again.

"She knows things."

"I bet she does."

"I bet you'd like to know what else came in that packet today." He said this in a snotty, superior tone designed to make Alex want to deny any such desire, a trap so Trefor could accuse him of not wanting to find Lindsay. So Alex declined to spring it and did not deny the truth.

"Of course I would like to know."

Trefor thought about that a moment, then said, "My faerie girlfriend tells me that, besides your earl charter and a personal letter from Robert, the packet held a letter from one of James' vassals. An intelligence report about another raiding party operating in the Borderlands. Scottish, by all accounts, but not under any banner recognized by Robert."

"Big deal. Tell me something that matters. The country-side is crawling with reivers and raiders. We just happen to be the largest and most official army of them out and about."

"Well, the reason such a thing was reported to James was not that there was yet another raiding party in the Marches, but that one of their number is a woman."

That perked Alex's interest. He'd heard of women accompanying their husbands on campaign, but they rarely fought and even when they did their husbands did not speak of it. "A woman on her own?"

"She calls herself a knight, they say, and she fights like one. James' vassal is totally boggled by this and says she's nearly seven feet tall and has black hair down past her shoulders. She's as mean as a viper and as strong as five men. And she paints herself."

Now Alex frowned. "Mean?" That didn't sound like Lindsay. "That can't be her. Lindsay was the one always griping at me that I was too violent. She gave up her disguise to marry me because she was tired of fighting. And she's tall for a woman, but she's not that tall. Just under six feet."

"If you were as short as these guys around here, that's tall enough to think she was seven foot. And people exaggerate. It's not like we got this on CNN. I think it's her. Tall, black hair, a woman who fights like a man . . ."

Alex considered that. Trefor had a point. It could be her, though it didn't seem much like her. "She paints herself?"

"The letter lacked details on that."

"Morag read the letter?"

"James read it. Morag listened in."

Alex frowned. "She reads minds?"

"No, she reads letters." He shrugged. "It's complicated."

"Ah. So, if I ever get a letter from anyone I shouldn't let her know until after I've read it?"

Trefor gave him a sour look. "Be glad to know this stuff."

"James would have told me what was in the letter."

"Maybe. Maybe it would have been just an amusing tidbit he would have forgotten as soon as something more important came up. Which, seeing as how he's the boss around here, pretty much everything in his day is more important than a woman reiver. More than likely he'd laugh it off as rumor gone off into fiction."

Alex was forced to acknowledge the point with a shrug, but said, "And we think it's true because . . . ?"

Frustration crept into Trefor's voice. "Because we know she's out there, somewhere, and we know she's tough enough to fight the way they say she does, and the physical description fits. You've got to go find her. You've got to dump James and go looking for my mother . . . *Dad.*"

A tight knot of frustration clenched Alex's heart. It was all he could do to not leap to his feet, jump on his horse, and ride off in search of Lindsay. But it was impossible. And Trefor would never believe that. He would never buy that Alex wanted to and couldn't. But deserting his duties went against not only his pledge to Robert but also everything he'd ever been taught by his father and by his military training. He said, "When I get a chance, I will."

Trefor gazed at him in silence, and Alex could feel the heat of hatred coming from him in waves. His son made a disgusted noise, then climbed to his feet and walked away.

Alex watched him go, and hated himself just as much as Trefor did.

CHAPTER 13

The feeling from the men was that Lindsay would panic and hold back in a fight. Her past performance was forgotten in the light of her revelation, and suddenly she was on probation again. Everything she did was analyzed for any sign of female fault and the least hesitation would be pointed to as unsuitability in battle. So she pressed harder than she ever had before when they'd thought her male. Her sword was quicker, her shouts louder, her eagerness to attack more plain than in any of the men present. It bordered on recklessness, but the need to prove herself more than before made her push the limits. No longer was it enough to appear determined; she had to appear bloodthirsty, and she found it difficult to achieve the appearance without becoming it. Battle anger became habitual.

She proved herself well. At night, after these raids she made as a woman, when the day was dissected around the fire, nobody complained about her. To be sure, there were one or two who even risked their own reputations to praise her skill and prowess. Some seemed surprised she had not suddenly become incompetent with a sword now that her gender was known, some were quiet and sullen, but none tried to suggest she hadn't been up to the task. She ate her meat with the men, drank her share of the mead, then rolled herself into her plaid with the hope she would have no more overt trouble from her compatriots.

She acquired a squire from one of the other knights who felt himself overburdened with help, and the young man eagerly managed her plunder. He was kept busy with several horses, an extra sword, and some axes. All else had been sold off, and she carried cash and jewels in a pouch at her side. After a while, she felt as if she were making progress in the world.

Except for her issues with Nemed. Over the next weeks the elfin king came around often, but Lindsay noticed he never mixed with the men. She saw him only from afar, in conference with An Reubair or simply watching them all from astride his horse in the distance. Often she would look up while they traveled and see the figure standing on a rise or near the edge of a forest, gazing at them as they passed, still as the trees and seemingly detached. Barely there, and unnoticed by the knights riding by. Perhaps he was watching the progress of his investment toward their goal. Or perhaps he was keeping an eye on her. The urge to wheel her horse and charge down on him to have it out was maddening. If only she could attack him as on a field of battle, she would have done it. Her hatred darkened her thoughts each time she saw him.

The elfin king stayed just far enough away that there was no hope of chasing him down. Were she to try, he would disappear before she could reach him, and the rest of the men would think her behavior erratic. Hysterical. *Feminine*. That would be the worst thing she could do in her situation. She rode on and awaited a real opportunity.

An Reubair offered to let her sleep by his fire, where she wouldn't be in competition with the ordinary knights for space, heat, and food, but she declined. Not only was she not interested in him, she especially didn't want to sleep near him lest anyone think she was slipping into his bedroll. Though these days she did lay her blankets closer to the fire than before, she remained at the particular fire appropriate to her rank and among the men whose support she needed while fighting. A year as Alex's squire had taught her much, and esprit de corps was a concept she understood well. Riding with these men, she only proceeded with her job and looked for an opportunity to kill Nemed.

The thing she found most annoying during these weeks took her by surprise, when her hormones kicked in to remind her that all work and no play would make Sir Lindsay a dull girl. Early on, when she'd still been lactating and bleeding from the birth, she'd had no interest in sex and no reaction to the physically fit men around her who frequently stripped for various reasons. But these days her hormones were settling down to normal and the weather was coming into summer. Warm scents of grass and trees, the smell of earth and new growth were heady. Dizzying. The men around her relieved themselves of their heavy armor and clothes.

The other knights were inclined to lie about the keep or sleep wearing only their trews—or sometimes nothing at all—and Lindsay found herself wanting to gaze upon them with appreciation. Some of them looked awfully good. Every one of them had battle scars, but during her years with Alex she'd become accustomed to that. None of these guys looked like modern bodybuilders, but two or three were so well muscled they rippled like football players when they moved, and she began to look forward to the days when those blokes would strip and sit by the fire to pick lice from themselves, just so she could watch.

It was a struggle not to stare openly at the bodies on display around her, and she limited herself to quick, sideways glances. It wouldn't do to stare. She couldn't let on she was as horny as they. Sometimes she found herself throbbing, and wouldn't they all have been so amused to know that? They'd surely take advantage, try to seduce her, and it would be that much more difficult not to cave to the temptation. And nobody needed the trouble that would cause.

Contrary to the opinion of Erica Jong, there was no such thing as a truly zipless fuck, and laying so much as a hand on one of her fellow reivers would result in unimaginable havoc among them all. There was no choice but to refrain.

But, oh, sometimes the temptation was horrible. Other days were not so bad and there were times when she hardly thought of it at all, but on two occasions she had to take a long walk to a cold stream and hope nobody would happen by.

Once she calculated the time passed since she'd last slept with her husband, and wished she hadn't, for the months after Alex's departure for his ship and the time she'd spent here totaled to nearly a year. No wonder she was beginning to yearn for the touch of a man's hand. A year was an awfully long time to go without.

Jenkins didn't count. What Jenkins had done wasn't sex; it had been violence, the same as if she had violated him with a stick. Which, now that she thought of it, might have been an idea. But she set the thought aside and put Jenkins from her mind. Jenkins didn't count, he was dead, had died in an appropriate manner, and that was the end of that.

Jenkins didn't count. Really.

Before, there had been Alex when the need became too much, and she'd resisted even him as long as she could. When they'd first been thrown together as knight and squire, strangers pretending to be cousins, she'd balked at feeling anything for him. Clearly he'd been in love with her, nearly since the day they'd met, it seemed. It had taken her much longer to return that love. Many nights of sleeping in the same tent, sometimes under the same blanket. During that time he was the only human being who knew who she really was, and over those months she became at first attracted, then attached. Love quickly followed lust once she'd allowed it, and her feelings for Alex never waned even after they'd returned home and she was no longer so dependent on him. Those feelings had never dimmed, and she often daydreamed of him: his scent, the sound of his voice low and soft in her ear, the feel of his lean body against hers. His breathing at night when it was the only sound to be heard, and the way the sound changed when he was aroused. Or thinking about her at all. In bed he'd been intense. Focused on her, as if the feel of her were all that would ever matter to him. He'd made her feel important.

The very fact that he loved her so well made her wish he were there instead of the motley Reubair crew, for his heart was more open than any man's she'd ever known. She had always been able to see into it as if it were a precious bit of glass made with swirls and whorls of color, endlessly fascinating. And as fragile. Oh, so fragile. Though he would deny it as hotly as he declared his love, it was plain she had a power to hurt him others did not, and where she was concerned he was to be handled gently. To the rest of the world he was invincible. As a knight he fought like a terrier and commanded his men fully and with firm hand. His strength had kept her sane when they'd found themselves in this place. Now, on her own, she longed horribly for that strength, in ways she hadn't even when he'd returned to his ship. Now she needed him as she'd never imagined she could need anyone, and the terror of never seeing him again grew on her and ate at her like a fungus.

One day in the countryside east of Carlisle, An Reubair fell back from his position at the front of his column and sidled up to her as they rode. He said, "Come with me," then reined off to the side.

Lindsay obeyed, though her heart surged with alarm. He guided her to a spot out of earshot of the other men, then turned to parallel the column's course at a walk. He said, "I have been watching you of late."

Her nose wrinkled. "Everyone has. Don't annoy me with your criticism. I've carried my weight."

"Aye, and then some. I admire it. Contrary to being critical, I value your strength."

Lindsay was silent. He should value it, and she wondered why he was telling her so. This pat-on-the-back conversation wasn't something he would do for his other knights, and she didn't like to be treated differently.

Especially when he added, "I would have such strength in my sons."

Oh. Now she knew his game. She nearly groaned, and stifled it. When she could trust her voice to not betray her disgust she said, "I wish you luck in finding a strong wife."

An Reubair seemed to take the hint and thought long on his next words as they rode on slowly after the column. Then he said, "I want you to know I am far more wealthy than I appear at the moment, for there are lands in Ireland unknown to human kings." She glanced over at him with eyebrows raised, and he replied to her unasked question. "The place is larger than any map will ever show. You humans have not conquered the so-called wee folk entirely, and more than likely never will." He straightened in his saddle, took a breath, and continued his pitch. "When I take a wife, she would want for naught. She would be a fortunate woman, well cared for. Well fed and clothed, and surrounded by servants. She would be required only to bear my sons."

A snort escaped Lindsay against her better judgment. *Only* to bear them. That was a scream. She said, dodging his point and the question he was about to ask, "And if they were daughters?"

Her commander shrugged. "Every man runs a risk of daughters. Even our Scottish king has had no luck in that. But I think you will have sons, and I would make you a happy wife and mother."

Now she wished to know how much An Reubair knew about Alex. How much had Nemed told him? Was he testing her? Did he know she was married already? For God's sake, did he know about the baby? Her mind flew to decide, for hesitation in her reply might tell him things she didn't want him to know, and she wasn't sure what she could afford to give away. "I daresay I'm already a wife." A moment's pause, then she admitted, "And a mother. I don't need your help in that."

He gave her a sharp glance, his surprise unmistakable. For a moment he even stuttered a bit of laughter in his shock. "You have children?"

"Child."

When he was able to continue, there was an offended edge to his voice. "And where is this child's father? What man allows his wife to traipse around the countryside in the company of other men, fighting like one? He should be flayed."

She looked over at him with a stare she hoped was filled with disdain, then informed him, "That would be Sir Alasdair an Dubhar of Eilean Aonarach. I'm his wife, and he's the father of my son. And as far as him *letting* me—"

"You're Marilyn MacNeil?" Now An Reubair peered at her hard.

Lindsay figured it wasn't good he had heard of her, but was pleased to note the genuine ring of surprise in his voice. Nemed hadn't told him anything; this was all news. "Aye."

He thought about that for a moment, then threw back his head and laughed. "Pawlowski. I should have known it; you became your own sister so MacNeil could marry his squire." The peals of his laughter rang long and hard, and Lindsay looked off toward the column of men. Some glanced back at them in curiosity.

She turned back toward Reubair in irritation. "*Knight*. I was knighted by Robert at Bannockburn." Lindsay didn't know why the distinction was so important to her, but it was. She'd earned the title, after all.

Reubair shrugged as if it were no matter to him and shouldn't be to her. "And why has Sir Alasdair turned you loose on the world? Or did you run away? No matter; divorce him, and I'll make you a far better husband. Even happier, let me kill him and do away with such a cowardly fool. The world would be the better for it." Typical faerie. Life was so much simpler for them in their selfishness.

"I need no other husband. We've been separated by circumstance; he is . . . elsewhere, and I search for my child who was stolen."

That subdued Reubair's anger at Alex. In a surprise turn, he took a more reasonable tone, almost as if he had a heart. It was an aspect of him Lindsay had never imagined could exist. "Stolen? By whom?"

Lindsay hesitated on the very brink of telling him she knew Nemed had the baby, but swallowed the words before she could make that mistake. "I don't know."

"Was there a changeling?"

She blinked that he would know that, and said, "Yes. An old faerie man. He told me my son had returned to the place of his conception."

"Och," he said. "Stolen. Recovering such a child is a difficult goal. Most who receive changelings never find their true children. They are taken away and sent to places where nobody would know them." Reubair was fey and selfish, but he also knew what she was up against.

"My son had dark hair like mine, but with the ears of the Danann."

An Reubair pulled up his horse and stared hard at her. She reined in and regarded him as blandly as she could. He nearly gaped at her. "Danann? And from where did he receive this blood? From his father?" His voice carried the conviction her reply would be negative.

"No. From me."

"Aye. Of course from you. I should have seen it. And I should have known when you killed Jenkins you were no ordinary woman."

Lindsay gave a snort of disgust and reined back around to kick her horse to a trot and rejoin the men. An Reubair spurred to head her off, and made her stop. She regarded him with the anger and frustration of having been slighted yet again. "Hear me: I'm far more human than fey, and I don't know magic. I killed Jenkins by my skill at fighting and my strength, not by trickery. Understand that, lest I find myself needing to prove it. On you, perhaps, this time. Are you sure you would want to risk it?"

A welter of things flickered in his eyes, and Lindsay thought for a moment he might like to take on the challenge. Why, she couldn't have said, and it was disconcerting. But finally he said, "Very well. Nevertheless, you

understand that if your son has the mark, he could be anywhere. And not by the will of Danu, but by the wiles of the
Bhrochan. Children stolen by the very wee are never returned. Not ever in the millennia they've existed. It is their
sport, and they're very good at it. Know that your son is lost
to you. Your husband is, as you say . . . elsewhere." Lindsay
noted that he'd noticed she wasn't telling him where Alex
was. "You are alone, and as strong as you are you have no
future as Sir Lindsay. You must attach—" At a cross look
from Lindsay he corrected himself in a more soothing
voice. "You must *ally* yourself with another husband."

He looked off toward the horizon, thinking, and his expression was one of frustration. Lindsay could sense real
emotion in him, as if it mattered to him that she make the
correct decision because it was correct, not just because he
wanted to own her. It further surprised her. His voice lowered and took on a reasonableness that was seductive for
its suggestion of respect. For the first time since he'd
learned her true gender he spoke to her as if she were a
thinking person. The way a man of his time would address
another man. Astonishment upon surprise gave her pause.
It appeared so genuine she wondered if she'd been wrong
about him.

Then she shook the thought away. There was an agenda
here, and he was pulling out stops, that was all. But she continued to listen without interrupting. "As a woman alone you
cannot survive long, even among men who once thought you
were one of them. You will never be one of them, and soon
they will understand that, like dogs who come to know their
master is not one of the pack. And they will turn on you.
They will resent that you keep your female delights to yourself at the same time you flaunt yourself among them. They
will either fight over you or abandon you, and if you have not
secured protection from one of them against the others you
will most likely die. Or be reduced to whoredom. Only I can
keep you from that fate, for I am the only one who can protect you from all of them."

"I've succeeded so far in my independence."

"It will last only as long as you remain strong and young. How old are you, Lindsay Pawlowski? What will you do when your bones begin to ache and your teeth begin to loosen in your head? What will happen the first time you falter with a sword in your hand? It must already be a great effort to appear as strong as a man. As aggressive. Even if you come by it naturally, it must still take all your power to keep up with the others. How long can you continue that way?"

"I intend to find my son and return home with him. It won't take long enough for that to matter."

Reubair snorted in exasperation. "You will *never* find your son!"

"Nemed will give him up. I'm sure of it."

He blinked. "Nemed? How do you know King Nemed?"

Lindsay bit her tongue. Now she'd made a hash of it. She said only, "I know of him. I've seen you talking to him, and I know you work for him. I expect he bankrolled this expedition."

"Bankroll?"

"He set you up with money, horses, wagons, such as that." A hunch came, and she added, "It's his land in Ireland you hold. You're his vassal."

A blink from him told her she'd guessed right. He said, "And you believe he has your son?"

"I do."

"I assure you he does not, for that is a task he would have given me. I would have known everything about you when we met, which I certainly did not." Fingers of doubt touched her spine, and she stared at him. "Surely it was the Bhrochan who took him. They're heathens and it's their way."

Again Lindsay reined her horse around, but this time, before she was out of earshot, Reubair said, "You realize, of course, had I known anything at all of your baby, I would have ransomed him to you for your hand." Lindsay reined back around and gaped at him. He continued. "Or at the very least for your quim. I aught but wish I had the son you so desire, to give him to you so you would give me one in return."

God help her, he was absolutely right. If he'd had something she wanted that much, he would certainly have used it against her. So would Nemed have. Sudden tears of obliterated hope surged and spilled, so inexorable she could only choke on them. With that single stroke, Reubair had laid to waste all she'd done in her quest for her son. Now she was seven hundred years from help or hope, and had not the faintest idea what to do or where to go from there. The realizations tumbled over her like stones from a ruined castle, crushing her.

An Reubair kneed his mount and went to her. "Ally yourself with me. I'll help you find your son."

With a panicky hand she wiped her face and looked away to the horizon. "You don't know any more than I do. You have proven that to me."

"The Bhrochan must have him. Those little madmen are a menace for young ones. They do it because it amuses them to see humans fret for their children. Despicable creatures." It was astonishing to find a streak in this man that almost resembled morality. Frightening that there was someone even he found disgusting.

Lindsay opened her mouth to tell him the baby must still be in the future, and she'd come through time for nothing, but then shut it, unwilling to blurt that story as well. She didn't want him to know her past with Nemed and how much she hated him. And if Reubair were to learn Alex was not in this century . . . She asked, "How can you make the Bhrochan tell where he is?"

"Och, I've lands in Ireland and a long history with those folks. They are not the most intelligent of beings. I know how to make them dance on a string the way they would have the rest of the world do for them. I can find your son. Or at least let you know of his fate."

"You would do that?"

"In return I would expect your hand. Marry me. Then

we'll search for the baby to raise as ours among the ones we would make."

Of course it was too much to ask that he bargain for something besides her freedom. More panic tried to claim Lindsay. Marry An Reubair? Make babies for him? The thought was repugnant. But she couldn't say no. She wanted to laugh in his face, maybe even spit in it, but she couldn't say no. She choked back more tears and scanned the horizon again as if looking for someone to save her. There was no rescuing cavalry, and though chivalry was popular in theory, it rarely resembled itself in practice. Finally she said, "Allow me to consider your offer with the care it deserves. Marriage is a thing not to be taken lightly under any circumstances, and especially under unusual ones such as these."

That brought a smile more wide than Lindsay thought appropriate for the enthusiasm she offered him. He said, "Aye. Think carefully. I'll await your reply with high anticipation." He nodded toward the column of riders, who had passed them and were beginning to move away. "Take your place among the men and think hard on what I've told you." Then he reined around and returned to his column.

CHAPTER 14

For the next several days it seemed An Reubair might have been wrong about the men. Lindsay ate with them, rode alongside them, and slept undisturbed among them. She hoped Reubair's unwelcome offer would slip by the wayside and not be addressed again, but that hope died when she noted him watching her, gazing from a distance at what she would do, and she knew he would never let it go. He appeared to be counting the days until she would give him a reply, and surely would come to her again soon. An answer would then be required.

Worse, the men began to prove him right. It was the night after the next raid that things began to shift in an ugly direction. Lindsay had fought well and come away with a fair amount of property that day. Spirits were high, and she was as pleased with herself as the men were with themselves. She felt well off, and as the evening's food and drink eased into her corners to make her feel comfortable and nearly sleepy, she listened to the talk around the fire with a sense of satisfaction. It brought to mind the days of sitting around with fellow reporters over ale in London, and some evenings the nostalgia was sharp enough to cut away some of the longing for Alex.

Simon was telling a story about the last girl he'd found willing to bed him, who had brought along her senile mother, for there had been nobody else to watch the old lady while they socialized. Lindsay laughed with the others over all the talking the woman had done while Simon had his way with her daughter. He declared the mother had been more of a distraction to him than the girl, whose amorous cries nearly drowned out the mother's conversation. They were a noisy pair. Simon insisted it was because of his immense prowess as a lover the girl had been able to ignore the prattling, for she was in paroxysms of ecstasy while the other woman rattled on about her dead husband. Certainly the girl had been entirely taken with him, and he suspected the mother would have liked to partake as well. Again Lindsay laughed with the others, picturing the scene in Simon's tent, the noisy girl with her oblivious mother reminiscing at full voice and him struggling to get his jollies in the midst of it. Simon glanced at her and said, "You laugh, but I would prove it to ye."

Lindsay laughed again, a bit louder than necessary as apprehension crept in.

"No, in earnest. I would prove to you I am the most exciting lover you could have."

"Not interested." Her voice went flat and all the humor left her.

"Oh, but one kiss should convince you. Just one kiss, and you'll be begging for more." There was chuckling among the others, and Simon seemed to take that as encouragement, a wide grin on his face.

"No."

"Just one." Simon scooted over toward her and leaned in as if to receive an offered kiss. Lindsay leaned away but kept her seat lest she be forced to leave the fire. Retreat was never a good idea among these men.

Her voice went even more firm. "I said, no."

But Simon only laughed and lunged at her, and his

sloppy mouth sought her lips. She jerked away and scrambled to her feet.

"Back off!" Before he could climb to his own feet, she
hauled off and tried to kick him in the head. But he grabbed
her foot and toppled her, then leapt onto her to deliver a hard,
slobbery wet kiss on her closed mouth.

She yanked her head sideways and gave a cry of disgust,
then pushed him off. Laughing, having made his score, he
acquiesced and went back to his own seat. Again the others
chuckled.

Now Lindsay was forced to decide how to react. She
could kill him, but he'd not harmed her physically and it
might be taken badly by the others if she indulged in such
an extreme response over one kiss. No, her dagger needed
to stay in her belt this time. Instead she stepped over to Simon where he sat on the ground, feinted a kick with her
right foot, then gave a hop as he went for it and clobbered
his face with her left. Simon fell flat on his back with a
bloody nose.

A murmur of consternation rose from the men, and
alarm skittered through Lindsay. They sounded more concerned for Simon's nose than the assault on her. Simon
dabbed at the trickle and looked at her as if she'd sucker
punched him.

One of the men muttered, "Och. There was no need to
break his nose."

Lindsay turned, appalled, and said, "I told you all that I
would not tolerate any man to lay a hand on me."

"It was only in fun." Simon spoke with closed sinuses,
as if he had a bad cold, and held one nostril closed with his
finger. Had he received the broken nose in battle, he would
have ignored it entirely and let the blood pour down his
face. But now his voice was petulant and surprised. His
whining made her want to kick him again.

"You fellows can have that sort of fun with each other,
but not with me." A nervous chuckle came from someone
near the wall at the thought of any of them kissing each
other. Her gaze swept the room. "Anyone who would try

that again will find himself kissing my dagger. Am I making myself clear?"

There was no response but silence. It was a sullen silence of disagreement, and Lindsay looked around at her fellow reivers.

"I said, am I making myself clear?" Alex's lieutenant voice echoed in her mind and she shook her head to clear it of him.

"Aye," said Simon, still dabbing his nose and looking at her crossly.

"Good." She sat back down in her spot and stared at the fire in the silence. Not good. This wasn't good at all. Her pulse raced. She tried to calm it and appear confident they would obey, but she had no such conviction.

During the next raid she fought with special intensity. Damned if she was going to let her fellow raiders treat her like a blow-up doll. They'd see how she fought, then give her the respect she deserved. She'd make sure of that.

But the next night the talk centered around a knight who had found a cache of silver coins buried in an enclosure, and whenever she opened her mouth to speak someone else overrode her. The respect she'd anticipated—that she knew she required to survive in this group—was gone. She ended the evening rolled in her plaid and thinking hard about what to do.

She also thought hard about Nemed. It was plain now he had nothing to do with the baby's disappearance, but she still hated the elfin bastard. There was no chance of forgetting what he'd done to her in the past, and she would still kill him if given the chance. Over those weeks she came to realize she was staying with the reivers in hopes of that chance as much as for the hope that Reubair would find a way to retrieve her son from the Bhrochan.

Assuming the very wee folk were the ones who had taken him. For all she knew at this point, the boy might have been taken by an ordinary human from the twenty-first century. Stolen from the hospital nursery like other missing children.

But what of the changeling and his talk of the baby's fate? If there was something Reubair could find out . . .

But would it be worth her freedom?

Lindsay thought hard, under the gaze of Nemed's vassal. He wanted her; it was plain in his eyes. She believed him when he said he had high regard for her strength. His hope was for strong children. His offer was straightforward and may even have been free of hidden strings. The face of the deal was bad enough without them. Her freedom in exchange for her son. She would become the property of An Reubair, chattel to live in a faerie land among the Danann.

She wondered what Danu herself would say about this. She still didn't know the purpose of the gift she'd been given by Danu. Knowing she was descended from the Danann brought new light to it, and Lindsay wished she had the book with her to examine more closely. The psalms had been left at the castle on Eilean Aonarach, and Lindsay wondered whether going there would be the thing to do. Did it carry any power other than inspiration? Could she contact the faerie through it? She had an awful lot of questions, and she could do with a chat.

Once again in the keep near Lochmaben, the men led by An Reubair rested from their forays. Lindsay found herself restless. The others lounged around fires and gossiped, but she had no use for the bragging these days. During the long summer light they sparred with each other, but it was worthless play. Lindsay wanted to return south and continue the resistance against the English. It was like wearing a hair shirt, an irritation embedded in her days. She itched to leave. Her body vibrated with the need. At every opportunity she joined sparring groups and fought seriously, not just to keep her skills sharp but to work off the need to swing her sword. It calmed her. She exhausted herself so she could sleep. So the dreams might stop. The nightmares she feared might not be just a product of her own mind.

Since Reubair's offer, at night she dreamed of her son, and of Nemed. Once again she held her newborn baby, tiny and sweet, eyes squinting and blinking in the bright hospital light, perfect mouth puckering, his head covered with a little blue knitted cap and a wisp of dark, downy baby hair peeking from under it at his forehead. In the dream she knew she would lose him. Even as she held him, she knew he would be gone the next day and there would be nothing left of him but a photograph. The ache was monstrous. That she'd let him out of her sight so he could be taken was guilt beyond comprehension. It paralyzed her. And there was Nemed, accusing. His hair lifted in the hot draft of the fire in his enormous hearth, and his cruel mouth curled as he spoke. He spoke to her of what would become of the child she hadn't even named. He told her the baby would be starved and beaten and drugged. He would be ridiculed. The only care he would receive in his life would be from people who did not love him, and it would be her fault. Most mornings she awoke with a face slick with tears, dripping into one ear. The grief brought an ache to her bones and blackness to her heart. It ate at her until the only sanctuary was to not feel at all.

The men who slept near her began to give her long, dark stares of doubt. Nobody asked, but she knew they were thinking she was weakening. She had to make the dreams stop. So she kept herself busy during the day, exhausting herself, and some nights she slept soundly enough to at least not remember the visitations of things she wanted to forget.

Sometimes she did forget in the intense struggle to maintain her place among the men. Finding men to spar with required little effort. The fights became harder and more aggressive as each of them ratcheted up the competition. Testing her. Soon Lindsay felt as if she were fighting for her life, and began to take injuries for it, giving them as well. To be sure, she began to intimidate some of the men, and comments arose that she'd lost her mind. A secret smile touched her lips whenever she heard that. Better to be thought crazy than weak, for all men feared a madwoman, but no man feared a normal one. Perhaps she wouldn't have to consider Reubair's offer after all. With luck, she could hold her own here and think of a way to approach the Bhrochan on her own.

But the faerie wouldn't let it go. One day while sparring, she looked up to find him there, his sword in one hand and the tip of it resting on the ground beside him. He said to her opponent, "Leave us." The man obeyed and took his sword to another challenge. An Reubair faced Lindsay with a grin on his face and a friendly stance. "Care to take me to task today?"

"You want to practice?"

He twirled his weapon in a lazy mulinette and hefted his shield in his other hand. "I want a good fight and will get the best one from you, I think. I see by the scars and fresh cuts on your hands you do not hold back anymore."

Her chin raised. "I never used to."

"You did. Now you don't. I want to see what you've taught yourself."

"Why should you care what I may know or not know? You say all you want is to know what sort of babies I make."

"And I would have a look at the one you've already made, to know better what to expect from you. Meanwhile, I like a challenge and will test your heart as well as your body." He took a stance with his sword held high, and she countered with a forward one, her shield and sword both held to the front.

"I'm likely to hurt you."

"That we shall see." With a flourish he attacked, and she fended easily with her shield. He was slow and sloppy, and she knew he was playing with her. Nobody in this company was that bad a swordsman. So she held up her guard and knew his real attack would come soon. When he came at her again, he was as thoughtless as before. Again she fended, and held her ground. Shields clashed with a wooden thud, and Reubair relented.

Her impatience rose, and she taunted. "Is that all you have to offer?" If he believed she thought he was really fighting, he might underestimate her as much as he wished to be underestimated himself.

Reubair attacked again, this time with all his skill and force. Fending wasn't so easy this time, and he backed her away. But she took the stroke with her shield and returned with her sword for a long exchange. Their swords clanged in the afternoon air, and Lindsay was glad to have the preliminaries done with. Then they separated and circled to eye each other for more openings. Lindsay feinted, but Reubair didn't go for it and she held back the real attack. Some more eyeing of each other, and she feinted again. Again he didn't go for it, but guarded the other side instead. A third time she feinted, and this time he went for it, but she still held back her real attack. He stumbled, but recovered quickly. Immediately she feinted to the other side, he went for it, and she made her real attack where she'd feinted before. Her sword slashed his surcoat and he staggered back in surprise.

"Oh ho! If your reach were any longer!" He appeared genuinely amused, and he came back on her with a series of attacks she fended until she was able to scurry to the side and begin circling, sword held to the rear, ready to swing at the next opportunity.

"I pulled that one."

"A lie, and an unworthy idea in any case. You spared me nothing, and you shouldn't. I don't need it."

"Very well. You'll bleed, then."

"Try to kill me."

"Then who would pay me?"

"Indeed, and who would find your baby?"

That was like a sock in the gut, and An Reubair took advantage of the moment. He attacked and backed her up in a hurry. Before she knew it, he thrust his sword through an opening to the side of her shield and stopped just short of stabbing her. She jumped back, but they both knew he'd scored a body hit. Had he been a real opponent, she might have been dead.

Reubair mulinetted his sword in a gesture of victory and stepped toward her. "See what I told you about holding your own? You have weaknesses the other men don't."

Other men? A smile touched Lindsay's mouth. Her commander's eyes flickered as he realized his error, and he continued. "In any case, you understand me, I'm certain. You are not a man and cannot stand up to the rigors of being one."

"I daresay I can. And have."

A shadow of anger crossed his face as she made herself clear she was not inclined to give up and marry him. "Your effort is pointless."

"My freedom is the most precious thing I have left to me and worth whatever effort might be required to maintain it."

"Worth more than your child?"

A twinge of guilt knotted her gut, and anger rose at the low blow. "You've not shown me anything to prove you even hold sway with the Bhrochan, let alone that they have him to begin with. I would be a fool to marry you on such a flimsy promise."

His cheeks flushed briefly with frustration and his lips pressed together as he glanced off to the side as if in search of a reply, but he took a deep breath and let it out slowly. He stepped closer and said in a voice gone quiet, soft, "'Tis an oath. I swear I will find your son if you would marry me."

Lindsay wasn't stupid, and knew his game, but this new tack was an assault from a direction she'd thought well protected and now she found it wide open. An oath, to Christian men of this time, was a cost to one's soul and answerable to God. An Reubair was laying himself open to a vulnerability he took seriously, and effectively offering himself to her. This was on the level of a twenty-first-century man uttering the words "I love you."

She ventured a look into his eyes and found him staring straight into hers. She had to look away, and mentally cursed herself for the weakness. Even worse, she realized that during the moment she'd locked eyes with him she'd nearly wanted him. Not quite, but nearly, and there was a dim stirring in her belly. She'd saved herself in time, before her betraying hormones could do their work on her resolve. Now she gazed at the trampled grass beneath her feet and reminded herself who this was. Nemed's vassal. The faerie commander of a troupe of reivers. A creature committed to taking what he could get and never mind who got in the way. A man who wanted her body but not her heart, and didn't feel the least compunction about using her vulnerability against her as blackmail. As much as he now sounded as if he felt something for her, she knew he could not and would never. She let out a cough, shook her head to clear it, and then looked back at him again. "Again, you ask me to take your word."

"On my soul."

She looked up. "Do you even have one?"

He feigned offense. At least, she assumed it was a feint. He laid a hand over his heart and tilted his head toward hers. "I must, for it cries out to you."

Lindsay had to laugh at that, and uttered a chuckle, but made the mistake of looking into his eyes again. The spark of humor in them caught her off guard once more, and for the briefest moment she considered his offer.

No. That was too much. It was time to make this stop. She scabbarded her sword, hefted her shield onto her shoulder, and without a word headed in the direction of the ruined keep.

Reubair hurried behind her and took her arm. She wrenched herself free and continued walking. He grabbed her again and she stopped to listen.

"Tell me what you would have me do to win you."

No. She wouldn't listen. She had to keep strong. But when the image of Alex came she thrust it aside. Alex wasn't here, and he was unlikely to ever be here. He was seven centuries in the future, and if she ever saw him again it wouldn't be in this lifetime. Only her will to be independent would keep her from caving and accepting this offer. No matter how much she wanted to find her baby, this was not the way to do it. She needed to find the Bhrochan herself and make them tell her what they'd done with him.

Which had been exactly what she'd thought about Nemed when the baby had turned up missing. How wrong had she been about that? There was no telling where she should look, and it was only Reubair's conviction the Bhrochan were no good that made him point to them as culprits.

It was time to get out of there. To stay with this company any longer would be to invite temptation. She turned to her commander and said, "I'm going. I can't stay here. I don't believe you really mean to find my son, and so I have to decline your offer. Since you seem to be right about the men not accepting me, then my only choice is to move on. I must restore my disguise and return to my search for my baby."

"No, stay."

"For what? As you've so thoroughly explained to me, there's nothing to keep me here. I've no hope of success among these men, so I can only go elsewhere."

"I can make you stay."

"You can kill me or restrain me. Hardly the same thing."

His lips pressed together, his fair cheeks flushed, and his eyes darkened with his customary anger. For a moment he looked as if he might hit her, but instead he glanced to the side as his jaw muscles worked. He was thinking, deciding. Finally he said, "I will find your son."

"I think not. You'll look for him, but only until I either leave or marry you."

"Then promise to marry me after I've found him."

An odd note of pleading in his voice caught her attention. He seemed truly afraid she would leave his company of knights. They both knew he wouldn't kill her if she did, and they both knew she had the advantage for that. Now he was offering all for a promise from her.

There were only two choices, as happened with nearly everything else in life. Stay or go. Accept or decline. Do or do not. She searched his face and found him looking straight across at her. There was no love, and that was a relief. But there also was nothing hidden. By all her skills at reading people, he seemed sincere.

In her silence, he pressed his case. "Stay and I will make certain the men will not annoy you anymore."

"I can't let you do that. You'll only make it worse. I have to make them stop on my own."

His face brightened. "Then you'll stay and accept my offer?"

She opened her mouth to say no, that wasn't what she meant, then closed it. It was time to decide, and she liked the idea of An Reubair joining the search without having to marry him first. Who knew what the future would hold? He could be an ally without having to be her husband. So she nodded.

CHAPTER 15

The large cavalry of James Douglas moved more slowly than Alex preferred, and it chafed him. In his service under Edward Bruce before Bannockburn, he'd commanded a small patrol that had made lightning strikes on convoys and performed reconnaissance in the Scottish Lowlands, and he'd liked the speed and freedom of it. Cutting through forests and avoiding established tracks made stealth far simpler, as well. James had always been more mobile than Robert and Edward, even when he'd commanded foot soldiers from the Highlands, but these days his numbers were still ponderous and heavy equipment, including a couple of captured siege engines, made their progress more slow than a small patrol would be. Alex found himself wanting to head south on his own, to cut into the heart of England.

"Tell James you want to take your men north." Trefor was at Alex's tent flap to present his great new idea. Then he added in a pointed tone, "My lord."

Alex looked up from the crude map in his hand, drawn by one of James' scouts. Hard to tell much from it, but if it was at all accurate he had misgivings about the terrain ahead. "North? Yeah, sure. This is me, telling James I want to head home in the middle of the campaign."

"There are English towns north of here." Trefor came all the way into the tent and closed the flap behind him, and Alex returned his attention to the map.

"More of them to the south. Fat and smug ones. Ones who think they're safe from us Scots."

"You're no Scot. You don't buy into this independence stuff, do you?"

Alex glanced at Trefor again. "You don't?"

"Why should I?"

"Well, you and I happen to know we're going to win." *Eventually.* The work they were doing just then wouldn't be finished for another decade or so, when the English king would be pushed back to his own country, but they would eventually win.

"You and James care about that stuff. Not me."

Alex nodded. "That's right. You don't believe in anything but getting your way."

Trefor's weight shifted in his impatience. "I want to meet my mother. So shoot me. She's reported north of here. If you don't take your men, I'll take mine."

"Bad idea. You don't have enough men to play John Wayne and charge to the rescue. Assuming this wendigo creature with the long hair and painted face really is your mother." He tried to imagine Lindsay with her face covered in woad, and couldn't.

"How can you think she's not?"

"I knew her. She's not like that. Lindsay was a tough woman, but she wasn't a maniac. She was . . ." Memories of his wife tumbled into Alex's head, and for a moment he couldn't speak for the emotions they stirred.

"Was. You said she *was*. Like she's dead."

Alex sighed. "I don't know what she is, dead or alive or even living in this century yet. But I do know she's not like the woman in that letter. She was . . . *is* . . . gentle at heart and not given to over-the-top displays of violence. She's giving and forgiving. She showed me how to know what was best for you . . ."

Trefor's eyes narrowed.

Alex sat up. "You couldn't know. There were circumstances you've never been told, and I don't care to go into it."

"Uh-huh."

The attitude chafed Alex, and he shifted in his seat. "But the bottom line on Lindsay is that this thing they talk about can't be her."

"I expect you wouldn't want her back if it was." Again the accusing voice.

"Of course I would. It's just not her. It can't be."

"I say it is, and I'm going to take my men and go find her."

"You'll be wiped out before you can get near her."

"A chance I've got to take." Trefor ducked out of the tent, and Alex set aside the map to rise and follow.

"Where are you going?"

"To wave bye-bye to James."

"No, you're not."

"I am."

"Trefor—"

A sharp pain slashed the back of Alex's head and a swooshing noise came from nowhere. A nearby tree went *thunk*. "Ow!" Alex's hand went to the pain and he ducked on instinct though it was far too late for that. He looked up at the tree, where a crossbow bolt stuck in the trunk, well embedded. Blood smeared his fingers. He'd been shot.

Alex turned to the direction from which the bolt had come, and heard rustling in the bracken and gorse among the forest trees. In an instant he was off and running through the brush, guided by the rustling and trampled bracken. But the attacker had a head start, and Alex couldn't catch more than a glimpse of green plaid off in the distance, only a tiny patch flashing once among branches and fronds. Then, as the fleeing man gained ground, the rustling came to an end, leaving Alex to follow the broken growth as best he could. He came to a burn.

There he stopped and listened, but heard nothing other than the running of water over rocks in the stream bed. He searched it for wet marks on otherwise dry stones at the surface, but found nothing. The rocks at the bottom were undisturbed. No sign anyone had even stepped into the water, and no indication of exit on the other side. So he retraced the trail, looking for a spot he may have missed where his attacker veered. Nothing. Again he stilled himself and listened. Nothing. Soon even the birds in the trees above went back to their birdly conversation. The quarry was lost.

Green plaid. Whoever it was had been wearing a green plaid. The color meant nothing, for green and brown patterns were commonly used for camouflage and none of the clans who wore tartan had yet caught on to the idea of sett patterns to identify themselves. But it did mean that the attacker had probably been a Highlander. Definitely not English, and probably not Lowland Scot, though some of Alex's Lowland knights wore plaids since coming to Eilean Aonarach.

A trickle tickled the back of Alex's neck, and he touched his fingers to find blood running freely from the scalp wound. It smarted but wasn't deep enough for the slightly nauseated feeling that would have suggested a bone wound and a nicked skull. He was lucky the bolt hadn't plunged straight into his ear and out the other side.

Alex wiped his smeared hand on his surcoat as he made his way back to camp, and only then realized Trefor had not followed him into the woods to chase the assailant. Some backup. When Alex emerged from the trees, he found a cluster of his men gathered around Trefor, who held the bolt he'd pulled from the tree. Hector, Gregor, and the others dropped their discussion of the missile and looked up at Alex as he approached.

Trefor said, "Didn't catch him?"

"Nope. Lost him at the burn. Good of you to help out."

Trefor grimaced, then handed over the bolt. "You're lucky."

"I'd be luckier if someone weren't shooting at me." Alex took the bolt to examine it. There was nothing un- usual about it, and no telling who had loosed it. He broke it over his knee and threw the pieces into a cluster of bracken, then touched a tender finger to the wound on the back of his head. The bleeding was slowing and would soon stop, having soaked his sark and the collar of his tunic. The damp, sticky linen and wool clinging to his neck gave him the creeps, so he headed for his tent to clean up, leaving the others to stand around and debate who the would-be assas- sin might be. He figured he needed stitches and ordered Gregor to find the woman among James' camp followers who was good at that.

Alex didn't like that Trefor seemed so nonchalant about this. He also didn't like that Mike was nowhere around. Mike didn't wear a plaid, green or otherwise, but that meant nothing. Whoever had shot that bolt would have donned the blanket to blend into the greenery, and could have got- ten it anywhere. There were plenty of plaids to be bor- rowed or stolen from Alex's knights.

The woman with needle and thread entered the tent be- hind Gregor, who brought a leather bowl filled with water and a linen cloth and set them on a folding camp table for Alex. The earl stripped to the waist and wet the cloth, then began dabbing blood from his neck and back. Gregor hur- ried to find a fresh shirt for him and wash out the spot on the tunic in the burn. Hector came from the talk with the other men, as Alex was bent over to have his scalp sewn back together.

"What in the name of all that is holy was that about?" Hector was nearly apoplectic.

The first poke of the needle smarted like fire. Alex drew a deep breath and knew it would become worse as she went and his skin sensitized to the pain. He concentrated on breathing. "Search me."

For a moment Hector puzzled over Alex's response, then he seemed to get it. "Ah. You say you don't know."

"Right. That was a complete surprise. Came from

nowhere." That he could have been taken so much by surprise made him feel a little stupid.

"I daresay, though, you might have an idea. A guess."

Alex could guess but didn't want to say. *Trefor.* He wondered whether Hector would make the same guess. "I couldn't say a name."

"Not out loud, in any case. But who else among us would do away with you? And you can be certain it was one of our own number."

Alex shut his eyes and let the pain of the stitches distract him from the knot in his gut. It loosened as expected and breathing became easier. "Sometimes it's hard for a man to know who his enemies are."

"Sometimes a man's enemies are the people closest to him."

Alex straightened to see Hector's face, and the woman with the thread attached to his head stood back and waited patiently until she could continue. He saw a sadness in Hector that told him his nominal brother also hated he was talking about another MacNeil.

"He was with me when it happened."

"He has men who obey him." *Mike.* Alex wished he knew where Mike was just then.

"Trefor didn't do it, and he had nothing to do with it." A minute ago Alex had been thinking the same thing as Hector, but now he couldn't countenance the idea that his son would try to have him killed. "He couldn't. I'm his father."

"Many sons have done away with their fathers, and Trefor is not known for his love for anyone other than that Bhrochan woman. He doesn't think of you as his father in any case. He thinks he has none, and therefore has no loyalty to you, nor the clan, nor anyone else but himself. And possibly Morag, but even at that I would have doubt."

"Trefor wouldn't sneak around like that. He'd come at me with a sword if he wanted to kill me. In fact, I bet he'd relish a public confrontation if he thought he could defeat me."

"You have more faith in him than anyone here."

Alex wondered what Hector had heard. "What do you know of it? What has been said?"

"James has mentioned him. It's been said that Trefor is your greatest weakness."

"I'm sure he meant politically, not physically."

"Is there a difference? All life is political. If Trefor wishes to see you dead, it surely is for his own advancement. What quicker and more sure way to have what he wants than to remove you from his path?"

"He wouldn't inherit. He knows he's not in line for my title, and could never be. Nobody would believe he's my son even if he tried to claim it, and the newly created title wouldn't go to anyone but a descendant."

"But the land. Does he understand that with no heir everything you have in addition to the title would revert to the crown on your death? The land, the lairdship, the castle? The *cairn*?" That last seemed to carry more weight with Hector than Alex might have expected, and he wondered what the story was about the stack of rocks over the remains of their ancestor. "Even your chattel would become the property of the king. Does he know that? He would gain nothing."

Alex replied, "Yes, he knows." But then he thought about that. Trefor knew it, but did Mike? And did Trefor truly understand that all land belonged to the king and use of it was strictly governed by one's relationship with that king? He remembered how long it had taken himself to fully comprehend property was not sacrosanct here as it was where he came from. The Magna Carta had been signed the century before, but they were still a long way from the concept that all men were created equal and entitled to life, liberty, and the pursuit of happiness. A man's home wasn't necessarily his castle, and even the castles changed hands with alarming ease. Could it be Trefor thought there was a way to slip into Eilean Aonarach after Alex's death?

If Trefor hadn't known the assault was coming, why

wasn't he more outraged than he was? It was a hard question to answer, and it gnawed at Alex the more he tried to find reasons for the behavior. "Mike," he said. "It's Mike who wants me dead."

"To what end?"

Alex shrugged and knew he was grasping at straws. "Nobody can say he's the brightest crayon in the box." Hector gave him a puzzled frown and Alex translated. "He's rather stupid."

"He fights well."

"He fights like a bear. He plunges in and flails about, and frightens off his opponents. One day he's going to encounter an Englishman who isn't a coward, and then he'll be dead."

Hector only grunted at that.

"In any case, I'm thinking Mike could be the one who shot at me."

"At Trefor's bidding."

"Maybe. Maybe not."

"Regardless, a wary eye should be kept on both."

Alex considered that, then slowly nodded. It was true; to ignore the possibility Trefor was capable of assassination would be stupidity. Blindness, and the worse for being willful. "Aye. They both must be watched." He bent back over for the woman to finish her work on his head.

Mike wasn't seen in camp that night until supper was over. Alex looked across at Trefor's fire when Mike strolled in as if he'd been out for exercise, and with his dagger hacked a chunk of cold meat from the bone that lay on a wooden platter near the flickering flame that had cooked it. Then he searched out a spot and flopped down to eat his food. Alex rose from his own fire with a stoneware jug hooked on one finger and went over on the pretext of socializing. Casually he handed off the jug of sweet English wine to Trefor as he sat.

"How's your head?" Trefor asked, then took a draught directly from the jug. He handed it to Mike, who sucked on it enough to appear very thirsty. The way he went at his meat suggested he was overly hungry as well.

Alex touched the back of his head and shrugged. "I've had worse. Good thing the bowman was a lousy shot. At that range he should have been able to kill me. The idiot probably couldn't hit the broad side of a barn." He shrugged again. "I've been shot at before, by guys with better aim and way bigger guns. No big deal." He watched out of the corner of his eye for Mike's reaction, but there wasn't so much as a flicker on the guy's face. Nothing. Not even a laugh at the poor, sorry assassin who couldn't shoot worth a damn. Mike wasn't showing guilt, but he wasn't showing anything else either. Could be he was hiding something, or could be he really didn't care about the incident. With that guy it was hard to tell if he was being discreet or just dense.

He turned to Mike and said, "So, Beavis, you missed all the excitement today."

That brought a slantways glance, but nothing more. Mike's attention was on his supper.

"What were you up to today? I bet nothing that interesting. I'll tell ya, getting shot at really keeps you on your toes and gets the blood moving."

"I was hanging out. You guys take a break, I take a break. That's fair enough, isn't it?"

Alex nodded. "Most of us use downtime for sparring. You get any practice in?"

"Yeah. Sparred with Henry Ellot. You can ask him."

Now Alex was getting an alibi. It firmed up his conviction that Mike had been the shooter. And Henry Ellot wore a green plaid. For that, Alex's own plaid was green shot with brown, but now he wondered whether Henry would have been able to put his hand on his today.

Trefor wasn't giving much away either. "You're lucky you're not dead."

Alex narrowed his eyes at Trefor and remembered the fortunate weather just before they'd left the island. "You say you have been taught to be lucky. All those Irish faeries you hang out with, I suppose."

"Luck is costly even when it just happens. Nothing in life is free, and there's always a price when you ask for something."

Alex knew that well, as sick as he'd been on returning to this century. "So you're saying you had nothing to do with the bolt missing me?"

"I did not. Had I known it was coming, I might not have anyway." Trefor's tone was flat. Matter-of-fact. Alex had the impression his son didn't care one way or the other what happened to him. He wasn't sure whether the sock in the gut the thought brought him was shock or disappointment, but he began to wonder why he'd ever felt he would walk through fire for this guy, his son. And the fully puzzling thing about it was that he knew he still would, the same way he would eat if hungry or make love to his wife if she were there. It would happen without question. This realization curled the edges of his soul, and he looked away from Trefor to the fire. The jug was handed back to him, and he took a long drink.

Then, with a sour glance at Mike he switched to Gaelic, though it wasn't Alex's strongest language. He hoped the reply would come also in Gaelic. "What is this luck thing you have? Tell me."

Moving only his eyes, Trefor looked at him and considered his answer. Then he glanced at Mike and back at Alex. He replied in the same language. "I have a talent for the craft. Not a strong one, but Morag has taught me one or two things. She's teaching me more."

"What was that I saw? Back at the castle. The weather thing."

"I made you lucky. For the day."

"Yourself. You made us all lucky, including yourself."

"Oh, but you were the fortunate one that day, and not me. It's far easier to do it for someone else than for one's self. And less likely to come back to bite one in the ass."

Alex frowned. "What does that mean? In what way?"

"Well, you'll notice it was unlucky to have encountered Sir James in Edinburgh while we were staking out the castle for Nemed."

Alex grunted in agreement, but said nothing.

Trefor held out his hands as if comparing weights in them like a scale. "See, you must understand that there is no taking in the universe without something to come fill its place. Every action has a reaction, though it isn't necessarily equal or opposite. You take luck, something else comes to occupy the void. It could be good, it could be bad. You never know. Making myself the lucky one puts me in the position of also taking the recoil. But if I make someone else the recipient, I'm in the clear."

Alex grunted again. "So someone else gets the bad luck later on."

"Don't pass judgment. You got your clear day. What I got was a splitting headache."

"Did I get my life saved today?"

Trefor's eyes narrowed at him. "Why do you think I knew that bolt was coming? You think I had something to do with it?"

Alex's face warmed, and he wanted to say no. But those words wouldn't come. He glanced at Mike and said, "Someone among my men, your men, or James' bunch tried to off me today. You've been a royal asshole to me since we met, so guess who I'm going to look to for someone who hates me."

"I'm pissed off; it doesn't mean I want to see you with a crossbow bolt through your skull."

"I can't be sure of that, can I?"

"Why would I—?"

"Trefor!" Morag ran into the firelight, her skirts in her fists and bare feet flying. She halted, and fairly jumped up and down in her excitement, still holding her skirts. Like a leprechaun dancing a jig. "Trefor, my love, I've something to tell you!" There was a sheen of sweat on her face and a pink glow of exertion; she'd run far, and it occurred to Alex

to wonder where she'd been and whether she'd been dancing again.

"What is it?" They were still speaking Gaelic. Trefor
reached over to draw Morag to him, and she settled in next
to where he sat. He put an arm around her and kissed her.

Morag looked over at Alex as if waiting for him to excuse himself and leave, but Trefor said, "Go ahead, and tell
it in Gaelic."

She heaved a great sigh. "Very well. I have news about
that woman knight they speak of."

Alex's hearing perked, and he listened carefully.

"Go on," said Trefor.

"I've learned the raiders she accompanies have faeries
among them."

Trefor and Alex both sighed, fairly impatient that
Morag thought this was a big deal. But she continued in
breathless excitement, insistent that this was important.
"Now I know who they are! 'Tis the troupe of the Danann
outcast who calls himself 'The Robber.'" She waited for a
reaction, but got none. Alex didn't get the significance she
seemed to attach to the information. Excited and impatient,
her hands flinging about in her agitation, she said, "Do ye
not see? Or know? He is a vassal of King Nemed!"

That name went straight to Alex's gut like a dagger. His
lips pressed together and he had to look away to calm himself. *Nemed.* The truth swam before his eyes, and he hated
to see it. He'd not believed the female knight covered in
paint and frightening men all across the countryside was
his wife, but now he was forced to consider it. This was too
close a coincidence to actually be one. Lindsay was with
Nemed. Not chasing him, but working for him, and that
tore Alex's heart quite in half. The woman was there willingly. Lindsay had joined the enemy, and he wondered how
long it had been that way.

Trefor looked over at him. "What's wrong?" He had
no clue.

Alex frowned at Morag. "It can't be true."

"'Tis," she said, and there was a note of triumph in her

voice that made Alex grind his teeth. "Face it, MacNeil, your wife is riding with a troupe of renegades led by us wee folk." Morag knew less than she thought she did, and Alex kept shut about his heartbreak. In fact, he fell silent entirely. He took a long slug of wine to hide that his voice had been choked off. Then he stared down the neck of the jug as if its black interior were the most interesting thing before him just then.

Nobody else seemed to have anything to say, either, until Trefor started the discussion back up. "So, Cruachan old chap, you know where she is now. You know where to find her." To his mind there was nothing else that needed saying. But Alex's head swam with many pertinent things he couldn't utter. Not to Trefor, not to anyone. He swirled the last of the wine in the bottom of the jug and kept silent.

"You know it's her," Trefor said to him.

"I do." He couldn't deny it any longer. But he didn't want to discuss it, so he looked around as if suddenly realizing the time. "I guess it's time to hit the sack. According to the latest from James, we move tomorrow."

"Which direction?"

Alex ignored the question and rose to return to his tent. He just didn't want to talk about Morag's news.

There was murmuring behind him as he went. Inside his tent he began to strip for bed. Gregor had laid out a bowl of water and a cloth, and though Alex wasn't in a mood for washing he made himself attend to it. He didn't get far, for Trefor's voice soon came at the tent flap.

"My lord, Alasdair."

Alex looked up from untying his trews. Usually Trefor just barged in, and never addressed him with any respect. This was new. He retied the string at the top of his trews. "Come in."

Trefor entered, restored the flap, and stepped farther in to speak discreetly. "You do intend to go looking for her?" It was a question, and his voice was mild. Also new.

"No."

"Why?"

"My business, not yours."

"Then I'll take my men in the morning." No anger, just flat fact.

"You won't like what you find." Alex felt flattened. As if his world had deflated in the instant he realized Lindsay was with Nemed.

"Then tell me what you think I'll find. I need to know, because I'm going in any case. I'd appreciate some information."

"Why do you think she needs rescuing?"

"Obviously she doesn't. What she needs is to know where we are. In case she's looking for us." He took a breath, then added, "For me, I mean. She might be looking for me."

"She's not."

"Why do you say that?"

"I just know."

"But—"

"I don't want to go into it. She's just not."

Trefor chewed on that for a moment, then said, "We need to be sure. And she needs to know we're here."

"If she gave a damn about us, she wouldn't be where she is. She would not have left London to come here." *She wouldn't be with that Nemed.* Alex eyed Trefor and wished he would just leave it alone. "There are things you don't know about, and are none of your business."

"They are my business. She's my mother."

"She's my wife. My responsibility. I know her better than you do, and I know why she's where she is. Let it go. Find her if you must, but don't be surprised if she tells you to drop dead when you get there."

"I can't believe that."

Alex grunted, and had to admit even to himself she probably wouldn't say that to Trefor. Maybe. He couldn't figure out what Lindsay was doing with that elf in the first place; he certainly couldn't be sure of anything else about her anymore. The nightmares he'd once had of the two of them together, sent to him by Nemed, came to mind and he shut his eyes to keep them out. He said, "Just trust me; there are things you don't know and don't want to know."

"Then I'll go. I do want to know, and I'll find out what those things are."

Alex frowned at him. "Why do you think she wants to be rescued?"

"I don't care what she wants. It's what I want."

"You want to find your mother shacked up with a slimy old elf?"

Trefor let go a short bark of laughter. "That's what you think? She's left you for Nemed?"

"That's nothing. For a while I thought he was your father." The look of shock on Trefor's face made him add, "Until I met you and saw how much you look like a MacNeil."

"I look like you."

"More like my brother. You're a ringer for him. It's . . . eerie."

Trefor didn't seem to have a reply for that, but cleared his throat and said, "Well. In any case, I'm going to find her. I think you should go with me."

"She won't want me to find her."

"You don't know that."

Of course Alex didn't know that. But even more he didn't want to take the risk of finding her and learning for a certainty she had left London to be with Nemed. This way he could harbor a tiny corner of belief she had gone in search of Trefor by herself. Desperate hope that it was, he needed to cling to it. "I just want to let it be. There's nothing I can do for her."

"*You don't know that.* You don't know that she isn't a prisoner. She could be held against her will."

"Lindsay? Right. Not unless she was locked up in chains." Or a cage. Nemed had put her in a cage once and threatened to kill her. How she could be working for him now confused the hell out of him.

"I think you owe it to her—and to yourself—to find out. Never mind what you owe to me."

"Why do you give a damn whether I go?"

Trefor's reply to that was immediate and matter-of-fact, and entirely reasonable in a Machiavellian sort of way. "You have more men than I do. There could be a fight. I need you there."

"I told you, let go of the John Wayne thing."

"If this guy is as nasty as you say, and if these raiders are the land pirates they appear to be, then there will be a fight if we get close. We run a risk. I want backup. I need your help to contact my mother and make sure she's all right. You're her husband and my father; I think you have an obligation to the both of us."

Alex considered that. Truly he did have an obligation to these two who were now his closest relations, but could it take precedence over his duty to Robert and James?

While he was thinking, Trefor added, "You want to split off from James. Tell him you see a necessity to patrol. You don't have to tell him which direction you're going, because you'll be going back and forth, sending dispatches by single rider. You don't like Douglas; you should jump on this opportunity to cut loose before he figures that out."

Alex had to smile at the thought of James ever giving a rat's ass whether anyone liked him. Nevertheless, he decided he liked the idea of splitting from the main army and said, "Fine. I'll go to James. We'll head north as soon as I can talk him into assigning us to patrol."

Trefor nodded. "Good. I expect we'll break away tomorrow."

"I expect so."

Without further discussion, Trefor ducked out the tent flap, leaving Alex to turn over in his mind what he thought he might find once he located Lindsay. Images tumbled in his head, and his gut soured. It surely wasn't going to be pleasant.

But he told himself he'd been wrong about her before and it was possible he was wrong again. She'd not deserved his doubts and now might be perfectly innocent of the things he was thinking. He took a deep breath, finished stripping, and resumed his bath, then slipped under the blankets on his pallet. There to dream self-inflicted night-mares of Nemed and Lindsay together.

CHAPTER 16

It took some talking to get James to agree to a patrol. The Earl of Douglas already thought of his army as mobile, and Alex suspected he also liked to always be the first to contact the enemy. That was reasonable; he was as hot for the plunder as anyone else and felt he had more right to it than lesser commanders. Again, reasonable by the standards of the day. Naturally he resisted the idea of sending forty men to wander the countryside on their own, but Alex was insistent. So insistent, his talk skated close to a hint he might simply take his men and go. It was a risk, but he figured he'd known James long enough to have a feel for how much pressure he'd tolerate. He watched the earl's face as he spoke, alert for signs of too much irritation. It was after several days of nudging that James finally came around to Alex's way of thinking and acquiesced to the request to split off from the main army.

They headed south, sent a dispatch to James regarding the territory he was approaching, then circled around and struck north and west toward Carlisle. Though they had heard the troupe of An Reubair was raiding the English

West March, in these days of slow travel and even slower communication they were still looking for a needle in a haystack. They might pass within a half mile of the raiders and never know it.

Then, tracing up a river unfamiliar to Alex, they came upon a town still smoking. In the midst of a thick forest, a remote village no bigger than a few houses gathered at a slow spot in the river had been burned to the ground and its inhabitants were beginning the process of rebuilding. At the approach of Scottish knights the hundred or so villagers took fright and scurried off to the woods. At a command from Alex, his and Trefor's forty men approaching up the riverside went into action.

"Get one, bring him back," said Alex, and Henry Ellot spurred away to cut off one of the men fleeing like a slow sheep running after a herd. His horse blocked the man's path, and when the villager tried to dodge around, Henry wheeled his mount to block him again.

"Halt!" shouted Henry.

The man obeyed, tensed to run at the first opportunity. He looked beyond Henry and waved away a small boy who shouted at him from the forest edge. The boy hesitated, then ran into the woods before any of Alex's men could catch him. The villager turned to Henry. "We've nothing more to take." The fellow's voice quavered with terror.

Henry said, "That's plain to see. My master wishes to speak with you. We want to know who was here. Talk only. It's information we need." He nodded toward Alex to indicate where he wanted the man to go. "Tell him, and know you speak to the Earl of Cruachan."

A light of surprise kindled in the man's face, and he looked over at Alex, who waited patiently with Trefor at his left and Hector to his right. It was probably the first time anyone had ever expressed concern over the predicament of the border families, and particularly the English villager would be surprised at benign interest from a Scottish earl. He glanced back at Henry, then turned to approach Alex with a trepidation born of long abuse from the north.

At a respectful distance within earshot, he stopped and went to one knee. "My lord," he said in a tone he might have used to speak to the king himself. He even seemed to be trembling. Alex may have been Scottish and therefore the enemy, but this guy obviously was interested in preserving his own skin in the midst of the earl's loyal men.

"Stand and look at me." Alex wanted to see his eyes, to know his mind. The detainee stood, and Alex continued, pointing with his chin at the destroyed houses. "Who did this?"

The man shrugged and shuffled his feet. "We cannot say. I don't know who they were."

"Describe them to me."

"I saw little." Fear rose to his eyes that he might not have enough information to please the earl.

"Tell me what you saw. Be truthful and thorough if you want to rejoin your family and friends."

The man paled, a feat Alex would have thought impossible, for the fellow had been deathly pale and distraught to begin with. Then he said, "They were Scottish."

Alex snorted, and lowered his head to peer into the man's face with disgust. "I know that. Be kind enough to tell me something new. I know you can do better than that. Give it some effort."

The villager's feet shifted in distress. "They were merciless. We did not resist them, but they burned our homes regardless. They took things they could not have truly wanted; we had no silver, nor anything of real value except to ourselves."

"Your livestock. They wanted the animals."

"Aye, and they burned all that would burn. You can see for yourselves there's naught left but ashes."

Alex found it difficult to imagine Lindsay participating in that sort of senseless destruction. It sickened him. "Go on. How many were there?"

"I did not stop to count them, and cannae count so high in any case."

"Were there as many as these you see before you?"

The villager looked around at Alex and Trefor's knights, and said, "Aye. As many, but likely no more."

"What else can you tell me? Anything, any small detail?"

The villager plundered his memory and opened his mouth to say something. He closed it, hesitating to say what was on his mind, thought some more, then finally said, "One of them was of the fey."

Alex did not move a muscle of his face. He said, "You believe in faeries?"

"Do you not, my lord?" Many didn't, for fear of those who would point the finger of accusation for heresy.

"Aye, I do." Alex had to admit that he did believe the wee folk existed, and had little use for those who would deny the patently true. "So one of them had pointed ears? Or did he do magic before your eyes?"

" 'Twas the ears. I saw one of the riders had ears that poked through his hair."

"Black hair?"

The villager shook his head. "Fair, my lord."

It wasn't Nemed, then, and Alex's gut untied some. He said, "Continue. Did you see a woman?"

The villager blinked. "How do you know of her?"

"Just tell me; was she there?"

"Aye. I thought her a vision, or a ghost perhaps, but since you tell me you know of such a creature then I expect she could be real. She was tall and thin, with hair longer than the men, spilling from below her helm and over her shoulders."

"What color hair?"

"Black. And she was as cold a killer as the rest. She fought like a madman, with a sword as keen and merciless as anyone might see on a battlefield. And her shouts were not those of a man. They were a high trilling, as have been reported by those returning from the crusades. They say the women of Islam sound thus. Mayhaps she was a warrior from southern realms. Them and their strange ways."

Alex knew the noise he was talking about, having been

to the Middle East, but couldn't associate it with Lindsay. If this warrior was his wife, she'd changed in ways he didn't understand. Ways he wasn't sure he wanted to understand. He asked, "She killed unarmed villagers?"

The man shook his head, and Alex was again relieved. "We were all too frightened to let her near. Nor any of the other rogues, neither. I can't say as we were eager to die for our livestock, and most ran away rather than face such a harridan."

Alex glanced around at the surrounding forest. "Which direction did they take in their retreat?"

Readily the man pointed upriver. "Thataway. You can see their tracks along the bank, though I expect they'll find a rocky place to confound those who would follow."

No doubt. It was a standard tactic when trying to shake pursuers, even when the victims of a raid were unlikely to give chase.

He was done here. He waved away the villager and said, "You may go."

The detainee dropped to one knee again and said in a hurry but in a voice thick with sincerity, "Thank you, my lord." Then he spun as he rose and ran away to rejoin his family.

Alex told Henry to reassemble the column of knights, and they moved on up the river in the direction indicated by the villager.

He'd told the truth. There was plenty of sign the raiders had passed this way, and this deep in the forest there were no alternate routes for several dozen horsemen and a herd of sheep and goats. But as the track rose the trees thinned and the river narrowed. Alex pressed on in the long midsummer twilight when they ordinarily would have stopped to eat and sleep. The trace would disappear as soon as the terrain became rocky, and he wanted to find which way the raiders had gone.

He found it while there was still good light. On a wide expanse of granite the trail seemed to disappear, and Alex halted the column. While his men set up camp within the

forest, he dismounted and set out on foot alone in search of
the trace that would indicate what route the raiders had
taken. The shoeless livestock left no prints, but the horses
left plenty of marks on the rock. When those disappeared,
Alex knew the group had put socks over their horses'
hooves. He stopped and cast around in various directions,
for this was where they would have changed direction if
they were going to. It wasn't long before he found a place
where spore had been picked up and some left behind. In a
crack there was a small bit of sheep dung he took up on his
gauntlet and smeared on the rock. Still damp. His pulse
quickened; they were close. He looked out over the area
and made a guess which way the raiders had taken. They
couldn't be far, but to race after them tonight would be too
risky. He would set out again at first light and possibly
catch up to them within the day.

Alex looked to it with a trepidation he hated to admit to
himself and would never let on to anyone else. Did he really want to see Lindsay with this bunch? If it really was
her, she'd certainly changed, and he couldn't guess how
much. He was afraid to know how much. He wondered if
Trefor hadn't been right, that he might not want her back.
And the thought tore his heart.

He made his way back to camp, and as he entered it he
found Trefor and Mike approaching his tent. To Alex's astonishment, Mike's hands were tied behind his back with a
hobble rope, and Trefor was shoving him every few steps,
making him stumble and complain. They were arguing, and
it was plain Mike was Trefor's prisoner. Alex asked,
"What's going on?"

"Tell him," said Trefor. His anger spilled from his voice
and his eyes, and his face was flushed red with it. Whatever
Mike had done, he'd obviously screwed up in a way he
never had before.

"Tref—"

"Tell him!"

Mike cringed, and looked at Alex with pleading eyes.
Alex was unmoved. Trefor gave Mike a good poke on the

shoulder. Finally Mike said, "I'm the one who shot the arrow."

Alex was surprised to hear this, but only because he'd not expected a confession. He'd figured Mike had done it, and was content to keep an eye on him to catch him at it if he tried anything like it again. Alex's eyebrows went up, and he looked to Trefor for details. Trefor obliged.

"He says he thought I wanted it. He didn't like the way we were being treated, and figured I wanted you dead for it. This brain trust here," he gave Mike another hard shove for good measure, "thought I would be the next Earl of Cruachan if you died."

"How could I know you wouldn't get the title?" Mike whined and cringed, and it turned Alex's stomach.

"And *then*," continued Trefor, outraged, "he came to me to let me know what a loyal friend he is." Another shove, and Mike nearly stumbled to the ground. "Bragging about how close he came to killing my father."

"Tref—"

"Stop it," said Alex. This was very bad, and neither Trefor nor Mike could have an inkling of how bad. Trefor should have kept this to himself and never made public what Mike had told him. Knights were gathering, muttering amongst themselves about it, Hector among them, explaining in Middle English what was being said by the modern Americans. Alex wished Hector had been elsewhere, for he was boggled to know what he was about to have to do, and knew Trefor would hate him all the more for it.

Alex's voice was level. Firm. He reached down to the soles of his feet for all the authority he could muster. "You have no clue what a terrible mistake you've made. Both of you." He looked to Trefor, then back at Mike. "First in shooting the bolt, and then confessing to it. What you've done is treason against your liege and that can't be taken lightly."

Mike's face was still blank, puzzled at the uproar and annoyed at the treatment he was getting from Trefor, but a glimmer of realization crossed Trefor's eyes. He knew what treason truly meant. He let go of Mike and took a step back.

Alex said to Mike, "What that means, you moron, is that I now have to hang you."

Mike let go a laugh. "Right." But when neither Alex nor Trefor laughed with him his face went white. "Huh?"

"I can't let you live, knowing that you took a potshot at me, and everyone knowing that I know. Even though you missed, I can't let anyone here think I would let an assassin live."

"Do what?" Mike looked to Trefor for a denial, but Trefor said nothing and only pursed his lower lip in his tension.

Alex said, "I told you guys you don't know what you're into. I told you that things were different here, and that you needed to listen to me to survive." He tilted his face toward Mike's and stressed, "Never mind that I *want* to hang you, I have to and there's nothing any one of us can do about it."

"He's one of mine. I'll have it done."

"Trefor!" Mike's voice went high. Panicky.

"You dumb bastard!" Trefor looked like he might cry, but held it in. "Nobody told you to shoot him."

"I missed."

"Which only means you're a bad shot. He's right; he can't let you live, or someone else might get the idea they can get away with an attempt like that. That's the way they think around here. You brought this on yourself."

"But I didn't kill him! You can't hang me for just shooting at him!"

Alex said, "People get hung here for stealing chickens. They get burned at the stake for stuff that's perfectly legal in the States. And you didn't just shoot a crossbow bolt in the direction of your friend's father. What you did was commit treason against your liege, a member of the peerage. Lee Harvey Oswald's got nothing on you. Except, maybe, he was a better aim."

"Trefor, don't let him do this." Mike began gasping, heaving for air that wasn't going to help.

"Shut up, Mike." Trefor was going nearly as pale as Mike, and his voice was cracking. He lowered his voice to Alex. "Is there a possibility of letting him, you know, escape?"

Alex glanced around at the curious knights watching to see what Alex would do. It was far too late to fool anyone. "No."

Mike continued to gasp, and turned circles as if in search of a way out of this mess.

Trefor grabbed him by the scruff of his tunic, hauled him back around to face Alex, and said, "All right, then. I'll have one of my men find a tree."

"No!" Mike began to cry.

"I said shut up!"

"I'll do it," Alex said quietly. Mike sobbed, and Alex continued as Trefor stared at the ground. "I'll have Henry assign one of the servants to string a rope." Mike collapsed to his knees, weeping, and Trefor let him stay there.

"Sir Henry!" Alex shouted. "Front and center! We have a situation!"

Henry hurried to present himself, and stared at the weeping prisoner as he listened to Alex's orders. He didn't appear particularly surprised at those orders, and when the earl was done he hauled Mike to his feet and shoved him away to arrange for the execution.

Alex watched Henry take Trefor's friend to his horse, and two of Alex's men helped him lift Mike onto the animal's bare back. The condemned made a sudden move to leap from the horse and escape, but several swords zinged from their scabbards and kept him in place. Henry led the horse by its halter toward the tree where the rope was being strung. Mike continued to weep and plead for his life at full voice, calling for Trefor to make them stop.

Alex and Trefor brought up the rear of those gathering to observe, and stopped just short of joining them at the tree. Once the rope was around Mike's neck, snug against his jaw, Alex called for the attention of all present. Taking responsibility for the execution, he made a speech that detailed the crime and outlined the reasons for punishment.

He stressed that this would be the fate of anyone else who might harbor thoughts of treason, against himself or any liege, for breaking one's oath of loyalty was the worst sort of betrayal and a mortal sin before God.

He glanced over at Trefor once as he spoke, and saw his expression had gone blank. Though his face was bloodless, stark white in his horror, his features were arranged carefully and without expression, even as his friend cried out that he should not let them do this. Alex found himself respecting Trefor's resolve. The guy had guts, was carrying through with what they both knew had to be done, and in that moment Alex had a surge of pride that he was a MacNeil.

Alex concluded his speech with a request that God have mercy on Mike's soul, then nodded toward the appointed executioner. The servant whacked the horse across the backside with a teamster's whip, and the animal bolted. Mike, in his terror, held on with his knees so his neck snapped, and then it was all over. The body dangled and swung until the executioner put out a hand to steady it, and all gazed in silence.

Then the quiet was broken by the voice of one of Alex's knights. "Long live the Earl of Cruachan." It was repeated by the rest of Alex's men, then they dispersed.

Trefor remained, staring at the ground as a urine stain spread across the trews of the dangling body. Alex watched him for a moment, then turned to go to his tent. Ellot would deal with the body. Trefor would deal with the loss of his friend.

The next day Alex took his men over the rocky slopes in the direction their quarry had taken, and found the spot where the raiders had reentered the forest. Sign reappeared, and the trail was even more fresh than Alex had hoped. They were able to go faster now, and Alex sent scouts ahead to bring back reports of the terrain. He needed to know the area in which they would meet up with An Reubair.

At midday, the sun high overhead and shining down in

dappled patterns through the forest trees, a scout came galloping back with breathless announcement. "My lord! My
lord, I've found them!"

Alex halted his column to listen to the report. The scout
reined in to a halt, his mount prancing and turning as the
knight spoke excitedly to the earl.

"They've stopped ahead. Not far. And they gear themselves for battle."

"They're going to fight us?"

"Nae." The scout nearly giggled with the glee this
brought him. "'Tis another village beyond they seek. Just
as the one we've recently left, they intend to attack and
reive the livestock. They haven't any knowledge we are
here."

Alex nodded. "Good. How far is the village from them?"

The scout shrugged. His excitement waned as he realized the earl wasn't as pleased as anticipated by the news.
"I cannae say. I know aught but what I overheard from my
place of hiding. They've secured their train and are even
now donning their armor and weapons."

Alex grunted and looked off down the track. He didn't
like this. Though he had surprise on his side, it was of little
value since the raiders were gearing up for a fight with
someone else and wouldn't be caught as flat-footed as he
would want. He considered hanging back, waiting until
they'd exhausted themselves on the village before them. A
valid tactic on the surface, for it would save lives among
his own men, but his men weren't the only lives at stake
here. In the back of his mind he heard Lindsay condemn-
ing the deliberate sacrifice of noncombatants. He and his
men were in a position to keep An Reubair from destroying
another village that had no garrison, occupied by simple
farmers and their families armed with pitchforks and sick-
les. By his own standards, taught to him by his father and
the United States Naval Academy, he was required to attack before the raiders made their assault if he could, to
save the unprotected village.

Trefor, beside him, said, "You said no John Wayne."

Alex, too deep in thought, had forgotten his son was there. The voice startled him out of his pondering and he wondered if the wee folk had perhaps taught Trefor a bit of mind reading. The magical had always made Alex nervous, for not much good had ever come of it, and he wished he could know what was going on in Trefor's mind. He said, "What do you mean?"

"I mean, you should let them attack the village and then catch them while they're busy. Ride down on them once they've exhausted themselves going after a bunch of sheep and cows."

"And the people of the village?"

"Collateral. And, if you think about it, English collateral. You're so hot to align yourself with all that is Scottish, maybe you should take advantage of the opportunity to stick it to King Edward. Those villagers are his lookout, aren't they?" He shrugged. "Not yours, in any case."

There was a time when Alex might have made that same argument, but he was no longer so sure. Lindsay had often chastised him for fitting into the medieval mindset too easily, and these days he was beginning to wonder if she hadn't been right. Using unarmed noncombatants as bait or targets was sometimes unavoidable, but this did not qualify so clearly as necessary, nor would it be accidental if Alex held off attacking for the sake of softening up the enemy.

Then he imagined the scene if An Reubair were allowed to attack first. An undefended village wouldn't be much of a resistance force and probably wouldn't do so well at softening anyone. He then decided. "You heard the guy in that other village. He said his people ran, rather than fight. This village might not resist, and that would make waiting pointless."

"But they might. And at the very least we could catch the enemy while they're busy rounding up the livestock and torching houses."

"No. You don't understand these guys. They're armed and headed for a fight. If they don't get one, they'll be frustrated.

Even more ready than they are now. Waiting is pointless. We'll go now. Attack before they get there."

Trefor shrugged. "Suit yourself. Just trying to be helpful."

"Your counsel is appreciated, but I've decided otherwise. Now order your men to follow us." He watched Trefor move off to comply, then passed the same order to Henry for his own men. They spurred off down the track at a gallop, in twos.

As it turned out, the MacNeil force reached the attacking raiders at the same time they all reached the village. Alex looked ahead to find the first house going up in flames, and villagers running this way and that, children screaming, women shouting and wailing. They were familiar sounds. There were thuds of sword against pitchfork or spade, but resistance was weak and wouldn't last. Alex searched the melee for Lindsay, looking to the raiders for any sign of a woman. He feared finding her as much as he hoped for it, and a sense of relief came as his gaze went from one to another and he saw no wild hair or painted face. He shouted to his men to charge, drew his sword, and the column of knights swept down on the raiders.

Committed to his task, he plunged into the midst of the fray with little thought but to put away as many of the enemy as possible. He lay about himself with his sword, wheeling his mount in the nearly constant shift of the fight.

Then he heard the ululating noise described by the villager. High-pitched, eerie among the shouts and cries of men. It froze his heart. He abandoned the opponent before him, wheeled, and spurred away toward the sound, straining his ears and eyes to find the source, his pulse thudding in his veins.

Then Alex saw her. Lindsay, without a doubt. Black, wavy hair below her helm, circling around to swing her sword at a villager on foot, it was his wife. His heart leapt to his throat to choke him, but he spurred onward to intercept. He thundered in to put his horse between her and her quarry, and they clanged swords as he rode past.

Abandoning her original opponent she came after him,

and he wheeled to find her at him, harrying and crowding. She didn't seem to recognize him. She was looking straight at him and didn't know who he was. Her face was twisted in an ugly snarl, her eyes filled with a rage he recognized in men he'd faced in battle. She swung on him, and he went to parry but then merely dodged. She overbalanced, and as she began to lose her seat, he came down hard on the hilt of her sword to help her along to the ground.

The tactic worked, and she fell. "Lindsay!" he shouted, but she either didn't hear or didn't recognize his voice. Or else she knew who he was and wished him dead, for when her horse moved away she gained her feet and attempted to hamstring his mount. But the animal reared and twisted, and she was forced to back away. When his mount came again to all fours, Alex dismounted and slapped it out of his way as he turned to confront his opponent. Lindsay hauled back for attack, and he fended. "Lindsay! It's me!"

But she saw only an enemy she needed to kill before he would kill her. He'd taught her that. Could she see who he was? Did she attack him, or only a faceless enemy? She swung on him and he was forced to shove her back as he parried. If she kept this up, one of them was going to do damage, and it would likely be her, for he would never swing on her to hurt her. Not his own wife. Not even if he were certain she knew it was him she was trying to kill.

So he took a chance though he might die for it. He dropped his shield and yanked his helmet off to throw it on the ground. "Lindsay!"

Lindsay hauled back to come at him again, but then the light of recognition finally came. She froze. Amid the fighting, surrounded by cries of rage and pain and the clank of sword against armor, she stood with her sword raised but still. Her jaw dropped, and Alex waited to see whether she would greet him or kill him.

"Oh . . . my God!" Her sword lowered and she dropped her own shield to the ground. "Alex! Oh . . ." In an instant she flew to embrace him with her free arm, and he held her to him with his. Then she burst into tears and said his name

into his ear over and over. It was the most delightful sound
he'd ever heard. Relief flooded him, rushing into all the
corners of him so that he had to swallow hard not to be
choked himself.

"Lindsay, I—"

"Sir Lindsay!" The voice was a man Alex didn't recognize, and he looked up to find a blond knight riding at them
with sword raised. Alex swung his sword around to stave
off the oncoming assailant, and Lindsay did likewise. The
attacker reined in hard and his mount skidded to a stop before two raised blades. He looked from one to the other,
and roared with anger, "What is the meaning of this?"

"He's my husband, Reubair. I'm through here." She
reached behind to take Alex's free hand in hers.

Alex glanced at her, and a smile tugged at his face. Then
he returned his attention to An Reubair and frowned to let
the guy know they were both serious.

The faerie knight gaped at Lindsay, then at Alex, and his
eyes narrowed. Then he glared at Lindsay again, his cheeks
flushed with rage. And perhaps something else. Alex had a
sense he'd come in on the middle of something, and puzzled over what it could be. Reubair's mount danced with
the excitement of the battle around them, and he reined in
tight to control the horse. "You. The negligent husband."

"An Dubhar to you, and I'll show you what that means
if you give me any guff. Get the hell away. Take your men
and leave this village."

Reubair shook his head and seethed with the anger of
one scorned. Again Alex wondered what was going on here.

Reubair said to Lindsay, "You would abandon your
quest? Renege on your pledge to me?"

What pledge?

"He is my husband. Before God and the world."

The anger on Reubair's face told Alex the pledge had
been a personal one, and very important to the faerie
knight. Whatever had gone on between these two was a
puzzle, and even more puzzling that Lindsay was blowing
the guy off so easily.

"Get away from here, Reubair, or I'll kill you." Not "*Alex* will kill you." She was ready to do it herself. Alex chanced a glance over at her. She meant business. Her mouth was set, and her eyes dull. Serious. Alex knew if this guy offered any more argument she would attack him.

Apparently Reubair knew it, too. He gathered his wits and seemed to come to a decision, then turned from Lindsay and addressed Alex.

"You may take back your wife, but I'll have my plunder. Fight me for it, or take the woman and run. 'Tis your choice. But if you choose the livestock and leave her unprotected, I will kill her." With that he wheeled his horse and charged away, again to the fray.

Easy choice. "Come," yelled Alex to Lindsay over the noise around them. He sheathed his sword and pulled her with him. She came along without a word as he recaptured his horse by the reins and drew it around to mount. He threw his own leg over and pulled himself up, then reached down for her. She also threw a leg up, pulled herself over, and seated herself behind him. He kicked the mount to a canter, away from the fighting. When they came to where the support wagon had been left, he reined in and reached back to help her down. Once she was dismounted, he wheeled to return to the skirmish.

"Wait! Alex!"

He wheeled again, coming full circle. "What?"

"Where are you going?"

"To finish my job."

"You've no helmet and no shield!"

"I also have no choice!" His horse kept trying to turn toward the battle, and he had to rein it around to face her. It pranced with the excitement of its rider and the commotion in the village.

"You're just going to leave me here?"

Irritation rose, and he said, "Yes. You're going to stay put, and listen to me for once, while I go back to my men and order a retreat. The villagers have all run off, their houses are all on fire, and their livestock aren't worth my men getting killed, thankyouverymuch. I'm going to call them off. So have a seat, shut up, and I'll be back shortly." He shook his head. "Jeez, you have not changed!"

She waved him on, and he reined around again, spurring his horse back to the village.

Quickly he called a retreat and made certain all his and Trefor's men made it away from the village. None had been killed, but there were several wounded. It would be seen later whether any of those wounds were mortal, but for now it appeared there were no real casualties among the MacNeils. Alex watched from a distance as the reivers made off with the livestock from the village. It was a sour feeling, but not much of a defeat. He'd found Lindsay, and that would make up for a lot of sheep lost by a village that was English, after all. When the last of the stragglers had passed him on the trail, he turned to follow them to where Lindsay and their pages waited with the support wagons.

There he dismounted and let Gregor take his horse as he searched the milling men for Lindsay. He found her, also searching the crowd for him, and he hurried toward her. When she saw him her face lit up and she threw off her helmet. They came together in a shuss of chain mail and leather, his mouth on hers in a joyous kiss of reunion. He held her to him, wonderful to feel her breathing in his arms, hers tight around his shoulders, her tongue, her lips on his in a way the two of them hadn't had in what seemed forever. Perhaps it had been forever, for he knew how malleable time could be, and he'd never before missed her the way he had in this absence. He let go his mouth to breathe and pressed his cheek to hers. He murmured into her ear, "I thought I'd lost you."

"I was going to go back to you. Apparently I won't."

A puzzled frown came over him, and he peered at her. "Huh?"

"Apparently I won't make it back and greet you when you come to London."

"Came to London. That was months ago."

Tears filled her eyes. "I'm sorry. I should have waited."

He nodded. "Uh, yeah. You should have." Then he kissed her again and hoped she understood he didn't care about anything but that she was with him again. She kissed him in return, and he hoped she felt the same way.

Soon it became apparent the men around them were staring. Alex straightened and addressed the curious. "My wife. You guys remember my wife."

Recognition lit in the eyes of the men who had known Lindsay as Lady Marilyn MacNeil, and she curtsied to them in her ragged man's clothing and filthy armor. Others frowned at her in an understandable puzzlement, then they all bowed to her and went about their business relinquishing their weapons and shields to the wagons and remounting to move on to the night's camp. They dispersed to their column, leaving Trefor standing where he'd been all along, staring at Lindsay and looking like a puppy left out in the cold. Alex nearly groaned, for he'd forgotten he had an important introduction to make.

He kept his arm around Lindsay's shoulders and murmured into her ear. "There's someone you need to meet, hon." She looked at him, eyebrows raised, waiting for him to go on. "He's our son."

Joy washed over her face. "You found the baby! Oh, my God, Alex!" She threw her arms around his neck. "Oh, thank God, you found our baby!"

"No, I didn't, I'm afraid." He pulled her off his neck and held her arms, nearly afraid she might hit him when she learned his news. "He found me. And that's him over there."

A deep frown creased her face, and her eyes narrowed to slits. "I'm sorry, what?"

"That's our son, standing over there."

She looked over at Trefor, whose expression suddenly turned as bland as Alex had ever seen. He betrayed nothing of what he felt, though Alex knew he must be seething, in agony to know what would happen next. Alex prayed she would take it well.

The reply to that prayer was "no." In fact, it was "no

way." Lindsay gaped at Trefor, then peered at Alex. "You're not serious."

"His name is Trefor. He came to me soon after I arrived here. Says faeries took him to the U.S. until he was twenty-seven, then sent him to Eilean Aonarach. He arrived a few days after I did."

Trefor said nothing and was as still as the trees around them.

"That *man*?" Lindsay shook her head. "That man says he's our son? No." She looked at Alex. "No, that is not my baby." Then her face crumpled into tears. "No, it can't be him. Tell him to go away. He's not my son; he can't be." With that she spun and retreated to the wagon where Gregor and the driver waited for the order to move on. She climbed onto the tarp covering it, and sat, waiting. A dark look at Alex told him she wasn't going to discuss the matter any further.

Trefor watched her retreat, his face still impassive except for a knot of muscle that stood out on his jaw. Alex couldn't see the pain he knew must be there.

Lindsay, perched on the wagon, laid her face in her palms. Her shoulders shook with sobs.

Alex watched Trefor return to his men, sauntering with insouciance for all he was worth, and sighed.

CHAPTER 17

The MacNeils retreated the way they'd come, letting An Reubair go the other direction. Alex glanced back frequently to his support wagons to check on Lindsay perched on the wooden seat next to the driver, but her expression seemed unchanged. He never found her looking at him, nor at Trefor. She wasn't talking to anyone, not Gregor, not the driver, not anyone, but only stared off to the left at the forest passing slowly by, a blank look on her face. Unreadable except for its very lack of emotion. Just like Trefor. Eerily like Trefor, for it brought home exactly how much he was like them both.

The column proceeded to a spot near the forest edge where the trees thinned some amid the beginnings of the rocky expanse they'd passed. There they stopped for the night. Alex supervised the encampment, and once his men were settled, pickets posted, and the company was on their way to being fed, he went to his tent to discard his armor and clean up for supper.

There he found Lindsay already cleaning up, stripped to the waist and tugging at wet hair with his comb. She wore filthy, worn trews, and a ragged, overstretched elastic bandage around her chest. She'd lost weight and seemed skinny to him. The last time he'd seen her she'd been heavy with the pregnancy, plump and healthy, her cheeks bright with roses and a smile on her face in anticipation of the birth. Life since then had plainly taken far more from her than just the baby. Muscles rippled across her shoulders and arms, and her waist was long and terribly narrow. Her trews hung low by their belt from her hips and appeared nearly ready to fall to the ground. The odd thought crossed his mind he should be glad he'd found her before she lost so much weight she disappeared entirely.

The faded and warped bandage, not as elastic as it had once been, was wrapped around her breasts and the ends tied around her neck to hold up her chest rather than hide it. No longer was she pressing her breasts flat and letting her shoulders slouch forward, and in a way he was glad, for he'd always hated that. He wondered how she'd managed to come out as a woman to the men in her raiding party. It could be she never had disguised herself, but that didn't make sense. She'd always been too paranoid about having to live like the other women in this time. She'd always preferred to take the abuse doled out to small, effeminate men rather than give up the freedom accorded to males.

For the moment, he put all that from his mind; he could think about it later. Now his wife was back with him, willingly it would seem, and he was glad. Ecstatic.

No, he was relieved. Only then did he realize how convinced he'd been she'd gone away with Nemed. That, also, he put from his mind, sorry he'd even thought it. He came up behind her and gently took the comb from her hand.

"Let me," he said softly. She relinquished the comb, and he began picking tangles from the long hair she'd just washed in his leathern bowl. The water was so filthy gray he couldn't see the bottom.

She said, "I kept dirty because I didn't want anyone to think I was fussy and effeminate."

"You don't need to explain. That's probably why they keep dirty, too."

She chuckled and nodded, and held still for him while he smoothed her tangles.

Once he was done combing out her hair, he picked up the linen cloth from the camp table, wet it, and began washing her. She shivered under the cold water, but otherwise held still as he ran the cloth over her smooth shoulders. He untied the knot at the back of her neck, and she removed the bandage so he would clean further. Then she dropped her trews and stepped out of them, leaving herself entirely naked. He kissed her wet neck, and she leaned into him as his cloth moved down her belly to her thighs. Her skin was as filthy as her clothes, and the water in the bowl grew darker as he went. He kissed each place on her as it became clean, soon kneeling behind her, then before her, and he ended by kissing her feet with heart-lifting reverence.

Then he stood to draw her toward his pallet, and she helped him off with his mail, tunic, boots, trews, and drawers. She kissed him as they lay atop his blankets, and he lost himself in the softness of her lips and tongue as she went to straddle him, then envelope him.

A long sigh escaped him and his sense of time and place disappeared. His world existed entirely within Lindsay. It had been so long, and he'd not realized it until now. The need to finish quickly was nearly unbearable; his mind crumbled, and he tried to roll her beneath him. But she resisted and pressed her palms to his arms to make him stay put. He groaned, then gasped as she moved hard against him. Then again. She began to slam against him, insistent, hard, thrusting with her hips the way he might have done her. Her belly flat against his, her muscles rippling against him, her breaths came in short puffs against his chest. She voiced them. Panting. Feral. Insistent. Faster now, and his head swam as she slammed against him and she tightened over him. His hips wanted to move, and they twitched against her, but she held him and made him keep still until a terrible shudder came over her and she uttered a cry, long and desperate. Sounding like pain.

Then she let go of his arms, he held her about the waist, and he finished in a few quick, satisfying movements. His body felt as if it were melted with hers, and he thought how impoverished were men like James and Hector, who did not love their wives. For the first time since returning to his ship, he felt whole.

She lay atop him, gasping for breath, and he held her there to feel her body still surrounding his, warm and damp and still a part of him he'd missed so terribly. He hugged her to him and murmured, "That was . . . interesting."

There was no reply. Then he realized she was holding her breath, and a moment later she let go an enormous sob. His heart fell, and he stroked her hair away from her face.

"What's the matter? It couldn't have been that bad."

She shook her head. He rolled her from him to lie beside him on the pallet, and gathered her into the hollow of his body. There she curled against his belly, her face pressed to his chest and her knees to his hip.

"Then what's wrong? What did I miss?"

It was a long wait for an answer, but he let her think for as long as she needed. He wasn't going to press her for her feelings about Trefor; he wasn't even sure how he felt about the guy, and he'd had months to figure it out. He couldn't expect her to have a handle on the whole mess so soon.

But when her reply came, it took him flat-footed. Her voice was low and flat, stripped of the feeling it should have had, and so quiet he could hear her tongue on her teeth. "You need to know I was raped."

It was like being knocked sideways with a mace. Half a dozen thoughts and emotions swarmed over him. Rage. Grief. Curiosity. Who had done it? Why? When? Could she be pregnant? It took him several moments to sort through his reaction and cobble together a coherent reply. Finally he was able to say, "I expect he's dead."

She nodded, and that calmed him somewhat. Then came

disappointment he wasn't going to be able to kill the guy himself.

She said, "Is that all you have to say?"

No. But it was all that came to mind he dared utter just then.

She asked, "How did you know he was dead?"

"Because you aren't. I know you well enough to know you must have fought him. If you were unsuccessful in stopping the assault, and he left you alive, you still wouldn't have let him go. I don't expect he lasted much longer than it took you to climb to your feet and tie up your trews. Am I right?"

"I stopped to eat first."

"Ah. Well, I guess if you were hungry that was the thing to do."

"It was a fair fight."

"Of course it was." He thought over his next words for another long moment. He could only hope for her to answer "Yes," but didn't expect it. He ventured, "Nemed?"

She tensed for a moment and looked up at him, then pressed her face to his chest again. "No. One of the reivers. Once they let me up, I went after him. Cut off his prick and balls, and threw the entire set into the fire."

Alex gasped. "Ow." His own testicles tried to climb up into his body and a nervous laugh rose, but he swallowed it. This wasn't a matter for laughter. He asked, "How long ago?"

"I'm not pregnant."

He wasn't sure how to answer that, for what he really wanted to know was how long she'd been dealing with this, but he managed, "Good."

The sobbing resumed and her tears wet his chest. The thing he wanted to ask now was whether she would be all right, but he didn't think he'd get an accurate reply on that soon. So he held her and let her cry for a bit, until the sobbing stopped and she began to wipe her eyes.

"I'm sorry. I don't mean to be a weenie."

Alex had to chuckle at that, and murmured, "Big day.

Lots to take in. I'm just glad you're here, and you can cry all you want." He wasn't all that far from tears himself, and kissed her head to keep himself from them.

"More to take in than you think," she said. "There's something else I need to tell you." She wiped her eyes and looked up at him again, and he tensed to know what the other news could be. "Apparently there's a góod possibility I'm one of the Danann."

Alex relaxed. "Oh. I knew that."

"How?"

He chuckled. "I've seen Trefor. He's my son, and I'm pretty sure I didn't give him those ears." For a brief moment he hoped she would take the opening to talk about Trefor, but she didn't. There was only silence, and he took heart in that she'd told him about her ancestry. "You didn't know?"

She shook her head. "Not a clue. Not until it was pointed out to me. I'm still not sure. I'm not certain I care for it either."

A smile touched Alex's mouth as he remembered there was something happy he could tell her. "Would it help to know you're a countess now?"

She rubbed one eye with the heel of her hand, and mumbled with a wet, swollen mouth, "Pardon?"

"Robert made me an earl. Faerie or not, you're now the Countess of Cruachan."

She leaned back to look him in the face as if she were checking to see whether he might be kidding.

"Seriously. I've got the letter of patent in my saddle bag if you want to see it."

"It's real?"

"Signed, sealed, and presented to me by Sir James Douglas in front of witnesses. Solid gold credibility."

"That's . . . wonderful."

"You don't sound pleased."

Her words stuttered and stumbled, and he had to wonder why. "I . . . well, I am. I'm . . . surprised . . . well, shocked, actually."

"Yeah. I'm probably the only American who will ever receive this honor except by inheritance. That must annoy you no end."

"No, that's not it. They think you're Hungarian."

"They think I'm Hector MacNeil's illegitimate half brother, son of the previous Laird of Barra, and I'm as Scottish as anyone else. My ostensible Hungarian mother has nothing to do with anything."

She made a small sound of agreement and finished wiping her eyes dry. "I suppose not."

Gregor blew through the tent flap, made a cursory obeisance, then returned to his feet and said, "My lord and lady, supper is ready. Shall I bring it?"

"Yes," said Alex, and sat up on the edge of the pallet as Gregor hurried away on the errand.

Lindsay sighed. "I'm never going to get used to the lack of privacy here.

Alex chuckled and rose up just enough to peel the top blanket from his bed and from under her, then draped it around her shoulders. "There. We'll get you some new clothes as soon as we can." He pointed with his chin to the pile next to the camp table. "Those rags are going on the fire."

She snuggled into the blanket, gave him a wan smile, and kissed him.

The next morning as the company prepared to move onward in their patrol, Trefor was nowhere to be seen. Though his men were still with the company, Trefor and Morag had made themselves scarce. Alex sat his horse as the company gathered, Lindsay by his side, astride one of his rounseys, glanced around for their AWOL son. Though her helmet and sword were with his in the wagon, she wore her chain mail over his spare linens, trews, and tunic. They waited, and it looked as if they might have to leave Trefor and Morag behind. Alex's feelings about that were mixed. It almost felt like a problem solved.

"Hector!" Alex called out. Hector, seated on his horse, looked over at him. "Where's Trefor?"

Hector glanced in the direction of the forest and shrugged. "I noticed him and his lady friend off in that direction not long ago."

Alex whistled to one of Trefor's men. "Go get your master. Tell him we've got better things to do than wait for him to finish playing patty-fingers with his girlfriend."

The knight gave him a sour look, but nevertheless said, "Aye, my lord," and tugged his reins to comply. But he pulled up as two figures emerged from the trees, Trefor and Morag, his arm around her shoulders. And though he stood straight, he also appeared to be leaning some considerable weight on her. Her tiny stature didn't lend itself to the task, and she stumbled a little. Trefor's face was deathly pale and clammy. At this distance his mouth seemed to have disappeared, for it was nearly as white as the rest of his face and pressed closed as if he feared vomiting.

"You all right?" called Alex.

"I'm fine. Let's go." He reached his horse and with care and enormous effort pulled himself up to mount. Then Morag mounted her own horse. Trefor sagged for a moment, then sat straight again in his saddle. "Let's go," he repeated.

"All right." Alex wasn't so sure, but they needed to proceed and Trefor's problem had to wait. They were headed to rejoin Sir James and would take some time finding the army.

But as luck would have it, a messenger from James found them before they got very far. That very afternoon as they reached the place where they would encamp for the night, one of James' squires found them and was escorted to where Alex sat his horse to oversee the work. The squire handed over a travel-worn packet of paper, then hung back to await orders regarding a reply. Alex unfolded the message and began deciphering James' horrible, medieval scrawl. Bad enough that the theory of penmanship was these days held only by monks who copied books, but the creative spelling and bizarre orthography of the times made messages such as this nearly as indecipherable as secret code for Alex. He frowned in concentration as he read.

Near as he could figure, James meant to tell him he was throwing in the towel in the south for the time being and heading back to Stirling for a while. This late in the summer, that probably meant he would winter there and venture south again next spring. The letter went on to release the MacNeils from service. They were to return to Eilean Aonarach until Robert would need them again.

Good. Alex had fully intended to return to James' army and continue fighting for the remainder of the summer, but was just as glad at this juncture to be able to go home and regroup. Not just to reorganize himself in his earldom and establish his authority over Cruachan, but perhaps also to work out some personal issues.

He looked over at Lindsay. There was a lot to work out.

Quickly he gave his brief reply of acknowledgment to James' messenger. As the rider moved off again on his mission, Alex noticed Trefor among his men overseeing his own encampment from horseback. He still looked ill. Recovering, but pale and slouching. His eyes closed as if resting for a moment, then he opened them to gaze off toward the forest. Alex wondered if he'd had a drinking binge the night before, but that didn't sound much like Trefor. The guy hated mead, there wasn't a great deal of wine to be had just then, whiskey didn't exist yet, and he'd always been able to hold his alcohol in any case. It would have taken a buttload of drink to make him this sick.

Then it clicked. *Luck.* It had been lucky the runner had found them, particularly on this very day. It had also been lucky the message brought by the runner was a release from James. They were now able to go home, which surely was where Trefor wanted to be. Trefor was sick because he'd been busy bringing Alex luck. Now Alex wondered how this was going to come back and bite him in the ass. He was pretty sure he didn't like Trefor messing with his karma, and wished he'd stop.

Alex walked his horse over toward Trefor and sidled close to speak in a low voice. "Okay, Mr. Luckybritches, nice work this morning. So how come you didn't just do your woo-woo stuff and have us accidentally find your mother instead of giving me all that crap about it?"

Trefor went sullen and glanced sideways at him. "Are you high? It damn near killed me to have you be found right away by a courier that was already looking for you. Finding Mom would have been a way bigger deal. That just wasn't within my power. Hell, if I could do stuff like that, I'd have stayed in the twenty-first century and gone to work for Donald Trump."

"How did you know there was a courier?"

"Morag."

"And she had nothing to do with James suddenly changing his plan?"

"No."

"Not that she's admitting, anyway."

"That, too. Besides," Trefor regarded Alex with the irritation that was beginning to seem habitual when talking to his father, "I wanted you to want to find her. It's my opinion you should have dropped everything the instant you knew she'd gone missing, and gone in search of her."

"You don't think I did exactly that?"

Trefor's face reddened with anger. "I know you didn't. I watched you out here, traipsing around with James like you were on vacation. The Plunder Tour of Northern England. Breakfast included with the room."

"That's hardly fair. I told you why I had to come south. Not to mention that if we hadn't come south—"

"But you weren't looking for *her*. And I wonder whether you have told her that yet."

Alex went silent. For one fleeting instant he wished to put his dagger through his son's throat, and his fingers even twitched to do it. The thought fled before a surge of shame, and he said, "She won't believe you."

"More's the pity for her having such faith in you."

"When we found her I was looking for her."

"Big deal. Have you told her you thought Nemed was my father?"

"Who are you, my marriage counselor?"

Trefor only gazed blandly at him.

When no reply came, Alex said, "We have some talking left to do."

"Talk fast. She needs to know this stuff."

"As I said, she won't believe you. You heard her; she doesn't believe you're her son. She can't get past the fact that you're not a baby."

Trefor's eyes darkened and glistened, and he looked away for a moment. Then he said in a constricted voice, "She's my mother, and the only one I'll ever have. I'm pretty much stuck with her."

"She's no more than a couple of years older than you, and unlike myself she was there when you were born. She saw you as a baby. She held you. You were a couple of days old when you were taken, so she undoubtedly nursed you. I don't think she's going to let go of that as easily as I did." Or as easily as he pretended to.

"She's got to."

"She might, but I'm not going to make her. She's my wife, and under my protection. I won't let you make her miserable."

"So I get to be miserable instead."

"Okay, who's the one wrapped up in his own needs? Now hear this, little man, you say anything to upset her, and I'll come after you. You say 'boo' to her, or approach her when she's not ready to see you, you'll answer to me. Got it?"

Trefor was silent for a long moment, fuming, his breathing hard and shallow. Then he said through his teeth, "Kiss my ass."

Alex said blandly, "Unlikely." With that, he spurred his horse to return to his own men and Lindsay.

All the way back to Eilean Aonarach, Lindsay avoided Trefor. If he hung to the front of the column, she reined in and fell back. If he came around the cook fire in front of the tent she shared with Alex at night, she withdrew and tied the flap closed tight enough so that Alex had a bitch of a time untying it later.

Over the course of the trip Alex talked to her about Trefor's life in foster care and how the future Morag had sent him to the past. She listened, but though she eventually accepted on principle Trefor was who he said he was, she nevertheless refused to treat him as her son. If Alex tried to get her to talk to him, she shut down and withdrew from him as well. Suddenly and thoroughly, as if he'd pushed a button. An "off" switch. He'd never encountered such a thing and had no clue how to deal with it. So he let her alone about Trefor and encouraged her to talk about her time with the raiders.

At night, with the camp quiet and the cook fires banked, they lay together on the pallet in their tent and whispered to each other. Under a full moon the fabric of the tent overhead glowed a dull gray and items inside were black silhouettes. Lindsay's head on his shoulder was dark on dark, but he could see her expression well enough for a serious talk.

"Lindsay, can I ask you some stuff?"

She nodded. She probably knew what was on his mind. Part of it, anyway.

"That blond guy who came up to us during the fight . . ."

"Reubair? He's a faerie, you know. You couldn't see it for his helmet, but he's one. There were several. All Danann."

"Yeah, I know. But . . ." Another question occurred, and he asked, "Hey, was the guy you killed one of the Danann?"

"No. He was human. Sort of. Mortal, at least."

"Why did he do it?"

Alex could feel her tense under his arm, and he knew he'd made a misstep. "You think I gave him a reason?"

"All right, let me rephrase. What, exactly, precipitated this particular exchange of rape and death?"

"He found out I wasn't a man, and took exception to it."

"Ah. You've said that's what would happen if you were discovered."

"And it did. I made him regret it with all his heart and soul, and the others were given to understand his behavior was unacceptable. End of story."

"All right."

"Anything else you need to know?"

A great many things. Alex returned to his original query. "What did that Reubair guy mean when he said 'negligent husband'? What had you told him about me?"

"I told him your name."

Just his name. "I have a reputation for negligence?"

"Reubair thinks you are. Not that I give a damn what he thinks."

"He said your leaving was your choice. And he sounded like he thought you were wrong in making it. Actually, he sounded like a jilted lover." The offended tone in the faerie's voice haunted him, and his imagination took flight with thoughts he struggled to rein in. Reubair had spoken of a "pledge," and that niggled at Alex. His fingers fiddled with a lock of hair against her forehead and he hoped for a denial.

She leaned back to regard his face in the darkness, then sighed, frustrated. "Is that what you think? That I was banging him?"

"Were you?"

"No! And I'm appalled you could think I ever would! I'm married to you, and I don't fool around with other men! I mean . . . do you sleep with other women? 'Cause if you have that little faith in the vows we took—twice—then perhaps there's been a terrible misunderstanding and—"

"I'm sorry. I just couldn't be certain."

"Why not?"

"I just . . ." There was no reply to make that didn't betray his insecurity. Then he realized he'd already blown any pretense of confidence. *Screw it.* He said, "I couldn't figure out why you left London."

"To find the baby." It was her "of course" voice.

"I couldn't be certain of that."

"Again, why not?"

"The photo. I saw the photograph of Trefor. With the ears."

"But you said our neighbor told you where I was."

"He told me the baby had been abducted and you left. I

didn't know what to believe. I saw the ears, and that was even more confusing. I knew he didn't get those ears from anyone human."

"And where did you think he got them?" Her voice went dark. Ominous. "Just exactly where did you think they came from, Alex?"

Alex hesitated long before answering, knowing how she was sure to react to this, then said, "Who do we know—did we know at the time—who has ears like that?"

"Nemed?" She sat up. "You thought *Nemed* was his father?"

"What was I supposed to believe?"

A snort of exasperation erupted from her. "Well, that's just it." She threw off the blankets. "That's just the very end of it."

Alex grabbed her arm before she could rise from the pallet. "Stop that. There's no other bed for you to go to, and it's too bloody cold out there for you to be huddling by a dead fire. Stay here."

She stayed, but continued. "Shame on you, Alex Mac-Neil, for thinking that!"

"All right. Shame on me. I'm sorry. I knew I was wrong when Trefor came to Eilean Aonarach and I saw his face. He's the image of my brother, Carl."

Lindsay seemed to deflate. "He is?"

"Yeah. For a moment when I first saw him, I thought he was Carl. It was spooky."

A silence fell, for Lindsay never liked to discuss the grown-up Trefor. Then she said, "Nemed is the one who told me I'm descended from the Danann."

"All right."

"You know Reubair works for Nemed."

"I do."

"I see."

"But you weren't with Reubair. Or Nemed."

"No. Reubair wanted me to marry him. I declined."

Alex chuckled. "You cut off a guy's balls and then got a proposal of marriage? Is he nuts?"

She chuckled at that also. "I think so. He thought I needed protection from the men and offered it in exchange for my making babies for him. I put him off."

"Because you were already married, or because you didn't want him?"

"Both. He was insistent, though. Rather full of himself as well."

"As faeries often are. You guys are the most stubborn creatures I've ever met."

"I'm not a faerie."

"Your son is. Magic and everything."

She turned away, and though she shivered in the cold she didn't come back under the blankets. "Let's not talk about him."

"We've got to eventually. We can't just ignore the elephant in the kitchen."

"I can't address that man out there." She looked over at the tent flap and gestured to it as if Trefor were standing outside the tent. "I can't accept that my baby doesn't exist anymore. It's like he's died." Tears rose to choke her, and her voice trailed off, high and weak.

"He's grown up, not dead."

"He's not . . ." She held her hands out, grasping at air as if trying to cradle a baby and failing. "He's not my child. He's a stranger. He's . . . for God's sake, he's only a year younger than I am. Every time he looks at me I can't imagine what's going through his mind. I don't want to imagine."

"He doesn't think of you that way. I know he doesn't. He wants you to be his mother."

"I can't. I don't know how. I never got to learn."

Alex would have liked to have told her it was instinct, but he knew it wasn't. Not for them. Instinct needed a child, and Trefor had never been one for them. Learning needed time, and that had been stolen from them. Nevertheless, he told her, "You'll learn."

"I'm not even thirty years old yet. I'm too young to have an adult son."

"So you've got plenty of time to figure it out."

"He doesn't."

Alex knew she was right. Trefor's childhood was gone, and with them both having left the twenty-first century it was irretrievable. "You're right. And you know what, that's something a mom would know."

For a moment there was silence, then came a snuffling. She laid her palms over her face and began to sob.

"Come," he said, and took her arm to draw her back onto the bed. "Come back and sleep. It'll be all right."

Lindsay lay back down, once again in the shelter of Alex's body, and he pulled the blankets back over them to get warm while she cried herself out. He had no clue whether anything would ever be all right, but for now he could only comfort her as best he might, then they both would let the issue dissolve for a while in the forgetfulness of slumber.

CHAPTER 18

On departure for the islands by boat from Oban, Hector returned to Barra, and Alex, Lindsay, and Trefor made their landing on Eilean Aonarach. Alex was eager to re-equip and reprovision for the trip to Cruachan, and curious what he would find there. While his boats were being unloaded at the quay, Alex summoned men from the village for a consultation. The messenger flew to his task, for the earl expressed a desire for Donnchadh and Alasdair Ruadh to report on the double. Lindsay disappeared with her servants into the laird's apartments beyond the meeting room to clean up and find something appropriate to wear in public as Lady Marilyn MacNeil, Countess of Cruachan. Alex supervised the unloading for a while, then went to his meeting with the village leaders.

In the room below the Great Hall in the castle keep Alex parked himself at the head of the large, highly polished table. A couple of tapestries hung on the walls, but those, the table, and the chairs were the only furnishing other than the thick layer of rushes on the floor. The floor covering was changed far more often than was usual in other castles, for though

Alex had become accustomed to rank odors he couldn't abide the health hazards of food waste thrown on floors and animal leavings left to be taken up with the old rushes. Dogs in his castle were trained to go outside, but the knights and servants who lived there resisted being trained not to throw bones and rinds on the floor. Today he looked around the poorly furnished room and realized he was going to have to fix it up. Now that he was an earl, there would be visits from people he would need to impress just to keep this place. It would be costly. He hoped the new island would bring good income.

Donnchadh MacConnell and his cousin Alasdair Ruadh MacConnell, having been apprised of their laird's recent elevation, made obeisance to Alex and then were invited to sit at the table. They settled into chairs of varying style and richness. Neither had rank or office that was acknowledged by the crown, but Alex recognized them as community leaders. He looked to them to know the minds of his vassals the same way he'd always tapped certain crewmen to know what was going on with the enlisted guys on shipboard. Knowledge was power.

Donnchadh was a tall, burly man, dark of hair and ruddy of face, who commanded a room with his size and resonant voice, but who also knew the value of a soft tread in the presence of his superiors. Alasdair Ruadh was in most ways opposite his cousin, being painfully skinny, red haired, and casual in manner. He was the village blacksmith and plainly knew the value of his skills, for he drove a hard bargain in all things. Alex kicked back in his large, heavy seat and requested Gregor to bring refreshment. The boy hurried away on his errand.

Donnchadh appeared a bit nervous, hesitant to speak, and Alex guessed he was hanging back to learn what sort of earl Alex would be. Alasdair leaned heavily on the table in an insouciant manner Alex knew meant he didn't give a damn whether Alex had become king.

"Cruachan," said Alex, and proceeded in Gaelic for, like most of the island inhabitants, Alasdair Ruadh spoke no English. "What do you guys know about it?"

Donnchadh smiled. "All that might be worth knowing, I think. My sister married away to the place."

That surprised Alex. "I never knew you had a sister."

"Three of them, two still living. One lives with her husband on the mainland, and the younger on Cruachan with her husband, who is a MacDonald." A steaming platter of meat arrived, rare and bleeding for it was early yet in the day, accompanied by a jug of mead. The men set to the repast without formality, and Alex found himself more hungry than he'd thought. The food tasted wonderful, having been seasoned from his kitchen rather than his supply wagon.

"MacConnells living there?" he ventured with a cheek full of meat.

"MacDonalds mostly. Some MacConnells, who are related to the Dhomhnallach and so traditionally side with them. Some MacNeils and lesser families, but the MacDonalds hold sway there, I think."

"Who lays claim to the island?"

"Yourself, my lord."

Alex chuckled. "I mean, who thinks they have a right to it besides me? There's always someone." Donnchadh and Alasdair Ruadh both chuckled heartily, for it was true. There was very little land anywhere in Scotland that wasn't disputed by someone.

The door behind him from the private apartments opened and he turned to watch Lindsay emerge. She'd cleaned up and now wore a fine, gray dress that showed off her figure. It was a bit loose on her for the weight she'd lost since last she'd worn it, but it still draped over her hips in a way that made him not want to ever look away. He stared, and wished Donnchadh and Alasdair Ruadh could be sent away and he would take her there on the table. But there was more important business at hand, and he forced his attention to it.

Donnchadh was thinking about Alex's question, then said, "I believe ye might have some trouble from the MacDonalds. They can be a mean, grasping lot, and surely did not take kindly when Robert laid claim to the place after the battle near Stirling."

"He didn't take it directly from them. Someone else had it."

"But neither did he give it back to them. The MacDonald felt he should have."

"But Robert didn't install another laird right away?"

Lindsay approached to occupy one of the chairs at the table. Donnchadh and Alasdair Ruadh fell silent. Alex said to her, "What?"

"Go on. I'm listening," she said.

Alex lowered his chin and hoped she would take the hint she should move along. He figured he knew what she was up to, and wished she would leave it alone. The men he had to deal with would not be comfortable with her around in a meeting like this. He knew she knew it, and he also knew she knew he knew it. She was neither stupid nor ignorant of the situation with these men and their culture. Particularly among these island Scots whose wives were barefoot and pregnant as a matter of course, and it was not a joke. Nor even an issue, for all the clansmen and their kin for hundreds of miles around took it as the natural way of the world.

But she only smiled at him and said, "Go on. You were saying about the families living on Cruachan. The ones who are getting a new master, and you want to know if you're going to have to evict any of them."

"I'm hoping not to have to."

"You hoped not to have to purge this island of Bretons, but when their allegiance to the MacLeods outweighed in their hearts their lawful obligation to you, it came to a fight. Now we need to know whether there will be a fight when we take our men to Cruachan." She turned to Donnchadh and asked, "Is there a castle?"

We? Alex now frowned at Lindsay, but she ignored him. *Our* men?

Donnchadh looked at her, then at Alex as if to inquire whether he was supposed to answer his Lady Cruachan's

query. Alex wished Lindsay would knock it off and leave
the room, but she pretended she didn't know she was making the villagers uncomfortable. Alex nodded to Donnchadh, who shook his head and replied to Lindsay. "Nae,
my lady, naught but a wee tower. A small keep on a bit of
rock but a furlong offshore. The place is quite wild, and the
population small."

Alex's hope of a large income from the place faded.

Lindsay continued her questioning. "Do the various
families fight amongst themselves?"

Donnchadh shrugged. "Nae. The families there have
their separate allegiances, but have lived more or less in
peace and in the interim since Robert's victory I've heard
of no outbreaks. With the MacDonalds so numerous, the
rest more than likely saw no use in making trouble. It's
cowed they are. I daresay, though, they'll be glad to have
the matter of their tribute settled. Hard to know who to
welcome when the crown is yet uneasy on the king's brow."

Alex had to grunt in agreement to that, and Alasdair Ruadh nodded.

"Are there any young men on Eilean Aonarach waiting
to marry for lack of a living?" asked the earl.

Donnchadh nodded. "Aye. Three of them."

"Four," said Alasdair Ruadh. "Brian's youngest son will
be fifteen soon, and has his eye on my daughter."

"Does he?" Donnchadh's eyebrows rose at this news.

"Indeed, and he's a good lad. I would be glad to see
them both in a new tenancy."

"You'd see them off to Cruachan? Brian being a MacNeil
and all, his son willnae be so welcomed by the MacDonalds."

"They'd prosper."

"And they wouldnae here?"

"There's room for them on Cruachan, and the earl will
make certain of peace from the MacDonalds there." He
nodded toward Alex as if to affirm his words.

Donnchadh looked to Alex, who said, "We'll work it
out. Everybody will have what they need."

Lindsay threw him a look, and he ignored it. He knew

someone was going to balk and cause problems or choose
the wrong side at one point or another. He would deal
with those things as they came. Meanwhile he needed to
assure these men—and the village they would report back
to at that evening's *céilidh*—that he had a handle on the
situation. He would do that with a lie if necessary.

"In any case," said Alex, "I'll need to take more than
just my knights with me when we go to Cruachan. You two
tell the villagers I want fifty volunteers to accompany me
as pikemen and archers. Fifty. Don't make me come draft
people."

Donnchadh and Alasdair Ruadh both laughed, and Donnchadh said, "Have no fear, my lord, for your village is filled
with men willing to fight for that land. Particularly the Mac-
Neils, who have long felt the place belonged to them."

Alex nodded, then called for pen and paper to have the
MacConnells draw a map of the island for him. There they
pored over the thing, talking into the afternoon of the lay
of the land, its features and resources, and the placements
of farm houses. Lindsay had the good grace to keep quiet
now, but did not leave the room and listened closely to all
that was said.

After the meeting, once the plate of beef had been demol-
ished, the jug of mead emptied, and the geography of Cruachan firmly embedded in Alex's memory, he and Lindsay
retired to their quarters and some privacy. Gregor poured
boiling water into the tub he'd prepared for his master, then
Alex dismissed Gregor and Mary to have his bath and a
talk with his wife. He began to strip, and his surcoat went
onto the floor. Lindsay lounged in a chair by the fire, her
legs crossed and one slippered toe poking from beneath
her dress hem.

"Don't do that again, Lindsay."

"Do what?"

"What you just did. Out there." He unbuckled his belt,
which also dropped to the floor, and he began to untie the
closure of his tunic. "Don't interfere in my business. I
know you want to live like—"

"Don't presume to know what I want. You've no idea, because you haven't asked."

The tunic came off and he tossed it onto the bed, and he gazed at her a moment, wondering what bug had crawled up her butt that she was suddenly so irritable. But he went on. "You're used to the way things were in London. In the future. It can't be like that here." His linen shirt came off over his head and he let it drop to the floor atop his surcoat.

"Of course not. It's not the same for you here either. The difference between us being that you're now a Scottish peer and I'm a bit of chattel."

"Don't start that."

"Don't pretend it's not true."

"It's not. You're my wife. And you're a countess. That's got to be a step up from writing human interest articles for the *London Times*."

"What I do in this castle is supervise servants who know their jobs better than I do. They come to me for orders, and I have to ask them what they usually do. Then I order them to do that. I daresay they think I'm fairly stupid. That's not even a step up from what I was doing for An Reubair."

Alex was disgusted to hear the faerie's name. "You'd rather be a man than a woman."

"No, I hated pretending to be a man. I hated the posturing and dominance games. You fellows can be unutterably silly with all that, you know, and I rather prefer not having to beat people up just to get their attention. I especially hated having to deny my anatomy. I mean, so what if I have to put a cloth into my drawers a few days a month? So what if I pee sitting down? What I liked was to be taken seriously. To be listened to and not ignored or condescended to. What I liked was to be included in the life going on around me. To have a voice in what would happen, particularly when it affected me. Is it too much to ask to be able to determine my life *and* get laid on occasion?"

"You have that."

"No, I do not." Anger began to redden her ears and neck, and the hard edge in her voice sharpened. "Not as long as I'm kept from knowing the details of what is going on. Not as long as I'm not kept informed."

Alex went silent at that, realizing she was right but having no idea what could be done about it.

She leaned forward in her chair and continued. "Just as much as when I was pretending to be a man, my life as Marilyn MacNeil was also a lie. Not to mention a crashing bore. Were I to go back to it, I would be banging my head against these stone walls within a fortnight." Her knuckles knocked against her forehead. "I couldn't stand to feel my brain turn to mush the way it did before. It was hell to be stuck here with nothing to do all day but worry you might not come back."

Backed against a wall, Alex lashed out. "Well, I'm sure your tenure with An Reubair was oh, so intellectually stimulating."

"As you've often said, nearly dying in battle keeps one on one's toes."

"Lindsay—"

"I want to be your partner in all things." She stood now, and stepped toward him. "Let me participate in your business."

"No. You have your own business."

"Yes, to support you. To look pretty for your friends who will then be impressed and give you land and let you help run the country. I remember you once denied having what you called 'political sensibilities.' Was it a conscious lie, or were you only fooling yourself?"

"I . . ." For a moment there was a mental whiplash effect as he saw his former American self superimposed over the Scottish earl he'd recently become. He had changed, but didn't want to stop and decide whether for the better or worse. "I'm not a lieutenant in the U.S. Navy anymore."

"I'll say you're not."

"I have to function within this society now. I can't give you authority. If I even appear weak, I'll be subject to resistance. It'll mean trouble. I can't let you weaken my control over my knights or my vassals."

"Alex, we'll be strong together. Two heads better than one, and all that. I'll fight by your side."

Alex blinked at that. *Fight?* "No. No way. You're not going into battle."

"Why not?"

"Just . . . no."

"Why not?"

"I couldn't fight effectively if I had to think about you being there."

"You did all right when I was your squire."

"We weren't married then."

"You didn't care about me then?" She knew better than that.

He blustered, in search of a reply, then said, "It's hard to explain. It's . . . you're part of me now. I'm responsible for you now in ways I wasn't then. You're my *wife*, for crying out loud. I can't let you ride into battle like that."

"And I'm supposed to be okay with you doing the same thing?" She crossed her arms and tilted her head in the manner of a chastising schoolteacher. "I think, dear, I'm going to have to put my foot down and say 'No more fighting for you.' Now that you're my husband and you're a part of me, I can't let you go charging off into the teeth of Edward's army."

"Lindsay—"

"Alex, stop it. Just stop being a pig for a moment, and listen to me."

He closed his mouth and pressed his lips together, forcing himself to listen to her though he knew he wasn't going to like any of what she would say. His gut refused to let his mind encompass the thought of her riding into battle. But he shut up for the moment so she could speak and then maybe shut up herself. Letting her talk herself out seemed the only way to get any peace.

"Alex," she said softly as she stepped closer to him, "I can't live this way. And we know neither of us can return to the future."

He did know that, for getting here had been too dicey.

Going back, even if they could find someone to send them, might kill them. Now he knew why Danu had sent him to Nemed to return them last spring, rather than send them herself. It was the only way they could have made the trip without that risk. Nemed was no longer an option, so they were stuck.

Lindsay continued. "I have to do something with my life, or go mad. I'm just not built to hang around and pretend to be busy. I must be doing something. Contributing."

"You do. You're the reason I have for wanting to fight well, live, and come home."

That brought a slight smile to her face and gave her brief pause, but then she said, "Merely existing to be in your thoughts and inspire you to greatness is a fine thing, but it doesn't keep me occupied or give me purpose."

"You're a writer. So write."

"About what? Alex, you're still asking me to live in a vacuum, and I'm telling you I can't do that. I won't do that. As in, you will lose me one way or another if you refuse me this."

Lose her. Yes, he knew she would leave if she decided she was unhappy enough. Unlike most pissed-off wives in this era, she knew how to live on her own and had the guts to do it. He sighed, defeated, and said, "What exactly is your plan?"

"I wish to be your partner. I want to accompany you on your campaigns. Fight by your side. Be with you and be your equal."

"No. You know that can't happen."

"As you keep reminding me, I'm a countess now. Wives of powerful men do it all the time."

"Yeah, when their husbands are dead or incapacitated. They take over when there's nobody else to do it, and more often than not they're allowed to hold the power because they're a placeholder for a minor male heir. We don't have one of those yet. Women accompany their husbands on campaign, but not as knights and rarely in armor. And those who have fought only bring ridicule on their husbands. It would be shameful for me to let you do this. I'd be laughed all the way back to Hungary."

"Then let them laugh. And let them blame it on your Hungarian side. You're a strong enough man to take it. You're powerful enough."

"Ha. Very tricky, Lindsay, but I'm not stupid. I know exactly how strong I am, and how strong I am not. It would be very difficult to withstand that sort of crap."

"But not impossible. And I can fight. You know I can. If I'm an asset, then who's to complain of it?"

Alex thought about that. She had a point. Unlike other women he'd seen on campaign, Lindsay could fight like a man. She would be a significant asset. But there was one thing more he wanted to know. "Why do you even *want* to do this? You never liked fighting before. You used to be on my case all the time for being bloodthirsty. How come you're all of a sudden hot to kill people?"

That caught her, and her shoulders slumped as she thought about her reply. "I don't really know. Except that when I was looking for my . . . looking for Trefor, I knew I had to do it. Fighting was the only way to accomplish my goal. I never liked it, and still won't, but it enabled me to be taken seriously. I was respected for it, even after Reubair's men learned I was a woman. And Alex," she regarded him from beneath her brow, "I was respected in a way I never experienced even in the twenty-first century. For a while, before they began to revert to hormonal dogs, I was accepted into their midst as one of them. And I liked that. I liked it a lot."

"You don't think my men are hormonal dogs? 'Cause I can tell you right now they are."

"But they are also your men. Not likely to make passes at your wife."

Alex grunted. Hard to argue with that.

He drew a deep, calming breath, let it out slowly, then said, "Only one thing."

"What's that?"

"If you come along, you can't fight as an equal. The

men would never stand for that." She started to protest, but he silenced her with a raised finger. "You know they won't. It's too close to where they live. A female knight would be too much a threat to who they think they are."

"And of course we're not talking about you."

He frowned and bypassed the remark. "If you come, on the battlefield you will have the status of a squire."

"I'm a knight."

"You're a woman, and if you go around telling people Robert knighted you, you will embarrass the king." He leaned over to get in her face. "We . . . don't . . . want . . . that." Then he straightened and continued. "If you come along, indeed, if you're going to function at all in my affairs, you'll need to take a secondary role in all of it." She opened her mouth again, and he rode over her. "Like it or not, fair or not, it's the way things are around here. You will be my other half, and in the eyes of everyone around us my lesser half, because that is the way they think and I can't change that. You will be my advisor, but not in the presence of other people. You can listen in on whatever suits you, but you will not speak until we are alone. You will never dispute with me in the presence of others. You will present a united front with me before everyone, for the slightest crack between us will invite a wedge from anyone who would cause me trouble. Cause *us* trouble. Do you get what I'm saying? Do you understand what must be done for you to get what you're asking for?"

She considered that, and he waited for her to think it through. She was a smart woman, and he had faith she would see his position. Then she said, "I understand. I know I'm asking to put you in an awkward position."

"And we need to do whatever we can to mitigate the inherent problems."

She nodded. "Then you agree with me."

"Agree that you should ride into battle? No. But I can see you won't be happy unless you do."

She went to him and slipped her arms around his neck. "I won't be completely sanguine until both of us are retired from fighting entirely. But I'll be less unhappy if I'm with you when you charge the enemy. I couldn't live knowing I'm guaranteed to outlive you."

Alex remembered the look on his mother's face when he'd told her he was going into the Navy like his father, and now Lindsay had those same wide, nearly tearful eyes and pressed-closed mouth. Back then he'd resented Mom's lack of faith he would stay alive, but after more than a decade of military life, combat flying, and medieval battle, he knew better. Lindsay was right. They'd both been right; he'd chosen a life that would surely end in an ugly, precipitous manner. He slipped his arms around her waist and she kissed him. Warm and sweet, soft and delicious. He let his hand slip down just far enough to feel the beginning of her cleft, where he knew it made her crazy to feel his fingers. Her arms slipped from his neck and she went to untie his trews.

"If I were to accompany you, you wouldn't have to make it all the way home for me to be there for you." She reached inside the trews for him and squeezed. "After a battle the earl and his squire could retire to their tent to comfort each other."

He reached for the fastenings of her dress. "Clean blood from each other."

"Celebrate that we're still both alive." She let his trews drop to the floor for him to step out of them. He went to pick her up, but she held his hands and said, "Uh-uh. Tub first."

Alex groaned and tried to kiss her and encourage her toward the bed, but she ducked away.

"Tub. Scrape clean the crusty places."

He grunted, and stepped into the lukewarm tub. It was tiny; just large enough for him to sit on the stone placed inside it, with his knees bent nearly to the surface of the water. And it teetered a little on the stone floor, so the water sloshed when he moved. Lindsay took the small pot from the fire and poured some more hot water from it to warm the tub. Alex reached for her skirt and slipped his hand up underneath it. Not for the first time he appreciated the custom of no underwear on women.

"Too bad this thing isn't big enough for both of us."

"You're the earl. And you know something about engineering. Build a bath house."

He made a thoughtful humming noise as he finished untying her dress and tugged it and her shift from her shoulders so they dropped to the floor as she bathed him. His head lay back against the edge of the tub and he watched her face as the cloth in her hand roamed his body. There was a bright look in her eye and a pleasant curl to her mouth, and it seemed she was relearning him. Rediscovering, and he was oh so pleased to let her. At his chest, she at first attempted to fluff the hair there, but it lay plastered flat with the water. So she gave up and leaned down to kiss him there. He took her face between his palms to kiss her, and her hand and cloth went between his knees and up his thigh to make him terribly impatient with her touch on what she liked to call his "naughty bits."

When she let him up from the tub and dried him off, he picked her up and deposited her on the bed, then climbed on after her. It was good to celebrate they were alive. They made love to each other, and he hoped they would be strong enough together to overcome the problems they would face in being together as partners instead of traditional medieval spouses. He thought he might be kidding himself, but for the moment, moving together as one, it seemed anything was possible.

CHAPTER 19

The castle was abuzz with preparations for the expedition to Cruachan. Alex had to place a moratorium on fishing until they would leave, for the MacConnells were traditionally allied with the MacDonalds and would surely carry to them the news of the earl's impending visit. Alex didn't want to sail smack into a welcoming committee of MacDonalds who might feel they had no need of a new liege. The MacConnells of Eilean Aonarach grumbled, even Donnchadh, who was usually more accepting of Alex's rule. He came to the Great Hall that night and was escorted to the head table while Alex and his knights lingered over supper. Lindsay sat to Alex's right, Trefor to his left. Alex leaned back to regard his visitor and consider his words.

"My lord." Donnchadh made his obeisance, then was bade to rise. "My lord, with all respect I cannae let you do this."

"Do what?"

"Curtail the fishing. You'll be taking food from the mouths of the children."

"I can't have the boats sailing off to Cruachan before I

can get there. They'll have to wait until I've secured the island."

"And how long will that be? How many days?"

"A week. Let us pack up and go, and then you can fish to your hearts' content."

Donnchadh glanced around in his distress, as if searching for help. "The summer wanes. The fishing needs to be done now."

"Haven't they been working all summer?"

"Oh, aye, and hard. 'Tis always a hard life for the fishermen and their wives. And each day they dinnae make a catch makes it even more difficult. Fewer fish, and if you don't mind my saying, it will also mean fewer of them on your own table come winter."

"Don't exaggerate."

"I do not. A week will put a hardship on us all."

Alex considered that but had to weigh it against his position with the MacDonalds of Cruachan. If their laird on the mainland were to send men, it would be an ugly mess for Alex to claim his land. People might die. "I need to be the one to bring news of the transfer of leadership. I can't let the MacDonalds put their heads together before I get there."

"Ye will have no trouble. I assure you."

"Yesterday you said otherwise."

Donnchadh pressed his lips together, and his eyes went dull with his frustration. "My lord, ye must have faith in your own people of Eilean Aonarach. We've promised allegiance to you. If you order the fishermen to keep away from Cruachan, they will obey. You can trust in it."

"Like I trusted in the Bretons, who then betrayed me to the MacLeods and invaded my castle in an attempt to murder my family."

"We are not Bretons. We are MacConnells and do not abide such cowardly practice."

"It only takes one. One boat to drift accidentally-on-purpose over to Cruachan and let slip word that the new earl is coming to take over. I can't let that happen."

"Most will welcome you."

"All will take the side they think is going to win, and you know that. Even if all I get is a public relations victory . . ." At Donnchadh's puzzled frown Alex elaborated. "Even if all that happens is that I win them over before there's a fight, then that is the best thing. I can't do that if I've got MacConnells passing gossip and folks forming opinions before I get there. I can't let the boats go out until I'm under way."

Donnchadh started to speak again but thought better of his words and shut his mouth tight. Alex understood his distress but didn't have an answer that would make him happy. The villager had nothing more to argue, and his shoulders sagged in defeat.

Then, just when Alex thought Donnchadh would give it up and accept the moratorium, Trefor opened his big, fat mouth.

"Aw, my lord, let them fish. They won't hurt anything." He looked sideways at Alex, with eyes filled with cold mischief. This was purposeful; he knew what he was doing, and he knew the trouble it would cause Alex.

Donnchadh looked to Trefor with an expression of hope, and Alex knew he was back to square one with the argument. He turned to Trefor in irritation and said in modern English, "Shut up." Not that he didn't know Donnchadh could figure out his meaning from the tone of his voice.

Trefor replied in Gaelic so Donnchadh would follow him easily, "He's right, my lord. No fishing for a whole week would be a hardship on the people. Your people. You're responsible for the welfare of this island."

Alex said, also in Gaelic so he wouldn't have to repeat himself to Donnchadh, "And I can't do that if I'm tied up subduing an island full of clansmen incited by the Mac-Connells and backed up by the MacDonald laird. It's not going to kill anyone to not fish for a week."

Now Donnchadh spoke, seeing an opening. "Oh, but it might, my lord. There could be such a lack as might mean starvation sufficient to kill the very young and the very old. The island is expecting three children to be born before Martinmas, and the widow of old man Fhearghas MacNeil grows feeble. Without sufficient food, this winter might be her last."

Alex's voice went hard, angry he had to argue this all over again. It meant he was going to leave his valued community leader with not only the question of the fishing unsettled in his mind, but also a question of his authority. He shut the discussion down. "Donnchadh, I've said all I'm going to. I'll take your words under advisement. That is all. You are dismissed."

Knots stood out on Donnchadh's jaw, and his face flushed. Damn Trefor for his butting in. Donnchadh bowed again, then turned and left.

Alex turned to Trefor and said through his teeth in modern English, "Try that again and I'll have you drug out into the bailey and hung from the arm over the stables' hayloft. And guess what, I can do that and nobody will say 'boo.' Your men can't defend you, 'cause they're outnumbered and outclassed. My guys would stomp yours just for the exercise. Do you get me? Open your mouth again, and I'll forget we're related."

"Like you give a damn on that account anyway."

Alex was angry enough to refuse to be guilted. "Well, you see my point, then. Falling back on the fact that you're my genetic heir would be an incredibly bad idea. So shut the hell up and act like you're not an idiot. Keep out of my business."

"That guy was right. You're starving the village."

Through clenched teeth, Alex replied, "Winter is months away. There are other resources. I'm not convinced the loss will be great enough to make so much difference as to outweigh the advantage to be obtained by the element of surprise in approaching Cruachan. Furthermore, though I shouldn't have to be explaining this to you, you little shit, as a MacConnell himself, Donnchadh's credibility here is somewhat strained. He makes a fairly good case for not starving the village, but as I said I'm not convinced. His loyalty has never been tested, and I don't want to be caught flat-footed if he decides a MacDonald regime would be to his advantage. Do you get it now? Do you fucking understand?"

Trefor took a long time to answer, glaring at Alex with anger that flamed in his eyes and flushed his cheeks. Finally he said, "Aye, my lord."

"Good." Alex turned forward again to address a bit of fat left on the plate before him, and sat back with it to chew as if nothing else were going on and his stomach weren't knotted up like a Celtic brooch swarming with distorted horses, dogs, and bears. He gave Lindsay a sideways look, where she sat with a large *cuach* of ale in her hands, sipping at it. "No comment from you?"

She reached over to place a hand on his arm. "Not in front of the boy, dear."

An amused smile tugged at his face, though he knew he was going to get an earful from her later.

And he was right. Though that evening he tried to avoid hearing it by keeping clear of the laird's chambers until she might be asleep, she sought him out and eventually found him on the quay outside the lower bailey, staring out over the heaving seas as the sun set over the western hills of his island. To the southwest, just over the horizon, lay Cruachan, whose name he now carried as earl.

He wondered what the place might be like. Donnchadh and Alasdair Ruadh had called it a "wilderness," and there were plenty of those around in these times when the English, Irish, and Scottish populations were still very small. And they would be even sparser once the coming plagues of this century were done with them. On the mainland of Scotland were still wolves and bears, and hunting was a good livelihood. He wondered how the people on Cruachan lived, or if they might be like the strange folks one often found in pockets in mountainous regions. Like American hillbillies who had lived secluded from cultural, and often technological, influence. It was an idle musing, for he would find out in a few days whether the MacDonalds of Cruachan were wild men or civilized.

A voice came from behind. Lindsay's, and it startled him. "I must admit there's a raw sort of beauty about this place one doesn't find in England."

He turned to find her bundled in a traveling cloak, hugging herself against the late evening chill, bits of hair loosed from her headdress drifting about her face in a blustering wind off the water. Her beauty made him smile, and he considered that any place might be specially graced if she were in it. "Out in California I've seen two-thousand-year-old trees as big around as a house and so tall I couldn't see the tops. I've seen mountainscapes and deserts that would take your breath away. Certain American scenery can make Scotland look positively ordinary." He turned to nod toward the purple sky where the sun had just disappeared beyond cliffs and rocky surf. "I've been pretty much everywhere, but this place is me. It's where my soul belongs. It's who I am and what I'm made of."

"Race memory?"

He shrugged. "Could be. Or destiny. You believe in a higher power; right now I think I could, too, if I tried."

"A higher power that took my baby away from me? He did that so you could return to your castle?"

Alex sighed, and went to put an arm around her shoulders and kiss her cheek. "Yeah, I hate it, too. Those blasted faeries . . ." He let that hang, and there was silence.

Then Lindsay spoke. "I came to talk about the fishermen."

"It's settled, hon. Don't give me grief about this. It has to be this way. I've got to weigh a week's fishing against the certainty of losing men if there's an uprising like we had before."

"Donnchadh was telling the truth about that old woman. She's likely to die if there is a hard winter. I talk to the villagers sometimes when they come to do odd jobs or sell things in the castle. They don't like to open up, particularly to the upper classes, and so it's often a bit dodgy to get any real information. One must be gentle and persistent, and it helps not to be the one threatening folks with hanging." Alex grunted at that, and she continued. "What Donnchadh neglected to tell you, probably because he didn't think you would be moved by it, is that the woman is highly thought of within the village and her loss would be considered an enormous tragedy. Furthermore, I would tend to agree with that. She's very old and at best has a very few years left to her, but her knowledge of the natural world is quite extensive and she teaches it. Medicine, home craft, animal husbandry, things like that. She bore twelve children, seven of whom grew to adulthood, and currently living and still residing in the village are two sons, nine grandsons, three granddaughters, and forty-seven great-grandchildren. With one on the way."

"I didn't make this decision because I thought the woman was worthless. I don't. I believe she'll live, and nobody will suffer for the lack of a few fish."

"I know you do. But the villagers do not. They're afraid. And there is something else you may or may not realize. Her descendants are also well thought of. Everybody hopes the new child will be a boy, because the sons stay within the clan and the daughters tend to marry away. The men are very brave and eager to fight well when they believe in the cause." She leaned toward him. "I don't need to point out to you the importance of their faith in their laird."

Alex considered that information. Keeping the vassals happy was a more important task than the history books would one day have it. To ignore the condition of so important a villager might come back to him in ways he couldn't foresee. And one he could foresee involved the loyalty of this woman's grandsons when they would be asked to defend his claim on Cruachan. "I see."

"Were you to remove your guards from the fishing boats and allow them to sail, nobody would think you weak or unwise. They would all recognize your compassion in this situation, and your trust in the fishermen who are loyal to you."

Alex snorted. "A fantasy in practice, even if more or

less true. It would only take one guy to mess me up." Lindsay opened her mouth to protest, but he put a finger on her lips and said, "*But* I think there may be something I can do. We'll step up the loading of the boats tomorrow and leave as quickly as possible. I'll tell the villagers to get their fifty guys together, and we'll leave tomorrow night instead of next week. No dilly-dallying."

Lindsay nodded. "That should do the trick, if you can make the preparations quickly."

"If we get the stuff on the boats as is, then we can take over that tower Donnchadh mentioned and make our preparations there. The men are in good shape and ready to fight; we might be able to drill on Cruachan before anything happens. Many of the horses aren't in such great fitness, but we can limit ourselves to only the better ones for this trip."

Lindsay smiled. "See, it'll work out—"

"Oh, look, it's the parental units."

Alex and Lindsay turned to find Trefor standing on the quay behind them. Alex glanced back out over the surf breaking against the stone below and decided he should rethink letting himself be found alone in a place where he couldn't hear approaching footsteps. Lindsay huddled tighter into her cloak and stared at her feet. Alex said to Trefor, "Need something?"

"I came to tell you you're going to kill that old lady."

"No, I'm not. I've figured out a way to let the boats go out tomorrow night. Anything else you want to gripe about?"

Trefor was nonplussed, but then said, "I'd like to talk to my mother, then, if I may."

"No."

Trefor addressed Lindsay. "Why won't you talk to me?"

She said nothing, and Alex wished she would. It would be so much simpler if she'd just face Trefor and have done with it. But he couldn't force her. Forcing her would do about as much good as trying to get toothpaste back into a tube. It would make a mess and accomplish nothing.

But Trefor either wasn't aware of that or didn't care. "Mom—"

"Don't call me that."

"You are my mother." Not pleading, but angry. The rage was gathering, and it was aimed at her.

"Stop it." Her body was tense, leaning into Alex. She was afraid of Trefor. Afraid of what he would say to her. Alex wished he would leave her alone. Her voice shook. "Please leave, Trefor."

"There, you've finally said my name." A sharp note of bitter victory sharpened his voice.

Alex said, "You heard her, then. She asked you to leave."

"Why? I don't get it."

Alex didn't get it either, but it was his place to defend Lindsay and if she wanted to approach this in her own time he would make sure she would be allowed.

"Mom—"

"*Trefor!*" Alex let go of Lindsay and took some steps toward his son. "Let it go. Just . . . leave her alone for now."

"But why—"

"Just go."

Trefor glared at him with a hatred so palpable Alex could almost smell it. And he was sorry for it. He didn't know what he felt for the guy, but it was painful and confusing. It made him want to smack him. To just haul off and knock him sideways for making him feel so awful. He gazed back with as stern a look as he had, and he hoped Trefor would listen this time and let them alone until Lindsay could straighten out her own feelings and face him. If ever that would happen.

Trefor glanced over at Lindsay, who still gazed down at her feet, then back at Alex. For a moment it looked as if he would try to get past Alex to speak to her, but finally he turned without a word and made his way from the quay and back up the long steps to the castle.

Alex let some moments pass before taking Lindsay's

hand and guiding her from the quay, darkened now that the sun was quite down. They went straight to the apartments, for it was late and the sun would be back up in only a few hours. Tomorrow was going to be a hard, busy day.

CHAPTER 20

Lindsay felt strangely comfortable in her chain mail. Two days ago she'd gone to the servant who did all the sewing for the castle and commissioned a bra to replace the ratty elastic bandage she'd been using. The garment was not entirely like the ones to be found in the twenty-first century, but was more like armor padding in the form of a tank top. Thick and quilted, it fit snugly around her rib cage and pressed her breasts rather than thrust them high to be seen. It neither hid them nor put them on display, but held them still and protected them from harm. It took some explaining to make the sewer understand what she wanted, but he was an industrious fellow and accomplished the task in good time.

Now she wore the thing beneath linens and silks from Alex's wardrobe, and her Psalter tucked in between her tunic and sark. The tiny book was like a talisman she carried in hopes of gleaning whatever power it might hold. At least it might remind her of her connection to Danu, and that was something. Over Alex's clothes she wore her own mail armor, and a surcoat of red and black bearing the stylized bald eagle element of Alex's arms. Her shield, newly painted, bore the complete arms: *bordure, compony azure and argent; gules, bald eagle displayed or; sable, a lymphad sail furled, oars in action, or.* In other words, the shield had a border of blue and silver to indicate Alex's ostensible illegitimate birth, a mythical bald eagle in gold against a red background, and below that a sailing ship in gold against a black background. The blue in the border was, of course, navy blue. To her, it seemed Alex had stopped just short of incorporating stars and stripes, and that amused her.

She stood among the men on the boat as it approached Cruachan. The deck was crowded, for Alex's boats were small and few. Lindsay and Alex stood at the bow of the lead boat, the men taking every available space behind them. The deck heaved beneath their feet. Donnchadh and his fifty villagers rode the boat behind, carrying pitchforks and hunting bows.

When the knights of Eilean Aonarach had first seen Lindsay in her armor, ready to sail to Cruachan, there had been a bit of an uproar. Though those who had fought under Alex before Bannockburn recognized her as the knight they'd once known as Lindsay Pawlowski, some of them had personal objection to the idea of a woman in chain mail regardless of how well she might have proven herself in battle. The shock was compounded by very mixed reactions at finding their compatriot still alive but not nearly who they'd thought he'd been, and there was a thick feeling of betrayal in the group. Stares and grumbling made the hairs on the back of Lindsay's head stand up. These guys seemed even less accepting of her than An Reubair's rough men of the lower nobility. Lindsay had expected better of men pledged to her husband.

Neither she nor Alex addressed the issue to the men, but only presented her as Alex's wife who would be accompanying them to Cruachan. Never mind that it was plain by her armor she intended to fight. Alex left it to the men to decide how to react and made it clear they were free to take their hired swords elsewhere. None left so far. It remained to be seen whether Lindsay's presence on the battlefield would be deemed a benefit. Again she would need to prove herself, and she wondered if there would ever come a time when her reputation would be enough for acceptance.

Now, approaching the island, the stares quit as more important concerns took their attention. The knights under Alex's command were no longer concerned about the moral weakness of the earl, and the earl's wife who had apparently lost her mind, and were focused on meeting what might turn out to be obedient vassals or a wild enemy. Nobody knew which way this would go. Lindsay felt a little relieved her husband's men had enough sense not to let their pride distract them from their job.

Like the rest of them, Lindsay hoped the change of regime would be peaceful, though a small corner of her balked at that hope. A tiny voice in the back of her mind niggled at her that she needed to demonstrate her ability to hold her own among the men, and this would be an opportune moment for it. Her pulse thudded in her ears as the boat landed at the tiny bit of rock on which the tower stood, and like the others she scanned the high, craggy horizon for greeters.

Alex looked out over the bow of the boat, also searching the shore for signs. Worry etched his face in ways only she would see. He'd arranged his face to be expressionless, and but for the tiny lines at the corners of his eyes and the one slightly raised eyebrow it would have been. His men could never know how he felt about anything, but she did.

Especially Trefor wouldn't know. He'd brought his men along in support of the earl and stood with them at a distance from Alex, where they clustered and watched the shore. Alex was ignoring him. Had been ignoring him the entire trip. It was hard to tell whether the earl was merely focused on the task at hand, or if he meant to cut Trefor dead, and thereby put him in his place. Whatever place that might be.

Trefor made it plain it was a place he didn't care for.

Lindsay watched him, taking glances to the side so he wouldn't see her staring. He seemed focused, like Alex, but he had a sullen look about him she didn't understand. An anger she found alarming.

It was hard to see him this way. Or any way at all, for that matter. She'd accepted this was the man her baby had become, but had no idea what that should mean to her. What had she ever been to him? What had she ever done for him that he should expect her to act like his mother? What on earth could she do for him now? What could it even matter to either of them?

Those thoughts sank her deep enough into sadness that she had to consciously pull herself out of it, take a deep breath, and peel her mind from it. This was not the time for wallowing in emotion, and she returned her full attention to the island and the tower. The MacNeils were armed, swords at their sides, prepared in case of attack once they landed.

The waiting keep was a fairly new structure. Tall and boxy, not like the crumbling, ancient tower in Lochmaben, and topped with a sharply crenellated battlement. It would shelter their men and horses, separating them from the possible dangers of the island, until they were ready to invade the island. At high tide the outcrop of rock on which it rested seemed like a tiny island, for the narrow arm that connected it to the main island was covered by a few feet of water. At low tide there would be a path from the tower to the island, rather less than the furlong Donnchadh had estimated, but still long enough to keep attackers at bay. A quay ran along the seaward side of the tower, where the boats would dispose of their cargo of men, horses, and supplies.

Lindsay looked to the horizon again. Still no clansmen to be seen.

Alex said, half to himself, "No welcoming committee. Not good." Lindsay knew he was right, since at least some islanders would surely have spotted them coming by now and the lack of welcome suggested the natives were hanging back. Waiting. Alex would need to approach with caution.

As soon as the first boat nudged up to the quay on the seaward side of the keep, guards on horseback were unloaded and deployed to the island, wading across the isthmus through waist-deep water and posting along the shoreline in a semicircle. The rest of the unloading went quickly and without mishap, and mostly in silence, almost surreptitiously. Horses, weapons, supplies, and men filled the tower in an intense bustle and clopping of hooves on the stone floor. The earl's men managed to unload all the animals and tack before a cry was heard from the pickets that an islander had been spotted.

Alex's head went up, and he listened. All the knights stopped to listen. At that moment Alex was on the second floor above the horses, supervising the allotment of sleeping space, but when the alarm shout came he broke off speaking to Henry Ellot, heard the call, then hurried up the stairs to see. Lindsay followed, and she was likewise followed by Ellot and Gregor.

Looking across from the battlement atop the tower, there didn't seem to be anything on the island but rocks and Alex's pickets. Alex shaded his eyes and mumbled a wish for binoculars. The knights on guard down there were all moving toward a single spot, and Lindsay looked at that spot. There she found a cluster of men gathered along the rocky top of the nearest ridge. Hard to pick out, they were so still, but they seemed as wild as Donnchadh had characterized them. In midsummer they of course would not be burdened with heavy clothing. Lindsay had seen the way people dressed on Eilean Aonarach, where tunics were few, women went barefoot, and children often went entirely without clothing, but these men wore far less than the men she'd seen. Here there were no proper belts other than rope, no trews or tunics, few boots, and their sarks were unadorned with anything resembling plaid or surcoat. Armor would more than likely be a distant dream to them. Their pale, light linen garments revealed thin, hard, large-jointed frames, and flapped gently in the wind at knees and arms. Where the fashion for most Scots was to be clean

shaven, these men wore full, bushy beards and long, unkempt hair. Lindsay had never seen anything like it, even
in these times and even on Eilean Aonarach where the culture was decidedly rustic. But for all their lack of clothing,
these men were armed more fully than even the knights
from Eilean Aonarach. They held swords, maces, and pikes
as well as farm tools such as those wielded by Alex's vassals. The gathering bristled with armament.

Not good.

"All right," said Alex. "Let's get down there and introduce ourselves. Henry, gather the men, get them mounted,
and we'll take them all out to the shore." He looked around
for Gregor, but the boy was already off to ready the earl's
horse.

Henry hurried back down the stairs while Alex looked
out across to the island again. The cluster of men had not
moved.

"Do you see anyone else?"

Lindsay scanned the horizon but found nothing. Down
by the shore . . . nothing. But then she spotted a cleft in the
rocks to the west along the shore, where there was movement. A line of well-armed men were creeping to flank the
MacNeil pickets. She patted Alex's arm to get his attention, then pointed. Alex grimaced.

"Crap." He removed his right gauntlet to blow a loud
whistle to the men below. When the pickets looked up he
waved them in the direction of the flanking movement, and
they then saw the line of islanders in the distance. The
knights adjusted their deployment accordingly, and the approaching line stopped. At that moment a file of Alex's
cavalry came riding from the tower and plunged into the
water along the isthmus. Behind them walked the Eilean
Aonarach villagers with their bows, scythes, axes, and pitchforks. When the islanders saw the numbers at hand, they
backed off in a hurry, melting away and into the rocky hills
like water soaking into the earth.

"You can't attack them, Alex. They don't know who we
are yet."

"Thank you, Jiminy Cricket. Who's side are you on?"

"I offer it only as a data point. They don't know who we are and don't know you have a charter from the king. They probably think we're random invaders testing their defenses."

Alex sighed. "Yeah. And it doesn't look like they're eager to find out otherwise, either. We've got to follow them. Get to the village before they have a chance to gather themselves."

"The men haven't eaten."

"Not a problem. Not with these guys. And with any luck we'll catch the village flat-footed so they'll listen, and they'll be sensible about this whole change of guard thing."

"Not if they're MacDonalds."

Alex bit his lip and shrugged, forced to agree. "So we'd better get going. Come on."

They went back downstairs, mounted, and rode out across the isthmus to lead the knights across the island and to the village. The fifty infantry followed.

According to Donnchadh MacConnell, only about half the island was what anyone would have called populated. There was some farmland, little pockets of tilled land tucked between forest and rock. But the folks who lived here existed more by fishing and hunting than through the bits of land they put to plow. The hills the knights and foot soldiers moved through were granite with a veneer of soil like webbing, stretches of green punctuated by gray rock, sometimes rolling, but in the distance the riders saw sharp peaks rise from the grass. They jutted to the sky like thick fingers. Or like walls surrounding a dark realm. These pastures were interspersed with low, forested places dark with growth and deep soil. The track they followed wended narrowly, the knights moving single file between the thickets of trees and underbrush. From where she rode with the squires, Lindsay watched Alex, looking around at his new domain, and she could almost see him thinking. This place was rich with game, and there was arable land going unused.

If the MacDonalds thought they had a claim to it, they would surely fight for it.

Alex would fight for it as well, and for more reason. Besides the farming and game, there was space here for the MacNeils of Eilean Aonarach to spread out. As clansmen, all MacNeils would prosper by resources and influence. Besides, the MacNeils' historical claim to the *cairn* meant the return of control of this island to the clan would bring prestige to himself as well as his people over whom he was laird and earl. And finally, as land attached to the earldom, it was essential to his status with the king. His title wasn't worth much without military control of the land and the people living on it. In personal terms, this place was worth far more to Alex than it would ever be to the MacDonald laird.

The company came onto an open area, tilled fields surrounding the village, and came to a halt just outside the tree line. The crop of oats was high and green, shimmering as the breeze blew across it. In the distance could be seen villagers gathering, their weapons waving this way and that as they milled about, waiting for the order from their leader. Lindsay wondered exactly who that leader was. Not that it mattered anymore. The group didn't appear in a mood to talk things out.

She looked over at Donnchadh, who was staring at the ground. As a MacConnell, normally allied with these Dhomhnallach, his loyalties were being tested today. By his subdued stance she gathered he was perhaps not as enthusiastic about this confrontation as the MacNeils around him. The next few hours were sure to reveal much about Donnchadh MacConnell.

Lindsay spurred her mount, trotted up to the front, and said to Alex, "If you send an emissary, don't send that Donnchadh MacConnell fellow. Send a MacNeil."

Alex stared out across the field, thinking hard. He said, "I'm going to go myself."

"I'll go with you."

He looked over at her and said flatly, "No."

"But—"

"No. And don't argue. Your presence would not be helpful at this time."

Lindsay understood him to mean she would be a distraction to the MacDonalds. "Take me with you, Alex." Her voice carried a sharp note of warning. She wasn't going to just let this go. "It's now or never. Let me be who I am."

His jaw clenched, he thought for a long moment, then said, "Fine. Come. But remember what I said the other day."

He gestured to Henry that he should stay with the men, then pointed to two other men to accompany himself and Lindsay to the village. The four took off at a canter down the track between the oat fields, Alex's banner flapping red and black and gold.

Many of the villagers scattered at their approach, but the core and the majority of the armed men stood fast to face the earl and his escort. Three of them walked out to meet the horsemen on the track. Alex and his knights slowed to a walk and the parties came together at a distance from the village. The one in the middle seemed to be in charge, a crusty old guy with a thick head of white hair and a bright light of challenge in his eye. He seemed to wish Alex would give him an excuse to attack. Rusty pike clenched in one hand, he planted it at his feet like a staff of office.

Lindsay watched the parlay as a member of Alex's bodyguard, alert for assault. She would kill anyone who might harm her husband, and kept a sharp eye to see what would happen.

Alex said to the old guy, "I am Sir Alasdair an Dubhar MacNeil, Earl of Cruachan, newly made by Robert Bruce, King of Scots."

That brought a chuckle from one of the lesser villagers, and the leader turned to deliver a stern look. Then he addressed Alex. "I am William MacDonald of the Dhomhnallach. I cannot recognize your fancied claim, for my allegiance is to my laird, The MacDonald." The man appeared a heathen, and was at best only a tacksman, but spoke with the intelligence and authority of a laird.

Alex had his charter in his saddlebags but didn't bother to show it. Most people in these parts couldn't read, and William MacDonald had made it plain he didn't care who had made Alex earl of this island. Instead Alex said, "I have the right to take the land by force of arms."

MacDonald raised his chin in challenge. They both knew this only meant Alex would have no interference from those allied with Bruce. The king's forces would not be brought to bear on this issue regardless of how it was thrashed out today, for not only was this squabble beneath the king's notice, but Robert and his army were busy in Ireland. But then Alex reminded MacDonald, "There are MacNeils living here."

"They have pledged to The MacDonald."

"They are lawfully bound to me, by order of the king. Your village will be divided if you resist."

"The MacNeils are of no account. Not for a number of centuries. We MacDonalds have held this place for a long time. We'll keep it longer, I think."

"Your MacDonalds will die."

"Of course we will. If sooner than later, then we will have won our homes at least. In any case, we cannot fail our laird and we will not succumb to your claim. You have no authority here. Leave us, or receive a fight."

"Then fight. I would have liked to keep loyal vassals but am happy to destroy rebellious ones."

A quick shadow of doubt passed over William MacDonald's eyes, but he then turned to his escort and gestured them to follow him back to the line of men waiting for them. The talk was ended.

Alex wheeled his mount and spurred back at a gallop to his men, his escort following. Thundering up to where the company waited, he reined in to a halt and said to Henry, "That's it. They're Dhomhnallach and they want to stay that way. They'll need more persuasion than just talk. They want us to just go away and let The MacDonald have their tribute. Unlikely, since we're going to kick their butts right now." He shouted to his men, "Line up! It's going to be a fight! We're going to knock their asses from here to Edinburgh!"

The knights gave a shout of enthusiasm as they arranged themselves for attack, and at the other side of the oat field the villagers also lined up. Their numbers were greater than Alex's company, and Lindsay hoped his professional cavalry would make up the disadvantage by their skill and experience in battle. But she knew the men on these islands had a tradition of fighting, and if Alex's men had an edge it would be a slight one. Lance tips wavered before the horses, ready to charge. Lindsay lined up with the squires to the rear, her own sword at the ready. She looked ahead, to where Alex sat his horse, his sword gleaming in the sun, and she said a brief prayer that he should live through the day. She had only a glance for Trefor, then looked away. She was afraid to know what she hoped for him.

A shout went up from the Cruachan villagers, and those men took off at a run into the oat fields. Alex shouted the order to charge, and his knights bolted in their line. Lindsay spurred her horse with her line of squires. Alex's MacNeil vassals followed on foot, shouting and holding their weapons aloft.

From the moment she met the enemy, she was intent only on staying alive and defeating the MacDonalds coming at her. Alex slipped from her mind as she rode into the midst of the teeming mob wielding iron and wood. She slashed at them, and though they were agile and quick, elusive, some were less quick than herself and were cut down by her sword. Men fell into the trampled oats, bloodied and crying out. Soon those left standing were panicked. Fierce at the start, the MacDonalds of Cruachan were outclassed and not as accustomed to battle as they'd thought. The knights overwhelmed them. The MacNeils found themselves chasing MacDonalds back to the village, leaving only a few stragglers to defend themselves. Unsuccessfully, for all who did not make the retreat died on the field.

In the strange way time had of compressing in battle, the encounter seemed to take only a few seconds, though it must have been nearly an hour. In the end the MacDonalds ran to their houses.

Lindsay pulled up her horse to let them go, but a cluster of several MacNeils gave a shout and ran after to chase them down and plunder the village.

"No!" she shouted, and spurred to head them off. Her sword overhead, she rode to block the MacNeil knights.

They reined in, puzzled. One of them shouted at her, "Plunder is our right!"

"They've surrendered. They're no longer the enemy; they're your master's vassals. You have no right. Stand down."

"You've no authority."

"More than you think. Before you defy me, be certain my husband will disagree with me. I know him well."

That gave all of them pause, then one by one they sheathed their swords and reined away from the village.

Panting with exertion but feeling as if she'd just warmed up, Lindsay looked around for Alex and found him on foot near the middle of the field, bent to examine a man who appeared dead. It was one of his knights. She spurred her mount toward him and leapt from her horse before it was quite stopped. "Alex!" She threw her arms around him.

He hugged her to him, the two of them clinking with their mail, and he kissed her. Relief he was alive made her go weak, and never mind being glad she'd survived herself. She kissed him back and clung to him lest she collapse to the ground.

"Get a room." Trefor was walking past, on his way to retrieve his horse.

Alex let go of Lindsay, turned, and walloped Trefor backhand with his spiked gauntlet.

"Ow!" Trefor pressed a hand to the side of his head, over a wound deep and bleeding in spite of the mail coif over it. His eyes went dull with anger and he drew his dagger.

Alex also drew his and said, "You're going to have some respect, or I'm going to kill you. Which will it be?"

"Come and get me, old man."

Lindsay wanted to shout at them to stop, but knew the only one who might even be distracted by her voice would be Alex, and that distraction might prove deadly. So she kept silent by biting her lips together. Then she drew her own dagger just so it would be handy. In case.

Alex circled, looking for an opening. Trefor appeared ready to kill his father, his eyes smoldering with anger he'd nurtured carefully all his life. He moved like Alex, for they were built the same. He held his knife the same way Alex did, having been taught by him. And Lindsay figured Trefor would not hesitate to kill Alex. She also knew Alex would never bring himself to do the same to Trefor, and it put him at a terrible disadvantage.

The men continued to circle, each in search of an avenue of attack. Trefor moved first, and thrust with a speed that made Lindsay gasp. Alex fended and the dagger missed its target, but slashed Alex at the wrist. Alex only grunted, jerked back on reflex, then replied immediately. He forced Trefor back a few steps, but Trefor refused to be panicked. The field was wide and there was nothing to trap him against, and he circled rather than be chased. Then he stopped after a few steps and stood ready.

Trefor came at Alex again and was deflected with a clink of blades. Alex shoved him off to the side, and he staggered. In an instant Trefor spun and attacked again, catching Alex's upper arm. He drove his dagger through the hauberk sleeve, and Alex let out a shout that was more surprise than pain. He retaliated in anger, his dagger slashing wildly back and forth, and only succeeded in making Trefor back off a few steps.

"Come back here."

"Come get me." Trefor smiled, and it made Lindsay want to smack him. God help her, it made her want to stab

him. She gripped her knife and knew she'd go after him if
he killed Alex.

Alex feinted, Trefor went for it fully, and Alex clobbered him aside his head with the butt of his dagger hilt.
Trefor dropped flat to the ground, dazed. Alex stomped on
his wrist, reached down, and grabbed Trefor's dagger. He
tossed it to Lindsay, who quickly wiped Alex's blood from
it onto her trews. Alex shoved Trefor onto his back with
one boot and stood over him with his dagger ready to attack if Trefor made the least move against him.

"All right, Mordred, here's the deal: you are going to
treat your mother with respect or you will answer to me. If
she ignores you, you will speak well of her. If she spits on
the floor at your approach, you will treat her with kind-
ness, reverence, and gentleness. If she slaps your face, you
will thank her for the attention. Am I making myself
clear?"

Trefor said nothing, but only glared at the earl.

Alex continued. "Understand this: I am not, and will
never be, your 'old man.' I am never going to grow feeble
except that you will be right behind me, also growing old
and feeble. There will never come a time when you will be
stronger than me; I will never be displaced by you."

Trefor started to climb to his feet, but Alex hauled back
his dagger for attack and growled at him to stay put. Trefor
obeyed and lay back down on the ground.

Alex sighed, took a deep breath, and looked out across
the trampled oats to the surrounding hills as if in search of
the words to say what would come next. Then he addressed
Trefor again. "I hate that this happened. I'd like to wring
the scrawny neck of every Bhrochan in Scotland for what
they did to us. You were taken from us; your childhood was
taken from all of us. It happened suddenly, and for Lindsay
and myself it happened only a few months ago. We haven't
had a chance to begin to deal with any of this. I mean, we
never even got to name you. We never got to find out what
it's like to be parents. You missed out on having a family

growing up, and we've missed out on being that family. And we've only just begun to glimpse what that will mean to us over the years." Alex's voice grew thick, though he still held his dagger at ready.

"Hate me if you want, Trefor, but I require you to cut my wife some slack. You will treat her with respect, and you will refrain from the smart remarks in her presence. For as long as the both of you live, you will obey her as a child even if that means leaving her the hell alone. Do that, and there can be a place for you in my domain. If you do not accept it, and if at any time you show the least sign of disloyalty to me, to her, or to anything MacNeil, I will destroy you. No hesitation, mercy, or remorse. Do you read me?"

Still Trefor only glared.

Alex brandished his dagger. "*Am I making myself clear?*"

Finally Trefor said, "Aye, my lord."

Alex stood straight, lowered his weapon, and sighed. "Good. Now get up out of the dirt and pay obeisance to the countess."

Trefor looked up at Lindsay, and the pain in his eyes broke her heart. But she said nothing as he rose to his feet then dropped to one knee. His voice quavered a bit. "My lady, I am your loyal servant."

He was her son. Tears rose to her eyes, but she swallowed them. "Rise, Trefor." He obeyed, then lifted his gaze to her eyes. They were the same age. She couldn't give him anything he needed, and he no longer needed any of the things she wanted to give him. Though she was his mother, to her he could only be one of her husband's household knights. She would give Alex an heir, other babies, and they would be her children. But not Trefor.

She handed back his dagger, and he sheathed it. Then he turned to retrieve his horse. As she watched him go, a single tear escaped her eye and she hurried to wipe it away. Then she went to Alex and made him remove his surcoat, hauberk, and sark to take a look at his wounded arm. She could let herself be absorbed in him, and the rest of the world might fade away.

Alex leaned down and kissed her cheek. His face pressed against hers, he said softly, "It'll be all right."

She replied, "No, it won't."

EPILOGUE

Trefor figured he was screwed. It had probably been a mistake to come here, to this medieval armpit of the universe, and now he wondered whether he should stay or leave or what. He stared down the length of the Great Hall at his parents, who sat at the head table, presiding over breakfast like royalty. It was party day; they were entertaining the Earl of Ross, James Douglas's friend and Edward Bruce's father-in-law. All the stops had been pulled out, and there was food everywhere. Fresh reeds on the floor, everyone dressed in their best dingy finery. Ol' Alasdair an Dubhar was doing his level best to become one of the gang, hobnobbing at Mach 3. Trefor nibbled on his meat, not particularly hungry, but wanting to look as if he were joining in.

The parental units seemed happy, all smiling and holding hands. Cruachan often leaned close to tell his countess things that made her laugh. The two seemed to have made a magic circle up there at the head table with their guests, one Trefor knew would never include him. That Gregor kid was there, standing attendance. The foster son. *Foster* son.

Irony upon insult upon injury. In all his childhood wishes
and dreams of his real parents, he'd never thought he could
have been displaced like that. Not by a *foster* kid. His
stomach was in a knot, and he gnashed at the meat he held
between his fingers.

Morag must be somewhere around, and he wondered
where. She liked to disappear at odd moments and then
reappear at even odder ones. He wondered where she'd got
off to this time; she hadn't been here in the castle when
they'd returned from Cruachan. The trip had taken a while,
though. Maybe she'd gotten bored and gone off to find
amusement. She'd be back. He could tell when a girl was
in love with him, and that one had it bad, though she'd
never admit it out loud. It made him smile to think how
tightly he had her wrapped around his little finger.

It had taken several weeks to organize the village on
Cruachan enough for Alasdair an Dubhar to return to his
castle. The resident MacDonalds were defeated, the families who'd participated in the rising tried and evicted, and
now the rebels were the responsibility of The MacDonald.
Their tenancies had been reassessed and some distributed
to those who had not participated in the rising, and that was
what had taken so long. Come spring new tenants would
begin clearing forest to build new farms. Much thought had
gone into the distribution of land. Other MacNeils would
be given tenancies there, most from Eilean Aonarach and a
few of the poorer folk from among Hector's MacNeils on
Barra. With the MacNeils and allied families now the majority on Cruachan, clan loyalties would consolidate Alex's
claim and also his alliance with Hector. It was left now to
decide who would be tacksman on Cruachan, and that was
what kept Trefor hanging around after that fight with his
father. That and the rumor King Robert might visit to con-
firm the new earldom with appropriate pomp and ceremony. That sounded like a fun party. Trefor thought it might
be pretty cool to meet Robert the Bruce, but even more it
might be good if ol' Alex made him tacksman and let him
run Cruachan. Even if Trefor couldn't call himself MacNeil,

which he never had until Morag found him and told him
his real name, making him tacksman would be the least the
earl could do. Yeah, sticking around was probably the best
thing. Pawlowski was as good a name as any. It at least was
his mother's maiden name and hadn't been given to him by
those who'd dumped him off.

He gazed long on the countess, and his heart beat faster.
His mother was beautiful, just as he'd always imagined
she'd be. The woman was strong and smart and interesting, and he longed for her attention in ways that he didn't
even want from Morag. The little redhead was delight-
fully fun, and helpful in many ways. He loved her, but not
in the bone-deep sort of way he looked to Lindsay Mac-
Neil. The countess scared him. He couldn't look away
from her. He would do anything for her if she would only
let him. She was his mother, after all. He was supposed to
care for her.

And, he realized, if Alex loved her half as much, then he
would be vulnerable because of her. Trefor tucked that
knowledge into the back of his head for later use.

Finally he looked away. Maybe he'd take a ride around
the island today. He'd not had a chance to check it out
when they'd arrived; it might be good to explore a little and
get to know the lay of the land. He stuffed the chunk of
meat into his mouth, picked another, and began eating and
chatting with the knight next to him.

The day was crisp and fall-like. Late August, but it was
plain winter would arrive early here compared to Tennessee. A pleasant breeze drifted among the trees of the forest through which he rode at a walk. There were only the
sounds of leaves swishing and dull, thudding hoofbeats on
the narrow track.

Morag's voice came from somewhere. "There ye are.
About time you came to find me!"

A grin splashed across his face and he looked around to
find her perched cross-legged in the crotch of a moss-

covered oak, wearing nothing but her golden rope belt and a smile. Her bright, coppery hair hung in wild curls that spilled over her shoulders, and her eyes glinted with high humor.

"There you are! Where have you been?"

"Right here, silly boy. Waiting for you to be done with those dreary mortals."

"I had business. I needed to attend—"

"Bah. Come play. The day is fine and ye must be stifling with all your clothes. A body should be freed of them on a day such as this."

Trefor grinned and reached for the ties of his tunic. In a few seconds he had it off, and his sark. Then he leapt from his horse. The breeze was a mite chillier than Morag made it out to be, but the goose bumps on him could also have been from the sight of her. She grinned, stood on the oak limb, and swung down from the tree. With a giggle she skipped away into the forest. Trefor hurried to relieve himself of his boots, trews, and drawers, then gave chase.

They ran through the woods, laughing, and Morag managed to stay just out of reach. A couple of times he nearly caught her, but she dodged from his grasp at the last second. It only made him laugh harder and chase in better earnest.

Then he caught her and held her to him. Unable to stop laughing, he tried to kiss her but managed little more than mashing her lips with his. Her laughter was out of control, and she was helpless in his arms. He landed a good, solid kiss, and her body warmed against his.

But then she slipped away from him and took off running again. He ran after but lost her in a thicket. Without slowing down he burst through it and figured he'd see her on the other side. Gorse scratched at his skin, but he barely noticed.

It was a small clearing, all grassy and surrounded in bracken. A fallen oak lay at one side, covered thickly with dark green moss that made it look as if it were melting into the grass. He looked around, but there was no Morag. Nor sign of her. His pulse raced, and he went to the log to see behind it. No Morag. He turned a circle, but still didn't see her.

There was a bit of rock sticking from the earth across from the log, and he went to it. No Morag hiding there, but he found a hole in the ground. It didn't look big, but that girl was small. She could fit just about anywhere. He knelt to peer into it and see what he might see. It was dark in there, which sort of figured since it was underground, but he thought he saw movement. His smile returned, and he leaned closer.

A force caught him from before and from behind and shoved, as if the very air were trying to stuff him into the hole. Too quick to resist, it blew him through the hole and he found himself tumbling into darkness. He landed with an *oof* on something soft. Above him, as his eyes adjusted to the darkness, he was able to discern roots. Big tree roots. Of course, he was underground. But there were voices. High, tittery ones, whispering all around. He sat up to see.

They were wee people. Bhrochan, he guessed, for they looked a lot like the several he'd seen in the States a year ago. Tiny folk with pointed ears like his, dressed in ragged tunics and trews. He held up a hand in greeting. "Hi."

One of them laughed, high and giggly and sounding like madness incarnate. She then leapt to her feet and did a little dance like a jig. "Oh, look! We're graced by a visit from our new prince!"

THE ULTIMATE IN FANTASY!

From magical tales of distant worlds to stories of those with abilities beyond the ordinary, Ace and Roc have everything you need to stretch your imagination to its limits.

Marion Zimmer Bradley/Diana Paxon

Guy Gavriel Kaye

Dennis McKiernan

Patricia McKillip

Robin McKinley

Sharon Shinn

Katherine Kurtz

Barb and J. C. Hendees

Elizabeth Bear

T. A. Barron

Brian Jacques

Robert Asprin

penguin.com

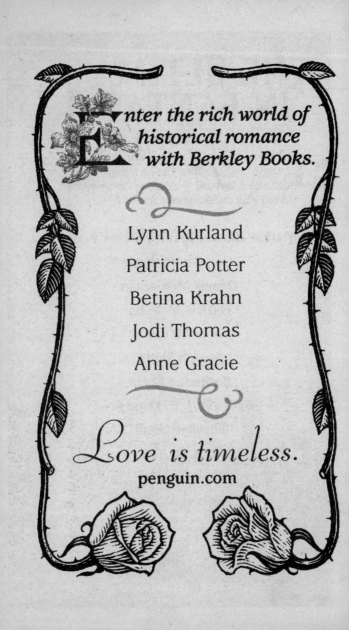

Enter the rich world of *historical romance* with Berkley Books.

Lynn Kurland

Patricia Potter

Betina Krahn

Jodi Thomas

Anne Gracie

Love is timeless.
penguin.com